I0667258

The
Hannover
Game

Book 1 in the Hannover Series

by

Mark J Diez

ISBN 978-0-9934155-0-0

Mark J Diez

www.MarkJDiez.com

Dedication

To my wife Marta Diez

I could never put into words what your love and
support have meant to me while writing this book

You are my inspiration and energy in life
This book exists because you believed it could

Your devoted husband

Mark 'my did it' Diez

x

Mark J Diez

Acknowledgements

As any author will attest, the writing of a book is in turns an enjoyable and difficult task. The influences and inspirations along the way are many and varied, but some stand out as pivotal.

Philip Dickinson - Foremost of these are my friend and inspiration, the author Philip Dickinson. The extensive feedback and guidance were worth more than all the gold in Moctezuma's halls.

Owen Benwell - Artist, designer and London garret flat mate. Thanks for the many and varied conversations on writing, art and life.

Lorelei Logsdon - My editor's insightful, informed and often humorous comments and feedback helped add a polish to the book that would have been sorely lacking without engaging her. The experience was more like being educated that edited, I am a better writer for the experience.

The Piccadilly Group - The PG Beta Readers did a great job in going through early versions of the manuscript; providing feedback and spotting schoolboy errors. Special thanks to Victoria Mercer and Duncan Small.

Mark J Diez

Israel – Egypt border
2007

~ 1 ~

Frost led the extraction team and their two guests further into the tunnels hewn into the sandstone base rock under the desert above.

Sand crunched under foot and a fine dust hung in the parched air, disturbed by the determined feet of the escapees.

"Keep moving!" Broer ordered, casting a glance back to the doctor and his wife who had started to slow down under the punishing pace they'd kept since entering the tunnels in Gaza.

Frost reached a junction and consulted a map once more. "To the right," he announced without stopping and headed on.

The woman gave a gasp as if surprised by the change of direction, but flanked by two operatives to their front and rear, she and her husband marched forward.

Another ten minutes passed, with changes in direction and the relentless pace maintained. Frost paused once more and, from behind the rear operatives, Broer let his frustration be known. "Frost, this isn't the tunnel, you idiot! We should have been at the extraction point already!" Broer cursed.

"I see light, we must be there," Frost replied.

"Get out of my way, ya fokken domkop!" Broer yelled in his native South African accent, pushing through and to the front of the group.

He headed forward, rifle aimed ahead to meet any response head on.

Near the end of the tunnel, he saw that it rose up to surface level, and through the opening he saw dusk was beginning to arrive. Laying on his front he crawled forward and saw they were not where they should be.

At a distance of around 300 feet away he saw the Egyptian border fence. *This tunnel must have come out under it at one point. But instead of finding all the tunnels, the Egyptians had just moved it backwards. Problem solved: let the Israelis deal with the smugglers.*

Broer shot back into the tunnel, raced up to Frost and slammed him hard into the wall. "You got us lost! My mission, and you fucked it up!"

"Broer! Stand down!" Byford shouted from behind the group.

As the most senior operative, Byford took ultimate responsibility for the success or failure of the mission. However, as this one was being used to train up Frost and Broer, they'd been leading it.

"Get a grip, assess the situation," Byford added.

Broer spat on the floor and headed back to the opening. They had to move fast to avoid being caught in the darkness that was drawing in.

He surveyed the area.

Through his rifle sight he saw that the nearest observation post looked to be over 600 feet away along the fence. He waited, but heard and saw nothing else. There were no lights or sophisticated detection systems to be seen, no noises from people or vehicles.

Crawling further out he saw a small trench under the fence ahead. It would need a quick dash for all seven operatives, along with the doctor and his wife.

He played the scenario through in his mind.

He'd go first with two front operatives to secure the fence. Then the doctor and his wife, under and out to freedom. The last two operatives and the old man, Byford, could follow.

It would have to do.

"Seven of us!" he cursed under his breath. He'd wanted three operatives, but Byford had overruled him. Shaking the thoughts off he slid back into the tunnel.

Broer explained the plan, dealing forcefully with various protests and appeals from the doctor and his wife, who were literally shaking with fear. Broer wondered if the doctor would piss himself. He'd seen it before.

"Frost, you follow me," Broer added, realising he'd completely left Frost out of his mental planning.

Broer and Frost made it to the fence with ease. Broer, leading, crashed side on into the base of the fence, half his body going in the ditch that had been dug out underneath it by the contraband smugglers.

He scrambled under and Frost followed.

Looking back, they saw to their horror that they were no more than 300 feet from a roadway and, just behind it, a series of small huts. As they looked, lights came on within the buildings.

"Move, move now!" Broer called to the operatives holding position at the tunnel entrance.

They shot forward, followed closely behind by the doctor and his wife, and then by the last two operatives.

As they ran forward, Broer reacted instinctively to a black form moving towards them, between the roadway and where they lay. He raised his rifle and starting firing.

Shots were returned, but not from a lone figure—there were at least three Israeli border guards bearing down on them.

In an instant, the night exploded into a maelstrom of automatic rifle fire, shouts and screams, flying dust, bursts of orange light from muzzle flashes and the whizzing sound of rounds passing dangerously close.

Broer ran forward, firing all the time at the shadowy figures. He saw one drop. Then he felt it. Time slowed, noises dulled. The battle mist had overcome him.

There were muffled shouts and harsh screams, flashes of light, the crack of gunfire. The scene around him made sense but there was a surreal nature to it.

He heard rounds wizz past and thud into the ground nearby. Something struck his leg, but even while falling he dismissed it. He hit the desert sand hard.

Looking up, another of the figures ahead dropped.

To his left, one of the operatives had gone around to flank the attackers. Broer saw the man firing and running towards the final figure, who was now turning to the oncoming threat.

Broer raised his rifle and, letting loose a long burst of rounds, cut the final defender down.

The gunfire stopped, but there was a new noise filling the air. Broer turned to the group back at the tunnel.

Blood and bodies littered the ground. Two operatives were dead, their bodies bleeding out into the sand, clothes and flesh torn up. Two others were crawling to the fence, limping and moaning from their injuries.

Byford jumped down from above the tunnel. The final kill had seen him take a minor injury to his shoulder. But the real disaster lay in front of him.

There, half way between the tunnel and the fence, encircled by the dead and the blood-stained sand, were the bodies of the doctor and his wife.

Wasting no time, Byford moved forward and with a grunt picked up the woman's body and placed it onto his back. He strained to get upright, but, steadying himself, walked forwards towards the fence, staggering under the weight.

Broer was having his own problems. He went to stand but a white hot pain from his lower back made him drop onto the ground again. Reaching around with his hand he touched a warm sticky liquid oozing from just above his backside.

He forced himself to bend his legs up from the knee, *Not paralyzed then.* "I'm hit!" he shouted.

Frost shot forward to Broer. "Can you stand?"

"Would I be lay around like this if I could," Broer said, seething with anger, wanting to kill Broer where he stood. He thought about the knife on his belt and Byford must have sensed his intention.

"Broer, stand down!"

He looked over to Byford, wanting to defy him, but thought better of it given his state.

"Get the other one!" Broer spat at Frost.

Broer watched him go back for the corpse of the last operative.

Frost would pay for this mess, but it could wait.

Once the shit storm had settled, his time would come.

London, England
2011

~ 2 ~

The police Sergeant looked out from behind the two rows of officers aligned in front of him. The solid wall they'd formed was enough to prevent the crowd moving down the main street and doing serious damage to the shops and offices there.

"Close shields!" the Sergeant shouted into his mouthpiece.

The crowd had swelled from perhaps five hundred to what appeared now to be well over a thousand.

As per the Riot Squad's plans, the mass of bodies were being directed along a route out of the city. If all went to plan, in thirty minutes or so, the crowd would be split up into two smaller groups, all heading in slightly different directions. The critical density of bodies would be lost and, being past any significant area of the city, the riot would fizzle out.

The carefully thought-out plans of the Riot Squad, however, were the last thing the Sergeant in charge was thinking about. His job was to follow another set of instructions given last minute, to separate and trap the group in the second half of this riotous mob. Simple enough.

"Beta group, stand ready," he ordered, as a line of police formed up on the opposite side of the street.

They placed their shields firmly edge to edge, as the Alpha group had just done on this side.

He watched the crowd moving along in between the lines. The noise was starting to build, a few braver marchers pushing at the police lines as they passed through and being pushed back.

Then he heard it—a series of blasts on a whistle followed by a foghorn being sounded. His officers had found their quarry and were in position.

In the middle of the crowd the Sergeant spotted his masked agent provocateur raise a canister of something up at arm's length and the foghorn sounded again.

"Yeh, yeh," the Sergeant muttered to himself, "I see you."

The man started spraying a cloud of liquid and gas into the air, then set it alight. As planned, the crowd around him immediately split, pushing back and sideways to get away from the unexpected burst of flame and heat.

People added screams to the shouting; the foghorn was being blasted long and loud, adding to the confusion and noise. Panicked, a few of the mob fell to the ground and people tried to avoid crushing the fallen, further stalling the crowd's progress away from the scene.

"Groups... Split them up!" the Sergeant barked down the microphone.

Instantly the front of both police lines raced out across the road towards their opposite sides, slicing through the gap in the crowd the ball of flame had created.

Each officer behind the one in front waited a brief moment and then followed close behind. The effect was like watching two giant snakes slithering in an unbroken line of protective scales, arching towards and then past each other.

In less than twenty seconds Alpha and Beta groups had formed two solid, shielded lines across the road, back to back, facing out to the now separated crowd.

"Alpha, walk them out," the Sergeant said.

The Alpha group started following behind the front part of the crowd, pushing the stragglers being left behind by those in front, who'd carried on walking, oblivious to the barrier that had just been set up.

He watched Alpha group walking them out of the riot area and away from the more important section of the crowd now firmly trapped and alive with anger. It was the best he could do not to laugh.

"Textbook," he mumbled, and turned his attention to step two of his instructions.

∞

Sir Anthear waited for the call to be answered; he heard a faint click, which told him the receiver had been picked up.

"Steven, are you seeing this?"

"Couldn't help but watch, sir," Steven replied.

"Ah, likewise. I trust everyone will do their bit correctly?"

"Well, sir, we've picked some of our best to make this happen. Let's watch the show and see, shall we? I'm sure it will be very entertaining," he said, hoping to reassure Anthear.

"Very well, Steven. Just one more thing: we have Lauren lined up for her visit later, I assume?" Anthear asked, a slight trace of worry in his voice that his prize may well be hooked but not properly landed.

"Fully briefed and standing by, sir. Really, everything is in hand," Steven said, again trying to ensure Anthear was made to feel everything was back under control.

"Very well, I'll talk to you tomorrow, then."

"Thank you, sir. Enjoy the show and I'll update you in the morning."

With that, Anthear hung up the call.

God almighty, first he messes up and then he starts implying others will, Steven thought. He switched his attention once again to the news and the riot being played out before him.

He knew everything had been planned and communicated just fine; the difficulty, as always, was in the execution. Coordinating a few pawns across the board was no problem. What was to come in the next weeks would be the difficult part.

He focused back on the TV. Any second now Frost should appear to cast the net.

∞

Frost looked across the crowd and saw David, about 30 feet behind the guy with the canister, still throwing flames into the air.

He saw the other two operatives slightly behind David and his accomplices, boxing them in and making sure they couldn't move backwards, while the one with the foghorn kept the assault of noise going, overwhelming their senses and adding to the chaos.

David had no clue he was already trapped.

Some others, not part of the charade, had started throwing things at the police line, just as expected. Stones, plants and their pots, tin cans, or anything they could get their hands on.

The psychologists at Hannover had predicted this perfectly.

Frost laughed out loud. "Sheep going along just as expected," he said to the officer in front of him, who couldn't hear a word over the shouting and chaos that was growing minute by minute.

The flame-throwing man was now trying to scorch the police shields. He ran out of whatever he was spraying and threw the empty canister against the police line, adding to the debris being pelted by the crowd. Frost saw it was time to act.

"Hey, blue, pop one off, let's get this done before we lose the window," Frost said into his microphone.

The police Sergeant felt his stomach tighten. He hated being called a blue by these Hannover guys, but it was a minor insult to suffer for the benefits he gained from collaboration.

He walked behind one of his officers who was dressed in full riot gear and holding a riot gun and put a hand on his shoulder. The officer leant towards his Sergeant, who shouted into his ear.

"Drop a canister in the gap behind the flamethrower guy."

The officer took a quick look back at the crowd and nodded. "Got it."

He loaded a metal canister into the gun, locked it, aimed high, and with a dull boom sent the canister towards the crowd with a hissing, fizzing noise.

It landed in the perfect spot, bounced under the feet of the crowd and started spewing its white cloud of noxious gas.

Those nearby gasped for air, coughing and crying while trying to cover their mouths and escape, but trapped between the police shield line in front and the crowd behind, no one was going anywhere.

Frost pulled his earpiece out and zipped up his jacket.

"Open up!" he said to the officers in front of him.

They opened a gap at the base of their shields. He crouched down and dived through and onto the floor, knocking into the crowd. A couple of protesters stepped back and picked him up, thinking he was one of their own, recently fallen.

"Bastards!" he shouted, slamming his shoulder into one of the officers who'd let him through, just for the amusement of the role-play.

He stepped back and pushed past the crowd. He used what space he had to move towards David.

"Pick it up! Pick it up and throw it back!" he shouted.

David looked at the canister through his watering eyes, grabbed it from the end not spewing gas out and hurled it over the shields and into the police line.

Frost ran up to David and patted him on the back several times, as if it would help with his coughing and crying, laughing loudly as if he were having a great time.

"Are we having fun yet?" he shouted at David, still laughing and resting his arm over the disoriented man's shoulders.

"Oh yeh, a real riot!" David shouted back, trying to recover a bit of equality in the encounter.

From behind the lines the Sergeant noted who Frost had singled out.

"Riot Squad, form up," he ordered over the radio.

Frost saw the Riot Squad, equipped with smaller round shields, faceguards and batons, take up position behind the police line. Any minute now the line would open up and the riot police would sweep in and start suppressing the crowd.

He looked over to the right of the line and saw the next piece in the game about to be played: his exit. A riot gun was raised and another canister was sent fizzing into the crowd to the right.

"Mine!" he shouted, knocking David on the arm before setting off running towards the canister.

"Bloody lunatic!" David shouted after him, as Frost vanished behind a line of riot police who had just burst through into the crowd.

David looked ahead and saw four policemen with batons raised and small shields against their chests running at him. Before he knew it the batons were hitting him, sending waves of pain coursing through his body.

He went to the ground with a hard thud as his chest hit the tarmac. A knee pressed against his spine and as his arms were pulled behind his back, the last thing he saw was the baton swinging down to his head.

∞

Sir Anthear flicked off the TV, gave a contented sigh and slid down into bed for a sound night's sleep.

Steven changed the channel, walked to the drinks cabinet and poured another glass of scotch.

He reached for the phone. "Lauren," he said as a hello.

"We're on for tomorrow then, I assume?" she asked.

"Yes, say 10am. Let David wake up and have his breakfast first. You have the paperwork?"

"I do," she replied. "I'll be there at 10 and see how he responds."

"Then I'll call at 10.30am. Goodnight," Steven said.

"Steven, wait!" Lauren said. "Are you sure about this?"

Steven sensed an uncommon tremble in her voice. "Of course I'm sure," he said.

~ 3 ~

"Wake up, wake up... we're here!"

David felt himself being shook as he struggled to open his eyes and realised that he was in some kind of van, lying down on hard wooden seats, facing the roof.

He swung his body around and, placing a foot on the floor, attempted to stand. His vision blurred as a painful throbbing emanated from the back of his head.

"Stay sitting down, you took a nasty blow to the head before you got arrested," the other person in the van told him.

"Who are you, where are we?" David asked.

"Quiet, they're opening the door," was the hushed reply.

The doors to the van were swung open by two officers in riot gear. A policeman in a white shirt stood between them.

"You, out," he said, pointing at David, and signalled for him to step out of the van.

The other man took David by the arm and started helping him towards the doors.

"Not you!" the officer barked.

The man let go of David, who stepped down onto the concrete floor of what seemed to be an enclosed garage or delivery bay. The van doors were slammed shut and the riot police disappeared from either side of the vehicle and back into the front seats.

"Through the door ahead, don't do anything silly," the officer warned.

"Where am I?" David asked meekly, as he obeyed the command and headed to the door.

"A police station," was the terse reply. "Let's get you booked in and processed."

David was shown to the duty desk, relieved of his loose possessions, including his belt and shoes, then made to sign an inventory form, before being marched off to a cell room.

"Take a seat, the doctor will be with you in a minute," the officer said.

A short while later David had been checked over, cleaned up and given a little food and drink to help him recover.

The painkiller the doctor had given him was the most welcome. He tried to sleep but couldn't, the pain in his head not letting him black out on his own terms this time.

He remained alone in the cell for the next few hours staring at the walls, images and sounds of the riot running around his mind. Eventually he drifted off to an unsettled sleep.

∞

"I'm here to see my client."

The police officer on the desk looked back at the woman who had just walked up to the duty desk and knew exactly who she was and why she was here.

"Well, as we only have one client in this morning, I guess it's him you're referring to," the officer said flatly.

"Show me through, then," she replied.

"Formalities first. Name?" the officer said, holding a pen above the registration book and staring the woman in the face.

Always the little games, she thought to herself.

The important police officers knew full well who she was and who had sent her, but the masquerade of pretence was always played out.

"Lauren Shields, council for David Rhett," she replied, attempting to skip a few questions.

"Right then, Ms. Shields," the officer said as he wrote the details in the registration book.

He put down the pen, picked up some keys from under the desk and stepped out from behind it.

"Take a seat, we'll get him in an interview room for you."

"Actually, the cell is just fine," she replied.

Though strictly against the law, he knew it wasn't worth fighting. In the cell everything would be on camera, but there would be no audio, which was just how *they* wanted it.

"Fine, follow me."

A few moments later she was in the cell alone with a confused-looking David.

"And who the hell are you then?" David asked with some force, staring at the woman now taking a seat at the end of his bunk.

Lauren gave him a gentle smile, careful to come across as concerned, but not to show insincere friendliness.

"David... I know this must all be a little confusing for you... but, together... I'm sure we can get this mess sorted out."

"You haven't answered my question," David replied, ignoring her comment.

"Ah, I'm sorry. I'm Lauren," she said, holding her hand out to him in her most feminine way.

He shook her hand and gave a nod. "So what do you want, Lauren?" he asked in return.

"Well..." she started. *You're an idiot for not realising I still haven't answered the question*, she added to herself. "We need to sort out the mess you're in and get you out of here."

"What mess? I was attacked and knocked out by the police!"

Lauren tipped her head to the side, showing a little neck to appear vulnerable.

"David, you were in the middle of a riot," she said while using her most concerned tone. "You threw a tear-gas canister at the police and some of them needed medical attention. Attacking the police is a criminal offence, you can be jailed for it!"

David looked stunned for a moment, thoughts racing around his mind.

"Ah, shit. It was some guy, he shouted at me to throw it back, I was in a panic!"

David stood up and put his hands to the back of his head, feeling the bump, a sense of dread washing over him. He knew in his heart that he could never spend another day in prison. A short stretch a few years ago had confirmed that to him.

Lauren looked on and inside was amused at how easy his fear of prison was to trigger, how easily he could be played with a little feminine softness.

That'll teach you for being too honest with people, she thought to herself.

"Oh, David, I know… I believe you, but the police have you on video with him. I'm afraid it looked like you were having a laugh and joke, it didn't look like you were panicking."

She clasped her hands together and placed them in her lap, looking up at him in his confusion.

"So now what?" he said in agitation, turning rapidly back to her.

As he did so, he saw how concerned she looked, and he felt his heart skip a beat as she jumped slightly from his outburst.

"Sorry, so you said something about sorting this mess out?" he said, this time more softly, "How can we do that?" he asked, once again sitting down on the bed.

She reached over and put her hand on his.

"David, I know some people who can make this go away. Not all the police are as blinded by the establishment as some. There are those who support your views."

She looked back to the door, conspiratorially lowering her voice at the same time.

David raised an eyebrow, unsure what to make of this woman with her hand on his, sitting so close and offering ways to give him a get-out-of-jail-free card.

"On the basis that there's no free lunches, what's the other side of the deal?" he asked.

She took her hand off his and placed it down on the bed between them.

"Well, of course, it's a favour for a favour. I help you... you help me," she said in whispered tones.

Casting her glance back to him, she saw his pupils dilate slightly as the rush of misplaced sexual excitement washed over him, manipulated as he was by her careful use of body language and conversation.

A moment went by in silence as he looked her in the eyes, feeling a rush of blood in his groin.

"OK, tell me what you want," he replied.

She gave a smile. "Come with me, I have something for you," she said, choosing her words carefully to wind him up even more.

She squeezed his hand, then stood to go to her briefcase on the small desk on the opposite wall.

Pulling out some papers, she beckoned him over.

∞

"Officer!" Lauren shouted to the policewoman standing just outside the cell door.

The officer opened the door and took a step inside.

"Need something, ma'am?"

"Yes, please take this signed statement and release papers to the front desk. My client would like to leave shortly," Lauren informed her.

Clearly a little confused, the officer took the papers from her and looked over them. A moment later she cast a suspicious gaze over David and Lauren.

"I see, well, OK then. Give me five minutes and then bring your client to the front desk," she said.

David and Lauren passed a few minutes with idle chatter about the incident that had gotten David arrested. David made a few feeble attempts to find out who had sent her, but she simply replied that David shouldn't worry about it and that they'd be in touch soon enough.

"Right, head out to the front desk and get yourself home," Lauren said, standing up to make it clear the conversation was over.

"OK, thanks, talk to you soon," David said, sounding hopeful. They shook hands and David headed out of the cell.

∞

Alone in the cell, Lauren sat down on the bed and closed her eyes.

An image of her favourite fantasy came to mind. Seeing herself in a prison cell, she was dressed as a warden, trapped with two prisoners.

One had the cell door tied closed with his shirt to prevent her leaving. The other moved towards her, and with a sick smile on his face, grabbed out at her and threw her onto the bunk.

She caught herself breathing hard and opened her eyes.

Smiling at the image, she stood up, gathered her things, and stepped out of the cell.

Looking up the hallway, she noticed David was already gone.

One born every minute, she thought.

She wondered how David didn't think it was suspicious that he had yet another offer of assistance, from yet another anonymous source, so soon after the first.

Arrogant or stupid, probably both, Lauren concluded in her own mind.

She heard the front desk's phone ringing, snapped out of her reflections and checked her watch. It was 10.30am exactly.

Turning away from the cell, she walked up the hallway to the front desk and saw the desk officer pick up the phone.

The desk officer replied to the caller.

"Yes, she's just here... a call for you," he said, holding out the telephone for her to take.

"Thanks," she responded.

Holding her hand over the receiver, she looked back at the desk officer and made it clear she was waiting for him to go away.

After a moment the officer got the message, gave Lauren a mild look of disdain and walked away from the desk.

She smiled to herself. She was used to that reaction and, unfazed, switched her attention to the phone.

"Hello, sir... yes he's just left and is very amenable to your offer of help now. Oh yes, of course you can, sir, take it from here by all means. No, no. All perfectly as planned and primed for you getting in contact when convenient."

∞

Sir Anthear, comfortable in the lounge chair of the Centenary Club, took a long draw on his cigar and continued listening to his long-term Hannover colleague Steven playing out his role as the Handler on the call to Lauren.

"Very good, Lauren, competent as ever," Steven said and nodded to Sir Anthear.

Steven once again spoke into the phone.

"Let's meet up tomorrow and we'll go through what behaviour we'll now be expecting from David and his merry band in return for our sponsorship."

With that, he hung up the call.

Lauren knew what the meeting tomorrow meant. Another project for someone and another fat consultancy fee for her.

Working for Hannover had proved a lot more fun than working for the mental health service, and the pay was way better too.

She hung up the call and just for the sport of continuing to annoy the desk officer, called out a thanks with a bright smile.

She waved the phone in the air a little to show that she'd finished with it before placing it on the desk, instead of on the hook.

Yes, very good indeed, she thought to herself as she headed out of the police station.

"A government spook," the desk officer said to his female colleague, who had just joined him at the front desk with a questioning look on her face. "Just before you ask," he concluded, replacing the handset.

"You've lost me. Who does she work for? MI5, 6 or someone else?"

"We're not told. It'll just be a phone call saying someone we have is going to be visited or we're to transfer them or something. For your future guidance, when that happens it's a case of ask no questions, get told no lies."

∞

Steven looked over to Sir Anthear.

"Well then, Sponsor, looks like your escaped fish is back in the net and ready to be drawn in a little further."

"Indeed it does, Steven, *handled* well as always. Lauren came through again, eh? She's quite the capable mind-fucker, isn't she? We'll have to watch her, she's probably psyching us, too," Sir Anthear said, managing to combine both a congratulatory and cautionary tone in one.

Steven raised his glass in agreement and they both drank a silent toast.

"Speaking of which, sir," Steven said, "I believe the girls will be arriving now. Shall we join our gentlemen friends in the Club room and see what Lady Thorisen has laid on for us this week?"

"Indeed, Steven. As you've so kindly helped me out of the hole I dug myself into, it would be rude to refuse your suggestion."

Sir Anthear gave a final hard suck on his cigar and stubbed it out, drank the last of his scotch and rose from the chair.

"Of course, one final piece of the puzzle remains for you—to get our man Byford back in the water," Anthear said, having turned to stare Steven directly in the eyes, impressing his authority on the situation in a moment of silence.

Though good friends with Sir Anthear, Steven was always sure to remember that he was not in charge. He was merely the Handler of any project Hannover wanted running, and Sir Anthear was the Sponsor.

That's why he always tried to stay one step ahead, like a good project manager should.

"Already working on it, sir. Once I hear in the positive that Byford's onboard, I'll take the next step with David and we'll be off."

Sir Anthear nodded in acknowledgement and let his usual pleasant demeanour return to his face. Straightening his clothing as if to draw the meeting to a formal close, he made for the door Steven was now holding open.

"Ah, well-bred ladies of connection but no money, happy to be part of their scratching and clawing for what we have," Anthear commented aloud.

Steven nodded Anthear through to the hallway. "Scratching and clawing, if you find the right girl, sir," he said, causing Anthear to give a muted laugh.

Steven followed his Sponsor out of the Lounge to the Club room and its weekly buffet of high-class treats.

~ 4 ~

David collected his things from the front desk of the police station, signed the paper confirming all his items were correct, and left as fast as he could.

Glad to be outside, he looked back at the station. 'Stone Hill Police Station', the sign read.

"Oh great, I'm miles away from home," he said aloud, raising his arms as he spoke, as if mirroring the protesting he'd done the night before.

Home was at least ten miles away. Looking in his wallet, he saw he had money, but not enough for a taxi. He checked his mobile phone and saw that the battery was dead.

"Grrreat... train it is, then," he said aloud once more and headed to the main road, hoping to find his way to the town centre or the train station.

Looking around, he couldn't see any signs for either. He realised he could have just asked in the police station, but he had wanted to get out of there and away from the police.

Thoughts of being locked up and maybe imprisoned came back and darkened his mind.

Was that Lauren woman right about prison? The police had certainly come straight for me, he reflected, thinking back to himself throwing the gas canister back at the police lines.

Realising he was standing on the street corner with his eyes half open, he shook the thoughts from his mind. He noticed a local shop, which he realised offered the opportunity to ask for directions.

Heading inside, he smelt the sweet and spicy aroma of Indian food. It was far more welcoming to him than the city streets, reminding him of his South Asian adventures.

The man behind the counter looked at him expectantly.

"Know where the station is?"

"The police station? It's round the corner, innit," the man replied in a local accent that took David by surprise.

"No, I know where that is, unfortunately—the train station."

"Oh, just keep walking down the main road and to the roundabout, where the two unfinished buildings are," the man told him, stretching his arm out and pointing his finger as if trying to reach around the door and outside.

"Thanks," David said, waving and leaving the shop.

He took to the street and carried on walking. In the distance he could see two tall buildings or, more accurately, the concrete shells of two buildings. They looked like apartment blocks, but no apartments were visible yet. A large sign on the building advertised them as The Mallards.

The Lame Ducks by the looks of it! he thought.

As he walked on towards the buildings, his mind went back to the night before.

The protest about global warming had been a good thing to do. Though a march through the financial centre of the city might be seen as a cliché these days, it was still the de facto way to get media attention.

David kept walking, running the events of the march through his mind, his arrest and the visitor, Lauren, offering him a way out. He wondered what the price was in return. 'A favour for a favour,' he recalled her saying to him.

"Yeh, I bet, but it's always a higher price to pay for the debtor," he said aloud to himself. He saw the train station, went in to buy a ticket and headed home.

An hour later David was in his bathroom, taking off his smelly clothes.

"Mary!" he shouted.

Since coming in he'd called her name three times but there had been no answer. He hadn't bothered to look around for her, instead heading straight upstairs to wash.

He turned the shower on, stripped and got into the cascade of water, feeling the warmth relax his muscles, reminding him that he'd not slept well in over two days.

Closing his eyes, he let the water ease him into a near-standing sleep.

The night before the march the group had been up late. Drinking, smoking and plotting into the small hours had become the norm before any event. He was mentally tired of it, physically tired of it and of the group, but giving it up wasn't an option right now.

His mind went back to the meeting they'd had before the march.

Brother Wolf was always trying to keep the group peaceful and join in any other protests and marches that would give them kudos in the eyes of other eco-warrior, environmentalist groups.

The peaceful thing was fine, David wanted the group low key. The kudos thing he couldn't care less about.

Greenpeace was planning a march through the city to protest fracking, and Wolf had suggested the group go along too. That was it, a simple decision that should have taken ten minutes, but no.

Instead of that, a group of about six had checked the route on the Greenpeace site, pulled up the area on Google maps, talked about how many police, how many people, if there'd be any press and cameras. On and on, as if any of it mattered.

David could feel the bile building up, thinking of the group. He pulled phlegm up out of his throat and spat towards the drain hole, not bothering to open his eyes to check where it landed.

Little had they known how many people would be there and how many police there would be. The event had been far bigger than any of them had expected.

David finished in the shower and headed to his bedroom. Looking at the room he could see Mary had been back last night, but where she was now didn't matter.

He pulled the curtains closed and dropped onto the bed. The duvet was cool against his naked body, and it felt relaxing.

The effect was short lived.

He was reminded of the bruise on the back of his head as it sent a few dull pains through his skull in protest at being pressed against the pillow. He rolled onto his side, partly pulled the duvet over himself and closed his eyes.

His ears were ringing and by the throbbing sensation in his limbs and face, he could feel that his blood pressure must be up from the tiredness.

Taking long, deep breaths, he willed his muscles to relax. Images of random places and events, sounds and sensations washed over him as he began to dream. Within a short time, he was asleep.

∞

"David!" Mary shouted as she came in the bedroom, seeing David asleep on the covers, duvet draped across his lower body.

"Mary..." he said, opening his eyes and trying to focus on what was around him.

"Where have you been? Your phone is off and no one knew where the police took you!"

"Didn't you ask them?" he said sarcastically.

"We couldn't," Mary snapped back. "Four of them lifted you up and took you straight behind the police lines. David, what happened?"

"Mary, slow down. I was knocked out, that's why they had to carry me. I've got an awful bruise," he said, touching the back of his head to show her where. "I was up at the Stone Hill station and just got back a while ago. What time is it?" he asked.

"It's 2pm, I've been calling everyone, even the hospitals!"

"God, Mary, relax, OK? I'm here now."

She looked at him with one of her hurt looks, but he knew she wouldn't make a big issue of it, just enough to show concern and stay on his right side.

"Get me a smoke," he said to her, pulling himself up to sit on the edge of the bed.

She went to the bedside cabinet and pulled out the working-box, as David had called it when they first met. Opening it, she saw that there were no joints ready.

"Hang on," she said, moving to sit in a chair under the window and then setting to work silently.

David watched her lay out a paper and sprinkle in some tobacco. It was rolling tobacco instead of normal brown, she knew he preferred it. It burned slower and smelt better.

She lifted out a resin block about the size of a man's thumb, heated and crumbled some of it onto the tobacco and then set about rolling the joint.

David watched her. He had always thought it cute but pointless, the way she rolled joints with such perfection. He felt it was uncommon for someone who smoked so many joints to pay such attention to what they looked like—but that was Mary, a nervous intensity about everything.

When it was rolled and sealed, Mary shoved some torn and rolled card into the end, wrapped the paper back inside the card tube and twisted the other end closed.

Just to finish this piece of artwork, she retrieved a small pair of scissors from the working box and snipped off half the twisted end.

Finally, she handed the joint to David. He looked at it in all its handcrafted perfection, popped it in his mouth, and held his hand out for a light.

"So what happened at the police station then?" she asked, now starting to roll a joint of her own.

David drew on the joint and held the smoke in for a few seconds, before exhaling towards the ceiling.

"I made a friend, it seems, that's what happened," he said.

Mary looked a little confused.

"What?"

David sat up, swung his legs out onto the floor and took an ashtray off the bedside cabinet.

"Yeh, I was visited by who really knows who, who offered to get me out of jail free as long as I did a favour in return for her favour," he said, turning back to Mary.

He knew the mention of a woman would set her on edge.

"Don't look so worried, Mary. I've no idea who she is; well, she's called Lauren, but I've no idea why she helped me get out without charge."

"Someone just offered to get you out of the police station and you don't know why or what they want?" Mary said.

David looked at her as she finished her second piece of master crafting.

"Yeh, I know. But after last night, when I threw that canister at the police... well, she suggested it could mean prison time."

"Prison! Rubbish, you didn't even do anything!"

"Except lob a tear-gas canister into the police lines, yeh, other than that I was practically spectating!"

Mary heard the anger in his voice and chose to stay quiet, lighting up her own joint and giving him time to feel the effects of his.

She watched him staring out of the window.

"Do you still think about it?" she asked.

A moment went by before David answered.

"Of course, but it was a shithole prison in a shithole country and things are different now. I'm just not keen to get even close to being locked up again."

Mary looked at him through the haze of their smoke.

Since coming back after his arrest in Thailand and six months in prison, he was weaker mentally and physically now, but angrier too. The tough, risk-taking man she'd known was gone, his sprit beaten and abused out of him in such a short time. Now, instead, here was someone who bullied and manipulated, always looking to lay risk and blame on others, while grabbing for whatever he could get.

"You think they'll come here? The police? There's a lot of stuff here, David," she said, breaking the silence.

He thought about it for a moment. He was safer these days after making a few contacts that helped to keep the heat away. Did Lauren know where he lived and what he did? How about the people she worked for?

"I don't know about the police bothering with us. We have a little protection now, and those who don't know us—well, they think we're just protesters," he replied.

Standing up, he walked naked over to where Mary was sitting. He could feel his cock starting to get hard. Walking around naked when Mary was dressed was an odd turn on he always enjoyed.

She seemed to him like some innocent young girl, and he was the wise old man, despite them being nearly the same age and her being a virtual drug addict now.

"Want some?" he said, smiling and stressing his groin muscles so that his now semi-erect penis lifted up towards her.

"Oi… David!" she protested, staring at his now straightened manhood.

He stood directly next to her, putting his free arm around to the back of her head. Mary kept looking at his cock, wondering what he was going to do. He grabbed his pyjama bottoms from the back of the chair and pulled them roughly up, the weight of her body stopping them, forcing her to lean forward.

"Hey, you can play later!" he said, quickly turning and walking away, leaving her feeling flustered at his actions.

"What should worry us is Lauren and whoever she works for," he said, sitting on the bed and pulling his pyjamas on.

He shook his head. "How did they know I was at the police station and she said they'd be in touch, but I never gave my number or address. So they obviously know a lot more about me than I do about them," he added. The thought of her frightened him.

Mary smoked the joint and looked at David pensively. She never did offer up any advice or suggestions.

He looked at her with his usual blank expression. *Do I have to do all the thinking in this relationship?* he thought to himself.

He thought about Lauren again. If she needed something doing, he needed someone to delegate it to; he couldn't take the risk on himself. He thought back to the march and had an idea.

"Mary, do we have a group meeting here tonight?"

"Yes, at 9pm. Why?"

"Good, I'd like to tell them what's happened since yesterday. I also want to find out who the guy was that came up to me in the crowd. Let's give Paul a call and see what he knows."

Mary stood up and walked off to the other side of the room, leaving a trail of smoke behind her.

"Here, let me get the phone," she said.

David raised his arms in the air as if commanding her to stop.

"No, it's OK. Let's go downstairs, I'm hungry."

Mary knew that was a not-very-subtle way of telling her to go and cook something.

She stubbed out her joint and blew a final cloud of smoke up to the ceiling.

"OK, let me cook some lunch up then," she said, heading out of the bedroom.

"Pizza and crisps is fine," he called out to her.

David stood, grabbed a T-shirt hanging off the back of the chair she'd been sitting in and headed downstairs.

∞

David went straight to the den—that's what they called it, anyway. It was more a spare room with all the crap in it, a desk for the laptop and a house phone.

There was barely room to move about.

The desk was against one wall with an office chair to sit in. Directly behind that was an old sofa they'd got off one of the group a few years back, which stretched from wall to wall.

The layout meant there was barely enough room to squeeze past the desk and get on the sofa, but people could use it so long as they kept their legs up.

The spare room crap was either hanging off nails in the walls or on a makeshift shelf David had put up across one corner.

Looking to the doorframe, he saw the most important feature of the room. Two plastic discs set into the wood, hiding the bars that had been slid through the wall. It was a novel way to secure the adjoining room's door in place and protect what Mary was most concerned about.

He reached out for the phone.

"Paul, hey. It's me, David."

"David, unexpected. To what do I owe the pleasure of this call, then?" the man on the other end of the line asked.

"I need you to find someone for me. Someone who was at the march the other day."

"You mean the riot?" Paul replied.

"That wasn't my idea, it just blew up as usual, probably your lot again."

He chuckled. "Maybe. So, who? Got a name?"

"Nope, but I do have a face."

The two men talked through the event and the moment Frost had come over to David, at the point that he'd thrown the tear-gas canister.

"That was pretty stupid of you, David. You do remember that if you break the conditions of your suspended sentence, you'll be locked up again?" Paul asked.

"I know that, it was just meant to be a march, I got wrapped up in the moment."

"Don't even be there in the moment," Paul warned.

"Help me find this guy and he can deal with those moments for me."

"Clever boy," Paul said. "You'll be on our video surveillance from the spotter crews we had out there. Give me until about midday tomorrow. Our lot will probably have him tagged by then anyway."

"Thanks. I'll come and see you a bit early this month and we can exchange gifts," David said.

"Sounds good to me," Paul said, a hint of seriousness in his voice.

David was convinced that Paul saw him as a small-time dealer and it needed to stay that way. The monthly gifts of cash and drugs were a small price to pay to keep the drug squad off his back.

David thought about the range of drugs he had around the house now.

Blocks of hash were to be expected, but the coke and heroin were on another level.

Mary was right, there was too much stuff in the house, but that was a problem for another time. There was nothing he could do to get rid of what he was holding onto.

He smelt the pizza and felt the hunger that had been building.

Time to eat.

He opened the desk drawer and took a couple of wraps of heroin. Mary would need her evening top-up soon. He could feel himself getting hard again as images of himself using Mary went through his mind.

"And time to get you wrecked for a good fucking, too," he added, standing up and heading to the kitchen.

~ 5 ~

Dr Kirby remembered when he'd been asked to the Hannover Club. It had been the first and only time he'd been to the club so far. A man fond of his food, the private feast that had been held in his honour had been a perfect welcome into Hannover. His mind took him back to the meal, how he'd leaned back in his seat and congratulated his hosts on the fine steak he'd eaten. He could taste and smell it again now.

Following a well-established custom, the welcome dinner had been arranged shortly after the ceremony marking him out as an initiate member of Hannover. The small number of men around him included only those who had either sponsored him to join or then voted in favour of him joining.

As far as he knew, none had voted against him—but on that point he hadn't cared. He was in, and that's what had mattered.

When approached about joining Hannover, he'd sensed he was being let into a secret inner circle, an overdue recognition of his talent as a chemist in the energy field. A rather brilliant one at that, at least in his own estimation. Being very well connected in the business hadn't hurt either.

However, as time went on, he'd come to realise he was only partly right about joining an inner circle—in truth, it was more of a very outer circle. Hannover was not some gentleman's club, despite the naming of the place he was about to visit for a second time. He'd come to learn that Hannover was part of the establishment, maybe even was *the* establishment from what he'd heard since joining.

Despite the disappointment of being a small fish in a very big pond, he'd felt he'd proved himself in the last year and was now wondering if this summons to the Hannover Club marked his time to be allowed further into the circle.

"Doctor Kirby," the stranger said as a greeting from across the room.

Kirby looked across at someone he guessed to be in his early 40s, slim without being thin and sporting a tan the likes of which Kirby had always felt only the wealthy and leisured could maintain. The well-to-do look was completed by a dark blue tailored suit and mop of oiled hair, finger-combed to one side. He smiled broadly from in front of one of two lounge chairs around a small table, positioned in the far corner of the room, opposite a lit fireplace—a setup in the Hannover Club that Dr Kirby guessed was the staging for all the really important conversations.

"Do come and sit down, terrible weather outside. Well, I see you're wet!" the man said as Dr Kirby approached. "The driver was supposed to have an umbrella," he continued, in part to Dr Kirby and in part as a statement to the aide showing him into the room.

"Really no bother, the UK is always wet and windy in autumn," Dr Kirby replied, offering his hand to the stranger.

"Ah yes, I do apologise." The man shook Kirby's hand and gave him a smile. "I'm Steven," he said.

"Nice to meet you, Steven. I haven't been in this room before, very snug," Dr Kirby commented while taking a seat.

The aide had already placed Kirby's hat and coat on a stand and had returned to the two men.

"May I get you anything, sirs?" the man asked.

"Something warming, I suggest. Are you a brandy man, doctor?" Steven asked.

"Not usually before dinner, but I think I can make an exception."

"Great choice, two brandies, then," Steven directed as an order to the aide, who walked off to fulfil the request.

"How have you been getting along this…what is it now, nearly two years since you joined us?" Steven asked.

"Almost exactly," Kirby confirmed.

"Is your Calling going well? Any problems with the things you're asked to help with?"

Kirby thought for a second, trying to assess if this was a general catch-up or if it was leading somewhere. He stuck with his view that the unusual nature of the meeting meant it was probably leading somewhere. Anyway, even if it wasn't the case right now, all conversations in Hannover led somewhere eventually.

Over the last couple of years, he'd been involved in minor activities with other Hannover members, who had been slowly revealed to him as opportunities arose. Most of the time, however, he'd politely refused to get involved with their activities if there was no obvious benefit to him.

"All just fine, thank you for asking, Steven. But, if I may be direct, I doubt we're here for a friendly catch-up. Get to the point, would you?"

With perfect timing, the aide brought over the drinks, deposited them on the table, gave a slight bow, turned and left the men alone in the room.

Steven had noted the comment. It was a perfect example of the breaks in etiquette Kirby had been making since joining. Despite attempts to help him adjust to the Hannover way of doing things, to include him in his level-group, as Hannover called the peer groups they built, Kirby had been consistently uninvolved and consistently had not adjusted to the Hannover way. Steven raised his glass, then swirled it around while inspecting the moving contents.

"To your health," he offered, taking a sip of the warmed brandy and sitting back in his chair to look directly at Dr Kirby.

Kirby responded by doing the same and waited for Steven to carry on talking, clearly comfortable with the silence.

"We've been approached by one of our members to help with a problem they have and I believe you may be able to resolve it," Steven said after a moment's pause. "I'm sure you know we have a very special interest in problem solving for our friends here at Hannover. However, do you know the way we go about problem solving, doctor?" Steven asked.

"I've started to get the idea, but do explain," Kirby said, choosing to keep his words brief.

"Very well. We devise what we refer to as a Project. We define the objectives and outcome, set the timescales, find the team and execute a plan. We even have a project sponsor and someone who handles the team. Nothing particularly unusual in all of this, just as you'd expect any organisation to run things," Steven explained, waving his hand in the air to ensure his words came across in a dismissive way.

"What *is* unusual, however, are...let's call them the project drivers and expected outcomes," Steven continued, now looking directly at Kirby to emphasise this was the bit he needed to carefully listen to. "There is always a significant issue driving someone to request a project. There is always a significant outcome expected. An outcome intended to reshape some other organisation, perhaps a portion of society, perhaps even the world," Steven stated in a flat and serious tone that made the hairs on the back of Kirby's neck stand up.

"I see," Kirby replied, trying to appear relaxed and not entirely sure he was doing a good job of it or of grasping the gravity of what had just been said.

"Do you, doctor?" Steven asked, continuing with his tone. "I ask because it hasn't appeared to me that you really understand you are part of an organisation, that really is, and has been for hundreds of years, changing and shaping the world."

Kirby took another sip of his brandy. There was a directness to Steven's statement that he didn't like the sound of.

"What I mean, Steven, is that I accept what you say, I've no reason to doubt you. Of course, I have no idea how this is done or what my role in it is," he said.

That's the problem, Steven thought to himself. He seized on the admission. "Of course you don't! You've shown that in your behaviour," he replied, causing Kirby to catch his breath in surprise at the pronounced change of tone. Steven continued, "So, let's talk about that, shall we?" Kirby nodded and said nothing. "Doctor, everyone in your industry knows that you're a world-class chemist and well connected. That's useful to us and the challenges our members face. However, one of our members has approached you about joining their company to help solve a problem, and sadly you refused."

Steven paused to let the point sink in and give Kirby a moment to reflect.

Kirby felt a mild panic rising. He'd tried to be too smart with his relationships in Hannover and it looked like the one-way benefit he'd been enjoying had caught up with him. His mind raced, thinking of who it could be. He hadn't been seriously approached in a few months, but there were often enquiries and offers of one type or another. Write papers, give talks, provide mentoring. He barely even thought about what people emailed or asked about before making his excuses. Then, suddenly, a face came to mind and he recalled the conversation, a Hannover conversation. When his face lit up, Steven continued.

"Yes, doctor, let's not name names but we're talking about Terminal Fuels. I'm sure your peers would have explained themselves well enough to get your engagement and avoid them having to come back to us to intervene. It seems however you weren't that interested in supporting that member of your level-group."

"Now I think I know who you mean and what you want to talk about. But let's not worry about my initial rejection and misunderstanding. That can be set aside. Do continue, Steven."

Steven nodded. "Whoever gets access to and can market your new bio-fuel formula is going to reshape the way the world looks at oil. The implications for the world are far-reaching indeed. Reduced carbon emissions, higher energy output, lower costs to process and a change in the geo-politics of the world. The list goes on, as they say. You surely understand the commercial and political effects, don't you, doctor?"

Kirby looked at Steven and for the second time his mind was racing. How had the man known about the new bio-fuel? Now it was apparent that his Hannover peers and Hannover in general knew about what was top-secret research.

As for Steven's question, the political implications weren't lost on him at all. To comply with the law, he'd contacted the Department of Energy and Climate Change—or just DECC as they were referred to—as soon as it looked like the research would succeed. They'd cautioned him to keep it secret and had remained in occasional contact, awaiting for him to confirm when the bio-fuel formula would be viable for production.

"I see, so someone at Terminal is a member of Hannover and so is someone at DECC—or maybe someone in DECC has been sneaking secrets to Terminal. Though I suspect the former, given how we operate," Kirby offered as a summary, attempting to both check his understanding and to show he had a better grip of the situation than he felt he had.

Whatever the case, he now knew what the purpose of this conversation was.

Kirby continued, "Given that, Hannover would like me to move from Cosgrove and take my know-how to Terminal?" he asked outright.

"Of course someone in the government could be a member of Hannover and simply have some other connection with Terminal," Steven responded, playing the logic game back with Kirby. "But," he continued, "you are generally correct. The request is to move from where you are now at Cosgrove Research and join Terminal Fuels, accepting their offer, which will be equally as generous despite the fact we've had to become directly involved."

Kirby thought for a moment. Saying no wasn't really an option, he was clearly being told, not asked. Refusing, apparently a second time, would have consequences he didn't want to explore.

"I'll need to see the offer and what the research budget will be. And as I have now, I need my own facility and a team of two researchers dedicated to my lab," he replied, in an attempt to appear somewhat in charge of the outcome of the conversation.

"Excellent! I knew you'd do what was needed," Steven said.

"Naturally. Now, before we go further, you should know there is just one problem with my research," said Dr Kirby.

Steven tipped his head and looked at the doctor, awaiting his explanation of the problem.

"It isn't stable. The mix turns into a gel, it doesn't break down fast enough to convert to a useful fuel." Kirby hesitated, nervous of how Steven would respond, but the man just waited for him to continue. "I haven't spoken about this to anyone. What we need is an enzyme to further process the fuel and move it to a stable state."

"I see, this is unfortunate news. Have you done any research around this or do you have any ideas about how to acquire the enzyme?" Steven asked.

"The research hasn't been successful, as you can no doubt guess, or I wouldn't be sitting here in embarrassment. However, enzymes are the Holy Grail of bio-fuel production; this is not a new problem."

"I assume you're saying an enzyme is already out there, doctor? One you could use?"

"Yes, it was invented years ago, by a brilliant Scandinavian chemist. Do you know the ship called the *MV Braer*?"

"Of course, doctor, it's now a wreck off the coast of Scotland somewhere, but wasn't that just carrying conventional fuel?"

"Yes indeed, light crude was its main cargo, but it had something else. An enzyme that could convert the heavier fuels. Half the reason the oil spill cleared so quickly was that the enzyme was active in the water, breaking the oil down and dispersing it. It's a long shot, but it may be that there are containers of the enzyme that didn't get mixed into the fuel, lying at the bottom of the ocean."

Steven looked thoughtfully across the room and then said, "This is unexpected, but may not be insurmountable. Let me see what I can do. Everything else must proceed as planned," Steven said. Before Kirby could interrupt, he continued. "From my side, Dr Kirby, there is just one other small detail: your research and any samples currently at the Cosgrove refinery where you are now are not to survive your leaving. It wouldn't do to have any record of the bio-fuel remain and your new friends embarrassed if they brought it to market."

Kirby took a few moments to realise what this new twist meant.

"How is that to be done?" Kirby asked. "There are vats and vats of the bio-fuel mix, ready-made for trials. The data is backed up on hard disks within the on-site data centre that I have no access to and papers of the research are likely on several desks. I can't run around and get rid of it all, can I?"

The doctor looked back at Steven, clearly confused as to what he wanted from him.

"Ah, you're right, of course. But don't worry about that, doctor—you just need to make sure you extract enough data and samples to take a complete set of your research with you. In the next few weeks, the project I spoke about will do the rest."

"You want me to steal the files and samples? Me?" Kirby asked with growing confusion and concern.

"The research is secret, doctor, and complex. Only you know fully what needs to be taken. You have access to it and no one will suspect your working with it. We can hardly send some random team of IT experts in to hack systems and hopefully collect the right files from the right places, along with collecting samples and expect no one to notice. We're not magicians, doctor!"

Steven sat back and calmed himself. This was Kirby through and through. The thing he didn't get was that he *was* Hannover: Hannover was the people in it. When Hannover needed something doing it was Hannover people that did it, not some mythical other team. Kirby needed to do his bit.

"When?" Kirby asked.

"Our engineers are already in position to address the data centre. Let's say the day after tomorrow."

"Right, that's quick," Kirby replied, realising for certain now there was only one expected outcome from this meeting.

~ 6 ~

In true form, Lauren arrived at the hotel five minutes before she'd been told to be there. As she stepped into the entrance to the restaurant she looked around but didn't see the Handler.

The restaurant looked as it had several years back, when she'd been summoned here to discuss her first engagement with Hannover.

The bar off to the left, tables to the right. Each of the dining tables with white linen and white tulips in the centre. The staff all smartly dressed with formal shirts and cufflinks, each sporting a white apron tied around their waist covering the top of their legs.

It was all very smart and very white, just how she imagined a restaurant on a cruise ship would look. Not that she'd actually ever had the time or inclination to take a cruise. With her various roles for various organisations, there was no time for distractions such as cruises.

She turned to speak to the waiter who was greeting guests as they arrived.

"Lauren Shields," she said.

He checked down a list on the pedestal in front of him.

"Ah yes, Miss Shields. Do follow me."

He crossed her name out, gestured for her to follow him and walked off towards the far end of the bar.

Around the corner were four tables, screened off from one another by wood and glass partitions. At the farthest table, Steven sat looking at Lauren as she approached. He thought she looked better than the last time they'd met. Her slim figure and long, dark hair made her look youthful, the flowing dress she wore made her look elegant.

Lauren saw him smile almost imperceptibly and as she reached the table he stood up to greet her.

"Your guest, sir," the waiter said and left them alone.

"Steven," Lauren said as a hello to her Handler.

"Hello, Lauren."

He gently placed a hand on her shoulder, leant in and kissed her on each cheek.

"How have you been keeping?" he said, gesturing for her to sit. "Good to speak on the phone the other day, but it's been too long since we've met face to face."

"Yes, it has," she replied as they both took their seats. "I'm surprised you asked me to come here, you're usually happy just to use the phone. I'm guessing this is a special case? You have a hard one you need a hand with, so you thought of me. How flattering," she said, now looking intently at him.

"Same old Lauren, I never could tell when you were joking or being serious. As it happens, it is a *very* special case, but let's order something to eat and get a few drinks before we dive into the details, shall we? I have a room here, so we can discuss business in private later."

"Good idea, I'm starving. But, already trying to get me up to your room, Steven? This may be a special case, but I'm not sure if I want to do it with you yet," she said, unable to stop a smile forming on her lips.

"There… that's what I mean!" Steven said. "Even I saw through that one! Take it seriously, will you?" he added, picking up his napkin and pretending to try and hit her with it.

She laughed out loud. "OK, OK. Anyway, you spotted me on that one—missed the other two, though!"

Steven handed her one of the menus and opened his to see what was on offer.

Flicking slowly through the pages, his thoughts drifted between the menu and recalling the time they'd first been here. Lauren had just been allowed into Hannover, sponsored by Sir Anthear himself.

He'd been told about her from an old contact, who had described her as extremely intelligent but low on moral norms. Perfect for Hannover. Getting a behavioural psychologist on the general staff those years ago had been controversial at the time, but it had paid off greatly and the team had grown since.

"I don't really like people, if I'm honest with you," she'd said at the meetings held to assess her, claiming not to hate them, but that, "it's just that most people are like dumb little pets, like trained puppies or sheep. Sheeple," she'd said.

Steven laughed at recalling her say the word and the dumbstruck faces of Anthear and him.

"What are you laughing at?" she asked, now hitting him back with her napkin this time.

"Sorry, sorry!" he said, laughing for a second time. "What have you chosen? I'm going for the lamb and a glass of white."

"Beef and a glass of red," she replied.

"Of course, Miss Contrary, I could have guessed."

They placed their order and the wine was poured. Alone with each other again, Steven took a sip of wine and moved his eyebrows to indicate that the wine was OK.

"It's a good job I can interpret your non-verbal communication," she said. "However, I'm not psychic, so tell me why I'm here and what you need help with."

Steven looked at her for a second.

"My god, that almost sounded like plain language! Or has your Neuro-linguistic Programming talk become so perfected I can't hear it anymore?" he joked, pulling another face to show a mix of confusion and surprise.

She looked back in mock disgust.

"I wanted you to… give it to me… straight," she said, pausing strategically as she spoke.

Steven held up his hands in a fake surrender.

"OK, OK, I'll tell you what's going on! Just please stop!"

Smiling, Lauren took a sip of her wine as if to toast the victory.

"I'm not going to give you all the details, of course, you know the drill."

"Yes, I know the routine."

"Do you remember Byford?" he asked.

She thought for a moment.

"The Scottish guy who lost his team and some civilians in Israel?"

"Egypt, but yes, the very same. As often happens, the story gets turned around. Strictly speaking, the civilians that got killed weren't his to take care of and it was two of his team that got taken out, not all of them. Anyway, the point is we're getting him back on a project. One of our guys has had a little chat with him and we expect him to come back to us sometime soon."

"And I met David the other day," she said, interrupting him.

"Sharp as always. As you've rightly guessed, he's also to do with this project, but I'm happy with where he is for now. David will soon get the attention of someone we'd like to have as a new friend, a bright young woman like yourself. However, unlike yourself, she has a bit of history I think we can work with, something that will resonate with Byford," he concluded, just as the waiter brought the food to the table.

"Now that looks good. Well-presented, perfect size, hot but not so hot you can't get your mouth around it."

It was now Lauren's turn to respond with a light-hearted look of disgust, rolling her eyes to the ceiling and sighing. "Steven! That was terrible."

"Hey, I can play your game sometimes!"

For the next quarter of an hour they sat enjoying the food and wine, and each other's company after so long apart, sharing occasional glances and smiles, saying nothing of note.

Steven looked up at Lauren, holding his gaze on her a few seconds too long.

"Yes?" she asked.

"Nothing, just been a while since I've been able to look at you."

She took a few more bites of food and then looked up at him again.

"I enjoyed our time, Steven, really I did."

"So did I—though I wasn't one of your sheeple, then?" he asked.

She gave a soft laugh, realising he'd remembered her saying that from those years ago.

"Yes, of course you are," she replied, reaching over and tapping him on the hand like she was placating a child. "I'm just not the settle-down-and-be-a-good-wife type. You're also in no position to go all middle-aged and fat."

He gave a sigh and raised his drink to her.

"Yes, all good points," he conceded. "Come on, I don't want to rush but we have business to talk about."

They picked up their glasses. Steven grabbed the wine bottle and headed to the room.

∞

Lauren looked around the room they had just entered. To her surprise, there wasn't, in fact, a bed.

The room was set up like an office, albeit a softly furnished one, matching the décor of the hotel. A desk and two chairs, floor-standing lamp and a few pictures on the walls.

"Oh, I'm not sure if I should feel insulted or flattered," she said.

"Honestly, you really expected this to be a cheap attempt at getting you into bed?" Steven asked. "Come and take a seat, we really do have business to take care of."

Lauren wandered over to the desk, sat herself down and nursed her drink on her lap. Steven filled his glass and offered Lauren a top up, which she gladly accepted.

"So tell me then, what can I help you with?"

"We have a number of subjects that we require profiles and strategies for. I need you to help me assess them based on the information I have here," Steven said, now pulling out a tablet PC from one of the drawers in the desk.

"OK, I'm intrigued, tell me more."

Steven flipped open the computer and started the camera. His face appeared on the screen. The computer's facial recognition software overlaid a grid of red lines and dots across his image of his face. The red dots danced around the image until they settled on key features such as his eyes and nose. After a few seconds, the grid of lines and dots went green and the computer unlocked.

"Here are the subjects' files. I'll transfer this system to you later, by the way," he said, now opening a series of folders and documents.

"This is Byford, who you already know. He's been our man for a good number of years. A capable operative who had a mission go wrong, got a few grey hairs and had someone close to him walk away, so he figured it was time to quit. We need him back and as I've said, I think we've found a way. The special someone he lost, who we've now found, is Mary. Here, this is her file. Surprisingly, we don't have that much on her, but what we do have should be useful to you," Steven said, switching to the folder containing information about Mary.

"Kept her hidden, did he?" Lauren asked.

"Yes and no. We of course knew all about his family when he joined us. Later on, when Byford went into his little mid-life crisis, Mary went off grid and we, along with Byford, lost track of her. Until our luck changed recently, that is."

He continued working through the folders.

"Frost, another operative, still active with us and a useful lever, worked with Byford in the past and the two of them keep in touch. The only other person of interest to me is David. I know you've prepped him, but we need some thoughts on how to *engage* him usefully, background on that is in the file too. Now, last but just as important: this is Melissa, almost nothing on her I'm afraid. She's an ASTU Officer, that's Anti-Subversion and Terrorism Unit. A new branch of police that is all about searching out organisations like ours."

"I'm aware of ASTU, they were formed after the Barton Incident, when that bridge was blown up."

"Correct, and they've been a small but noticeable thorn in our side ever since," Steven said.

Lauren continued, "If I'm reading this right, you want some basic behavioural psychology applying to most of them. A little something to move them in the right direction—you've no doubt planned that, too?" she said.

"Of course," Steven replied in a slightly mocking tone. "You can flick through the scenario documents later. The math boffins have gone over them and assigned a series of probabilities based on various behaviours, given certain events and their effect on the outcomes modelled for each scenario. It's achieving those outcomes that I want strategies for, starting with the most desirable scenario…"

"Where everyone does what you want them to?" she said, interrupting.

"Of course," Steven said again. "But give me actions and reactions for each subject in each scenario. I want to know what actions we should be able to get a certain participant subject to do, given a certain situation we can create and what the expected reaction should be from the target subject. The math is all well and good but I want a playbook with alternate paths to the desired outcome, should a certain action—reaction not go as planned. Make sense?" Steven asked, spinning the computer around for Lauren to see more clearly.

He sat back in his own chair and took a long drink of wine.

"I see. Hannover really has taken my advice onboard, then. I was worried that being so frank about how usefully simple-minded people are would be too much. I'm glad you were there, Steven, so in tune with my way of thinking."

"I'll take that as a compliment," he replied, showing his usual good humour.

It was true, to a degree—they both had a somewhat non-typical view of people, which probably helped them get on so well.

"Steven, level with me, what's really going on here? This is a lot of moving parts, I've never seen so many people needing profiling at the same time."

He looked at her for a few seconds, uncertain how to summarise what he knew. There was also a lot he didn't know.

"Lauren, it's as I've said. You're still the best..."

"Not what, Steven, why. This analysis can be done by anyone, but why these people?" she asked, interrupting him.

"I disagree, this isn't a regular profiling job, it needs your skills. As usual, there's a lot I don't know, Lauren," he began. "I heard a rumour that the Department for Energy and Climate Change called in a favour. They want some research...spirited away, shall we say. To do that they need to use our know-how and discretion. If I'm correct, a minor member of our group is the chemist with the research." Steven turned away, worried his face would betray that he knew a little more than he was letting on.

"I see," Lauren said, still thinking through the bigger picture. "But, that doesn't explain Byford, or David for that matter," she added.

"Oh, that's an easy one," Steven said. "David's girlfriend is Mary."

Lauren let out a noise that said she had some insight into the depth of the situation.

"Ah, an eye for an eye, is it?" Lauren asked.

"Something like that. I don't know how all this wires together right now. I'm getting pushed as much as I'm pulling. But Byford needs to come back into the fold and get his beloved Mary back—David can be thrown to the wolves for all I care."

"All right, now I see a little of the why. I can give you what you need and you can even have your math geeks run over the scenarios again to see how probable they become, with more real-world motivation in place," she said, now looking at the picture of Melissa on the screen.

She looked at the picture more closely. "And what about this one? Name and picture, nothing more?" she asked.

Steven looked at Lauren for a second.

"A Sir Anthear lead. She's your real challenge. I should be able to get you more on her later. For now, I just want you to keep her off our backs. However, Sir Anthear wants you to convince her to join us," he said, keeping his gaze on hers.

Lauren looked directly at Steven.

"Is that a joke! He wants to get an ASTU Officer to not only turn a blind eye to this lot, but also defect to Hannover for the shits and giggles of it?"

Steven almost spat his wine out with sudden laughter.

"Lauren, you're the best damn psychologist we have."

"I'm the only one you have!"

"Yes, yes, I know. Well, we do have profilers. Point is, if anyone can work out how to get her onboard, you can. Anthear will be in touch in a few days, he's got a way to get you near her so you can do your thing."

"How near?"

"Arm in arm. Anthear thinks he has a way to get you *inside* ASTU."

Lauren sat back and waved her hand around in the air, pretending to be casting magic spells.

"Exactly that!" Steven said in a jovial tone.

"How do we even know about her, what do we know, why do we care?"

Steven raised his hands in the air.

"Search me. Contact of Anthear's told him about her; what, why, where, who, I don't ask," he said.

"Good little puppy," Lauren mocked.

Steven got up, poured the last of the wine and walked away from the desk, leaving Lauren lost in thought.

"So, Anthear has a co-conspirator inside the ASTU, which would technically *be* subversion, wouldn't it? Oh, the irony," Lauren said.

"ASTU probably is Hannover! You should know by now, it's rabbit holes all the way down with us!"

"With a lion's den for yours truly at the bottom. This is a dangerous game Hannover is playing this time, Steven."

"Just get her to join, after that she's another story," Steven said.

Lauren continued to look at the picture of Melissa.

She looked young, maybe in her mid-twenties, a mix of slightly vulnerable and sharply intelligent. Lauren thought she also looked mixed race; Asian and European, perhaps. There was a slight tan to her skin and her long, dark hair seemed unusual for a native Caucasian. To be ASTU she would have to be one of the brightest. When ASTU formed, it had been by invitation only. Since then the recruits had been known as the best of the best.

Creating a few scenarios and suggesting some things to do to encourage people to move in a generally planned direction was one thing; brainwashing someone of Melissa's intelligence was another. People had free will, they were unpredictable.

Melissa would need to have a few hot buttons that could be pressed.

Steven stood quietly away from her, happy to let her think and to have the opportunity to look at her, enjoying watching her lost in thought.

"OK, but my usual daily rate of 1500 pounds and access to whatever Hannover staff and resources I need," she said, turning to see Steven over by the far wall, staring back at her, his back resting against a large door she had missed earlier.

"Of course, my dear," he said in a gentle tone.

"Now as you don't seem to need time to sleep on it," he said, spinning around and opening the door wide to reveal the room behind was the bedroom adjoined to this suite, "perhaps I can invite you for a nightcap?"

Lauren's eyes widened at the surprise, but she stood up and walked casually towards the door.

"I knew you wouldn't disappoint me, Steven," she said, gently brushing her hand against his chest as she swept past him and into the room.

~ 7 ~

From his vantage point of a gazebo on a small hill, Frost watched Byford running around the lake for the third time. He knew he'd be finishing his daily exercise soon and heading past him—at least, that's what he'd done these last few days that Frost had been spying on him.

Frost was content to wait. He hadn't been to this part of Spain before and was surprised that the weather was warm at this time of year.

Málaga is a lot different than Bilbao in October, he thought to himself, taking another deep breath of cool, clean air. *Like being in the mountains, a lot better than London.* Off to his left, a mother suddenly bellowed something at a boy of about five, who she was just picking up off the floor. As she wiped off whatever dirt was on his clothes she continued to berate him in Spanish.

"Man, Spanish chicks, gotta love 'em," he said out loud in her general direction, giving her a smile and a nod as she looked over to him.

She gave a slightly embarrassed smile in return and dragged the child off in the direction they had been both originally going.

Frost checked her backside out for a second and turned back to watching Byford, who was nowhere to be seen.

"Balls…" he said, then stood up to get a better view of the path around the lake. Byford was definitely not there. Frost turned and stepped onto the path the mother and child headed down just a minute before.

Unfortunately, the path he was now on was crossed by another which Byford was running up, directly towards Frost. Realising his hiding was over, Frost stood and waited for Byford to reach him, with a big grin on his face in anticipation of his old colleague's surprise.

Byford was no more than five metres away when he looked up, saw Frost and stopped dead in his tracks.

"Byford!" Frost bellowed at him in a long, drawn-out greeting, arms wide open and a grin still on his face.

"What the hell?" blurted a fatigued Byford, now in obvious shock and disbelief at seeing Frost.

"Eh, nice to see you too, mate! Been a while, eh?"

"What the hell are you doing here?" Byford demanded.

"Easy, obviously it's not a social call but no need to get all upset. Just here to have a little chat," Frost said in order to relax Byford, not wanting the moment of reunion to go the wrong way.

Byford had over ten years of experience on Frost and a reputation for being a capable operative. Just because he was older didn't mean he'd gone to seed, and looking at him now, Frost could see he kept himself fairly mission ready.

"I thought I'd made it clear I was out three years ago," Byford said, now walking up the hill past Frost.

Frost turned and followed him.

"Yeh, my mistake, I can see you're a proper retired person, aren't you? Strolling around, enjoying the sun, going fat and soft."

"Force of habit, too many years keeping ready for idiots like you to get in touch. Doesn't mean I'm keeping ready now, though, I told you I'm done with all that shit."

Frost walked with Byford in silence for a few minutes as he headed towards his home.

"I guess you're not just going to go away, are you?" Byford asked.

"No, mate, you know the drill. Anyway, surely you've got a bit of time for an old pal? Maybe a beer or two eh? The occasional email between us is all well and good, but it's good to see you face to face," Frost replied.

Byford turned and looked Frost squarely in the eyes. He was right; it *was* good to see his friend in person.

"Aye, you too, pal, you too," he said, slapping his old friend on the shoulder and smiling broadly.

"Just a shame I'm here on official business," Frost said.

After a short walk, punctuated by general talk and admiration of the place they were in, they arrived at a block of flats and Byford pulled his keys from his shorts.

Frost aired his confusion. "Thought you were living in a house a bit further from here?"

Byford turned and in a smug tone said, "Oh, been following me have you? Always were a bit sloppy, Frost, that's a house I'm house-sitting for someone. When you think your target's gone to ground, don't piss off back to the titty bars straight away in the future, eh?"

"Yeah, you got me!" Frost retorted with a snort that told Byford he'd guessed correctly.

Inside the flat, Byford headed straight for the fridge, grabbed two cans of beer and threw one to Frost. They cracked them open and raised them towards each other.

"Well, a bit of a shock, but good to see you, Frost," Byford offered as a crude toast.

"You too, buddy."

They knocked their cans together and took a long drink.

"I'm going to shower. Relax and don't make yourself too at home," Byford said and walked off down the hallway.

Frost went straight to the fridge, grabbed another can and some roast chicken, which he guessed was from last night's dinner.

"Nice one," he muttered to himself and headed back to the living room with his supplies.

He heard the shower running and looked around the living room for anything of interest—on a shelf above the TV was a picture of Mary.

"Bingo," Frost said aloud, "but you can wait till later."

He wandered out to the patio, sat down at the table and tucked in to Byford's leftover chicken as he looked out over the sea. In the distance, the blue-green ocean sparkled in the morning sun. Frost discarded his plate onto the patio table and drained his beer. He closed his eyes and felt the sun warm his skin and a gentle breeze play over his face. The sounds and feelings began to blend together and the world faded away.

"Hey! I thought I said don't make yourself too at home?" Byford announced from the patio door, catching Frost by surprise.

"Bloody hell, think I was falling asleep then," Frost replied, pulling himself up in the seat.

Byford placed another beer on the table for Frost, pulled up a chair and sat down to his side, facing the same direction.

"Ha! I do the same. Good views, eh? You can see the transporter ships and sail boats some days or just watch the clouds, it's a great place to watch the sea," Byford said, a relaxed tone echoing in his voice.

"Can't disagree there, boss, certainly relaxing, but is this really it for you now? I mean just hiding here when you've got a bunch of loose threads to tie up?" Frost asked, knowing full well Byford would know what he meant.

The last project Byford had led had turned into a complete disaster. It was only his long reputation of delivering results over the years that had saved him from being ousted from Hannover completely.

Instead, he had taken a self-enforced break, saving the Sponsor or Handler the embarrassment of making him take one.

Best to get out of the way of Hannover and allow them time to move on without him being a constant point of conversation.

"Well, I expected someone to come visiting eventually, not like you can really hide from Hannover, is it?" Byford replied at last.

"Nope. And like I said, this isn't a social visit."

Byford took a deep breath and sighed. "Go on then, what's happening?"

Frost leaned over to Byford as if trying to ensure no one nearby could hear.

"Well, official word is they want you to lead a team on a little distraction project. Bunch of new joiners that need putting through their paces. Couple are graduate intakes too," Frost said, casting a glance over to Byford.

He knew Byford had done distraction projects before; projects that were just covers for the real projects were pretty common. But leading a team of new joiners was another thing, everyone in Hannover disliked that. Hannover's recent decision to take on people with no military training had also not gone down well with the older members.

"Jesus, great. So what's this, a return trial by fire? See if I can carry out a project successfully and with a bunch of amateurs? Fantastic. Did you need to leave soon? Don't let me stop you!"

"Don't be so down on this one, mate," Frost said.

Byford looked over to Frost with a look that said *this better be good.*

"That's the official word, but rumour is it's a bit more complicated. I've heard this is not only a distraction project, but a get-back at some prick who refused the approach from a Sir Anthear project."

"What? Anthear approached someone direct? What was that about?" Byford said in a tone that left no doubt about the seriousness of the breach of protocol.

"This is where it gets interesting and where you need to listen up. You know Sir Anthear always thought of you as his man, even though strictly it's the Handler, Steven, who pimps you out. Well, Anthear found out about some guy called David, who's running some kind of eco-warrior outfit."

Byford looked visibly confused by the tale so far.

"Fascinating. And?"

Frost continued to the punch-line he was struggling to get to for fear of Byford's reaction.

"Yeh. They seem like a lot of noise and not much action to me, but guess who David's girlfriend is?"

"Amaze me," Byford said, maintaining his nonchalant tone.

Frost hesitated for a second.

"Mary."

Byford was midway raising the beer to his mouth but stopped suddenly and his heart skipped a beat.

"*My* Mary?" Byford said, spitting a little beer out at the same time, though as it came from Frost, he already knew the answer.

"No, the virgin bloody Mary. Of course it's your Mary, you dopey git."

Byford stood up and took a few paces back and forth.

"Holy crap, they found her?" he eventually managed.

Frost seized the moment.

"You know Hannover take care of their own. Yes, they found Mary, my team's been on these eco's for about three months now."

"Two years I've been looking with no leads and now you tell me you've known where she was for three months! Why didn't you say something, why didn't you grab her?" Byford demanded, standing over Frost and glaring down at him.

"I can't take an unauthorized action, can I? And, mate, she knew where you were all the time, didn't she, but she never reached out to you."

Byford stepped back from over Frost. He was right. She could have contacted him whenever she'd wanted to.

"Also, I'm afraid she's got herself into a bit of a situation with her personal life and health."

Byford stood staring into the distance for a few more seconds and then took a gulp of beer.

"What situation?"

"David, as well as being a fucking do-gooder leader of these eco warriors by day, just happens to be a drug dealer by night. He's dominating her emotionally, now he's got her hooked on shit and, well, she's stuck if you get my drift. Thinks she loves the guy and maybe she does in some twisted way, but she also needs him for the drugs. So, we can't just rip her out of there for several reasons."

Byford stood in silence, looking out to sea, thinking of Mary and imagining the state she could be in, images of the healthy woman he used to know, then images of a physically ruined woman went through his mind.

After what seemed an eternity he finally responded.

"I get it, we can't just go in there and grab her if Anthear's got this David marked."

Frost replied in agreement. "No chance, and Hannover won't just go in there and get her out of the goodness of their hearts, either, you know that."

"Jesus, ever feel you're being gamed?"

"Yeh, of course you are, mate, but that's the game we signed up for," Frost said, as a way of saying it was something they both knew and had accepted.

"She's been lost to me for nearly two years, what makes you think she'll welcome me with open arms?"

Byford sat down, placed his head into his hands and let out a deep sigh.

"Come on, Byford, that's not like you. It's never too late. With a little cleverness and help, you might earn yourself a second chance with her."

Byford raised his head and fell back into his seat again, head facing the darkening sky. Frost looked over at Byford and made a last appeal.

"One last job, it'll be easy for you with a good crew."

"A new, clueless crew."

"Perhaps, but you get your mandate to sort the bastard out, get Mary back and sort her out too. Loose ends tied up. They might let you leave for good, honourable discharge for exemplary conduct and retire off."

Byford straightened himself in his chair and reached over for his beer.

"Looks like I've just been gifted an opportunity here, eh?" Byford said.

"The perfect gift for the man who has everything, except what he wants most."

"Indeed," Byford replied, with an air of finality.

The two men sat in silence and watched the sun finish setting behind the sea, a final blaze of orange light vanishing beneath the distant horizon, giving way to the dusk.

"Fine, tell the Handler we're on. I'll go over to London next week and have a little chat with him to get the details straight. One detail's for sure, I need you backing me up."

"Officially or not, I wouldn't have it any other way!" Frost replied.

"All right then, here's to one last job."

Frost raised his beer and tapped it against Byford's.

"One last job."

~ 8 ~

Kirby sat at his desk in the office he held as head of research for Cosgrove Research hitting the refresh key on the browser and waiting for the website he was using to finish reloading.

Checking the time, he saw it was 1pm exactly. He hit refresh one more time and it failed. His heart leapt—that was the signal to tell him *they* were now expecting him to move.

He looked up from his laptop to ensure he was not being watched from the lab. Most of the assistants were on lunch and those that were still working could be seen happily carrying on inspecting and testing samples.

"Here we go then... first step," he murmured to himself.

Taking a data pen out of his trouser pocket, he slid it into the computer's USB port and, once it registered, he began copying all the data files he'd been carefully organising over the last few weeks.

Data on the designs for genetically engineered plants which were sources of desirable chemicals, molecular designs and details of compounds, distillation instructions, mixing procedures and more.

All of it slowly moving over to the data pen.

Thinking ahead to what post-production data should be useful, Kirby had also included a copy of test results from samples and burns of the fuel they'd performed.

With the network down, there would be no record of what he was about to do, none of the usual servers connected to monitor what data was going where.

He continued to make it look like as if he were working at the computer while the data transfer carried on.

The technician at Hannover had told him that all he needed to do was copy the files and then wait for a message on his screen to say everything was complete.

He waited for what felt like an eternity, flicking his eyes between the lab and screen, checking the progress bar as it moved at an intolerably slow pace.

Small beads of sweat started to form on his brow and be felt the humidity rising under his shirt.

Then, suddenly, the message appeared.

'Done' was all it said. He clicked 'OK' and the file-transfer window closed.

If all had worked as planned he now had the last 5 years of bio-fuel research on the data pen and the log of any copying would be nonexistent.

Kirby pulled the data pen from the computer, slid it back into his pocket and checked the time: 1.08pm.

8 minutes, was that all?

He felt excitement at the thought of what he had just stolen, a silent power at what he now possessed. It was not only his own research, but everything of those before him. It was nearly priceless, and he just happened to know someone who'd pay a fine price for it, too. One more thing to do.

He checked his watch again. At exactly 2pm the network would come back up.

Step one at one and step two by two, he thought to himself, reflecting on the fact they'd picked an easy way for him to remember what time he had to get this done by.

Kirby sat back, took a tissue off the desk and wiped the fine sheen of sweat from his brow, wafting his shirt to help cool his body. He knew he was no hero, but the thought of what he was going to get out of doing this was enough motivation to finish the appointed tasks.

Satisfied he was now a little calmer, he looked up and across the lab. The assistants and the lead researcher had come back in from lunch earlier than expected.

Whatever, time for step two.

He stood up from his desk and headed across the lab to the men, carrying some printouts he'd prepared earlier.

"Hello, gentlemen," he said to the two in the far corner.

These two were on centrifuges, their job simply to separate and catalogue the mixtures that were being trialled.

"I notice from the results over the last week that batch mixtures are varying quite a lot. Any thoughts on why?" he asked.

They looked at each other and both betrayed a look of slight worry and confusion.

"Not sure, doctor," the older man said, stepping in to take the flak that was about to come.

"You're not sure? Don't you look at the results?" Kirby asked.

"Well, as you know, we record results, we don't analyse them," the man said.

"I could get a machine to do that! What about you?" Kirby asked the younger man.

"No idea either, doctor. We run the centrifuges five times a day, that's over fifty samples. I don't recall the values over the days or weeks, I'm afraid," he said, giving Kirby the precise excuse he was looking for.

"Just what I'd expect! The samples should essentially be the same, that's the point of the isolated vats and mixtures! Give me some vials," he said to the researchers before they could add any more to the conversation. "I will go and run the samples off each vat myself!"

The younger man jumped off his chair, then jogged around the table to clumsily grab a handful of vials from a rack on the far wall.

"I need eighteen!" Kirby shouted at him across the table, causing the man to turn back around and collect some more vials. "Three samples per vat, which I trust you've been doing?"

The man came rapidly back around to Kirby and held the vials out for him to take. Kirby looked at the vials, then up at the man.

"In a vial case perhaps?"

The man repeated his jog around the table, vials clutched between his hands. Back at the far wall, he saw a padded case on a shelf but couldn't reach it for holding the vials.

"Help, maybe!" Kirby said to the older researcher, who'd been sitting silently the last few minutes watching the exchange between the other two men.

The older researcher sprang into action, jumping off his chair and going around the table to grab the case. He opened it, laid it down and the young man dropped the vials into the interior padding. They both fitted the vials into pre-cut slots, snapped the case closed and the younger researcher handed the case to Kirby.

"Good!" Kirby said, turning and walking off to the east corridor and towards the vats.

The two men watched him go.

"My god, is he autistic or something? He sits there rocking on his chair, mumbling to himself, then has these outbursts," the young assistant said.

The older man laughed and turned back to his work.

"They don't call him Rain Man for nothing," he replied.

The vats of experimental bio-fuel mixes were located about three hundred feet away from the lab. Requiring a walk through the facility, then outside to the storage area.

Kirby walked the length of the east wing and checked his watch: 1.22pm. Any second now the pass-card-operated door lock should go green to show it was unlocked; right now it was glowing red.

"Come on!" he murmured to himself, aware he barely had time to get the next step done by 2.00pm.

With the benefit of a hacked CCTV system that watched over the facility, the engineer who was orchestrating the switching off and on of the various systems watched Kirby walking down the east wing. He saw him a few steps away from the door to the outside, typed a command on his computer and unlocked the door.

Kirby saw the electronic door access light go green. He breathed a sigh of relief and pushed the door open. He'd been told he'd be watched and helped, but where and how he hadn't been told in detail.

Hannover all over, half information and even less trust, he thought as he stepped out of the building and into the afternoon air. It felt cool as he breathed it in and, as always, it had the pungent aroma of what to Kirby smelt like cooking oil that had gone rancid.

Glancing around for anyone who might notice him going to the vats, he saw no one and felt another wave of relief. Though like those inside he didn't have to worry about being challenged, he preferred to carry out his task without an audience.

He looked across the roadway in front of him and to the six tall, black-painted vats. The huge cylinder-shaped tanks reminded him of oversized oil drums, appropriate for what they contained, he'd thought to himself on occasion. Stepping away from the door he made his way along the paved pathway to the road and towards the vats.

They were perhaps five metres across and thirty metres high. Thick pipes ran from the top of each vat, all heading off in the same direction, towards the distillation plant someway behind. All the vats were contained within a high wall, with a chain-mesh gate in the middle of the wall, facing towards Kirby as he approached.

How Hannover were going to 'disappear' all of this was beyond him.

He saw the pass-card reader on the gate was red and stared at it, willing it to turn green. As if hearing his wish, the light turned from red to green, unlocking the gate as he was just a couple of feet away. Hairs pricked up on the back of his neck thinking of himself being so closely watched by some unknown observer.

The gate creaked open a little as the lock was switched off. Kirby swung it open and passed through, taking a final look around to see if anyone had seen him. Convinced that no one had, he pulled the gate shut and, hearing the lock re-engage, moved to the side and hid against the surrounding brick wall. It felt good to be out of the watchful eye of CCTV.

In front of him were the containers of bio-fuel, each containing a different experimental mixture.

The pipes and cables above cast a spider's web of shadows onto the ground, ground that was blackened and gelatinous from the many small spills of oil that had occurred over the years. That was how the facility managed to smell like it did: the oil and chemicals were as much a part of the surrounding ground as the ground itself.

He looked at the base of the closest container and saw the sample tap from where he could fill the vials he was carrying. Stepping quietly over to it and keeping aware if anyone might be around him, he then reminded himself it was perfectly normal for the lab staff to be here. Kirby felt himself relax at the thought.

He placed the case down and clicked it open. Removing a vial, he unscrewed the top and presented it to the thin spout of the metal tap. Slowly opening the valve, the greenish black liquid poured out and filled the vial.

Once filled, he closed the valve, fastened the vial and wrote on the label 'Vat 1: e2-f8-a5', the vat number and code for the mixture that could be matched to the research papers he'd stolen.

Kirby made his way around the vats, filling all of the sample vials, three for each vat, and labelling and replacing them into the case.

"Where are you, you idiot?" the engineer asked to the screen he was monitoring.

Kirby had gone off camera when he had entered the compound nearly half an hour ago.

"You should be out by now!"

The engineer reached for a two-way radio on his desk.

"Groundsman, any movement?"

A few seconds of static followed. "Checking..." came the reply, followed by a click and the hiss of more static.

The Groundsman was in fact one of the facility's security staff, the person who'd helped Hannover understand how to access the security systems they were now hacked into. He left the security cabin at the rear gate of the facility, where the tankers and supply trucks came through to feed the research or take away fuels ready for use by the various oil companies. The cabin was no more than sixty metres away from the storage area he knew Kirby should have left about five minutes ago.

He walked down the tarmac roadway, past parked trucks and crates stacked with oil drums. Nearing the storage area, he saw no sign of Kirby.

"Gates closed," he said into the radio.

"I can see that, where's Father Christmas?" the engineer asked back.

Enjoying the visceral nature of the job, a great change from the administration of the lab, Kirby approached to the final vat and realised he'd not been watching the time.

"Good lord!" he said aloud, checking his watch: 1.55pm. "I'm late!" He filled the last of the vials as fast as he could, labelling and placing them back into the case.

His task was to be finished by 2.00pm, with him at the gate for when it opened.

He slammed the case shut, stood quickly and jogged around the vat and back to the gate. He reached it and saw the pass-card reader was showing red.

"Crap," he exclaimed, pulling on the gate.

In a panic, Kirby instinctively went to use his pass-card and open the gate. The Groundsman took his last few steps to the gate and appeared suddenly in front of it.

"Wait!" he said, seeing what Kirby was about to do, making him jump with surprise.

The guard raised the radio and turned to the camera on the building Kirby had exited earlier.

"Knock knock," he said.

The gate clicked open and, after taking a moment to register he could come out, Kirby swung it wide and left the storage area.

"Afternoon, doctor," the Groundsman said casually. Before a shocked Kirby could reply, he turned and walked off back to the cabin.

In a moment of insight, he realised he was not only being watched and assisted from afar; there were others with Hannover connections inside the facility.

Why don't they just tell us who's who sometimes! he thought as he watched the man walk off.

The engineer was exasperated. *Come on, snap out of it and get back to the lab, you idiot,* the engineer thought to himself, watching Kirby on the camera.

He saw Kirby close his mouth and turn, headed back to the doorway he'd come out of earlier.

As he approached, the pass-key turned green as before. He stepped in, closed the door and headed to the lab.

When he arrived, the staff made little eye contact, which was just fine for him.

He went straight to his office, placed the case on the floor by his desk and sat down to regain his composure. Hannover had obviously prepared the ground a little more then he'd realised. He'd imagined he was alone, and yet clearly there were others who knew about him, but he knew nothing about them.

A secret organisation indeed, he thought to himself, recalling the image of the spider's web pattern around the vats. *Very fitting*, he added.

Kirby spent the rest of the afternoon working in his office, occasionally checking that the data pen was still in his pocket and trying not to look suspiciously at the case full of vials by his desk.

Around 6.00pm the lab was finally empty, all the staff heading home without a word.

Kirby jumped up and went to where the young researcher had got the vials for him earlier in the day. He took another eighteen from the vial rack and placed them into a washing machine underneath the table next to a collection of dirty vials, dishes and other lab equipment needing a clean down.

Slamming the door shut, he selected a wash programme and turned the machine on. It started the washing cycle.

"There's your vials back," he said to the empty room, but thinking of the researcher who'd empty it in the morning.

Kirby went back to his desk, snapped open the sample case and checked the vials one last time. This was it then, he wasn't just copying data and taking samples, he was really going to steal them.

Leaning down under his desk he retrieved his backpack, one he always used to bring his laptop and other items to work. He removed the vials from the sample case and placed them into the backpack packet and zipped it closed. With the vials secure he checked his pocket one last time.

He whipped off his lab-coat, threw the backpack over his shoulder, grabbed the empty vial case and deposited it near the sink. He made his way out of the lab, the heist complete and valuables secured on his person.

Breaking into a smile as he passed security, Kirby got into his car and drove from the facility, feeling like a bank robber who'd escaped with the loot.

He arrived home just as a light rain began to fall.

~ 9 ~

The doorman on the Hannover Club looked just as he always did: long woolen overcoat, scarf, suit, shiny shoes and gloved hands clasped in front of him. Byford thought these people couldn't be any more obvious, especially with their physical build, the look on their faces and radio earpieces obvious to the world.

"Afternoon," he said to the doorman as he stepped up to the main door.

"Afternoon, sir," the man replied and opened the door for Byford.

Byford had never seen this one before, but there were no casual visitors to the Club and the Handler had no doubt briefed the staff that someone would be coming at an appointed time.

Byford stepped into the reception hall and was greeted by the concierge, at least that's what he thought this person was supposed to be.

"Good afternoon, mister...?"

"Byford."

"Ah, yes, of course, mister Costana will be with you shortly, mister Byford. He's asked for you to wait in here," the concierge said, extending his arm out to guide Byford to a door on his right.

Byford went through into the small reception room and with no further pleasantries, the concierge closed the door behind him.

Not back in the family yet, Byford, he thought to himself.

The room looked like most others in the Hannover Club. A few large, well-padded leather lounge chairs, a heavy wooden table, some brass lamps and, in this one, some of the less-perfect paintings that Hannover possessed.

Byford studied one of a young woman who was sitting on a stone ledge holding a bow, one hand over the top of her eyes as if looking into the distance and protecting her eyes from the glare of the sun.

"A Pre-Raphaelite, or at least an attempt at the style," a voice said from behind him.

Byford turned around to see mister Costana had come into the room by another door.

"Hello, sir."

"Good to see you, Byford," Costana said, shaking Byford by the hand and giving him a warm smile.

"Are you an art person?" Costana asked.

"No, not really, but this caught my eye. What or who is it of?"

"It's by an unknown artist, mimicking what's called the Pre-Raphaelite style, a romantic style recalling Greco-Roman mythology, an attempt to reconnect to the gods and nature, to take people back to a simpler time before the industrial revolution."

Byford made a thoughtful sound and nodded. Costana took that as a cue to carry on.

"You see how she looks Roman or Greek in her flowing clothes, the golden crescent standing atop her hair band and so on. Do you know what the painting means, Byford?"

Byford thought for a second but felt nothing insightful come to his mind.

"Not a clue, sir."

"Well, fair enough. It's all a metaphor, and while a reasonable attempt, it's not perfect. Look at her little finger," Costana said, pointing to the little finger on the hand the woman had raised to shield her eyes from the sun.

"Oh yes, how do you bend your finger like that?" Byford asked.

"You don't. Also, the arm is too long, the grip on the bow is wrong and the waist band would never sit like that."

"Why does Hannover have such a bad example then?" Byford asked.

"I painted it," Costana said with a smile towards Byford. "But anyway," he continued, drawing the talk of paintings to a close and turning directly to Byford, "engaging, but nothing to do with why we're here, so let's get onto that, shall we?"

"Good idea, sir. Obviously I asked to meet with you about the interesting news Frost gave me a few days ago," Byford said, somewhat relieved to be finished with the chit-chat.

"Yes indeed, Byford. Come through to my office," Costana said, now waving Byford through just like the concierge had done earlier.

The room's décor was the same stately style as the reception area's: a stately desk at one end with formal chairs in front, and a nearby set of four of the lounge chairs he'd seen before. There was more art on the walls and a collection of old books in a glass case to the far side.

Costana walked behind the desk and sat down. Byford took a seat in front.

"I haven't forgotten the usual civilities," Costana said, handing Byford a cup of tea off a tray placed to the side of the desk.

Byford took a sip.

Milk and two sugars, he thought.

It reminded him just how much Hannover ensured they knew about their people.

"We have a project for you to deliver on, which needs to take place in the next week or so. Exact time scales to be confirmed once we've lined a few pieces up. It will involve you working with a new team, which should be fine as the project objectives are clear cut, and involve a target that is not expecting an event they have to respond to," Costana said.

"So this is a civilian target then, sir?"

Strictly speaking, all Hannover's targets were civilian. This militaristic allusion was meant to ask if the target was capable of making an armed response, whether they expected to or not. While all targets might be civilian, they weren't all peaceful, law-abiding ones.

"Yes, Byford. It is in the civilian domain, so will not have a high level of security that you would need to counter. Is that clearer?" Costana explained, recognising Byford was only asking to ensure no blame for any confusion was placed on himself.

"Much clearer, sir," Byford said.

"Good. As I've said, there's a few pieces to align before we carry out the work, so you'll have time to acquaint yourself with your new team. You'll have to drill them somewhat to get their readiness closer to your liking, before we provide you the full brief and you execute the project."

"Where is the team to be trained, sir?"

Costana smiled and said, "You're going home for a couple of weeks, Byford. The team will be heading up to one of our houses on the Shetlands; South Island, to be precise. A flight and boat have been arranged for you midday tomorrow. The story is you're a diving instructor and they're your pupils. Not too far off the truth."

Byford thought about the Shetlands. He had indeed be born and raised on the harsh islands, but he hadn't been there in over twenty years.

"How long did you say I had to train them, sir?"

"Just under two weeks, didn't I say that already?"

"Ah, sorry, sir. Must have missed it," Byford replied.

Two weeks to prepare the team wasn't long, and that would mean they weren't as green as was being suggested.

"So, they need to learn swimming. Anything else? No weapons drills, skydiving, espionage…?"

"Yes, very droll, Byford. Q will be here with your Batman belt in just a moment," Costana said with what looked like a hint of humour from the otherwise dry character Byford had become used to. "You'll get your high-level brief now and full instructions when you're on-site tomorrow. All over our encrypted communications channel as usual. You have the cipher memorised, correct?"

"I don't, sir. I've been out for two years," Byford replied in a matter-of-fact tone.

Costana gave a look of what to Byford seemed like mild disgust at being reminded of this fact.

"Well, in any case you'll get the brief tomorrow, by email. We'll go through some points now, though."

Costana picked up the phone and dialed a number. "Costana here, can you bring up a laptop and arrange for a cipher briefing tonight?"

Byford couldn't make out the reply, but Costana thanked the person on the other end and hung up.

"A new laptop will be at the desk outside when you leave and you need to go to Austin House to get a new cipher key tonight. I'll have the brief emailed to you before you leave for the airport."

While the two men drank their tea, Costana described the project Byford had been given. He outlined the team skills, their experience, strengths and weaknesses. He told Byford why the location had been chosen, given Dr Kirby's need to use long-submerged enzyme samples. Once in his flow, Costana even went as far as suggesting what the nature of the main mission was. One thing that wasn't mentioned was the reason Byford was here—Mary.

"Sir, what about this David?" Byford asked. "Where does he fit into this?"

"Yes, of course. As expected, your loyal friend has been giving away secrets."

Byford ignored the disingenuous comment. Hannover would have told Frost to lure him into doing the mission by telling him about Mary. That was the game.

"David was approached some time ago. Not for who he is, but for who he knew. Foolishly, he refused our advances and tried to use his awareness of us to his advantage. It doesn't work that way around, as well you know. Suffice to say, this does not end well for David. But his loss will be your gain."

Costana's words were both a portent and a reminder of who dealt the cards and made the rules.

"In which case, let the game commence, sir," Byford replied, quoting the translated motto of Hannover he recalled was written in the Great Hall, in the very building where they were.

Costana broke into a smile. "Yes, indeed. Iacta alea esto! And what a fine game it is."

The overview concluded and Byford's agreement secured, Costana stood and walked over to the door of his office.

"All right then, Byford. Head on out and I'll talk to you again when you're ensconced on your native soil."

"Thank you, sir," Byford replied and shook hands with Costana as a farewell.

"By the way. What is it a metaphor for exactly, the painting?"

"Ah, well, this is what art does to you, Byford. I see you are an art man after all. What do you think when you look at the painting? Has she shot an arrow and is now observing the distance to see if it struck home, or is she watching and waiting for her quarry, and has yet to even cast an arrow? Is she a metaphor or is it her posture or the arrow? What's the significance of the sun in her eyes and the moon on her head? Who knows, Byford! I'll let you ponder it yourself and you can see what meaning it has for you!" Costana said, clearly amused with his own words.

"Well, sir, I suppose I could do that, but then again…"

Costana gave a short laugh and patted Byford on the arm.

"Fair enough, Byford. Travel safe and we'll be in touch shortly to introduce your mission in full and your new team."

With that, Byford left the office, walked through the reception room and past the painting. He gave it one last look as he passed, then left the room with no further inspiration revealing itself.

At the reception he was handed the new laptop Costana had requested.

"Cipher briefing arranged for 2100 hours at Austin House, sir," the man handing him the laptop said.

"OK, thanks," Byford replied, quickly signing to acknowledge receipt of the device. With that he headed out of the Hannover Club and home to the London house he'd not seen for over a year.

~ 10 ~

The visitors started to arrive around 7pm. Mary greeted them at the door while David stayed out of the way in the den. After the quick exchange of the usual pleasantries they were allowed in, being showed down to the basement.

The meeting wasn't until 9pm; but the problem with people like this, David reflected, was that they thought themselves to be more than friends of the host. It was one more thing, amongst a growing list, that David had begun to find more and more annoying these last few months. He overheard a few of the group asking where he was and how he was.

Mary dealt with their questions as instructed.

"Plenty of time for all that," she said. "He'll tell you all what happened later. Let's get a few drinks and relax first."

It was the usual pattern and easy to distract them with. They'd arrive and bring a few bottles of wine and beer, then in the basement they could start drinking and smoking, some of them doing a little more. In truth, most of the dealing David was doing now had started by supplying members of the group, most of whom wanted to enjoy the drugs but didn't have the balls to seek out a street dealer. Well here he was, happy to take advantage.

For the next hour or so David heard others arriving, but he was too absorbed in what he was doing to pay much attention to the chatter at the door.

He'd opened up his connection to the Tor browser on his computer, a way to surf the internet anonymously. In addition he was using a piece of software to further encrypt his website requests and data. This extra step shouldn't have been needed, but recent reports of Tor being hacked made him reticent to rely on it alone. Double-bagging, as Wolf had called it.

Wolf had shown him to surf outside the normal internet, on the Darknet, but also to hide the unique address of his computer. That way, no one would be able to trace his surfing, what websites and forums he went to. It made sense even if he didn't understand it.

Given the events the last few days and most especially since meeting Lauren, he thought it even more important to hide what he was doing from prying eyes. Though on reflection, he realised Lauren clearly already had knowledge of what he did and how to get hold of him.

He searched out anything he could find about the riot. He visited the usual sites that provided illegally gained content. A search engine that collated the Darknet content was the first stop.

He looked for hacked surveillance camera feeds, tapped police radio transmissions, emails that had been intercepted and names of anyone that may be related to the event. There were scant references to the night, mostly police emails and a few stolen news reports that had probably already been published.

Most of what he found referenced Greenpeace, the numbers who turned up, arrests made and names of known activists. Then he found it—a link to a police surveillance video showing the march. This would be far more informative than the ground-level view they'd been showing on TV. He watched and saw the groups being split, the front one getting walked away and the group at the back become more violent as the minutes passed.

He saw himself in the crowd, throwing the tear-gas canister back at the police. He cursed himself again for his stupidity. A moment later there was the person he'd been searching for.

"Got you!"

The video rolled on and David continued to watch in morbid fascination.

He saw the riot police burst through the lines and head straight towards him. He watched aghast as they surrounded him, knocked him down with no attempt to restrain him, and then dragged him out of the crowd and through the police lines. Almost out of shot of the camera, a van was waiting for him.

The film rolled on but David had stopped watching. He stood up and stepped away from the desk.

"Holy shit," he said aloud to no one.

The arrest was all planned, right down to the police van, ready to take him away.

David picked up the phone again.

"Two calls in the same night?" Paul asked.

"Yeh, I know. I just sent you an email on your private account. There's a link to a video, but you'll need to Tor in to see it," David replied.

"Interesting, what's it of?"

"Me getting my head smashed in, but that's just the highlight. Watch a few seconds from four minutes onwards. The guy who runs over to me is the guy I want to know more about."

There was a moment of silence on the other end of the line.

"OK, I've got it. Give me a second to get the video up," Paul said. "By the way, don't send me emails about this stuff from your normal account if you're trying to stay hidden. I have your details here in the email header."

David wasn't even sure what that meant, but agreed to be more careful in the future.

"OK, I see him. Friendly guy. You sure you never saw him before, then? He sure looks like he knows you," Paul said.

"Sure of it. Can you use this to find him?"

"Almost guaranteed. I'll ping you a message to your phone when I have it."

Paul hung up and looked at the man on screen, frozen in mid greeting to David.

"So who are you, then? Not going to ruin my little party, are you?"

David placed the phone down.

At least now he had a chance of finding out who the guy was and quickly. He disconnected all his software and closed down the computer.

It was just after 8.30pm, and it was time to go and mingle. As their leader and dealer he could at least enjoy having a little fun with his guests while he sold them his wares. They might not be useful protesters, but they were useful for that at least.

He stepped out of the den and saw no one was in the hallway. From the noise coming from the basement he guessed everyone was already here anyway. He locked the front door and turned the hallway lights off, then headed down to the basement.

It was easy to make a grand entrance. The basement was essentially two big rooms where he'd knocked down the dividing wall. As such, the stairs ran down the wall so everyone could see who was coming and going. Who was coming could also see everyone in the room, too, which David liked.

There were a couple of sofas against the back walls, a makeshift bar and a few tables near the middle of the floor. Scattered around were huge cushions masquerading as chairs, and the look was finished off by strategically placed lamps. The whole place was designed more like a nightclub lounge than a space for a serious group to meet.

"Hey everyone! Did we have fun yesterday or what?" he said as he walked down the last few steps, greeting them with his arms open as if ready to receive their praise.

A number of people called out his name as a return greeting, and a couple of the men came up and slapped him on the back and shoulders.

He was handed a beer, which he raised up to everyone in the form of a toast.

"Cheers, everyone, well done on yesterday!"

Beers were raised and the cheers returned. He could tell by the look on a few faces that they were already drunk or drugged enough to not even remember yesterday.

"David, how are you, bro?" Brother Wolf asked.

With a joint and beer in one hand, he held out his other hand, palm up, towards David.

David swung down his outstretched hand and gave Wolf's hand a slap.

"You got hit pretty bad, went down straight away, man. Some of us tried to get in the way of the police, to stop them dragging you away but they were away with you before we could do anything."

"Hey, Wolf, no problem, man. I think they were a little bit pissed at me throwing that canister back!"

"Yeh, man! We saw you do that and couldn't believe it, what the hell got into you!" Wolf said, flailing his arms about his head and leaning back as if swooning over at the idea of what David had done.

David didn't reply, instead indicating he was going to greet some of the others who were there and walked away. *Good, so at least they think I did that on purpose*, he thought as he walked away.

He saw Mary in her favourite spot, propped up against the back wall, sitting on her favourite cushion. Next to her were a couple he recognised by sight only. "Hey, Mary," he said, pulling up a free chair to sit down with them.

"David," she said, standing to lean over and kiss him on the head. She sat back down. "Colin and Louise," she indicated, waving her hand at the couple next to her by way of introduction.

Colin looked like a straight—dressed normally, trimmed beard. But Louise was obviously a long-term activist. He could almost smell it on her, sense her attitude. Of more interest, her pierced nose and gaunt complexion marked her out to David's experienced drug-dealer eyes as yet another junkie.

"Mary was telling us the police kept you overnight," the woman said.

David noticed how she seemed to twitch and struggle to move her mouth as she spoke.

"Yep, got back just a few hours ago. They gave me a hell of a grilling in the station, wanted to know all about who I was and what group I was with," he said, lying for the fun of getting them worried and to play up his adventures in their eyes.

"Damn, what did you tell them?" the man asked.

"Nothing of course!" David replied, acting offended at the idea.

He was already enjoying this. Doing his best to get in with the girl and alienate the boyfriend. It was a favourite pastime. David knew that Colin was too straight to make a scene and maybe that would be to David's advantage later.

David reached out his hand to Mary and, addressing them all, said, "Listen, you guys relax for a bit longer, we'll do the meeting stuff in about ten minutes."

He got up and walked off to speak to Wolf again.

"Hey, mate," he said to Wolf, grabbing his arm and motioning him to follow him to a quiet area near the makeshift bar.

"Listen, did you see the guy who came over to me before I got arrested?" he asked.

"Not me, no. But some of the crew asked who he was, they thought you knew him," Wolf said.

"Jesus, does everyone think that? I never saw the guy before then. But I do want to know who he is," David said.

"Well, that should be easy. I heard a couple of the guys hung around him after you were dragged away. He was asking where you'd gone, seemed proper concerned. I think some of them might have his number or something."

David looked shocked. "Crap, I never even thought of that," he said. "OK, let's ask them."

David took an empty bottle from off the bar and clanged it against the other one he was holding.

He kept doing that until everyone in the room had stopped talking and was looking at him.

"Thanks for coming, everyone. The other night was great and despite how it ended for me," he said, giving a theatrical smile and rubbing the back of his head, "it was a successful protest!"

He raised his bottle to the cheers of the group.

"We're not done yet, though: the fight goes on and we have a lot more work to do to get the message across," he said to further cheers.

"By the way, did anyone else get arrested?" he asked, realising he knew nothing of what happened after he was taken away.

A few confirmed that neither they nor anyone they knew had been arrested.

"Great, just me then!" he said with a strained tone, causing more cheers and laughter.

"Well, OK, good. Let's get down to business. It looks like we made a couple of contacts that night, one of whom was the guy who came over to me from the crowd. Did anyone find out who he was?"

Nick, an old regular of the group, raised his hand.

"He said he was called Frost, I got his number here somewhere," Nick said, stretching out so he could get into the front pocket of his jeans from his seated position. "I have it here I think."

David couldn't believe his luck. Maybe now he could get a real activist into the group, not one of these half-arsed layabouts. If the cops really were targeting him now, he needed a patsy to run interference and take the spotlight.

"Yeh, here it is. Frost... that was it. Not tried the number though," Nick said, holding the scrap of paper up.

David took it from him.

"That's great, he looks like just the type of guy we could do with in the group. I'll contact him tomorrow," David said.

"Now, bigger news. I made another contact at the police station. I managed to get away with no charges against me, despite the dramatic arrest and exit," he said to sounds of surprise from the group. "It seems we may have made a friend in a high place, possibly a sponsor of sorts," he added.

There was a combination of surprise and silence across the room, and then Wolf spoke up.

"A sponsor? What does that mean?" he asked, all eyes still fixed on David, who was enjoying his moment of power.

"A sponsor, a supporter, someone who's on our side and can help us out in some way. Who and what, I don't know precisely yet. What I do know is they got me out of jail free, no passing go and no paying a fine," he said. "Don't overthink it, Wolf," he added, seeing Wolf was mulling over the badly propositioned game reference and not the real message.

Wolf snapped out of his reflections. "What do they want from us?" he asked, again seeming to be the mouthpiece for the group.

"Nothing yet, they'll be in touch soon and I'll let you know. For now, enjoy the good news that we're not on our own anymore!" David raised his voice as he finished speaking and raised his beer bottle again as a salute.

Most echoed his cheers and gesture; he noticed that some didn't, but chose to ignore them.

"OK, that's the official stuff for tonight, everyone relax and have a few beers. You deserve it!"

He walked off through the room and back to Mary.

When he got to Mary, she was alone with Louise, sitting next to her where Colin had been earlier.

"Hello, ladies, how you doing? No Colin?" he asked, sitting himself down in front of them both.

"He had to go, early to work tomorrow," Louise said.

David smiled inside. "Ah, shame, I was just going to suggest we get this party started properly," he said, pulling out the two wraps of heroin he'd taken from the drawer earlier and holding them out, one to each of the women.

They cast a glance at each other and David knew they were recognising and acknowledging each other's addiction. He quickly closed his hands around the wraps. *Like kids in a candy store.*

"You're with friends here, Louise, don't sweat it," he said softly. "Come on, let's go somewhere more private."

He stood and headed to the stairs, which led back up out of the basement. Out of the corner of his eye he saw the two women stand up and follow him. An image of himself as the Pied Piper leading rats to their doom came into his mind.

He smiled to himself again, took a left turn at the top of the basement stairs and headed up the steps to the first floor, back to the bedroom he and Mary had been in a few hours before.

~ 11 ~

David reached over to the bedside cabinet, stretching over a sleeping Mary, and grabbed his phone. The tone he'd just heard told him a new message had just come through. He rubbed and blinked his eyes to clear the sleepy haze from them, and squinted at the phone's screen through the remaining fog in his eyes.

The message was from an unknown contact. 'Found your man. Give me a call' was all it said, and he didn't need to guess who it was from. David slid down and off the end of the bed to avoid waking Mary and, standing up, realised that Louise was asleep on the floor, covered by an old duvet he figured was long thrown out.

He stepped over her and headed out of the room, more pressing matters on his mind than trying to recall what had happened the previous night.

"Paul, thanks for getting on this so quickly," David said, thinking it never hurt to be polite to the guy, even if he was being continually blackmailed by him. "What did you find out?"

"Morning, David. Yeh, well I got him, seems he is called Frost but much else is a bit unclear," Paul said.

"Unclear, what do you mean?"

"I've not been able to pull that much on him, seems someone has decided to erase or hide some of this guy's past. The usual checks don't go through, so I can't tell you where he lives or anything close to that." Paul continued, "This record is a stub, just a small record kept for reference, which means it looks like this guy is ex-army and likely ex-police, but what branch I can't find out. There's a dead-end thread that suggests he got kicked out of whatever department he was in recently."

"What did he get kicked out for?" David asked.

"Seems he's a bit of a loose cannon, not exactly the type to be a good boy and do as he's told. But then I guess you saw that the other day. Only bit of information of use is that he was undercover with a group like yours and went native."

"Well, that is interesting," David replied.

"Figured you'd like that," Paul said.

"OK, any idea how to get hold of him?" Even though he already knew, it didn't hurt to double check.

"Why the hell are you so interested in him, all urgently too?"

David's mind went blank. Maybe he was going too fast, desperate to use Frost to satisfy Lauren's unknown demands, but he felt scared. Scared of crossing Paul, scared of who Lauren was and what she'd want. He just couldn't go back to prison; he wished he'd never gone to the march.

"Seems like a good guy for us, that's all. Better him than me out there, eh?" David said, hoping to appeal to Paul's desire to keep his cash cow safe.

"True, bloody stupid what you did. To answer your earlier question," Paul continued, "I suggest you just stay visible, he'll find you."

"OK, thanks, Paul, I owe you," David said.

"Yup," was the terse reply.

"By the way, are we still good?" David asked.

"Yes, why?"

"Just, on the video it looks like I was targeted, which our arrangement is meant to avoid," David said.

"I don't run the whole force, if you stick your head up like that you'll get it knocked down eventually. Which, given you're still on probation, isn't bloody wise. Let's be clear, our arrangement is about your side business, not your whining about the state of the planet. If we weren't good, you'd know about it," Paul said and with that the line went dead.

∞

"You gave them your number?" Byford asked.

"Yeh, mate, seemed the best way, we're in a hurry after all," Frost replied.

"Jesus, I appreciate the keenness but a little subtlety wouldn't go amiss either."

Frost looked out over the river at the city beyond, enjoying his morning coffee and the freshness of the air.

"Well, that David, he's not the sharpest tool in the box, is he? I figured he needed a way to get hold of me, a bit more direct than your idea. Anyway, it would be odd just to act all mysterious when his mates came over to me. Especially after I was seen helping him out and after the blues lifted him. Funny as fuck when they knocked him out!" Frost said.

Byford ignored Frost's soldier view of the world and amusement at others getting into fights. Instead, he thought about Frost giving his number to one of the eco's. He'd arranged with contacts outside Hannover to get Frost a new back story available on police files. Not a moment too soon, he was informed just an hour ago the profile was accessed late last night.

Things were moving faster than he expected, but in the right direction.

On balance it really didn't matter how they'd found Frost in the end. So long as they did and it was believable.

"Right, well, heads up, we tagged the file on the new you and it got picked up last night," Byford said.

"Crap, that was fast. He's got contacts then?"

"Yeh, but we don't know who accessed it. The internet service provider, location, etc. were all garbage and, anyway, it doesn't matter. As you gave out your number it's only a matter of time until someone passes it to him," Byford said.

"But no guarantee he'll call, mate," Frost said.

"He'll call. David wants friends and he's obviously interested, or he'd never have had the file pulled. Now you have a back story, try and remember it!" Byford said.

"Yeh, yeh. 12 months undercover, got a bird pregnant who was part of the target group, defected to my undercover life, got found out by my police handlers and kicked out of the force," Frost recounted rapidly to show he'd memorised it well.

"Good, but keep it simple. They'll believe it; heck, David will want to believe it," Byford said.

"No worries, mate, I wouldn't be the first undercover copper to go native, happens all the time. I'll just wait for the call."

∞

"Wolf, hey it's me," David said over the phone. "How do you feel about Frost?" he asked, without any further preamble.

"I have no idea, David," Wolf said flatly.

"You have time for breakfast? Let's meet up at the Café on Bridge St., in half an hour?" David asked.

Wolf was about to protest, but being used to David's ways he thought better of it. Also, he was suddenly intrigued by David's interest in Frost.

"Sure, I'll see you there in 30 minutes," Wolf replied.

He grabbed his coat, headed out the door and set off walking to the café.

David was already there when Wolf arrived, sitting in a corner enjoying a full English breakfast and a steaming cup of tea.

Just like him not to bother waiting or offer to buy for you, even if you thought he'd invited you.

Wolf walked up to David.

"Hey, mate, let me just order something to eat... be with you in a minute," he said, walking past David and heading to the counter to order.

The man taking orders was a living cliché. White T-shirt stained with grease, overweight and with barely acceptable hygiene. Some would consider it a guarantee of a good greasy-spoon breakfast, enjoyable if you didn't overthink the health risks. Fortunately, Wolf wasn't one to do that.

"Full English, extra fried bread and cup of tea, please."

The man took the order, gave Wolf his change and swiftly followed it up with the tea. Wolf picked up the cup, walked over to David and set himself down in a chair opposite him.

"So, what's this about then?" he asked.

David came right out and said what was on his mind.

"I got the Frost's number from Nick, last night at the house. I was thinking of calling him and seeing if he was interested in joining us."

"Well, you know Mary introduced him to you at the march back in May, right?" Wolf asked.

"Did she? I don't remember that at all," David replied.

"Not important I guess, we're a big crowd, bound to bump into some of the same faces. I thought he was a buyer or someone you'd rallied with before," Wolf said.

"God, maybe. So many faces come and go I don't pay attention to half of them," David replied, looking slightly distant as if trying to remember the event of first meeting Frost.

Truth was he dealt puff and charlie to so many people he only bothered remembering who was who when they were buying. He didn't remember Frost so he mustn't have been buying, David concluded in his mind.

"Besides he's obviously in the activist community and knows Mary in passing; what the hell is so interesting about him that you drag me here to discuss it? What do you want from him, David?" Wolf asked, wanting to get to the heart of the matter.

"I'm in shit, mate," David said. "When I got arrested I thought I was done for, but someone paid me a visit and got me out of there. However, she's going to want something in return."

"What the hell! You can't do anything, it's bad enough you went back to selling stuff. If you don't keep your nose clean you know what happens. Just tell her no! Do you even know anything about Frost?" Wolf asked.

"I can't just tell her no! As for Frost, it seems he's a bit of an action man. Seemingly ex-military or police according to my sources." David made a point of adding the last part about sources for extra effect; he felt it never hurt to imply you had people in high places.

"What? If he's ex-forces or police isn't that a risk, how would that help us?" Wolf asked.

"Good question."

The waitress came over with Wolf's breakfast.

"Wow, you are the hungry wolf this morning, aren't you," David quipped.

Wolf started into his breakfast without a word, giving David some space to answer the real question.

"The most important thing is he'll know how they work, he'll know their tactics. Just like the other day at the demonstration. It looked to me like he knew when they were going to use the tear gas and when they were going to storm out of the lines at us," David said.

"You've still not answered my question," Wolf said.

"He does it, whatever it is Lauren wants. Then if things go wrong, my nose is clean," David said, stating plainly what he was thinking.

"Right, now I'm with you. Well, he isn't afraid of action, that's for certain. I guess someone like that could help keep us safe when we're out, give us a little guidance in the field," Wolf said, between bites of food and large slurps of tea.

David watched him talk and eat in mild amazement.

"Remind me to ask why they call you Wolf at some point; oh, actually…" he said, tucking into his own food.

The two men carried on eating in silence for a few minutes.

"To play devil's advocate, have we thought about why he may be a shill for the police? Let's eliminate why we're sure he's not a plant by them or someone else for that matter," Wolf said.

David thought about it for a while, running scenarios around in his mind, but it didn't make sense.

"I have someone on the inside in the police, pretty senior, he thinks the guy's records are legit."

"You have a copper in your pocket, man are you kidding me? That's the first time you told me that!" Wolf said, sounding genuinely surprised.

"Yeh, a little guardian angel for us and the business, but I'm not sure he's the one in the pocket."

"So, assuming this insider of yours has something going on with you"—Wolf held up his hands for effect—"and I don't want to know what, we can assume he'd do his due diligence. So… we should bring him on board."

It took David a moment to realise what Wolf had just said.

"Exactly, but I wanted to make sure it seemed right. You don't have any concerns? I thought you'd be more cautious."

"Yeh, I'm concerned, but you need cover or all of us are in trouble! Also, if you had him checked out that's something else again. So yeh, bring him in and see what he's like. In any event, you can use him for this special job you have to do and keep him out of everything else." Wolf said.

While they finished their food the two men spent the next half hour in idle chatter about the recent demonstration, ideas for the group and general man talk.

"OK, Wolf, I'll give him a call this afternoon," David said as they both stood to leave.

"Cool, let me know how it goes," Wolf replied as he pulled on his coat.

He gave David a pat on the arm, a gesture of reassurance, then headed off.

Alone now, David's thoughts turned to what he'd say to Frost.

He pulled out his wallet and retrieved the piece of paper with Frost's number on it.

Looking at it for a brief moment he recalled Frost's face but gained no inspiration as to what to say.

Jesus, relax! he told himself, realising he was practically obsessing about getting Frost on board, fearful of what was coming next from Lauren. It seemed Frost would be just the kind of guy he might need, especially if she came up with something tricky for them to do.

He looked around as if expecting her to appear at any moment. The thought of her saying she'd find him when needed made him feel like he was being watched.

David walked away from the café and headed to a gravel-covered surface car park across the street. It was away from the road and offered a place to talk without being overheard. Not that he knew of anyone who might be listening in, but a little healthy paranoia never hurt.

Instantly, Lauren's face came to mind again, as if to suggest to him that *someone* was listening.

At the car park, he pulled out the piece of paper again, dialed the number and took a deep breath. The phone rang a few times, and then Frost answered.

"Hello?"

"Hey, Frost, it's David. The guy from the demo the other day," David said in his friendliest tone.

"You've lost me, I met a few people that day," Frost replied.

"Canister-throwing guy, or arrested-and-taken-away guy, depends what you find most memorable."

"Ahh, that guy! Sorry about that, mate, I didn't expect them to single you out like that, you weren't the only one throwing stuff at them," Frost said.

"No problem, it was all fun... well, except for the bruising," David replied, trying to keep the tone light. "Listen, what are you up to today? I was wondering if we could meet up."

"This afternoon maybe, what did you want to talk about?" Frost asked.

"Well, I'd rather talk face to face."

"Sure, but I like to know what I'm letting myself in for. Not being funny, mate, but I'm guessing this isn't a casual tea and biscuits you want to meet for," Frost said.

David thought for a moment, looked around and saw no one so decided to risk a bit of information.

"That's all right, understandable," he said. "Listen, after I was arrested I was released almost straight away in the morning. I had a special visitor who sorted things out and said she'd be in touch in a few days. A little help for a little help and all that."

"OK, mysterious. So how can I help?" Frost asked.

"I'm figuring you like to be involved in exciting events like the other day, and I'm guessing she'll be wanting to get our help with something. Something other than walking around the streets shouting at the police. A little bird tells me you're quite capable in your own way, so I figured you might be interested in using your talents," David said.

"Very resourceful of you. Yeh, I might be interested but I don't work for free and I don't camp outside research labs with pictures of sliced-up bunny rabbits. There's bigger fish to fry, you know what I mean?"

"Hey, I hear you, neither do I. I'm of a mind that if we're going to do this we should be looking to get the message across in a bigger way too. As I said, I suspect she won't want us just waving placards around, so this could be the bigger game."

"All right then, sounds like you need my help. You know the Arlington bus station? There's a bar, the Black Horse, opposite. Let's meet at 3pm today," Frost said.

"I know the station, I'll find the pub," David replied.

"OK, see you later."

David pulled the phone away from his ear, checked the display and made sure the call was ended.

Frost took off his headphones, reached over to his laptop and stopped the recording.

"You never know what might be handy," he said to himself, saving the file to a folder named 'Project X.'

It was a habit Frost had developed to make sure there was enough dirt stored away on the people and projects he got involved in, just in case. That way, if anything went wrong, Hannover couldn't hang him out to dry. Not likely to happen, he'd often thought; but after all, he was just a foot soldier, not a high-ranking member pulling the strings. Insurance was always wise to keep.

Frost picked up the headset again and dialed another number.

"Hey, buddy," came the reply when Byford answered.

"Now then, mate, guess who just rang?" Frost said.

"Are you on the laptop?"

"Yes, of course, all safe and encrypted on our James Bond spy equipment," Frost said, making the usual joking references often used by Hannover operatives. Byford ignored it.

"So, what did he have to say for himself, then?" Byford asked.

"Not much, wants to meet this afternoon and go through stuff. Spilled the beans about Lauren though, he's itching to get into some new action by the sound of it," Frost said.

"She used her real name?"

"Well, he never said her name, but we all know who the Handler's favourite girl is," Frost replied.

"OK, you meet with him this afternoon and let him schmooze you into joining. I'm heading up to meet the new team tonight, so I will contact you in the next few days to see how you're doing," Byford said. "But remember, stay low and stay out of Lauren's way too, assuming it is her. Oh, and no comms off the net, we can't risk anyone picking up on anything."

"Sure thing, I'll be his new best friend in no time and let you know what more I learn about Mary. I just hope the timing of all this is good. When's D-Day at your end?" Frost asked.

"Two weeks and counting, so we need our game plan set up by mid-week next week," Byford said.

"Right, mate, that's not long but I'll see what I can do. Talk later."

"Thanks, Frost, take care," Byford said and hung up the phone.

Frost clicked 'end' on the call software and saved the file.

~ 12 ~

Byford placed the cipher key into the laptop's USB port and the system came alive.

No more than 1cm in size and looking like a wireless dongle for a mouse or other device, it unlocked the hidden partition on the laptop, which gave access to Hannover data and applications. Without it, the laptop booted up with the normal operating system and worked just like any other PC.

As he'd been instructed, he looked at the camera on his laptop and saw his face appear on the screen. A web of red lines and dots danced across the image of his face, before the points settled on his main features and the mesh of lines and dots turned green.

A seemingly garbled message came up on screen and Byford thought through the cipher he'd been briefed on the night before. Typing in what should be the unencrypted message, he saw the words 'Access Granted' appear on the screen, and this further layer of security was passed.

The communicator software was showing '1 unread message.'

He opened the message and saw the mission pre-briefing he was expecting. As usual, information from Hannover was on a need-to-know, as-and-when-you-need-to-know basis.

The entire document was encrypted in what the Hannover boffins had said was an unbreakable cipher. In fact, the message itself was not the only thing encrypted—the encrypted message was further encrypted. Meaning anyone intercepting it would have to crack two ciphers to read the message.

That assumed they could get onto the Darknet and find the servers where the communications were taking place.

For the likes of Byford, getting to these messages was made possible by the laptops and cipher keys Hannover issued their field agents. All of which were primed to destroy their hard-drives with a small explosive, in the event a user didn't authenticate successfully via the face recognition software.

He'd also been told that trying to take them apart had similar explosive effects. Something another operative was rumoured to have proven when he'd dropped his laptop, splitting the case and setting off the fireworks.

Byford did a quick read through the document he'd been provided.

The main thing of interest was the travel time: he was to be flown out to the Shetlands at 11am this morning. He re-read the first few pages again—collection at 9am, flight at 11am, no personal items to be taken and no equipment needed. It was 7am, two hours left to pack and be ready for when the Hannover driver arrived to take him to the airport.

Byford showered and put on his travel clothes of jeans, T-shirt and fleece.

He took his watch, ring, passport and wallet and placed them into a small safe in his closet, then locked it shut, sliding a wooden panel back in place to hide the safe.

It was a routine practiced over many years.

He thought about what the new team members would turn up with, misinterpreting exactly what 'no personal items' would mean. In the years past, he'd seen everything from lucky charms to mobile phones to family photos. All of which would compromise the individual and potentially the team in the event they were lost or the operative was caught.

He went back downstairs and checked the laptop for any further messages. There was the message from Steven as promised, the sender identified only as 'H', for Handler.

'Amber status. Confirm in a few days. Good luck' was all it read.

Amber was the state that told Byford the run-up to the mission had begun, all preparations would start and the team were to be made ready, awaiting the confirmed 'Green light Go' status. At that point, all communications would go silent and the mission would be carried out come hell or high water.

He deleted the message from the system, took out the cipher key and reaching into his underpants, slid it into a small pocket just under his scrotum. Another odd practice he'd adopted.

If captured or searched, few tough guys were going to fondle his genitals to see if there was something hidden there. Even if they took his pants off, the little pocket would look like part of the underwear seams. So went the theory, anyway; hopefully he'd never have to find out.

That was something else he recalled needing to explain to the new team, who would no doubt have the cipher keys rattling around in their pockets or probably still inserted in the machines.

In which case they would boot straight to the face-scanning software.

"Jesus!" he said to himself, thinking about what he'd face, shaping the new team and leading a mission with them straight afterwards.

Two weeks of stress.

He checked the clock on the wall: 8.50am.

Looking around the house he did a final confirmation that all lights and the cooker were off and doors locked.

He'd only been back here a few days and was already off, but still, it felt like home again, even if his preference was for Spain now. The contrast of the regular life he lead between missions, compared to what he'd be doing in a couple of weeks, never ceased to humour him.

Byford heard a beep of a horn outside and without further ceremony, grabbed his laptop bag and headed out of the house and to the car.

"You seem familiar, do I know you?" Byford said to the driver, through his open window.

"I'm new to this area, must be someone who looks like me," the driver replied. "Do we need to stop off anywhere?" the driver asked.

"Straight there," Byford said, without saying where *there* was.

"Very good, sir," the driver replied, the planned dialogue out of the way.

Byford had never been convinced these scripts, as they were referred to, were secure in any way, but they gave passenger and driver some level of confidence each was who they were meant to be.

The drive to the airport passed without conversation and with no telephone to distract himself with, Byford took the time to think over the information he'd read in the briefing.

The location for training was the Shetlands, South Island; he'd stay there with the team for just under two weeks.

Byford recalled being there years ago. It was a small house, secluded and near the coast. There was room for about five people with their swimming and sailing gear.

The best thing there for swim training was the large amount of wrecks. The coast around the Shetlands was treacherous, scores of ships had been lost there for hundreds of years and were still being lost there today. Along with that there was plenty of coast along which to do fitness training, night manoeuvres and to practice all the other skills they'd need, away from curious eyes.

Though it was a short mission as far as Byford knew, this team needed all the skills of a tight military unit in two weeks.

"Bloody hell…" he said aloud, again cursing the job that was ahead of him.

"Sorry, sir?" the driver asked.

"Nothing, just talking to myself," Byford replied, returning to his thoughts.

They arrived at the airport. A small private one outside central London, able to take jets and carry passengers. There existed an unwritten agreement that the airport didn't ask too many questions about passengers and flights, so long as fees were paid.

As the car pulled up to the jet, he was surprised to see an operative near the plane and the stairs down ready to have him board straight away. Leaving the car, he headed over to the steps.

"Morning, mister Byford," the operative said, waving him on board. "We're ready to leave as soon as you're on board, sir."

Byford ran up the steps and headed into the cabin. There he was met by a stewardess, who greeted him and showed him his seat. It was one of just four seats in the cabin, behind a table with a continental breakfast laid out on it.

A car to collect him and a jet with breakfast laid on. *Someone's laying on the royal treatment for sure*, he thought to himself.

A stewardess greeted him and showed him to his seat. On the opposite table, he noticed a few crumbs. He sat and strapped himself in just as the jet started to move off for the flight to the Shetlands.

"How long is the flight?" he asked.

"Just about an hour, sir," she replied and walked off into the flight deck.

The flight quickly levelled off and the stewardess reappeared in the cabin, offering Byford tea or coffee.

"Who else is on board?" Byford asked, alluding to the untidy table opposite from him.

"Mister Daler, sir. This is his plane," she said, pouring the coffee.

Byford reached for his coffee, he smelt it and recognised a rich medium Arabica roast. "Ah, someone's been doing their homework," he said as a compliment to the stewardess.

She smiled in acknowledgement and again returned to the flight deck, leaving Byford to enjoy his breakfast and the views.

About quarter of an hour into the flight, it was the turn of a tall, middle-aged man to appear from the flight deck and make himself known to Byford.

"Hello, mister Byford. I'm Daler, owner of the research plant you and your team will be visiting in a few days," Daler said with an easy tone, offering him his hand.

Byford shook it and gave a half smile as greeting. "Well, slightly unexpected," Byford said, waving Daler to the chair in front of him.

Daler sat and looked Byford straight in the eyes. If Byford was meant to be intimidated, it didn't work. He was more taken with how well dressed Daler was, in a dark blue suit, tie, crisp white shirt and cufflinks. Byford thought he looked a bit too well-groomed to be running a refinery.

Na'er trust a dandy, son, his late father had once told him.

Looking at Daler, Byford didn't trust him one bit.

He could feel himself already annoyed that Daler was here at all. Experience told him a sponsor doing this was a sign of an egoist. Most were intimidated enough by Hannover to avoid meddling with how they did what they did.

Daler smiled, realising that Byford was not going to play the game.

"Yes, and I thought that while we had some time in private, I could give you a little insight into the facility. Your Handler of course approved this or I wouldn't be here," Daler said.

"No, you wouldn't be," Byford replied, now staring Daler in the eyes. "Well, go ahead. We're landing in under 20 minutes, so you haven't much time."

"Indeed," Daler replied.

"You may wonder why I want you to attack my facility and steal my research," Daler said.

Byford said nothing but noted the snippet of information Daler had just given away. It revealed a lot. This was clearly no distraction job, not if they were stealing research too. This was a cover up, real action. That also meant the team Byford was to train wasn't as green as he'd been anticipating.

Daler noted Byford's silence and continued.

"Truth be told, it's for a number of reasons. The most personal being that the majority of research has nothing to do with Dr Kirby. The good doctor, who is about to walk away with all the know-how and claim all the glory, only joined us recently. Relatively speaking. But despite that, one by one, he's managed to get the board of directors over to his side."

"I thought *you* owned the company, so why worry about the board? Anyway, the fact we're having this conversation says you sanctioned the action and are in with Hannover. We wouldn't be face to face otherwise. So where *exactly* is the problem?" Byford asked.

"There are several problems! The first is that it was a good friend of mine who did most of the research. A good friend who is now dead, and he would not have wanted the research to be... horse traded by a *thief*... for career and financial advancement," Daler said, almost spitting.

"So your dead friend wanted to save the world with his new bio-fuel, stick it to the oil companies and now his legacy is being trashed by a chancer, who's going to steal the formulas and the glory?" Byford said, goading Daler a little to test his character.

"Correct, in part. It's Kirby's intent to make the bio-fuel formula available commercially. He doesn't want to save the world, you understand; just make a name for himself, to get rich in the process no doubt. Stealing five years of research he never did, I might add. It's his push for profit that's got the board all engaged with him and it's very, very stupid. I've only managed to contain them as I still hold the majority of shares!"

"I'm still lost. Did you approach Hannover with this project?" Byford asked, still wondering what the problem was.

Daler stood up and paced away from the table a few steps. After several moments of staring out of the window at the sky, he turned back to Byford.

"Yes, I approached Hannover after it became obvious I couldn't get Dr Kirby to go quietly out of the way, via a move to Terminal Fuels. A company in which I also have a considerable share, in case you're wondering. Kirby persisted, the board granted larger research facilities and he began in earnest to find a bio-fuel formula that was stable and marketable."

Byford thought about the mission briefing he had quickly looked over, but couldn't recall anything about the research; full details were still to come. He took a guess.

"You want your finest researcher to move to a pure oil company, who will moth-ball the bio fuel and so halt research on your friends work. He said he wouldn't go, because he wants to complete the research I guess. So now we're about to shut down that research, force him to Standard, grabbing the formula ourselves... to give it to Terminal? Colour me confused. This is why I'm not interested in explanations. Why the hell do I need to know all this anyway?" Byford asked.

Daler gave a soft laugh.

"Byford, the research and materials must make it safely *out* of Cosgrove Research, but must never make it *to* Terminal. The products of the research hitting the market was never the intended outcome. Do you know what would happen if bio-fuel actually replaced oil-based fuel? No!" Daler exclaimed.

"So, what would happen?" Byford asked, leaving the issue of securing the research to one side, out of interest for what was going around Daler's mind.

Daler walked back and sat in his chair, resting his hands on his lap.

"Why do you think we even bothered doing the research, if we were never going to do anything with it?" he asked.

Byford looked at him with his best blank expression. "Enlighten me."

"Three million pounds a year research and development funding from the Department of Energy and Climate Change, that's why. Three million to keep them informed of the energy options the UK has via research from companies like ours. Jonathon and I, he's the friend I mentioned, couldn't believe our luck. They wanted basic accounting, that was all, which we happily cooked up. The money could then be spent on whatever we wanted, really. Almost zero accountability and to be kept secret. Probably what killed him off, he had a penchant for cocaine and dancing ladies."

Daler laughed at the thought and it seemed to brighten in his demeanour, remembering his dead friend's vices.

"Why?" Byford asked.

Daler looked at him, seeming slightly confused.

"I've no idea, useless with the ladies I guess and just too much high living for a man of his age."

"No, no. I mean, why doesn't the DECC, want the bio-fuels to replace oil?"

"Oh, I'm with you!"

Daler leant his elbows on the table, fingers steepled, chin resting on his thumbs.

A moment passed with him looking at the clouds through the window.

He turned to Byford.

"Oil, or more precisely energy, is power, mister Byford. Those who control it have the means to control the world and do as they wish. They of course being the great nation of the USA, using their tool of control, the US dollar. It's the world's global reserve currency, after all, and the USA need it to stay that way; a deficit of billions of dollars every month makes it imperative. If you introduce alternatives to oil and the dollar, that reduces their power, which pisses Uncle Sam off no end."

Daler sat back in his chair, now clearly in the flow of conversation.

"Why do you think Saddam Hussein was taken out? He was going to trade oil in currencies other than the US dollar, the Euro I believe was his preferred choice. You can't have that, it devalues the dollar. Get rid of him, maintain the dollar's value and take his oil as a bonus. Why do you think they got rid of Gaddafi? He was planning to accept payment for oil in gold, via an African gold dinar for god's sake. You think the UK or US has enough gold to use for oil purchases or would even want to? It would cause a chain reaction. Imagine the Saudis following suit. Never going to happen, US dollar or nothing. Same problem, same solution. Get rid of him, take his oil and 144 tonnes of gold in his vaults by all accounts. A double bonus and a very strong message to the world!"

"I heard these type of conspiracies but never thought this stuff was real," Byford said.

"You're not supposed to think it's really the truth of things, go back to sleep, little man!" Daler replied. "We actually have six viable formulas, you know? But none will hit the market unless *they* say they want it to. That's what Dr Kirby doesn't realise, partly because he can't be told of course. It's why I've set him up to go to my other company. I'm not being an ass, I'm trying to save his life. If he convinces the board to commercialise it or if he goes anywhere else with it, to another company for example, I won't need to sue him. He won't see the next sunrise, I guarantee you that," Daler said.

He turned to face Byford directly.

"So now you know why this is so important. Byford, you are to intercept Dr Kirby and take the research from him, before he arrives at Standard or does anything stupid. This may not be explicit in your instructions, but it is essential."

"Well, now I see why you're telling me all this. If he goes walk-about then you're on the line too," Byford said.

"We cannot simply hope Kirby will arrive safely to Standard Oils where we can pick it up, too much is at risk if the research fell into the wrong hands. I need Kirby tucked away at Standard and the research to disappear en route."

Byford looked at Daler, now understanding what this conversation had been for. Though initially annoyed at Daler being there, he'd given so much away Byford was pleased that the conversation had taken place.

"Of course you do. The money from the Department is nice and living isn't too bad either, eh? But to be clear, if it's not in my instructions, I won't be doing anything. Just so that's clear."

Daler sat back in his chair once more.

"Well then, I shall have to speak to your Handler again."

"You do that."

As if having been waiting for the conversation to end, the stewardess came out of the cockpit and greeted the two men.

"Ten minutes to landing, gentlemen," she said, clearing the breakfast items away and returning to the galley.

Daler stood and took a seat at the opposite table, fastened his seat-belt and resumed looking out of the window at the clouds.

~ 13 ~

The two men sat back in the car seats, pressing against them in a vain attempt to make themselves more comfortable.

"God these seats are uncomfortable, my arse is going to sleep. How long is he going to be in there?" a fat Carter asked his thinner companion Jones.

"Until he comes out, I guess," was the sarcastic reply. "Feel free to stretch your fat legs for a bit, burn a few calories while you're at it."

"Yeh, and get piss wet through while I'm at it."

For the next few hours, the men sat and watched Kirby's house through the deluge of rain, variously complaining about uncomfortable seats, the weather and a lack of food.

∞

"Jon... Kirby here, how are you doing?" Kirby asked over the phone.

"Well, it's been a while. I haven't heard from you since you left us for your new friends at Cosgrove Research," came the reply. "To what do I owe the honour?"

"I have something that may be of interest to you. Why don't we meet up and discuss, I'm sure you'll be interested," Kirby said.

Given he was Chief Chemist for Standard Oil, Jon Federman was only too familiar with the story of Dr Kirby's spurious professional rise. As far as Federman was concerned, Kirby had got where he had by being a first-class shit and not a first-class chemist. What made the call alarming, though, was that he'd already been warned to expect it.

"I'm shocked. You have a chequered history here, but I'd be keen to see what you have on offer," Federman said. Whatever Kirby would come offering might be something to be suspicious of but he was also intrigued to see what it was he was offering.

"Where shall I meet you?" Kirby asked, ignoring the loaded comment.

"Come to my house in an hour. My wife is cooking lamb and we're having it with a nice Rioja I've drawn from the cellar."

"Uh oh, the mad scientist is on the run," Jones said, nodding towards Kirby, who'd just emerged from his house and was rapidly heading to his car.

The two men watched Kirby throw a black case onto the front passenger seat and climb into the car.

"Look sharp, he's heading off somewhere right now," Carter said.

"I can see that."

Jones started the car and waited for Kirby to pull off.

For the next half an hour, they followed Kirby at a distance which was too close for either of their liking.

"Bloody weather," Jones cursed.

Kirby arrived at a residential area in a leafy suburb that was obviously for the well to do.

"Blimey, look at this place, it's like one of those housing estates off an American movie," Carter said.

Jones whistled in agreement. "Aye, it's where the rich boys live."

"Which is where exactly?" Carter asked.

"Willow Bough Drive apparently. Dial it in, will you? Let's see who we have here," Jones said.

"OK, but watch him," Carter replied as he opened up a small laptop he pulled from the door-well.

Jones watched Dr. Kirby step out of the car with the briefcase in hand and head across the road. He went only about 30 metres down the street before heading up a driveway and towards someone's front door.

"Got the list, give me a number," Carter said, having opened a list of residents from an electoral register.

Jones pulled out an old brass sailor's telescope from his coat pocket, expanded it and looked at the door Kirby had just entered.

"Jesus, I'm working with Inspector Gadget!" Carter said. "What's the number?"

"57, who's that?" Jones asked, compressing the telescope and putting it back in his pocket.

"Let's see. Oh dear, a mister Federman."

Jones raised his eyebrows in surprise. "As in Federman of Standard Oil?"

"The very same," Carter replied.

"Shit, that's not good."

"No, it's not. You better call the boss, pronto," Carter agreed.

Jones dialed the number and waited sullenly for the Handler to pick up. The dialing tone ended too quickly. "Hello, sir, I'm afraid the courier got the wrong address..." he said, not needing to add any more.

"You have a name?" Steven asked.

"Federman, sir."

There was a moment's silence where Jones could hear the Handler attempting to compose himself, which despite his obvious efforts didn't accomplish much.

"Idiot! Just as I thought he would. Get him as soon as he comes out. I'll sort out the recipient, you make sure the problem with Dr Kirby ends tonight. This is three strikes, am I understood?" Steven said.

"Understood, sir," Jones replied.

Steven slammed down the phone.

"Yep, he's pissed off."

"Time to administer a little sense to the good doctor, is it?" Carter asked.

"A bit more serious than that; it's game over for the doctor. We take him as soon as he gets out."

∞

With dinner commenced and pleasantries out of the way, Federman had moved on to asking Kirby the real reason for his visit. "It's perfectly fine, my wife and I are partners at all levels," Federman reassured him.

For the next few minutes Kirby described the research and fuel samples he'd taken, adding that his goal was to move to a company that would bring the fuels to market, and that while he'd been working to convince the board at Cosgrove Research, his main worry was it would never happen there.

"I see. You have all necessary samples and research secured to reproduce the fuel?"

"Of course. Well, there are in fact several formulas that are viable commercially. I have everything needed to replicate the most complete one at your facility. The rewards to Standard would be incredible, to yourself too."

"I understand this, doctor, but the risks are also very great. Is the Department of Energy aware of the formulas?" Federman asked.

His wife spoke before Kirby could respond. "You can't just walk away from Cosgrove and into Standard with products the DECC are aware of," she added, making it clear she understood her husband's business well.

"Yes, they are aware, but there is something you must simply trust me on about this."

Federman looked across to his wife and back to Kirby.

"And what would that be?"

"I have already been told to remove samples and research before I am to go to Terminal Fuels."

Federman stopped chewing his lamb and looked again at his wife.

More composed, she continued as if the bomb shell Kirby had revealed had not gone off.

"Do you understand what I mean?" Kirby asked.

"We understand perfectly!" she replied before her husband could do so, already sensing his building anger. "Someone has requested you to leave Cosgrove Research, with their most promising DECC registered research, and head over to Terminal for a position they have obviously secured for you. Meanwhile, you've decided to barter with my husband by offering this all to Standard Oil in return for a no doubt handsome package. Is that roughly correct, doctor?"

Kirby shifted uncomfortably in his seat, taken aback at the easy exposure of what he'd thought was a subtle plan.

"You're generally correct, but as I've mentioned, this is the most complete formula. The board at Cosgrove moves too slowly, despite my work to move their thinking on. It's just a matter of time before someone else comes up with something viable and goes commercial. Given your husband and I have such a long history and that I know he's a decisive man, I felt duty bound to approach him."

Federman had begun eating again while listening to his wife, but at Kirby's last statement he almost choked, slamming his cutlery down on the table.

"Duty bound!" Federman shouted. "The whole industry knows you got where you are by stealing others' research and here you are again! I don't even want to know who you're working for, it's illegal and DECC will have your balls for it, mine too!"

Federman stood, sliding his chair backwards and slamming his palm onto the table. "Get out of my house, right now!"

Kirby did as instructed without saying a word, panic rising in his mind as he realised the depth of his miscalculation.

∞

"Doctor Kirby, get in!" Carter ordered.

Kirby hesitated for a moment, still confused from the sudden change of circumstance and ejection from Federman's house.

He saw the look on the man's face and decided to do as told.

Carter slammed the door shut behind Kirby and climbed into the front passenger seat. The driver pulled out and drove the three of them away from the house.

"Where are you taking me?" Kirby asked, leaning forward towards the men.

The man in the front passenger seat suddenly turned and, lurching over his seat, reached out towards Kirby, grabbing him by the collar and pulling his face towards his own.

Kirby's mouth fell open and he squinted with fright, dropping his document folder to the floor involuntarily.

"Shut the fuck up! Shut the fuck up and stay in your seat!" the man shouted, so loudly that Kirby's ears rang with the sound of it.

Kirby felt the man push him away slightly without releasing his grip.

"I demand to know who you are! I have friends—"

Kirby didn't get to finish the sentence. Carter pulled Kirby back towards him and smashed his head into Kirby's nose. "Shut the fuck up!" he shouted again.

Kirby saw stars and let out a scream as Carter released his grip. He dropped back into the seat, raising his hand to his face. Blood streamed from his broken nose into his open mouth and he felt it running down the back of his throat, the harsh iron taste making him cough.

"Bleed on my seats and I'll throw you out of the fucking car!" Jones added, looking back at Kirby via his rear-view mirror, seeing him writhing about in pain from the violence Carter had just dealt out.

Kirby took a handkerchief from his raincoat and tried to stem the gushing fluids coming from his injury, the rising panic and adrenaline easing the pain he would have otherwise felt.

They drove through the darkness and rain, eventually pulling off the main road and onto a gravel track that Kirby saw ran parallel to the shipping canal at the edge of the city. The car bounced and swerved down the track, past dark fields of overgrown vegetation to his right and rusted, broken chain-link fence to his left bordering the canal.

A few minutes later they passed under a motorway bridge, driving between the high concrete pillars and roadway above. The driver killed the lights and drove on a few hundred yards more in the near darkness.

Kirby could feel beads of sweat start to drop from his forehead, his heart pounding in his chest, fearing what was to come.

The car drew to a halt and the two men leapt out.

A few hundred yards later, they skidded to a halt and the two men leapt from the car.

Carter swung the rear door open and grabbed at Kirby, who was weakly holding up his arms to prevent himself being dragged from the car.

"Come here, you snivelling shit!" Carter said, grabbing Kirby by the arms and hair, dragging him out and marching him away from the car.

Jones had gone to the boot of the car. "These?" he shouted to his companion, holding up two baseball bats.

"Just bring one," was the response.

Kirby was thrown headlong onto the ground and felt the impact jar his entire body. "Why are you doing this!" he screamed.

The reply coming from Carter was a gloved fist slamming into the right side of Kirby's head. "I said shut the fuck up!"

"He's a bit old, I guess beating him half to death isn't going to take much at this rate," Jones said, in a clinically calm voice that contrasted with his screaming friend. He walked over and handed Carter the baseball bat.

"Now listen, doctor Kirby, the reason for this is you're a prick. My calm but unreasonable friend here would like to beat you to death for being such a prick, but Hannover wants you alive for some reason. That's a lucky break you got there, but it's not a get out of jail free card. No one, and I mean no one, screws Hannover!" Jones said.

"I didn't tell him anything!" Kirby whimpered up at the man.

"Did I say talk or lie?" Carter asked.

"Now now, we don't care, we have our instructions and you're to learn your lesson," Jones told him, holding his hand up to prevent Carter doing any more shouting or punching.

"OK then, I think a little pop and crack will do it," Jones said.

With silent agreement, Carter swung the baseball bat with practiced accuracy into Kirby's left knee and an audible pop was heard and his knee cap snapped off.

Kirby screamed out again and rolled forward, reaching for his leg.

As he did so, Jones swung his foot with perfect timing up at Kirby's face, smashing into his jaw and sending him flailing backwards to the ground.

Once again the baseball bat was raised and this time it came smashing down into Kirby's ribs. The cracking sound was accompanied by the whooshing of air and Kirby was left shaking and crying with the pain and shock of his sudden injuries.

The two men nodded to each other in recognition of the efficiency of their work.

Jones reached down and grabbed a wide eyed and whimpering Kirby by his collars. "That's your lesson for now," he shouted, "the deal has been done. Doctor Kirby, you've broken your word and paid the price. So we're all straight again. Go to Terminal, keep your head down or you'll see the *really* ugly face of Hannover!"

Kirby was dropped a final time to the wet ground and left to the pain and injury inflicted on him.

~ 14 ~

"Good evening, my love," Anthear said as he came up behind his wife and planted a kiss on her head.

He took off his coat and scarf and threw them down over the arm of the sofa. He then took a large bundle of cash from his jacket and placed it on the drawing-room table before heading over to the drinks cabinet.

"Looks like you came out on top again, dear. I see why you're home early," his wife said, looking over at him from behind her magazine.

"Why, I'm home early only to see my beautiful wife! But yes, you're right, I did, my love. Blackjack is certainly paying off lately."

"Who's doing the paying?" she asked, tilting her head down and looking at him over her reading glasses.

Ignoring the question, he finished making himself a Martini with ice and, having noticed his wife was without a drink, made her favourite evening drink, a gin and tonic with slice of lemon.

He walked over to her chair, placed her drink on the table next to her and sat down opposite from her on the sofa.

"Some you lose, some you win," he said, sipping at his drink. "The house always wins in the long run, but some are certainly losing more than others lately."

"I assume you're referring to Andrew? His wife cornered me at the ladies club yesterday. What an absolute bore that woman is," she said.

"I assure you, my dear, Andrew is also a bore and owes more than just us. We may be old school friends, but we're not his keepers, are we? Anyway, I offered to square his debts to us in return for something else of substance. I'm sure he'll come up with something. His wife needn't worry about not affording lunch for herself at the ladies club or piano lessons for little Jane."

"Very good, dear, I really can't be hearing anymore from her about her husband's gambling or philandering for that matter. I'm sorry, but she knew what he was like when they married," she said.

"Indeed she did, my love," he replied in agreement.

Anthear and his wife continued to chat, sharing gossip of people they knew, the events of the day and the goings on of the ladies club and snippets of things at the Hannover club.

The ringing of the phone disturbed them.

"Who'd be calling just before supper?" his wife asked.

"Hmm, I wonder…" Anthear replied with a sigh, looking at the phone.

"Answer it then, dear," she said.

Anthear got up, crossed the room and picked up the phone.

"Well, Andrew, I was just talking about you. Didn't expect to be hearing from you so soon," he said a little loudly, by way of announcing who it was to his wife.

She pulled her face in recognition and Anthear continued.

"What's the occasion of the call then?" he asked.

"I've been thinking about what you said. I have something you might be interested in, someone actually. One of my staff here at ASTU," Andrew replied.

"Do tell."

"Her name is Melissa, she's a new recruit to ASTU, came over from MI5 on a transfer about 12 months ago. Bright but edgy, probably won't last with us to be honest, she's already been labelled as a retention risk, but she might be useful to you. In fact, you might want her on your side as you and your friends certainly wouldn't be wanting her on your back," Andrew said.

New talent was always something Hannover was on the lookout for, female talent all the more. The days of the James Bond hero type was an idea stuck in the 70's and women had proven themselves more reliable—less macho 'balls to the wall', as he'd heard it described.

However, the fact that Melissa had already been presented to him meant the value of Andrew's lead wasn't quite as high as Andrew was no doubt hoping it would be. That aside it was interesting to hear the same name again.

"I appreciate the lead on Melissa," Anthear said, once again at a level that would ensure his wife overheard, "but please don't assume what my friends or I would be worried about."

Andrew caught the warning. "Ah, my apologies, no assumptions intended. Merely pointing you towards someone of note."

Happy that Andrew wasn't going to misplay yet another hand, Anthear continued. "Has she done any field work yet?"

"Yes, three cases so far and closed them all, with help of course."

"OK, well if an event came up where you had some prior notice, placing her on the case so we could observe her would be appreciated," Anthear said.

"Got something on the drawing board?"

"Don't worry about that. I'll let you know as and when," Anthear replied.

"OK, but once an ASTU team is assigned to your event, it's game on, you know? I'll keep Melissa free to get her assigned, but I don't control these people once they're off," Andrew said.

"Very well, then I believe our agreement is this: she gets assigned, and if we can work with her, we're all straight again," Anthear said.

"Agreed. Let me know when, but make it soon please. I can't hold her forever."

"A matter of days. Keep her available and we'll have something set up before you know it."

"Thanks," Andrew replied and hung up the phone.

"Well, she is a popular girl. However, that was rather generous of you, wasn't it, given he's giving you nothing?" Anthear's wife said, deducing what the conversation was about.

"Well, catch 22. If we take on Melissa, he'll assume it's because he pointed her out and expect a trade in return. If we don't trade, he may work out someone else must have presented her."

"Well timed on his part then, good to see he got lucky for once," Anthear's wife observed.

"Very true, my love! Now, supper?"

∞

The next day, Anthear decided to check in on his recent placement within ASTU.

"How is the new role going, settling in?" he asked.

"Hello, sir. Boring as hell, I now remember why I don't do full-time employment anymore. Too much bureaucracy and bullshit," Lauren said.

"Ah yes, I remember those days. Tell me what you've learned about the team at ASTU, then," he asked.

Fortunately, he'd called on her encrypted mobile or it would have been likely the call to or from the building was being monitored by ASTU intelligence, just as she expected all email to be monitored. It made it harder to report back to Hannover, but fortunately they were always technically one step ahead.

She brought Anthear up to speed on the ASTU personnel she'd had contact with, details recorded in their files and major projects she'd heard about or been asked to recommend staff for.

He asked the occasional question and made noises to show he was listening. When the conversation appeared to be waning, he got to the real point of interest.

"Oh, before I go—what about this Melissa, any progress on her? We got a second recommendation about her last night."

Anthear had avoided asking about Melissa for the entire call and now he was about to bring the call to an end, had raised it as an aside. As expected.

Lauren was always mildly amused by the predictability of people and their behaviour; amused, but perhaps leaning more towards seeing them as pathetic and weak.

Words she'd often used to describe her subjects, but only to likeminded and equally manipulative psychologists of course. Calling people subjects was frowned on in the profession these days, and calling them pathetic would mean instant excommunication. Not that Lauren cared about the concerns of the other so-called *professionals*.

As for this quirk of leaving the important things to the end of a conversation: she hated very many quirks, but this one annoyed her the most. *Pathetic*, she thought to herself, then smiled to change the tone of her voice.

"Interesting that someone else pointed her out, though a little slow, as we've had our eye on her for a while. I think she's been working her way to us for some time; not that she knows that, of course," Lauren said.

"Agreed, it looks like she's one to go for. Beyond the basic brief you received, have you got any further background on her yet? Is this someone with, shall we say, 'a history', that could be useful context to colour her view of us favourably?" Anthear asked.

"No need to explain, Sir Anthear, I fully understand your concerns in ensuring she's safe to approach," Lauren said, actually meaning 'no need to spell it out to me like I'm a moron.'

She continued, "According to her file she has a very colourful background."

Lauren walked around to her desk and pulled up a file on her computer.

"She's described as mildly aggressive, someone who doesn't mince her words. Mixed race too, a Spanish and Chinese mix but now a naturalised Brit. Father was from Shanghai and got kicked out of Spain after he split with the mother. Mother remarried an Englishman and they moved to England when Melissa was three. There, they've lived happily ever after it seems."

"OK, that's a bit more colourful than I expected already. Any contact with the father?"

"Doesn't say, which means no. Covers her more recent background though. Just before graduating from University she's approached by MI5—her ability with Spanish, English and Chinese along with her academic record and psychological profile seemingly marked her out as a person to recruit. After a few years at MI5, the Anti-Subversion and Terrorism department was formed, and here she is," Lauren said.

"Well, well, so she's never actually met her father, that is interesting," Anthear said, half to himself.

"Why is that so interesting?" Lauren asked.

"Don't worry about that. Just always a useful thing." Anthear paused for a moment and then continued. "Right, I suggest you recommend her for the little project we'll have going soon. Let's try her out on our terms, give her a piece of work that is on the fringes of typical for her and see how she responds. If you can, create a reason for a debrief with you when she returns, that'll allow us to check that she's moving in the right direction," Anthear said.

"No problem, sir. Once I get word, I'll assess the nature of the assignment and come to the conclusion that Melissa is a good match, then we can take it from there," Lauren said.

"Perfect, talk soon." With that Anthear ended the call.

∞

"Steven, it's me!" Lauren announced over the phone.

"Unexpected, everything OK?"

"I've just had Sir bloody Anthear on the phone asking about Melissa! Apparently someone else in ASTU has now mentioned her."

"What the hell is he doing? He's the Sponsor, he should be coming through to me with this stuff. How am I supposed to know what's going on when he does this!"

"I know, he's worrying me, breaking protocol again. We work the way we do for a reason! Steven, he's got something for this Melissa and now seemed interested in her father. Do you know who he is?"

"Haven't got a clue, but it sounds like I need to find out. I may consider him somewhat of a friend, but Anthear's a manipulative bastard who doesn't give a crap about anyone unless they matter," Steven replied.

"Two people mentioning her? When does that happen, he's already up to something."

"Just be careful in there, Lauren. He's the boss, so go along with what Anthear wants and let's see how this plays out. It may just be coincidence."

"In Hannover?" Lauren interjected.

Steven continued, "If I can find anything out about why he's so interested in her, I'll do so. You'll understand if I keep you ignorant on it, though?"

"Of course, and please do. I've done well so far just by knowing what I need to!"

~ 15 ~

The plane drifted down steadily towards the runway at Sumburgh Airport.

A smooth landing and steady taxi to a remote stand and they had arrived at the Shetlands, the first step of the journey to come, now complete.

As the cabin door opened the fresh, crisp air of the Shetlands poured in, making the stewardess rush to put her long coat on.

To Byford it was like bathing in refreshing water. He filled his lungs deep with the air and could smell the land and sea combined into an earthy, salty fragrance. He found it invigorating after so long away.

The cockpit opened and the captain stepped out, walking straight past Byford without a word or glance his way. Daler then got up, went into the cockpit and closed the door.

"Thank you, sir," the stewardess said as she gestured for Byford to leave the plane.

He grabbed the last of his things, headed down the steps and climbed straight into a waiting car.

"Just to the ferry?" the driver asked.

"Yes please," Byford said in response.

The ferry to the South Island would be the second leg of his journey, before reaching the house and meeting the team once they arrived. As he watched the passing scenery through the car window, Byford reflected on being given an evening alone before the team arrived next day.

It was some time to read up on the full mission, which would be in the next email. More importantly, it was welcome time to ensure all was in order, that he was in order.

He was grateful for it.

One thing was swatting up on a mission statement so the details were known. It was another thing altogether to be mission ready and primed to respond to whatever wasn't in the plan, the unexpected that always happened.

People, situations, equipment, weather, incorrect information—it was all there to trip you up. Being prepared for the unexpected was half the mission. This one was straightforward enough, but it was dangerous to be complacent. He'd learnt from hard experience.

Byford saw the harbour come into view and snapped out of his reflections.

"We made good timing, ferry leaves shortly," the driver said.

"Great," Byford replied, seeing the boat loading its last few passengers.

They pulled up just near the ramp to get on board and in a practiced set of actions, the driver jumped out of the car, swung the door open for Byford to leave, wished him a good journey and handed him a ticket for the ferry.

"Ah, thank you, very well organised," Byford said, nodding politely and walking off to the ferry.

The short trip across the water was uneventful and the boat's pilot kept a steady pace towards the distant shore.

Byford looked out across the landscape and watched the last rays of light spilling across the horizon as the sun began to dip below the far hills, touching their peaks and setting them alight with an explosion of orange and yellow.

He took in another deep breath of sea air and this time felt a wave of relaxation wash over him.

It really was good to be back.

The boat arrived at the docks, and as he stood to get off the pilot raised his hand.

"Your stop is next," he said.

Byford felt a tinge of annoyance at being herded along. It was the Hannover way, but always made him feel things were not under his control.

"Is this help, or babysitting?" he said to himself under his breath, mind wandering to the Handler, imagining him giving instructions to control and watch every step Byford made.

"Sorry, sir?" the pilot asked as he came back to the wheel.

"Nothing, where are we going?"

"The drop off is a beach, at the cliffs below the house. All a bit cloak and dagger but they asked I get you on location without having the village noticing when you went up there."

Within a quarter of an hour or so they arrived at the beach. Dusk was nearly over and the last of the day's light almost exhausted.

A small stack of rocks covered by sand acted as a jetty for Byford to climb onto from the boat.

"Just up the hill," the pilot said, gesturing with his hand to a pathless hillside of scrub and rocks.

From just behind the peak of the hill Byford could see the house.

"Great, thanks," he replied.

The pilot's posture suddenly changed. He fixed Byford with a stern look and, standing stiffly, offered Byford a handshake.

"Good luck to you and your team, sir."

"Thanks again," Byford replied, noting the sudden military air of the man.

With the first tangible sense of the mission having begun, Byford turned and headed up the hill to the house.

It was a short walk up from the beach to the house.

He stopped around 30 metres away and stepped backwards against the soft branches of a decorative pine tree.

A question that hadn't been answered was *how* he'd get into the house.

He waited and watched, but the house was dark, with no signs of movement from inside.

Byford slowly and quietly moved off to his left, circling around towards the back of the house, careful to maintain his distance and listen for any telltale noises of other people.

By the time he'd reached a point where he could see the back of the house, he'd seen and heard nothing.

His military instincts were suddenly alive once more.

Without planning to, he went down into a crouched position, breathing gently and listening carefully, trying to place every creak, tap and rustle.

He heard only nature and nothing that sounded like people going about their unnatural business.

Satisfied, he circled around to the front of the house and followed the same routine—again nothing. By now it was virtually pitch black and the house was becoming hard to see, even at this short distance.

Heading to the front door, he reached out and tried the handle, but the door was locked. Looking down he noticed a faint reddish glow emanating from underneath the handle, creating a subtle area of light on his skin.

He'd seen this once before, a hidden electronic lock. *No wonder they sent me at night*, he thought to himself. Placing down the backpack he was carrying, Byford pulled his trouser waist band forward and, reaching into his underwear, retrieved the small dongle used for the laptop.

Crouching, he looked under the door handle, saw a small slot and inserted the device. A low click and the door was unlocked.

Once inside, he locked the door behind himself and took the key that had been left on a hook screwed into the door frame.

'Site door activation at 20:13 hours, positive match to expected occupant. Monitoring ended as per your request,' the systems operative typed and sent an encrypted message to the Handler.

They clicked 'Close Connection' on their screen and the remote surveillance ended, just as the in-person assistance had done half an hour before.

Byford meanwhile, had already made it to the kitchen, grabbed the biggest knife he could find and had commenced a sweep of the house.

Satisfied he was alone and that all doors and windows were secure, he felt himself relax and starting breathing normally again.

After cooking up some food and enjoying a few of the beers that had been provided for him, he fired up the laptop and checked for messages.

There was one, but it wasn't what he was expecting.

Instead of full and final details about the mission in just under two weeks, there was a task to complete beforehand.

As he read through the message, it became clear why he'd been sent to this location. Within a mile of the house that was to be their base was a ship wreck that contained valuable items to be recovered. Those valuable items were on the biggest, most recent wreck the islands had seen: the *MV Braer*.

It was 100,000 tonnes of oil tanker when it had been afloat; today, it was wrecked off a place called Garths Ness, right on the south tip of the island they were on.

Sitting a few metres below the surface, it was ideal to dive in. This unexpected side task needed a little more than just diving skills however.

The message contained instructions about the recovery of containers, stored in the cargo hold within the ship. The instructions stated they were labelled 'Enzyme 114.'

Various notes had been provided about the likely condition of the ship, location and description of the containers. There was also a note about a delivery that would be made to him before the dive.

His experience told him that the vague wording meant he was being sent explosives or weapons, or both. Things were warming up.

As Byford read through the remainder of the message, he thought of the team profiles. Buckby would be useful for her skills cracking locks and doors, Lagis knew marine demolition if Buckby got stuck and, as a route finder, Carlson should be useful mapping a route in and out. Finally, Daniels would prove invaluable for his understanding of electronics.

It looked like Hannover had put together a good mix—time would tell.

~ 16 ~

Frost checked his watch: 3.25pm. By rights, David should already be in the Arlington.

He'd know that when he got through the traffic and finally arrived at the pub.

"Aww, come on!" he cursed at the stationary cars.

The satnav said he was just a few minutes away, but at this rate he'd be lucky to get there before David gave up and left.

The rain continued to pour down, hammering against the windshield and obscuring the view ahead. The failing light wasn't helping, either.

A full 20 minutes later, he arrived at the pub and pulled into the car park. Racing inside to avoid a complete soaking, he wiped the rain off his face and looked around the bar.

Thankfully, David was easy to spot—he was sitting opposite the door, nursing a half-empty pint.

Frost held his arms out and shook the rain from his hands, making it a gesture towards David, as if blaming him for the rain.

"Wet out?" David asked, laughing and getting up to greet Frost.

"Just a bit!" he replied, shaking hands with David.

They both took seats at the bar and David ordered two pints for each of them, drinking down the remainder of his old pint.

"Let's take these round the back room, we can talk there and have a game of darts, if you're up for it?" David asked.

"Not played in years, but let's give it a go!" Frost replied.

They headed to the snug, small room that could fit about 20 people, but it was currently empty of anyone. Just a few seats and tables around the walls, along with the promised dart board.

As they stepped in, David turned and locked the door. "Don't want any of the yokels disturbing us," he said.

Frost did a quick assessment of the situation.

The door lock was no problem, he could easily smash the door open if he needed to get out in a hurry. As for David, despite the way he walked—a kind of forward-lurching swagger, as if he was about to attack someone at any moment—Frost could now see he was in no way the threat he liked to portray. Up close, anyone could see David was not in the best physical shape. To Frost he looked weak and unfit; he doubted the guy could win a playground fight, let alone a pub brawl.

As for the way he drank down the beer, that told Frost his new friend was bordering on alcoholic, probably with a little something else on top, judging by his yellowing teeth.

"So, what's the story, mate?" Frost asked, wandering over to the dart board and opening it, ready for play.

"First things first..." David said, picking up the darts.

The two men went through a socialising ritual, playing a round of darts, drinking their beer and talking about anything but what they'd come here to discuss.

"So listen," David finally said, to Frost's relief, "I'll let you have this one, you're well ahead of me anyway!" He waved his hand dismissively at the dart board.

He continued, "Come on, let's talk about what we came here for and see if you want to join in the fun." He gestured for them to sit down at a nearby table.

"Sounds good, I've been curious since you called me," Frost replied, taking a seat.

"My little group is all into the idea of activism, but that's it mostly, just the idea," David began. "That's a problem for me, because beyond a few marches and sticking some posters up, they really can't be arsed to do anything substantial. You know what I mean?" he asked.

"Yeh, I think so. They're well into the idea of being all about it, but that's it. Don't tell me, they love talking about it, getting angry together, smoking your shit and then falling asleep?"

"Blimey! Have you been round my house before!" David said, pretending to look puzzled at how Frost understood the group so well.

"Mate, there's too many people like that in the world, eco activist types are no different. Do you have any real activists, people you can trust?" Frost asked.

"I've got one, that's it. Brother Wolf, I think you've met him, a good guy, but a bit light-weight, if you know what I mean," David replied.

Frost let a brief moment pass between them, as if reflecting on his own situation. Looking slightly distant to increase the effect.

"Well, I know how that feels. I used to think I knew who to trust... but things change," Frost said.

"Tell me about it," David said.

"Don't get spooked, but I used to be in the Met Police, undercover no less. I kind of screwed up though, by firstly losing my faith in the pointlessness of what we were doing and secondly, falling for a girl I was supposed to be nailing for criminal offences; not, you know…"

"Actually nailing?" David asked, finishing the sentence for Frost.

"Yeh, something like that. Getting busted for dealing didn't help either, even if it was my girl's fault!" he replied.

Frost continued, "Before that, I was army. Paratroop Regiment for nine years. So 13 years later here I am on civvy street, wandering around on my own again. All those years and literally not a steadfast friend to show for it. Oh, some of the army lads get in touch every now and then for a drink, but no one's close anymore. To be honest, I guess I'm pretty fucking angry about it."

David could hardly contain his excitement at what he was hearing.

Ex-forces and ex-police, now rejected by both and gone native.

Having Frost appear now was like Christmas and Easter together.

"Well then, mate, third time lucky maybe. I need a guy like you on my side and I stick by people. You can trust me on that one. My girl, Mary, and Brother Wolf will have your back too," David said.

"Sounds all right for a starter, but if I'm to trust in you, give me something to work with as well," Frost said, demanding similar disclosure from David, curious what he'd give away.

"I'll level with you then. I have two problems, actually make it three. First is the group and the threat of being called on again by my new lady friend, which I fully expect her to do. Guaranteed she'll want a job doing by the group, in return for giving me the get-out-of-jail-free card. Fuck knows who she works for, but she was a bit full on and confident with it all, totally playing me. She's totally done this before," David said.

"She sounds a piece of work. So, you want me to help out with whatever she needs doing?" Frost asked.

"Exactly. Like I said before, it won't be shouting at the police and sticking up posters, of that I'm sure."

"Hmm… well, could be right up my street. What was problem two and three?"

"Problem two is that most of the group won't go for anything beyond the usual. I can get together maybe five people for something special, including you and me. The rest I wouldn't trust to… well, nothing. I just wouldn't trust them," David said.

"Don't sweat it, if she wants something funky done, we want a team of around five anyway. Any more becomes a problem. Third?" Frost asked.

"Thirdly and most importantly, I don't actually give a shit about the group doing anything more than what we do now," David said, looking directly at Frost.

Frost pulled the corners of his mouth, as if acknowledging the revelation of a deep secret.

"Oh, clever boy. David has something else going on, does he?" Frost asked, raising his glass to David and taking a large gulp of the beer.

"Damn straight I do. Nothing too heavy, just selling a bit of puff and charlie, maybe one or two other things, but it keeps me in cash and keeps some of the group around me happy. Meanwhile they provide cover for my comings and goings, an explanation for the people I hang around with. So you see what a total pain in the arse my unexpected visitor was?"

Frost stayed silent for a moment, taking in what he'd been told against what he already knew, so as to not mix up the two.

"How much are you shifting a month?" he asked.

"About £5k usually, up to £15k in summer or at new year," David replied, being more open than Frost could have hoped.

"Good figures, not huge but I see why you want the cover of the group," Frost said.

Doing quick math in his head, Frost worked out that shifting £5k meant a mix of about 2-to-3 kilograms of resin and maybe 50 grams of charlie, depending on the prices he could get.

It was a lot for one guy. To deal it when needed, he guessed half that would always be at David's place. Where exactly was something to discover and valuable information to pass on.

"I appreciate your openness, mate," Frost said. "Listen, I'm happy to help manage the problem with your lady friend. Let's take this somewhere a bit more private and discuss what we're going to do about her, eh? I feel like someone's going to walk in at any moment."

"Yeh, let's head to mine, you can sample some of the treats I keep there. Mary's mate Claire might be home too," David said, raising his eyebrows at Frost and slapping him on the shoulder.

Frost agreed and the two gave a toast, marking their new relationship and understanding of each other.

Images of Frost leading the job Lauren wanted done, getting caught and taking the blame all raced through David's mind.

Schmuck, David thought to himself as they got up to leave.

∞

"Mary?" David shouted as he and Frost got in.

"Up here!" came the reply from upstairs.

"We're in the den!" came a shout from another voice.

"Hey Claire!" David shouted back, before turning to Frost. "You're in luck," he said, then shouted back upstairs, "I've got company, we're going to the basement for a few beers and a smoke. Come and join us if you like, but give us 30 minutes, OK?"

"Yeh, yeh... OK," came a mixed reply from both of them answering over each other.

David and Frost went to the basement, grabbed some beers from the fridge and set themselves down on sofas opposite each other.

"Nice place," Frost said.

"Yeh, a little place of privacy to keep my nefarious dealings away from nosy eyes," David replied. "And look what we have here!" he added, producing a wrap of charlie with one hand and a bag of skunk in another. "Magic!" David exclaimed, causing Frost to laugh.

"Shit, that was actually quite clever!"

David threw both bags on the table between them, followed by papers, a mirror, a blade and other paraphernalia from a box under the table.

"Show us what you've learned then," he said, sitting back to watch Frost at work.

If that was meant to be a test or challenge, David was in for a surprise. Frost took the papers and gear, rolled a perfect joint that looked machine made and offered it back to David.

David gave an appreciative look and got down to enjoying what he placed before them both.

From that point on, the night switched into party mode.

Frost took advantage of David's supply, snorting coke and smoking dope like he'd not done in years. Even with his tolerance, built up over the years of drinking and other abuse in the army, he was grateful for the combination keeping him level, as one brought him down and the other back up.

At some point Mary and Claire had come down to the basement.

Frost could see Mary was already wrecked and looked like she was often in this state. It was the first time he got more than a casual glance at her in the last months. He could see her hair and skin were in poor condition and she was unhealthily thin.

Claire wasn't in much of a better state—they both reminded Frost of crack whores. Bodies and minds going to ruin.

After a few beers and joints, someone put music on, club tunes that set the girls off to dancing about with each other.

David got up, went behind Mary and started dancing with her.

He nodded at Frost to get behind Claire and do the same, but before he could Claire had shouted for him to get up with her.

They danced, filled the air with more smoke, laughed, messed about with each other, played card games, snorted more coke and drank more beer.

A few hours later the music had ended, the light were dim and they were all crashed out on the sofas.

All except Frost.

As the night had gone on, he'd switched to beer and when going to pee drank water to clear his head. He played along with the others and fed them fresh joints and drink, faking his own continued excessive consumption.

Now they were out for the count, David with Mary draped over him, both stripped down to their underwear, after a last round of strip poker.

That hadn't gone well for Frost; he'd ended up naked and covering his privates with a cushion as the game continued. Much to the amusement of everyone else. Claire had grabbed a few handfuls several times, but the thoughts of sex with her hadn't evoked much of a reaction. Thankfully, the drink and drugs had been a believable excuse.

At least this had all led to him being accepted. David appeared completely relaxed with him, a good rapport built in a few hours of carefully managed interaction.

What now caught Frost's eye was not the semi nakedness or the drugs that were both laying around, but David's necklace.

It had been snapped off in the partying, much to David's annoyance.

Mary had caught her hand in the chain as David swung her around to mimic taking her from behind. He'd instantly become angry, grabbing Mary around the neck and choking her slightly.

"Look what you've done! Pick it up!" he'd shouted.

What Frost was later to learn in the gossip afterwards was that the necklace contained a small piece of umbilical cord from David's dead son. The baby apparently had survived for just a few days. It explained the bond Mary had formed with him, beyond the need for drugs.

Frost could now see it on the table between them. It would be the perfect 'token', something that he'd been instructed to get for Byford.

Sliding himself out from under Claire, he rolled her to the back of the sofa and waited to ensure she was still asleep.

Satisfied she was, he turned his body until he was sitting on the sofa facing David and Mary, listening to their breathing. Reaching forward as slowly and carefully as he could, for papers and a bag of skunk, setting them up in front of himself.

The necklace that was his real goal was lying opposite him, next to a lighter that would make a legitimate next item to pick up. He took his time, rolling a joint and making sure those in front of him really were asleep.

The handiwork done, he popped the joint between his lips, quickly stood and leant forward, putting one hand on the far side of the table, blocking David's view should he open his eyes. With his free hand he scooped up the lighter and bracelet in one circular motion.

Satisfied his theft had gone unseen, he walked off up the stairs and towards the rear garden, carefully depositing his stolen treasure in his coat on the way out.

Outside, he noticed his heart beating heavily and took a few deep breaths to settle it again.

Feeling composed, he lit the joint and he drew in a mix of sweet-flavoured smoke and fresh morning air.

"Got you, you fucker," he said to himself, blowing out a soft cloud towards the morning sky.

~ 17 ~

The ferry pulled up to the dock and the two-man crew busied themselves with securing the boat. A small walkway was placed over the edge of the boat and dock for the passengers to alight.

The rain, which had started in the early morning, had continued unabated. Dark grey clouds hung low over the island, hiding the tops of the highest hills in the near distance.

"OK, folks, out you go," said the second crew member, who'd wisely stayed inside.

He slid open the metal doorway, letting in the rain and wind.

One by one, the passengers stepped carefully out and onto the dock, variously unfolding umbrellas and pulling up hoods.

A tall man with a cropped grey beard stood nearby, sheltered under a large umbrella.

"Diving school?" he shouted in their general direction.

"Yeh, me!" Lagis said.

"Me too," came the reply from Daniels.

"Over to the bus," the man said, pointing over at an unmarked white van about 20 metres away.

Carlson and Buckby made themselves known and were shortly also in the back of the van.

The man closed the doors behind them.

Sitting on crude wooden benches, they were all left to shake off the rain and greet each other politely but cautiously, unsure of who the others really were.

The man jumped into the front seat.

"You sure picked a fine day to start your training up here!" he said.

As he spoke, the head of a collie dog appeared over the front passenger seat and was immediately followed by a bark, as if the dog was in agreement.

"She's called Ochre, by the way," the man said, shouting backwards to his passengers and pulling off from the car park.

"Oprah? That's a funny name for a dog," Lagis said.

"Oh, good one! Haven't heard that in a while," the man replied.

"Isn't she dead?" Daniels joked, getting no response.

The man broke the awkward silence. "You all divers, then, or first time?"

"First time for me. I heard there were shallow waters and plenty of wrecks here. So, a good place to start," Daniels said.

"Well, I'm an experienced diver and if you're just learning here, then you've got a steep learning curve ahead of you."

"Oh right," Daniels replied, "Isn't a steep learning curve quick? I'm more into shallows, as I said," he added, attempting to add his own humour.

Buckby silently appreciated his comment, deciding Daniels was a little more erudite than he was letting on. For a few moments there was another awkward silence that amused Buckby more than his failed attempts at humour.

"Ah, don't you worry. This diving school teaches anyone and the weather will calm down by tomorrow. We've got plenty of shallow bays for you to paddle around in and a lot of wrecks for you others to have a look at. Something for everyone here! Isn't that right, Ochre?" the man said in as reassuring a tone as he could manage.

The dog barked her agreement once again, causing the man to laugh while vigorously stroking her on the head.

"How far is the school?" Buckby asked.

"We're coming up to it now," the man replied.

Buckby checked her watch, it had taken less than 15 minutes from the docks; when she got time alone later, she'd check exactly where they were.

The van took a sharp turn up a gravel drive and stopped outside a cottage.

"Here we are!" the driver announced.

He leapt out of the van and into the rain, followed by his dog, this time not bothering with his umbrella. The man opened the back door and swung it wide.

"Here we are, teacher's waiting!"

The four students climbed out and he pointed them towards the house, where Byford was waiting at the front door.

"Come in, come in!" Byford called out to them.

He was wearing thick-rimmed glasses and a woolen cardigan, making him look ten years older than he really was.

The man shouted a farewell and good luck to them as he climbed back into the van, cursing his dog for getting the seats muddy and wet. The dog barked and they drove off.

Once inside, Byford directed them all to the kitchen area, where an open fire and large table with pots of tea and coffee awaited.

"There's tea and coffee here, plenty of stew and dumplings on the stove and, if you prefer, there's a few beers in the fridge," he said. "Make yourselves at home. I'll leave you to it while I go grab the paperwork and sign you all in."

He gave a smile and went to head out of the kitchen.

Just before he left, he turned back and said, "Oh, I will need any mobiles you have. Turn them off and hand them to me, please."

Though a little surprised with the sudden change of demeanour, they did as instructed and handed the phones over.

"Thanks, back shortly," he said and left the kitchen.

"OK, that was unexpected," Daniels said to no one in particular.

Left alone, a brief look passed between Lagis and Buckby, both of whom seemed to be wondering if the other was an experienced operative.

Buckby thought about who was who. Judging by the behaviour of Daniels and Carlson they were either very green or actually civilians, but the chances of a civilian being here now seemed minimal.

She'd heard that the intake to Hannover had expanded beyond ex-military and police, which could sometimes work, but if these two were Hannover operatives, she was already concerned.

The instructor who'd just left them to supper was certainly Hannover, but in what role, she'd have to wait and see. She concluded to herself that everyone here must be Hannover or they would never have got through the door.

Reassured, she stood up to see the food on offer.

Now in the office the house contained, Byford flicked on the cameras for the kitchen area and took in a multi-angle view of the new arrivals on a small screen to the side of the desk he was at.

Scrolling down the report on his laptop, he identified each of them as the operatives he was expecting.

He continued watching. Lagis and Buckby were matching their profiles, staying cautious and aware, while Daniels and Carlson were behaving like college kids.

The Handler hadn't been joking when he'd said the team were new. Not only new to each other, but to Hannover by the looks of it.

Looking back at the screen he saw Carlson punch Daniels on the shoulder as they jostled to grab beers from the fridge.

Satisfied they were the people he was expecting, he dropped the doddering old man persona and adopted his real role as the Lead. He took off his cardigan, swapping it for a fleece, put down the glasses and put on a baseball cap. To finish off, he pulled off his ill-fitting jeans that had been covering his running trousers.

It was probably a pointless ritual, but many years in Hannover had engrained in him a need to always be masking his true identity and true intent.

Byford sighed and regained his thoughts. Ready to commence the training, he went downstairs and back into the kitchen unannounced, where the new team were busy eating and drinking.

"Right, I see you're settled in, but time to stop dicking about," he said, taking all by surprise. "I'm Byford, the Lead on this mission and you are the *potential* team."

"Ah, I was wondering," Buckby said.

"Yes, so you can relax—we're all Hannover here, but you two can get with it and stop acting like college boys," Byford said, looking over to Carlson and Daniels. "And I take tea with two sugars, by the way," he added, waiting to see who got up first.

After a few moments it was Lagis who responded, "Allow me."

"Thanks. Now all of you, after you finish eating, hand in everything you're carrying, the lot. No personal items or possessions are to be used after tonight. You are not to use or carry any of your own stuff, be that clothes, wallets, laptops, whatever. Not even your own toothbrush or jewellery, be that worn, pierced or otherwise. If it wasn't issued by us, hand it in. Is that clear?" Byford asked, looking around at them all.

After getting general agreement, he continued.

"Good, we have a changing room and store on the ground floor here. I'll issue your basic kit and you unload and change in there. The rest of your kit is in your room, anything else we'll issue as we go along. Hide anything and I will kick you off the team," he warned.

With that, he sat down and enjoyed the tea Lagis had made, washing down some of the stew and talking to the team about their swim experience, jobs with Hannover and generally getting the measure of who he'd been sent.

As he already knew from the brief, Daniels was not as green as he made out but was enjoying playing the role of the new guy. Buckby was the most no-nonsense one of them all. She seemed only mildly interested in socialising and was clearly forming her own view of the team.

After some time, Byford was satisfied he had the basic measure of them. The training over the next days would show him how they really were.

"Right, let's get you lot re-kitted," he said. "Daniels, with me, please, and bring your backpack. You can come back and finish off in a few minutes," he added, noting Daniels was in mid bite.

Walking out of the kitchen, Byford opened one of the doors off the hallway which opened into a small room with shelves and metal storage boxes.

Daniels walked in behind him. "How does this work then?" he asked.

"You go in the changing room there, take this kit," Byford said, handing him a deep plastic tray with a small bundle of clothes and running shoes.

"As I mentioned earlier, take everything off and put it all in the tray, then come back out dressed in this gear."

Daniels did as told, changing into black combat trousers, T-shirt and training shoes. Being only 5' 5" but stockily built, he was a little surprised it all fitted well.

He came out to see Byford with a hand-held metal detector, similar to those used in airports.

"Stand over here, arms out," he was told.

Daniels did as instructed and Byford scanned him for any metal.

"OK, wait here, don't move, keep your arms up," he said.

Daniels again did so and Byford went into the changing room to inspect what had been left there. Finding nothing, he came back to Daniels.

"OK, relax. Send in Buckby."

Without a word, Daniels dropped his arms, turned and left the room.

Byford placed the tray into one of the metal storage boxes, threw in the mobile Daniels had given him earlier and snapped the locks shut.

Shortly after, all the team were all changed and dressed the same.

Back in the kitchen, Byford allowed the team have their fill of food and drink.

"Right, I'll show you your rooms. At 2000 hours we'll start some basic training, so I can check where you're at physically. Run and swim today only, but get ready for it tomorrow as we don't have much time to train and prepare. See you in a couple of hours," Byford said.

After showing the team their rooms he left them to their own devices.

∞

Buckby looked around her room.

It was comfortable, if simple. Bed, desk, shelves and a rug on the polished wood floor.

She noted an abundance of bedding and thought about a good night's sleep. Since being called on to attend the mission, her sleep had been broken to say the least.

"Rustic, I suppose," she said to herself, reflecting again on the room.

She wandered over to the window and looked out across the garden and scrubland leading down to the sea.

From her vantage point, it looked like the sea was about a mile away.

She thought about what she'd seen coming in on the ferry and the drive to the house. They were definitely on the south end of this island and not far from the small port the ferry had landed at.

"Shetlands for sure," Carlson announced through the open door, as if reading her mind.

Buckby turned to see Carlson standing in her doorway.

"What's that, you worked out where we are then?" she asked.

"I guessed it was Shetlands, lot of diving here and Edinburgh airport is the usual place to head out from. A short Westerly hop after landing and the ferry across the water, not hard to guess," Carlson replied. "Anyway, I pulled it up on the map app when we landed at Sumburgh."

"Ah well, that would make the guessing easier. A little obvious, though, isn't it?" she asked.

"Hidden in plain sight. If we sneak off to some remote location, the cover of being a tourist diving school doesn't make sense," he said.

"I guess," she replied.

"Anyway, was just checking the rooms; all equipped the same. I'm going to have a nap before we start running about. I'm figuring from here in we're at full throttle," Carlson said.

"OK, catch you later."

With that, she closed her door, drew the curtains and lay on the bed to join in with the collective team nap.

~ 18 ~

"This kind of analysis is pointless, it can't tell you what you want it to tell you," Lauren said, "but I've taken a bit of extra liberty with the scenarios I provide."

Lauren held her clasped hand out and, opening it, dropped a data stick into Steven's lap.

"If it covers the main things Sir Anthear wants, then I'm happy," he replied.

He reached down to the side of the chair and picked up his laptop, flipping it open and inserting the data stick. There was silence between the two of them while he took in the highlights of Lauren's report.

"So Byford doesn't stay?" he asked in a dull tone.

"No. Based on the information you've provided me and his behaviour in the recent past, I can't see why he would stay. In fact, if he gets Mary back, which is his personal objective, he's even more likely to leave," she said.

"Great. Well, that was the only leverage we had to get him back. Do you have something in here that turns that scenario around?" Steven asked.

"Yes, of course I do, two things in fact. Firstly, you need a shared trigger event to fundamentally change their relationship, from the point of the event forward. Secondly, you need to shift Byford's opinion of Hannover from being that of an employer to that of a benefactor. People leave employers, they stay and support benefactors."

Steven looked at her, thinking through what she'd said, imagining what these two things she'd described might be like in reality.

"Steven, stop daydreaming and turn to page 12," she said, which he immediately did.

A few more silent minutes passed between them.

"Hmm... interesting. Well, this David is disposable, as you know from Sir Anthear's current opinion of him," Steven said, confirming he'd read the first alternate scenario Lauren had created. "I'm not entirely sure he'll panic quite as much as you suggest, though."

"Steven, read between the lines a little, you hopeless literalist. Byford took the mission because he wants Mary back, but it's not enough to re-secure him."

"Go on," Steven said, prompting for further explanation.

"In addition to doing what I suggest in the report, and I know you have the contacts to get done what I suggest, Byford will be up to something too. Combined, David will react. Closest to him is Mary, who will bear the brunt of that reaction. If bad enough, that's your trigger event. David's unlikely to kill her, so you get what you need to affect Byford," Lauren said, hoping spelling it out for Steven would be enough.

"OK, I get it. Drip, drip, drip from all angles until David goes over the edge," he replied to confirm his understanding. "How unlikely is unlikely, by the way?" Steven asked, tuning into the word Lauren had used.

"I've estimated 80%. There is always a possibility David will overreact, perhaps killing her unintentionally, or that someone else will intervene and cause her death," she said.

"You should have worked for a life insurance company with that cold, calculating assessment skill you have there."

"Actually, I used to, but it gets boring fast."

"Why am I not surprised. Now, what about Sir Anthear's new interest, Melissa?" he asked.

"She's a bit more interesting, given she's a lot brighter and more complex than David," Lauren said.

"The summary here says highly volatile, 30% chance of reversion. Is that even a word?" Steven asked.

Looking up at Lauren he raised one eyebrow and lowered his mouth.

It was a playful gesture Lauren had seen a few times before, when her explanations had been less than clear to him.

"Can you explain this to me in plain English, please?" he added, giving a smile.

Laughing, she reached out and patted him on the knee.

"There there, Steven. It means she's got attachment issues. Daddy wasn't very present in her life and Mummy felt boarding school in Hong Kong would be good for her," Lauren explained.

Scanning the report again, Steven said "I see, but her father, who was it... Guang, got kicked out of the UK *after* the divorce. In which case what were they all doing in Hong Kong, I wonder?"

"You're correct and it's a good question. He acquired persona non grata status after his Triad connections were discovered. They all went to Hong Kong before the handover, which was interesting timing. Some say the Chinese government wanted him to hand over his illicit business there, to help set up his underground network there before the handover," she said.

"I see, but bring it round to Melissa for me again— or Xifeng, is that her real name?" Steven asked.

"Yes, Xifeng means 'western phoenix', quite poetic. Melissa was her mother's choice. The reversion risk is based on the fact that *Melissa* has been unable to form longstanding relationships. Her father and mother both leave or dump her, we see her move universities, get pulled from MI5 and we know she's single. There's no hobbies or clubs, no church or ladies group, not even a library card. Nothing. She's a loner, who if approached in the wrong way, might get spooked."

Steven sat silently, taking in what Lauren had said and reading through the report. Lauren watched his face change and saw his eyes squint ever so slightly. She'd observed him like this before. The moment when his seemingly simplistic questions, asked as if he didn't get what was being discussed, led him to a greater insight than those who'd simply take everything at face value.

"Conversely our approach, if done right, might be seen as a natural next step for her. Especially if you can make her think this is where she was meant to be after so much uncertainty," he said. "Destiny manifest, her path revealed," he added dramatically, looking up to Lauren.

She found herself accepting his words as if they were a decree not to be questioned.

"What else do I need to know about in here?" he asked, turning his attention back to the report.

"There is one more thing: Frost. You know he's a close friend of Byford?" she asked.

"Naturally. What of it?"

"The risk is that Frost and Byford aren't the only ones who have history. The ever-interested Anti-Subversion and Terrorism Unit have one of our own too. You recall Broer, I'm sure."

At the mention of his name, Steven looked up at Lauren directly.

"Broer is working for ASTU?"

"Yes, and you know the colourful threats that went between Broer and Frost when they came back from Israel," Lauren replied.

Steven's mind swam back to the events of the past. The death threats that had come at the end of a bloody fist fight had not been about Hannover, but the failed mission that Byford had ran with Broer.

After months of rehabilitation the first thing Broer did on his return was to hospitalize Frost, and though Frost recovered and came back to work, Broer made clear death threats before he had vanished. Now Steven knew where Broer had vanished to.

He had to face the facts—Broer could have told ASTU almost anything. He'd be on the hunt for Frost and would try to crack the group and possibly parts of Hannover.

"A clever move on his part, but this complicates things," he said at last, sitting back into his chair.

"Yes it does, but read the whole report. I propose some strategies where we might use this to our advantage," she said.

"How so?" Steven asked in a low voice, mirroring his concern.

"We need to draw people together. If we can get Melissa assigned to the project as Anthear wants, then we need to leave a suggestion of Hannover being involved. If we do that, Broer will make sure he's assigned too. When that happens, we can expect Broer to become distracted from the ASTU team's mission, back onto his personal agenda. This behaviour should affect Melissa, ideally unsettling her when she's needing to feel secure in her new family. If we can engineer conflict between Broer and Frost that will perhaps motivate Byford in the longer term," she explained.

Steven leant towards her in his chair. He hadn't thought past the current project and its immediate objectives, but here she was doing what she did best.

"That's why I can't just rely on those dry mathematicians, no imagination," he said, confirming his acceptance of her own thread spinning.

She laughed. "Well, some would argue that they have a lack of imagination! They must have amazing imaginations to work with such abstract ideas all day."

"Fair point!" Steven said. He continued, "OK, we have many more pieces to line up than I thought. Byford should have started training the team already. We'll need to move fast on your recommendations. I'll work on David, you get ready to do your thing with Melissa. I'll go and brief Sir Anthear and make sure he knows we're on top of it," Steven said.

"Yes do, I don't want another one to one conversation and if he takes things into his own hands again, he'll have another failed mission on his hands. Page 25 for that scenario, by that way."

~ 19 ~

It was 2000hrs exactly when muster was announced with the blasting of a sports whistle, sounded by Byford, already outside on the front lawn.

Within minutes the team were outside and, without prompting, formed a straight line in front of him, awaiting instructions.

He looked like the classic army physical training instructor. He was adorned with a whistle around his neck and, oddly, a pair of swimming goggles hanging there too.

The rain had now stopped, leaving the damp air crisp and fresh. An early evening breeze had risen from the south, bringing with it the smell of the sea.

"Good," Byford said once the team were in line. "First thing is a brisk run. We'll do a circular route and finish off with a quick swim in the bay back there, before heading back here for the last of the exercises."

"Sir," Daniels said, now adopting a more formal tone of reference that Byford appreciated, "won't it be dark when we're swimming?" he asked, having noted the light was already beginning to fade.

"Depends how fast you all run, doesn't it," Byford replied.

Without further instruction, Byford signalled for them to follow him and started to jog away.

"Like I said, full on from here in, not even a warm up," Carlson whispered to Buckby.

The team ran along at a quick pace, though easily keeping up with Byford. At first they'd followed the road they'd used earlier when they were travelling to the house, then they'd cut onto scrubby moorland headed for the top of a hill about a mile away.

Byford noticed that Daniels seemed to be in his element.

His short, stocky legs were perfect for running over the scrub and moorland they'd been crossing, whereas Buckby, with her height, was struggling.

The going was tough enough for all of them, but Byford had made it harder by adding in a few natural obstacles to contend with.

The first was a small stream, running heavier after the rain. The steep sides of the stream bank, rising over 10 feet on either side, prevented them from climbing out to dry ground.

Splashing their way upstream they arrived at a small waterfall, perhaps 20 feet high and just a few feet across. Though not huge, with the high banks of the river blocking them and this obstacle in front they now had a very wet way ahead.

"Up you go!" Byford shouted, before they had a chance to guess what the next challenge was.

One by one the team climbed the waterfall, grasping at anything that would hold them, while being hosed by the freezing water.

Meanwhile, Byford had climbed around the obstacle using a combination of rocks and large roots he'd become familiar with over the years.

"Old git," Lagis mumbled under his breath.

"Squeeze out what water you can and let's move," Byford said, once everyone was at the top.

The team did as instructed and, once ready, Byford got them moving again before anyone had the chance to suffer from the cold.

They ran on without any sign of Byford tiring. Along hillside edges, over fences and dry stone walls, up the gravel track of a disused farm and out the other side to a small valley with a pine tree wood either side.

By now the light was fading fast and the constant twists and turns had the team disoriented.

Byford stopped running and turned to face them.

"Doing well, all of you. Good work," he said to the team.

"Now, you need to go through the woods ahead of us until you reach the bay. Find and follow the stream down to the shore. Once there you'll see where you are. Swim across the bay and I'll see you at the house. Last one back gets cut!"

The team looked at each other for a moment and, guessing they were now in competition, Carlson sprinted away for the woodland ahead.

The rest of the team followed at a pace and Byford watched them disappear down the hillside into the trees, Carlson being rapidly caught by the long-legged Buckby, who was shouting his name as she chased him.

Byford looked to the west and could see the sun touching the horizon. In ten minutes the island would be pitch black and if he'd timed it right, the team would be safely across the bay. If not, he'd be needing his goggles after all.

He took one last glance at them, seeing Buckby almost catching Carlson. Hopefully they'd realise the point of the exercise was not about who could run the fastest.

With that thought in mind he doubled back the way they'd came and crossed a nearby hill, dropping down towards the house.

"Stop your running, you moron!" Buckby shouted at the nearly sprinting Carlson.

He was obviously used to cross-country running, bounding along using rocks and trees, grabbing branches to lever himself through tight spots and jumping across depressions in the ground.

Despite his ape-like progress, he was no match for Buckby's raw speed.

About two feet behind him, she dove forward and tried to grab at his shoulders. The move was mistimed, and instead she raked his back with her fingers and landed flat on the ground behind him, barely avoiding his heel kicking her in the face. Even with this, it achieved what she'd wanted.

Carlson lost his balance with dramatic effect, flailing forward and landing face down into the pine needles carpeting the ground. His forward momentum caused his legs to swing over his body and he crumpled to the ground like a rag doll.

Buckby picked herself up from her soft fall and dived on top of him, grabbing his shoulder and dragging his head up. "It's a test, you dick! We finish together."

Laughing, Carlson looked at Buckby and spat several times to remove the pine needles that were lodged in his mouth.

Letting go of him she stood up and stayed ready, in case he decided to retaliate.

Instead of attacking her, he rolled over and sat up to wipe the remainder of the forest floor from his face and eyes. "Jesus, there's no messing with you, is there!" he said, Buckby now standing over him in a threatening posture.

Before she replied, Lagis and Daniels arrived on the scene.

"All right?" Lagis asked.

"Yeh, fine," Buckby replied, "Listen, we need to finish together so no one can be cut," she said to them all.

"How do you know that?" Daniels asked.

"Look, you're new to this. If we don't come back as a team, he won't cut one of us, he'll cut all of us. For those of you who've not been Hannover long or at all, that's how it works," she said.

Lagis jumped in. "OK, we stick together and finish together. Let's get moving. By the looks of it, he's set us up to be crossing the bay in the dark and I for one don't like the idea of it. We swim together and run together to the house," he concluded, more as an instruction to the whole team than as a point being shared for discussion.

"Let's go then," Buckby agreed.

Lagis and Buckby waited for Daniels and Carlson to start running down to the bay and then followed.

"Just in case you're wrong, when we get to the house we should form up on the lawn and wait till he sees us. That way he won't know who to cut even if he wanted to," Lagis said to Buckby.

She nodded her agreement and started for the bay.

∞

Byford reached the house and after a quick check that nothing untoward had happened while they were out, he let himself in and went straight for a shower.

By now the team should have reached the bay, in fact they should be halfway across it.

Though a short swim, the darkness and the night-time tide would be a challenge.

This run with its little obstacles was no more than what they'd face on the mission, although this was a few hours of training and the mission would take minutes.

If the challenges they'd faced this afternoon were beyond them, then they really weren't ready.

He let the warm water wash over him, the heat bringing life and energy back into his body.

Though still fit and active for his age, he'd started to feel the cold and prefer the warmth more with every passing year.

The joints in his fingers began to ease up and the chill around his forehead began to ease. He dried and dressed, then went downstairs to the kitchen, putting on the kettle and awaiting the return of the team.

Wandering into the main room, he couldn't resist looking out through the window to see if any had arrived back. He saw no one in the darkness that was now fully settled on the island.

Hopefully they'd all made it across the bay safely.

Concern crossed his mind about the wisdom of timing it so they'd be in the dark near the end of the exercise. He just had to wait and see if the team would rally together and bond as quickly as he hoped.

But right now, they were late.

∞

As anticipated, the light failed the team as they were about halfway across the bay.

The rocks had been easy enough to climb into the water from, but now only a distant silhouette against the evening sky was their guide to point they had to reach to climb back out.

At this distance, perhaps still half a mile, there was no sign of a beach; it all looked like cliffs.

The team swam on through the growing gloom.

A splash and muffled cry from her right alerted Buckby that Lagis was in trouble.

It was now almost impossible to make anyone out in the darkness, but the occasional glint of moonlight through the slowly clearing clouds created enough contrast to make out heads and arms, disturbed water and wakes of the swimmers.

Buckby spun about and dove under the water where Lagis had just gone down, no more than six feet away from her.

She was underwater for a few seconds, swimming blind in the darkness, when Lagis's thrashing arm hit her body several times and then punched her directly on the nose.

Holding back the pain to avoid breathing water, she tried to grab his arm, but he continued to swing around wildly. Instead she felt for his head and, on feeling the touch of his hair, reached down and grabbed the collar of his clothing.

Kicking hard, she swam herself and Lagis to the surface. They burst out of the water, gasping for air and spitting brine.

"On my leg!" Lagis shouted, spluttering more water from his mouth, before sinking again.

Daniels and Carlson were immediately around him and taking a shoulder each, supported him while they treaded water.

Buckby swam around to the leg Lagis was trying to lift and on seeing it, understood how he'd been pulled under.

The bay they were swimming through was relatively shallow and rocky, a haven for marine life.

She'd skimmed by a few of the fish that had made it their home, but Lagis had attracted a bigger admirer.

There, attached to his lower leg was a common octopus. Not huge, but weighing in at about 10lbs, it was enough to pull a swimmer under in a panic.

Buckby placed her hand around the creature's body and squeezed as tightly as she could, as if strangling some human foe.

The tentacled arms started to release from Lagis.

She pulled hard, separating it from his leg, and with a cry tossed it as far as she could before it took a hold on her.

All the swimmers were now exhausted from the fight.

"Relax, float and get your breath," Buckby told them.

All, including herself, did as told.

"Never seen anyone taken out by Cthulhu before," Carlson joked while treading water.

"Let's go. Swim to the right of that headland, it looks flat, hopefully a beach," Buckby said.

∞

Byford lay on the cliff edge, overlooking the bay the team were struggling to swim across. The night-vision binoculars he was using helped, but it was still hard to make them out. However, he was able to watch Buckby take the lead and made a mental note of her management of the unexpected test that had just been presented to the team.

At least this had now confirmed his belief: she was Lead material. Something to remember for the future.

He lowered the binoculars, pulled off the swimming goggles from around his neck and made back for the house. His gut instinct to come and check had been right, but thankfully he hadn't needed to get wet.

∞

The rest of the swim was uneventful.

Breaks in the clouds allowed some light to swim by and as suspected, the differing shade of the distant outlines was the beach Buckby had hoped for.

"God, I'm knackered and fucking freezing," Daniels cursed as the team hauled themselves onto the small sandy beach.

"Get up and let's run the last stretch as a team," Lagis said, slapping Daniels—who was squatting down, arms around himself and visibly shaking—on the back..

Buckby once again took the lead. "Let's move or we'll get hypothermia being in the water so long."

They jogged up the grassy hill away from the ocean and shortly arrived at the house.

"Line up," she ordered as they reached the house.

The team did as instructed and while doing so triggered a security light, illuminating them and catching Byford's attention from within the house.

He leapt up and went quickly outside to check on the arrivals. "I see, all back, together, in one piece after that excitement?" he said, now inspecting the team as they dripped onto the lawn.

There was no reply except for heavy breathing and the rustle of wet clothes as the team shivered and dripped where they stood.

"You're done for tonight. Get in and change before you catch your death," he said, waving the team into the house.

Byford went in and to the office. Checking his watch, he sat and waited for an expected phone call. A few minutes later, the phone rang.

"Now then! How's it going with the kiddies?" Frost said in his usual high-spirited form.

"Good to hear from you, all going well?" Byford asked.

"Yeh, I got that 'little something' you asked for. Want me to brown bag it?" he asked, making reference to passing on items without Hannover knowing.

"No, no need for spy tactics. Get the office to send one of their boys up," Byford said.

"You sure? They'll check it."

Byford thought for a second. Of course Hannover would check anything sent to one of their own properties, by one of their own agents, with their own courier.

In this case, Byford didn't expect it to have any repercussions. They'd expect him to be in touch with Frost, were probably already whispering about the call right now in some darkened operations centre.

"Send it through," he said at last.

"On its way. Talk soon, boss," Frost replied before hanging up the phone.

~ 20 ~

Byford had continued training the team over the last week. A mix of fitness, equipment use, teamwork and, of course, swimming.

Though usually it would be just a few days of preparation and then deployment on the mission, these were a new unit. That meant drilling them for slightly longer to ensure they'd fit into the Hannover way of doing things—and fit with each other.

His assessments of the team were coming together and all looked like they'd be fine. A fact he was happy about after the schoolboy errors he'd seen some of them commit on the first few training sessions.

Lagis and Buckby were continuing to prove themselves the most competent and steady. However, Daniels and Carlson had been the opposite of that from day one.

They were just hard work.

Daniels was here because he was a technology expert and with work was keeping up physically. Carlson was the other side of the coin. A military veteran, a Close Reconnaissance Soldier.

The brief from Hannover had been clear.

Carlson was a loner who thrived on risk and adrenaline; as such he'd be the one to keep on a tight rein.

Hannover needed both brains and brawn, preferably in the same person. To varying degrees, they all had what was needed.

Time would tell if they had it as a team.

The planned deploy date was now close, closer than he'd suggested to them, but there was something they needed to complete first.

That was the side mission: to recover the containers on the *MV Braer*. Though all had proved themselves in the water, they hadn't proved they could swim under difficult tactical conditions.

∞

Byford stood from the dining table where he and the team were enjoying a simple supper of toast and tea. "Final day tomorrow," he said.

The team looked around at one another; having never been told how long the training was going to be, they shared a mutual sense of surprise at being told it was almost over.

"So, have we all made it?" Lagis asked.

"Not yet, you can still fail and get kicked from this team and Hannover, right to the last minute. Your training was meant to be two weeks, but it's being cut short as the mission has been set up earlier than expected. This team is still first choice, but as you no doubt expect, there's a back-up in case I say you're not ready," Byford lied.

"Are we ready?" Buckby asked.

"Mostly, but some of you need to pull your fingers out to make sure."

"What's the plan for tomorrow?" Lagis asked.

"A special swim. I'll brief you in the morning. Have a lie in; we're not setting out until mid-afternoon." With that, Byford picked up his drink, grabbed a piece of toast from the central pile and got up to leave. "Enjoy your last supper and I'll see you down here 11.30am latest," he added.

The team gave various wishes of good night and acknowledgements of tomorrow's meeting time, then watched Byford leave the kitchen.

"What do you make of that then?" Carlson asked, breaking his customary silence.

"Maybe he's going to read before bed," Lagis quipped.

"Very funny. I mean the final test and there being another team. I never guessed that."

Buckby shifted in her seat, sitting more erect in a way the team had learned meant she was about to express her opinion.

"You have to be kidding me. I told you when we started: the whole team is being evaluated. One fails, all fail and they deploy another team. They can't deploy unstable teams, can they?"

Except for the noise of continued eating, the team fell silent.

She stood to leave. "Anyway, I'll see you all in the morning, have a good night," she said, and left for bed.

Carlson got up, walked over to cupboard under the sink and presented a bottle of brandy that had been hidden away behind various cleaning products.

"Our leaders have gone to the land of slumber, now the mice can play."

"Where the hell did you find that?" Daniels asked.

"Exactly where it was, looks like Byford is an old soaker or a previous team managed to sneak the bottle in, I found it a few days ago."

"Make sure it's not cleaning fluid!" Lagis said.

Daniels stood to fetch glasses for the three of them. "Don't be a party pooper, Lagis; Carlson has done us a good turn here."

He came back and placed them glasses on the table. "Pour away!"

Carlson did as instructed.

The three men raised their glasses and cheered each other as they drank.

Lagis choked. "Ugh! Seen better days!"

"You're such a wimp, Lagis," Carlson said, pulling his face in reaction to the drink, "but you might be right!"

A few shots later, Lagis decided to call it a night. "Right, time for bed for me too. This will sure help me sleep, though," he continued, tipping a shot into his now lukewarm tea. "Night, chaps, don't get too wrecked for the wreck tomorrow." And with that, he left Carlson and Daniels alone.

"Off to see his girlfriend?" Carlson said to Daniels, starting to laugh.

"Probably!" he replied, laughing in unison and raising his glass in salute to the absent Lagis.

∞

The morning was gloriously sunny.

As Byford descended the stairs, he could hear the birds singing in the garden.

The rain clouds that had been a feature since the team first arrived were now gone, replaced by a light blue sky and a bright sun.

Though the sky here was never the azure blue of where he now called home, it was enough to lift Byford's spirits.

"Morning, all," he said as a greeting to the team.

As expected, they had assembled in the kitchen, which had quickly been established as the main communal space.

With no other word, he busied himself making his morning coffee. He could feel the tension in the room, the team waiting for him to say more, but he was happy to let them wait.

He finished making the coffee, turned and headed out of the kitchen.

"Living room at midday sharp," he said as he departed.

∞

At exactly midday, the team had all filed into the living room to see Byford standing near the front window, with a large black sports bag on the floor in front of him.

"Good, take a seat," he said, indicating to the sofa and chairs positioned around a small coffee table.

They did as instructed.

From the bag he pulled out a blueprint of the *Braer* and spread it out on the coffee table, flattening the creases of the thick paper. The *Braer* was displayed as a white-line drawing, sliced perfectly in half lengthways, to reveal the decks of the ship from top to bottom.

"This is where we're going today," he said. "More accurately, we're going here," he added, jabbing a finger at a large area under the top deck of the ship, exactly beneath the ship's bridge.

After giving them a moment to take in what details made sense to them, Byford continued.

"The wreck broke in two when it went down. This storage area is believed to be exposed to the sea and that's where our prize is. We're after yellow containers, about the size of a large fire extinguisher. They should be in racks, here and here," he said, pointing out a series of cylindrical shapes drawn along one of the walls of the storage area.

"Ah, that's what they are," Carlson said. "What's in them?"

"Nothing of interest to ourselves, but of interest to our project sponsors, of course," Byford replied. "We go in, get them, hand them over. That's what we've been asked to do and that's what we will do."

Byford lifted the bag from the floor and dropped it onto the table. "We had a special delivery of a few essentials last night."

"So I wasn't dreaming about hearing voices then," Buckby said.

"Not at all. I'll issue your main equipment out later, but here's a few items we need to be clear on how to use," Byford said, first pulling out a set of thick straps for carrying items found undersea, followed by small explosive charges and wire.

"OK, now you're talking," Lagis said. "Stretchable charge with linking wire, if I'm not mistaken. Are we expecting to be making our own holes to get these containers out?"

"Very likely. All of you should be aware that the wreck is unstable and the sea here is difficult to swim in. It looks like a calm day today, but even so, the currents are strong. The water will be clear enough, but the wreck will be silted-up. We might need to loosen the racks a little to get at our prize and doing that presents risks."

Carlson pulled the blueprint off the table and, seeing he was starting to apply his skills, Byford retrieved other documents from the bag.

"Here," he said, passing them over to Carlson. "Pictures of the *Braer* breaking up before sinking, sea-floor maps and maps of the currents and tides. Should be all you need to plan the swim route."

"You read my mind," Carlson said in return, unfolding and inspecting the documents.

"Take these," Byford said to Lagis, as he reached for the charges and wires on the table and placed them in front of him.

Lagis took the items and inspected them. He pulled one end of the charge gently, confirming it was packed as a lattice of metal and explosive, allowing it to expand like a concertina.

"Clever," he said in admiration.

"I want you to show Daniels how to wire them. He's the electronics guy and needs to learn this side of his trade," Byford said, indicating for Daniels to come closer.

"Right, we'll meet back here in one hour and go through the plans you've come up with and set off," Byford said to Carlson and Lagis.

He turned to Buckby.

"You come with me, bring the straps. Let's get you ready to swim," he said, leading her from the room.

∞

The hour to prepare flew by and before the team knew it, they were arriving at the water for their first real job as a team.

The small beach between two rocky outcrops was a good spot to enter the water.

Byford kept scanning around the coast and nearby hills as the team continued to equip their diving gear. Though he didn't expect any casual passers-by to recognise most of the equipment, it was best to make sure no one inadvertently discovered them.

"We've got about two hours until nightfall, so let's make this quick," Byford said to the assembled team. "Follow Carlson to the location and make sure you're watching Lagis when he does his thing!"

Carlson walked backwards into the surf to avoid tripping up on his fins. When in the water, he placed his full-face mask on and tried the built-in radio. "Buckby to team—thumbs up if OK. Over," he said.

The team laughed at the joke and gave him the thumbs up. Taunting Buckby as being 'the boss' had become standard fare over the last week or so.

They finished fitting their own fins and securing their equipment, then followed him into the water.

Byford gave a final check around and, satisfied they were unseen, entered the sea.

A few feet under, echoes of waves hitting the shore reverberated through the water. Water that was as expected: cold and clear, but with strong tides that bobbed the team around as they swam.

At this point, the *Braer* was invisible, laying about 150 feet away from the beach and just a few feet down.

"Guide us in," Byford said over the radio, instructing Carlson to swim on.

Carlson followed the coast for a while, then descended further.

To Byford's relief, the three others were swimming in perfect formation, side by side with a couple of metres between them. Finally, the training had started to pay off.

The visibility started to drop the deeper they went, the water turning murky and silt starting to float past their masks.

"Watch your distance, Carlson," Byford warned, fearing he was paying no attention to those following him.

A second later—"We've arrived," Carlson announced.

As the team swam to join him, the *Braer* came into view before them. Carlson had brought them to exactly where they needed to be.

The ship was a dark hulk of rusting, silt-coated metal. Laying partially on its side, it was snapped in two near the bridge. The separated halves leaving a gaping hole maybe 30 metres wide, exposing the inner oil storage tank and pipework.

To their left, the vast length of the ship vanished into the gloom.

"No trouble getting in then," Lagis said as the swimmers gathered a short distance from the ship, treading water and awaiting instructions.

"Carlson, storage area?" Byford asked.

"Not exposed. Beyond that bulkhead. On the right," he replied, signalling with his hand towards the ship.

The communication system was working, but it required talking slowly and carefully.

Byford kicked and turned his body to face where Carlson had pointed. "What am I looking at?"

Carlson replied, "That wall of steel. The bulkhead is intact. Storage is behind there. Under the bridge. We need to get in there," he replied between breaths of air.

"Got it. Lead on," Byford said.

Carlson lead the way again, swimming further down and towards the place he'd pointed out.

Without prompting, the team followed.

From near the floor of the shattered tanker, the bridge towered over them.

The bulkhead, stretching across the entire width of the ship, was an imposing sight.

"It's like the gates of Mordor," Daniels said.

Carlson was not in a mood for humour. "Lagis. I need shaped charges where I show you. Daniels, come and wire them up."

The three men swam away from the group and towards the middle of the steel that was blocking their progress.

Carlson swam from point to point indicating where to place the charges.

Lagis retrieved the charges and stretched them in long lines as instructed. Next to each he placed a small mine, to be used as the explosive trigger. The flashing LED lights were visible to the team as each mine was armed.

Meanwhile, to ensure they'd all blow at the same time, Daniels started to cross-wire the mines.

Satisfied the job was being done properly, Lagis swam back to the waiting group, to present Byford with the remote trigger.

Daniels wound the last of the wire around the contacts on the mine. He flicked the arming switch on the trigger mine and pushed off from the bulkhead, propelling himself quickly back to the team.

"All done," he said as he swam to them. "Mine is armed."

Lagis tensed—he saw the red light on the remote trigger he was holding and realised the mistake Daniels had made. "Timer!" he bellowed over the communication set.

Daniels had made the same mistake in practice at the house, setting the trigger instead of the timer. He was thinking like an electrician, and now it was too late.

"Carlson, get out..." was all Lagis managed to add before a flash of light stung their eyes and the pressure wave hit them all full force.

Disoriented, kicking and flailing in a cauldron of bubbles, they fought to recover themselves.

Byford dragged his mask back into position, holding his breath and blasting air into it from the tank to clear the water.

Buckby kicked out to the sea floor, chasing a fin that was dropping towards the broken deck.

"Carlson! Carlson!" Byford shouted at last.

He looked towards the hole that was now torn through the metal of the bulkhead to see Lagis swimming towards it.

"He's inside! Sucked in. Drop in pressure," he said.

Byford looked up to see Daniels start to move from a floating position.

"Daniels. Report!"

A second passed and then Daniels said, "I'm OK! I'm OK! Swim on," he replied, recovering himself into an upright position.

"All of you. Get to the gap. Now!" Byford shouted over the communication system.

They swam with all the speed they could find.

When they arrived, Lagis was barely visible in the gloom.

He had Carlson upright against a framework of metal tubes. Silt and bits of debris floated around them. "Unconscious. Can't tell if injured," he said.

"Breathing?" Byford asked.

"Yes."

"Lagis. Daniels. Swim him out. Buckby, to me!" Byford ordered.

The two men each placed an arm of the stricken man over their shoulders and carefully swam through the gap and up to the surface.

Byford flicked on a light attached to his suit and swam further into the space they had entered.

The light reflected in the eyes of several fish, who shot past the swimmers and out into open ocean.

Silt continued to drift around as Byford moved deeper into the gloom. Buckby turned her own light on and followed carefully behind.

Against the wall in front of him, Byford saw what he was searching for. "Here," he said, pointing ahead.

Buckby approached and saw the framework of pipes secured to the wall, holding the containers they'd come here for. "Biohazard. Enzyme 114?" she asked, reaching out to a container and brushing the silt and marine detritus off it.

"Yes. Don't mention these details to the team," Byford said.

"Won't they hear us?" Buckby asked, pointing to her mouth.

"Too far now. Metal walls, too."

Byford swam to the containers nearest to him and, pulling out his diving knife, hammered the heel against a metal buckle holding a strap in place. A few hits and it popped open. Pulling the container free, he inspected it and saw it was still sealed.

"Get one more," he said.

Buckby checked and discarded several others before finding one in good condition.

With a container each, secured by the webbing straps they'd brought, they made for the surface.

∞

Changed and recovered, the team assembled in the living room.

"I don't need to tell you that was a stupid error, it could have got you and others killed!" he said to Daniels, who stood there and wisely said nothing in reply.

Byford continued, "Listen and learn properly. You know your stuff, but you can't just keep your head in that forever. You have to learn new skills. That applies to all of you!" he warned, turning to the team.

Again, no one spoke.

"Understand this, any of you screw up like that again and you'll be out. That includes you, Lagis! If you'd have taught him properly this wouldn't have happened. In your case, Carlson, you got lucky, but you also need to watch your situation. It was no time for sightseeing down there; you're part of a goddamn team!" Byford told them, not hiding a single ounce of his anger and waiting for any sign of dissent.

One thing was to be made clear: the team would shape themselves in exactly the way he demanded.

That was the Hannover way; that was his way.

The team acknowledged their understanding by their silence.

"This stays with us," he said, more calmly, "but it's one chance only. Anyone screws up again and you're out."

∞

Byford flipped open the laptop, went through the authentication process and opened his email.

This time, the email he'd been anticipating was there.

"About time," he said aloud.

Looking at the email attachment, there was all the expected information for the real assignment. This was the complete mission statement, not the overview brief he'd read at home in London.

Here he now had target details with photos, dates, equipment, primary and secondary objectives, route, capture risks, kill risks, deployment method, mode of extraction and so on.

There was even a weather forecast, moon phase, tide table and sea temperature chart.

He read through it twice, taking in what the task he was required to do really was.

He lingered on the final part of the message:

"Provide a blank reply to confirm green light on your team.
No further messages to follow.
You're on your own now, good luck."

He sat back and thought about the team. Buckby had shined. Despite their failings, the others had proved that they were up to the task.

Tonight he'd speak to Buckby privately and make sure he could stay in touch. Though against the rules, everyone needed allies in the Hannover world.

Byford hit 'Send' on the blank reply, snapped the laptop shut and headed to bed.

~ 21 ~

"All well, I trust?"

Steven stood as Sir Anthear entered the office. Though not strictly Hannover protocol, it always seemed appropriate to Steven.

"Yes, sir, Byford has it all in hand. Observations say the team has been active on the island and that he's had contact from Frost as expected."

"Ah, well that's good and to be expected, as you say. What was the communiqué?"

"Frost sent him a necklace and locket, sir. That was it."

"Intriguing. Do we know what it is for?"

"No, sir, not at this point, though it was inspected and contained some skin. Either foreskin or umbilical cord was the guess. A small amount was taken for analysis."

"Curiouser and curiouser, and unpleasant either way. On any account, line up your other pieces and let's get the side show rolling, shall we?"

"I'll brief Lauren tonight and she can do the same with David tomorrow, sir."

"I see, umm… why not today, as in right away precisely?"

"Lauren is embedded at ASTU."

"Ah of course, how forgetful of me. Very well, I shall leave the logistics down to you as always. Brief them well this time, Steven, we don't want our man Byford making any slip-ups on this one."

"Understood, sir."

Sir Anthear smiled and nodded to his Handler, then turned and left the office as abruptly as he came in.

∞

"Lauren, good evening. How was the day at work?"

"What, are we married now? What's burning you, Steven?" Lauren asked, in her usual direct manner.

"I need to meet with you later this evening. Usual place?"

"Is that wise?"

"It'll be fine. See you at 9pm?" Steven asked.

"No point in me asking why, I guess?"

"You already know, but the specifics I'll cover when we meet."

"OK, 9pm. Ciao."

A knock at the door drew Steven's attention.

"Come in," he announced.

An aide entered the room, carrying a sealed brown envelope.

"A message, sir," she said as she reached the desk, holding the item out for Steven to take.

Once she had left, he opened it and removed the contents, a single piece of paper showing analysis results.

It confirmed that David and Mary had a child, but Steven recalled no intelligence saying there was a child ever seen with them.

"That is interesting," Steven said slowly, trying to think how this new fact might be of use. "Hmm... no need to upset the apple cart," he decided and dropped the envelope into his desk drawer.

He checked his watch—it was time to go.

∞

"Well, you look great," Steven said, announcing his late arrival to Lauren, who was already seated at the table they'd used less than a week earlier.

"Trying to hide your tardy timekeeping with charm, Steven?"

"Fair comment, but the observation still stands."

"I've ordered," she told him.

"Was that a rhetorical question on the phone earlier then?" he asked.

It took her a moment to connect with what he was saying.

"Ah! Cheeky sod, we are not an old married couple. You always eat and drink the same thing, it's not hard to choose for you. Very boring."

"I prefer to call it reliable and consistent," he said in as posh and dismissive tone as he could manage.

They shared their usual laughter and some light conversation while waiting for the food to arrive.

"Jamón Jabugo good choice," Steven said as he finished the last of his food, sitting back and enjoying the flavour of the last piece.

"The jewel of Spanish cuisine, as I believe you called it once."

"Well remembered. Acorn fed, pure breed, pata negra. Nothing to beat it," he replied, eyes closed and a contented look on his face.

"A que te recuerda?" she asked him rhetorically, knowing who he was thinking of.

"Si, a mi abuela."

Lauren had been there when the woman he called Grandma had died, back when they had first became close. The woman had always pandered to his childhood love of Jamón and chicken.

She saw Steven compose himself again, and then he looked directly at her.

"Come on, let's talk business in the back room."

"Ah, not sneaking me upstairs this time?" she asked, trying to lighten his mood.

"Not today, I'm afraid," he replied, the memory of his loss many years ago still darkening his mood.

The room they entered was on the same floor as where they had dined. An innocuous looking door off one end of the dining room led to a neat-looking corridor, which in turn led to back-rooms in which guests could conduct business and entertainment in private.

They placed their drinks down onto a small coffee table and sat facing each other.

"It's time for you to contact David again," Steven began.

"Ah, I was wondering."

"Yes, we're days away from the main event happening and David and his band of merry men need to be ready. We need them briefed and confirmed as willing to attend. Do you anticipate any problems?"

Lauren sat quietly, thinking, looking away towards the wall to the side of her.

She reflected on the conversation she'd had with David at the police station, his apparent understanding that he would be called on.

That wasn't what played on her mind.

"Do you really need him as your sacrificial lamb?" she asked, still staring into the distance.

Steven looked at her and while he enjoyed the freedom to view her face, which he'd always found beautiful, he was in no mood for playful chat.

"Yes, he must be there and he must fulfil his assigned role. You need to convince him to do so when required. You've done the analysis, Lauren, and we've mapped out the events. Sir Anthear is quite clear on his expectations and plans cannot be changed now."

"We don't even know what his expectations are."

"We know enough to fulfil our roles. We'll provide David with what little information and help he'll need to do his job and that's that."

Lauren was now looking directly at Steven.

At times like this she felt helpless against his will, his stubbornness.

For a smart man, it always shocked her how blindly obedient he was to Hannover. It was why he'd risen through the ranks, but also why they had never had a true relationship.

At least, that was what she told herself.

Taking a deep breath, she let her instinct to battle him dissipate.

"OK, what do I tell him?"

"The action is tomorrow night," Steven said.

"Jesus, are you kidding? Actually…don't answer that."

Steven continued, explaining the location, times and actions required from David and his group.

"Any back-up?" Lauren asked.

"No, they are to consider everyone hostile. Get in, flood the place, get out."

"Fine, that won't be a hard sell, David is borderline paranoid aggressive anyway. He'll probably relish being asked to go outside the law. Do we have anyone on the inside, any *family men* loitering around?"

Lauren's reference to a code phrase used by Hannover operatives when encountering a team brought the first smile of the evening to Steven's face.

He raised both hands from his chair and pulled his mouth down, in a gesture Lauren had seen many times.

"Maybe yes, maybe no."

She playfully kicked out at his leg, but failed to make contact with him.

"Call him now," Steven said, pulling out a phone from his jacket pocket and handing it directly to her.

Though her blood pressure was rising from his continued direct attitude, his mood wasn't yet light enough to push him by refusing.

She took the phone and hit dial, knowing the number would already be there to call.

"David... it's Lauren, how are you?"

Steven could hear David's voice but it was low and tinny, not allowing him to make out what was being said.

Lauren explained what was needed and used her best empathic and soothing tones in response to David's numerous and expected complaints.

"Yes, the equipment is at the edge of the trees, it will look like trash dumped there. Carry it through to the fence. That's right, just open the pipes and release what's in the tanks, nothing more."

Steven could tell she was winning David over.

"OK, good luck," Lauren said and disconnected the call.

"A little confusion as expected, but he's all good to go."

"Three of them are going?" Steven asked, checking what he'd heard.

"Yes, no surprise there. David was never going alone. Does it affect plans?"

"Hmm, true. Well no, two or three, it doesn't matter. Everything is timed well and this action's pretty simple."

Lauren could see Steven was running through his mind information she had not been privy to.

"It's the frustrating thing about all this for me. Everyone down the chain knows less and less about what's really going on up the chain. Does it not annoy you, Steven?"

"I've stopped worrying up, I just worry down now. My job is to get the job done through the team and make sure the pieces are in place; that makes success likely. If I do that, those up the chain are happy. Just that on this one, David makes me nervous—mainly because in truth there are two actions. We're playing the David action and the refinery action."

Steven paused in a way that told Lauren he had caught himself saying aloud what was not really for her ears.

"It's about timing, though. If those upstairs want Byford back, David's the trigger. These two are sticks that need rubbing against each other to create the spark, and this joint action will do that," Lauren said, as if reassuring Steven she understood.

"Very true, my dear," he replied.

Steven picked up his neglected glass and drained the Martini from it.

"Well, we're done here. Drink?" he said, waving the empty glass in the air.

∞

"David, man, will you listen to yourself, that last protest was a massive step as it was and it ended dramatically for you! There's a reason no one's done what you're proposing and that's because it's too extreme, it's practically terrorism!"

David was used to Brother Wolf's initially negative response to any idea or plan that went beyond waving placards around.

Though he was a good eco activist, he was the Mother Earth, peace-and-love kind, despite enjoying the occasional rally and near riot.

David on the other hand couldn't care less about the eco activism, he just wanted to convince those around him that he did. That and deal with the task that had now come from Lauren.

He also had a surprise to share.

"Why not do it?" he asked, not only to Wolf but to the entire group. "We have to hit them where it hurts, we have to…" but he was cut off before he could finish.

"I'm up for it, but how? Tell me how."

As planned, the question and interruption had come from Frost.

David was pleased he was already playing his part as they'd discussed.

He stood up from the cushion he'd been sitting on, leaving the rest of the group of about fourteen people, sat or sprawled around as they had been for the last hour.

The basement of David's house was the perfect place to meet for them. It felt safe and secret, hidden away from the straights of society and the constant gaze of authority.

David noted that half of them were high, and most had been drinking. The mix of disgust and frustration he felt towards them had been growing with every passing day. *Fucking tree huggers*, he thought to himself.

Even though he mostly wanted them as cover for his illicit dealings, he'd become progressively more disillusioned with the activist crowd.

Most were all talk and no action. Middle-class kids with an easy life and some weird guilt complex about being looked after by mummy and daddy.

That was his theory, anyway; Frost was more like what he wanted and he was glad he'd asked how they could get the latest activism idea to happen.

Not that he felt it was optional, this had to happen. Composing his mind, he gave a slight smile to ensure any tell-tale look was hidden away.

"I'll tell you how," he said to Frost, pausing for effect to look around the group.

"We recently acquired a—well, let's call her a supporter. I think we're about to have the means and the know-how to start doing some very interesting things. The refinery is how we prove ourselves."

He waited to let the words sink in, and then came the acid test.

"Who's up for joining me?"

David looked around the room and waited for a response, but the response wasn't forthcoming.

"Come on, people. This is a call to arms and we stand at a fork in the road. Which direction we take now will decide our future and whether we make a difference in this world or not. I've never been one for fighting, but the time comes for everyone to stand up for what they believe. This world of ours may not have long to go, and I'm not about to hide away now when she needs us most!"

David ended his rabble-rousing speech expecting a cheering response, but was met with looks of confusion and weak agreement.

Fucking tree huggers, he thought to himself once again.

"Count me in," Colin said.

"Well, thank you. At least someone has the balls. Who else? I need one or two more."

"OK, I'll come as well," Brother Wolf said, surprising David.

"Great, thank you too. You all just chill out, yeh, and don't trouble yourselves. Guys, Frost, come on, let's go through the details." And with that, he left the rest of the group to their own devices.

~ 22 ~

The old fishing boat bobbed around in the gentle swell of the sea, its mast lights the only illumination high above the decks.

Nets stretched out both sides into the water, held by bright orange buoys that ensured a distance of at least 200 feet between the *Sea Mist* and any other boat that might pass by.

The moonless night provided a dark sea in the bay, and a clear view of the harbour about a mile away meant the refinery was even more visible, in all its sparkling and smoke-belching beauty.

The *Sea Mist* leaned gently and a final soft splash emanated from its port side.

Even with a dry-suit on, the water was cold.

They were an improvement on the old wetsuits; but still, this was the North Sea and the permanent cold of the water seeped through, even where the water didn't.

The sea was just alive enough to hide any ripples made by the group of divers now in the water.

Daniels pressed his feet against the boat and pushed gently away. The most experienced of the team, he was immediately in his element once in the sea.

There was no gear snags and no shock from the cold water when it hit his blacked-out face.

Unlike Buckby. As the tallest of the team, she should have had the easiest task of getting overboard and into the water. Yet her taller frame, while making her a natural swimmer, meant the gear was harder to lock together.

She was still trying to tease off a strap from the miniature tank attached to her side, which had caught around the charges secured to her chest.

The tanks were each the size of a soda bottle, slotted into what looked like a police gun holster.

It was a new piece of equipment for her and the fitting of it hadn't gone well.

Jesus, I hope she doesn't pull a pin out, Daniels thought to himself.

"Buckby, stand fast, let me get it," he whispered across the water.

She started gently treading water and waited for him to swim over and untangle her.

"Fuck off, just before you say anything smart," she warned.

Amused, Daniels lifted the strap and pulled it tight to stop it moving again.

"There ya go, you look great now," he taunted.

A raised middle finger was the only response he received.

"OK, lovebirds, let's focus on why we're here."

The attention of the divers turned to Byford, the Lead they'd come to respect as much as his serious temperament when crossed.

There was a different feeling amongst them now. A bond, a readiness.

When they'd gathered two weeks ago in the Shetlands, they had been just four potential recruits.

The task on the *Braer* wreck had been their training ground, a way for the Handler to make sure they were a cohesive team who could achieve their tasks. That Byford hadn't lost it.

In their minds, Byford had transitioned from being their instructor to becoming their Lead diver and, despite their strengths and weaknesses they were no longer recruits—they were a trained team ready for their mission.

All were turned to him, awaiting his orders.

"Daniels with Buckby, Lagis with Carlson, I'll take point," he stated in his usual direct manner.

It was reassuring that the old man had a willingness to lead missions. They might still not know his background, but he was competent and he was the Lead. They'd learned to obey and that was all that mattered.

"Look ahead at the two red lights to the east of the refinery—that's where we'll get on shore. Swim under the second buoy, then split," he said, nodding the net to his side.

He waited for them to look and take in the sight.

"Daniels take left, Lagis go right of target and all of you keep 50 feet behind me."

That was the end of the instruction.

Byford gave a thumbs-up to check if they all understood him and they copied the gesture.

He fitted his mouth piece, swam perhaps 30 feet away from them and sank beneath the surface of the water.

Small ripples leading to the net in front of them told the two pairs of divers it was time to move.

Daniels signalled to Buckby and then he dropped vertically down into the water.

Buckby followed a few seconds later and her long frame soon allowed her to catch up with him. She saw him swim towards the gap in the net, about fifteen feet down in the water.

Lagis and Carlson followed half a minute afterward—the mission was underway.

The two groups followed the direction Byford was going in, each keeping the ones in front just in view.

After a period of easy swimming, Byford could see the seabed beginning to rise beneath him, a dark shadow barely lit by the light of the refinery filtering into the water.

There was always a calmness and comfort about being in the water, and the seabed felt as safe as land to him, maybe more so.

He let his fingers gently touch the sand as he swam slowly on.

Hopefully the others were behind him and would now be breaking off in their given directions, hitting their appointed spots on the shoreline as he'd instructed.

As he swam the last few feet to shore the seabed rose more sharply, and with both hands on the sand he walked his flattened body forward, using the remaining buoyancy of the now shallow waters.

His head broke through and, resting with his body in the water and head out—his turtle posture, as he called it—he looked at the scene before him.

The refinery was the biggest he'd seen, probably two miles wide along the shore, and he couldn't tell how deep—maybe a mile from what he'd seen from the boat. The descriptions in the brief didn't do it justice.

A row of long huts, with wooden walls and corrugated steel roofs, were nearest to the shore side, bordered by a wall and a chain-link fence closer towards the shore where he was now resting.

Grass and small bushes grew around the fence's base, a spiral of razor wire sitting at the top.

Behind the huts was a maze of towers, chimney stacks, pipes, gantries, storage vessels and cranes, all studded at random points with a constellation of lights.

The stench of oils and chemicals hung in the air and a little was even tainting the water he was lying in, creating a rainbow of colours around his hands.

He noticed a slight movement from his left side and, looking over, saw that Daniels had reached the shore about fifty feet away.

Checking to his right, he saw Lagis.

He felt a sense of relief which cleared the initial worries from his mind.

About a hundred feet ahead was the fence they needed to breach. A quick but quiet dash to the shadows beneath it was needed.

He raised his hand, aimed it at the fence and then rocked his hand back and forth twice.

Instantly, the two groups lifted themselves out of the water and, keeping low, headed directly to the fence and the relative cover it provided.

Checking around to see if they had been observed and noting nothing change in the dark scenery around, he gave another signal.

Removing forearm length cutters which were secured to their thighs, Daniels and Carlson proceeded to cut the fence from the bottom up, opening a way in just big enough for the team to get through.

With the entry point made, the team members squeezed through and placed themselves against the wall.

Not before Daniels, short but well built, had become entangled in the fence, one of the spikes of wire he'd just made piercing his suit and holding him fast.

He spun to the ground with the momentum of his forward motion, making a wet slapping noise as he hit the floor.

"Daniels, you poisoned dwarf, get up!" Buckby whispered.

Without a word, Daniels unhooked himself and headed over to Buckby and the safety of the wall.

With the show over, Byford left the water and made for the other gap in the fence, cautious of encountering the same problem.

He burst through with practiced ease, stepping forward and landing on his knees next to Lagis and Carlson.

"Switch out your gear," he whispered to them. Turning to Daniels and Buckby, he mouthed the same words silently while rolling his clenched fists over each other.

The team members did as instructed.

They re-secured their cutters, took off their fins and strapped them on their lower backs. In a matter of seconds, they removed and secured their masks, gloves and hoods, then became still again, awaiting further instruction.

Byford saw they were ready and pointed to the top of the wall, waited for a split second, and then lowered his hand.

This time Daniels and Lagis took the lead, jumping up to face the wall with arms and palms outstretched. They raised a foot and with perfect timing were helped up by the cradled hands of Buckby and Carlson, pushing them upwards.

Helped up, they grabbed the top of the wall and pulled themselves onto it.

Just as in training, they spun around and each reached an arm down, which was variously grabbed by Buckby and Carlson.

In an instant, Byford ran over to the wall.

Carlson reappeared and Byford was pulled up and over the wall.

The scene before them was exactly as had been described during training.

Ahead of them, in the near distance, they could see the main objective.

If all went to plan, they'd be watching the burning wreckage of the plant from the skies in less than 15 minutes.

~ 23 ~

"There," David said, pointing to a pile of rubble and rubbish that looked like it had been hastily dumped off the back of a van.

"That fly-tipped crap?" Colin asked.

"Yeh, that carpet at the back. Wolf, go get it."

Brother Wolf ran out of the tree line they'd been following along and picked up the rolled-up carpet.

Heavier than expected, he resorted to half carrying, half dragging it along the ground and back to the two waiting men.

"Too long to pick up."

They carefully unrolled it to see that the other items they needed were inside.

David handed them out and grabbed one end of the carpet.

"Let's get over that fence and be done. Quicker the better."

∞

"We're in," Buckby said, pushing open the hard plastic door that had a second before been sealing off the telecoms substation.

Byford and Daniels shot into the room.

"Clear!" she heard Byford say and joined them inside.

Lagis and Carlson took up positions outside to watch for anyone discovering the intrusion.

"Got it?" Buckby asked Daniels, who was already at a junction box full of wires, connections and flashing LED lights.

"Patience," he replied.

They waited in silence as he probed across pairs of wires, using a handheld device with a display of dancing lines.

Pulling out a scrap of paper, he partially unfolded it and referred to a schematic roughly drawn in pencil.

"Confirmed, T3 to T5," he said, as if waiting for a second opinion.

Byford picked up on his hesitancy, but the mistake at the *Braer* needed to be history.

"Daniels, do your stuff. Snip it!" Byford told him.

The look on Daniel's face confirmed Byford's suspicions. He replaced the paper, pulled out a small pair of wire snips and cut the wire between the two connections. "Done, cameras down," he said.

The three of them left the room, closed the door behind them and headed for a roadway ahead.

∞

David and Colin grabbed one end each of the rolled-up carpet.

Swinging their load back and forth a few times, they held onto a corner each and launched it up and over the fence.

The carpet unrolled over the top of the fence and unfurled the remainder of itself on the other side.

A wave of metallic rattling echoed along the fence as the barbed wire shook with the force of the carpet hitting it.

The two men ran back to the bushes they'd been hiding in.

Frost dropping at the last minute was still playing on David's mind. He'd wanted Frost to lead this, to keep himself out of harm's way. With Frost out, he'd had no choice but to attend himself.

At least Wolf had offered to do it alone with Colin, understanding the risk David was running. It was just too important, though. No, he'd lead it, get it over with and get rid of Lauren.

"That worked, covers it nicely," Brother Wolf said.

"Your turn. Get over there and fasten it together," David said in reply, giving Wolf a pat on the back.

Wolf broke from the cover of the bushes and headed for the fence.

Pulling zip-ties from his pocket, he threaded them through the fence links and the foot-holes cut into the carpet, making the improvised ladder more secure to climb on.

As soon as he was done, he climbed up and over the fence, dropping silently to the other side.

"Go!" David said to Colin, who shot forward and followed in Wolf's footsteps.

As he swung himself over the top of the fence, David saw him rolling his legs away from the protection of the carpet and over the exposed barbed wire.

Anticipating what was to come next, he shot forward just as he saw Colin trap his clothing and flesh on the barbs of the wire.

Confident in his athletic move, Colin had already started to let go of the carpet, expecting his legs to swing over and then land down onto the ground in one easy move.

He gave a muffled scream of pain as his leg was trapped, causing him to lurch head first to the ground.

As he dropped, the cruel barbs bit even deeper, tearing at his flesh and sending a red-hot pain searing through his leg.

The cloth and flesh freed itself from the barbs as David made it to the bottom of the fence, just as the man crashed to the ground.

David cautiously made his way over the fence, while Wolf pulled the limping Colin to the edge of the nearest building.

"What the hell was that!" David said angrily, yet as quietly as he could.

"The fence sunk down under my arms, I thought it was rigid. Whose stupid idea was it to use a carpet!" Colin said, breathing deep and getting a grip of the pain.

"Are you bad? There's a lot of blood," Wolf said.

"Fuck it, give me your scarf and some zip ties," Colin said to Wolf, who handed them over.

Colin wrapped the scarf around his wounded thigh and, once done, used some of the zip-ties to hold it in place, rolling the scarf over the top and bottom to keep it in place.

"Let's go," he said once done, standing and starting to hobble off.

"Well, that's what I like to see," David said.

"Where do we need to get to?" Wolf asked.

"We've gone through this! We just need to get to the Silos over there, open the valves and flood the place with the stuff that's in there. Then we get out of here and leave them to clean up the mess," David said.

It was exactly what he'd told them back at the house, but Wolf was always one to ask what he should have already known.

"Yeh, let's keep to those buildings and stay out of the way," Colin said.

"How do we know the cameras have been cut?" Wolf asked.

"We don't, just keep your masks on and trust that the others have done their job," David said, already moving off for the dark shadows cast by the buildings ahead.

∞

"Move on," Byford said to the waiting Lagis and Carlson as he came out of the telecoms room.

They immediately stood up and ran towards their new objective, a roadway about 500 metres ahead.

To get there they would pass through a set of low, flat-roofed buildings they'd first seen from off-shore.

Lagis and Carlson took up position at the corner of the first two buildings and signalled all was clear. Byford instructed Buckby and Daniels to move out.

They ran past Lagis and Carlson, found the next two strategic hiding points and gave the same signal back to their colleagues. This pattern was repeated, and the team slowly but stealthily making their way forward.

Byford, ever cautious, let them lead on, watching for danger coming from behind.

After a few minutes they were spread out, lying down in the shadows once more, looking across the road to the second leg of their journey.

"On?" Lagis asked.

"Wait," Byford replied.

∞

"When does the football highlights start?" the younger guard asked his colleague.

"I think you'll find that's 'do', and it's in 20 minutes."

He checked his watch.

"Balls, we have patrol at half past, right when the highlights start. I've got an idea, let's do it now. You do the front half and I'll do the back half. We'll be back by half-past in time to see what happened today," he said.

The older guard looked at his colleague over the rim of his spectacles.

"I suppose that would work," he agreed. "You head out now and start from the last check-point in. Click the radio when you get there and I'll head out this side."

With that, the younger guard put on his jacket, grabbed a torch and headed out.

∞

"We have incoming," Buckby said.

The team watched as a man ran down the road towards them, flashlight in one hand and a black device in the other.

He approached a building, held the device against the wall and the team heard a low electronic beep. The man then turned and continued running down the road towards them.

"What are we doing?" Carlson asked.

"Waiting. Stay where you are," Byford replied.

The man was now directly opposite them and almost staggered as he caught sight of Daniels lay in the shadows.

He held his hands up to show he was no threat.

"Family man! Family man!" he said, using the code word he'd been given.

Unseen, Byford gave a low shout.

"Get home!"

There was a moment's hesitation while the man registered the response and started running again.

"He's our gatekeeper. Watch out for a flash of light ahead in a few minutes," Byford said to the team.

"Is he armed, what's he carrying?" Daniels asked.

"Nothing, electronic reader for his patrol points," Byford said.

The guard recorded his presence at some additional check-points and then reached the storage compound ahead of the team, unlocked the gate and went inside to record his arrival there.

As he left, he gave two flashes of his torch towards the general direction of where the team were lying.

He turned back towards the guard house, leaving the gate unlocked.

"We're clear. Straight on, no stopping!" Byford said to the team.

Buckby stood up and looked back at her partner.

Daniels got the cue and leapt to his feet, shot across the road and into the shadows of the nearest building.

Buckby wasted no time and quickly followed him.

A second later Lagis and Carlson did the same.

With the team now across the road and heading towards the main objective in the distance, Byford checked to make sure that they remained unseen. Satisfied, he followed.

The team kept moving as they headed towards the silos. They darted in and out of the shadows, using the ground or the edges of building as cover.

A sense of urgency and expectation was now upon them.

Within a few minutes they had reached the edge of another roadway.

Nearby they could see container trucks parked up for the night, a building with a sign 'Research Lab 1' and the rear-gate guard house to where the 'Family Man' had returned.

"Check it, visual," Byford said to Lagis, pointing at the guard house.

Lagis pulled out a small pair of binoculars and observed the guard house for a few moments.

"It's our man and he's back in his hole," he said.

"One or two?" Byford asked.

Lagis looked again for a few moments.

"I see one only."

"OK, there's two of them, so the other is roving," Byford said, "Listen up, we have a wanderer and potential compromise. In and out and back to the extract in your pairs. 15 minutes from my mark or we leave without you."

The team nodded their understanding and variously checked their watches and began to loosen the equipment they were about to use.

"Lagis, lead on!"

Lagis shot up immediately and was followed by Carlson. The two men raced across the road and through the gate ahead, making it safely into the storage area.

A second later, Carlson gave the OK and Daniels and Buckby disappeared into the storage area.

As usual, Byford waited a few moments to check all was clear, and then followed the team.

∞

"You! Stop where you are!" the guard shouted as he flashed his torch towards the group, who were pressed into the shadows of the wall to the back of the storage area.

The three of them froze in the hope that the guard would think he was mistaken, but he was heading straight for them.

"Fuck!" Colin said to no one in particular.

"If he comes to us, grab him," David said as low as he could.

"Grab him?" Colin asked.

"As in deck the fucker!" David replied.

A few seconds later, the guard was bearing down on Wolf, who was closest to him.

"Stand up and don't move!" the guard shouted.

Wolf stood up and took a few steps away from the crouched men.

"OK, OK, mate. No harm done," he said, now standing still and holding his hands in the air.

"What are you doing here?" the guard asked, now a just a few metres from Wolf.

"I was just going to break a few lights and stuff," he said, blurting out the first thing that came to mind.

The guard had now stopped and was weighing up what Wolf had said when he saw the two others jump up from the ground and race towards him.

He turned to run, but it was too late to escape.

Colin dived towards him and wrapped his arms around the man's legs, slamming him to the ground in a perfect rugby tackle.

He held him there as David raced to his front and started to pound on the back of his head and back with both his fists in a whirlwind of fury.

Colin let go of the now whimpering man and stood up, kicking him hard in the ribs.

An audible crack was followed by a muffled scream.

David had turned the man's head and was now smashing him in the face repeatedly with his right fist.

He gave a final cry and spat blood as Colin kicked him again with all his force.

The two men stopped now, seeing that the guard was no longer going to put up a fight.

∞

"Keep going, finish off," Byford whispered to the team, who had turned to check with him what they were to do.

He couldn't believe the commotion that was going on just on the other side of the wall. He'd been briefed that David and his friends would be on site, but what had they just done?

What's more, they were early and Byford's team remaining a secret from them was now at risk.

He carried on listening as he watched his team dart in and out of the silos and pipes.

∞

"What the hell! Is he dead?" Wolf asked, visibly shocked, his voice shaking.

"Shut up, Wolf!" Colin said, now checking if the man was breathing, "Relax, he's alive."

"For now! We can't leave him here to bleed to death!" Wolf said.

"Fine, drag him to the guard house," David replied.

"What, and say here's your mate, he had a little accident?" Colin asked.

"No, we'll just dump him outside. They'll find him soon enough. Come on!" he said.

The two men picked the guard up by his shoulders and David grabbed him by his legs.

∞

"We're done," Daniels said to Byford as he and Buckby came back to him.

"Get back to extraction, check your exit. Sounds like they've gone off but make sure," he said, tipping his head to the wall from behind which the disturbance had been heard a minute ago.

The two of them nodded their understanding and headed away and towards the gate.

Lagis took a palm-sized, plastic-clad charge from his webbing.

"Place it at the top where the main feed pipe is, I can use it as a pilot light for the rest of them," head said to Carlson, handing him the device.

Carlson looked up and saw an outlet pipe just above head height, the main feed pipe being about 15 feet up. Shaking his head, he placed the mine between his teeth and jumped up to the outlet pipe.

Grabbing it, he swung back and forth to build some momentum, then jerked his body up until his waist sat level with the pipe.

A few moves later he was standing on the pipe and reaching up to the main feed pipe Lagis had pointed out.

He took the mine from his mouth and, flipping it upside down, stuck it to the side of the silo, where the pipe disappeared.

With a low clang, its magnetic base stuck fast.

Finally, he pulled out a strip of plastic from its side, which uncovered the positive end of the battery inside and brought the small LED display to life.

"On line," he said to Lagis in a low voice.

"Good. Let's go to the boss and get out of here."

Carlson went to retrace his moves, balancing against the silo and lowering his body.

This time however, the move went wrong.

He felt his body tipping too far backwards and tried to grab the pipe to prevent himself falling.

Instead, he lurched forward while his body dropped.

As he fell, his head slammed into the bar, flicking him backwards.

The failed climb down ended as he slammed perfectly flat into the wooden decking around the silos, the sound of splintering wood echoing off the walls.

Byford shot over to the two men, and when he arrived Lagis was already checking the damage.

"He's concussed," Lagis said.

"Can you walk?" Byford asked the stunned Carlson.

All he could manage was a feeble 'yes' as he tried to stand.

Lagis put an arm around him and lifted him to his feet.

"Here, all in place and on line," Lagis said to Byford, handing him what looked like a small mobile phone displaying six horizontal bars, all showing green and the word 'ready' on them.

"Slide to unlock, tap to unleash hell," he continued, "Be sure I'm not here when you do it."

"Great, both of you get out of here and back to the extraction point."

Lagis nodded to show he'd understood and headed towards the gate leading out of the storage area, doing his best to propel his colleague along.

Byford waited until Lagis and Carlson were out of sight.

Unzipping a side pocket on his trousers, he took out a thin chain necklace and locket.

Turning it in his hands and thinking of Mary, he gathered it into a ball, then tossed it up and over to the opposite side of the wall.

He turned his attention to the handheld device.

Sliding the display as instructed, he tapped all 6 green bars one after the other.

Contrary to what Lagis had been told, the explosives did not go off the instant the buttons were tapped. Instead the entire display turned orange and a single word appeared: 'Primed.'

Though a subtle thing, keeping the power to end a mission out of the hands of the foot soldiers was the Hannover way, in every degree.

Byford flipped the device over, took off the back and extracted the battery. Turning, he threw it as hard as he could over the wall he'd previously tossed the necklace. No one, by any unexpected turn of events, was going to prevent him closing this mission.

Placing the remaining items into a side pouch, he stood and made his way out of the storage area.

∞

"Who's that?" David asked, pointing to a figure running across the road from the Silos.

"Who cares, they're leaving where we need to be, so let's get this done," Wolf said and immediately headed back towards the storage area.

Colin and David looked at each other, surprised at Wolf's response.

"Blimey, Wolf has finally smelt blood!" Colin said.

The three men made it to the gate without further incident and, going inside, saw no one was there.

"Running man left the gate open," David said.

"Obviously," Colin replied.

"As in, he didn't have to break in, dickhead," David said.

"Again, whatever. Let's start at the back and open up these things there first," Wolf said, once again not waiting for a reply.

The two men followed him to the furthest silo.

"Open a pipe at the back or we'll get covered in this shit," David said to Colin, who had now produced a wrench from the back of his trousers.

"You had that up your arse all this time?" Wolf asked.

"Funny man, I had it up my belt as you well know."

Wolf moved around the silo until he found what looked like a tap. He flipped it up, and a stream of dark liquid gushed out.

"This," he said, looking at Colin.

Colin moved to the tap and started to unfasten a bolt secured to the underneath.

A few hard turns later, the tap fell off and fluid was pouring out.

"Great, do the rest," David said and Colin set to work.

∞

The team were now sheltered out of sight around the buildings at the extraction point.

Byford was the first to see the blinking red lights in the sky, still some distance away.

As he reached the roadway they'd crossed about 20 minutes earlier, he stopped and hid in the shadows around buildings next to him.

He could see that the team were all present at the extraction point.

Carlson was pressed up against one of the buildings and its concrete steps, lying on his back and not moving.

Lagis was crouched next to him. Even in the darkness, Byford could make out a look of worry on his face.

Carlson was going into shock by the looks of it.

Byford could see the helicopters were well across the bay now and their thud-thud noise was growing louder.

He shot forward across the road and towards the prone Carlson.

"Get ready!" he said. "Carlson goes into the first chopper."

No sooner had he said this than his voice was drowned out by the deafening noise of the first helicopter dropping from the darkening sky and into the space between the buildings.

The pilot stopped inches above the ground.

The sudden appearance, noise and billowing wind from the helicopter made it seem like some screaming mythical creature had just descended from the sky.

Byford grabbed at Carlson and caught hold of his clothes and gear straps on one shoulder. Lagis did the same and they dragged the man to the helicopter's door.

With a grunt they placed him inside, and he rolled and tried to stand. Before he could, Lagis jumped on board and the helicopter began to rise instantly. Byford saw Lagis dragging the still prone Carlson safely into the chopper.

He took shelter once again against the buildings as the growing noise of the second helicopter could be heard.

∞

"Jesus, that must be the police!" Colin shouted.

"Shit!" David said.

He started to run to the entrance of the silos and then immediately back again, clearly in a panic.

Where Wolf had found his courage earlier, it now seemed lost.

"They must have dropped police off! Why did it land and take off again?" he asked.

"We need to get out of here right now!" Colin said. "Look."

He pointed up to the sky at a second helicopter rising in the air in the near distance.

"Two choppers, that's like eight policemen."

He stepped out from behind the fourth silo he'd now opened a valve on.

"Probably found the guard's body!"

Fuel was flooding out of the silos, the wet splashing noise of the fuel hitting the ground bouncing off the walls around them.

A dark pool of the fluid had accumulated into a viscous, black pond and was now streaming away in a thick rivulet, out of the gateway and onto the road.

"Come on!" David shouted at them both, already heading for the way out.

The three of them moved as fast as they could, panic overtaking them as the thought of police racing towards them filled their minds.

In a few seconds they were back at the fence and David leapt up to kick his way back over to the other side using their improvised ladder.

Colin was next, but his injured leg was already going stiff from his injury.

"I'll push you," Wolf said.

Colin put his good leg up as far as he could, trying to reach the highest possible hole and gripped the carpet. With a shove from Wolf he was on top of the fence in one clean move.

Once all three were on the ground, David put his arm around Colin and supported him, walking as fast as possible away from where they were.

∞

Byford looked up as his ride started to descend.

Not even strictly a helicopter, it looked more like something a hobbyist would construct in their garage. The aircraft frame exposed all the moving parts and the pilot was clearly visible through a glass canopy barely large enough to protect both the pilot and the passengers from the wind.

It landed with a soft *wish-wish* noise.

Stepping onto the tubular frame of the aircraft, Byford buckled himself into his seat and they rose to about 30 feet straight up. The pilot handed Byford a device similar to the one he'd disassembled earlier.

"This one's live," he cautioned over the noise.

While rising, Byford had unhooked a night-vision unit from behind him and slid it over his eyes.

There in the distance, he could see the three patsies making their way down from the fence.

Perfect timing, he thought to himself.

Once they were on the ground, he triggered the first explosive.

The shock of the explosion threw all three of the escapees to the ground.

David cried out as airborne fragments from the now broken wall smashed into his back, sending him down even harder.

They turned in shock to look back at the rising cloud of smoke and at the smashed wall, through which they could see the silo was ruptured almost to its full height. A torrent of fuel was rapidly emptying onto the ground, flooding the storage areas and rushing out of the gateway.

"Get up! Get up now!" Wolf shouted to them, finding his courage once again.

"Get up and run!" he ordered, now not caring about trying to hide their presence given the whole world would be bearing down on them very soon.

They staggered to their feet, bruised and deafened, making their way as fast as they could through the back field that had led them to the refinery fence, no more than an hour ago.

∞

"Did you get him?" the pilot asked as they turned and headed out over the bay.

"Hmm, not sure," Byford replied, removing the night-vision goggles and switching his attention to the RIB positioned out in the bay.

He clicked off his seatbelt and prepared to drop into the sea below.

In the distance, three more explosions erupted and, this time, the fuel burst into flame, sending a roiling orange-and-red fireball high into the night sky.

Mission complete.

Thank god, Byford thought, and dropped into the sea.

~ 24 ~

Mary threw her back against the hallway wall as the three men burst through the front door. They looked dishevelled, dirty, panicked.

"David, what happened?"

"Shut up! Move!" he screamed at her, racing past her and immediately going downstairs into the basement. Wolf and Colin followed directly after him.

"It's OK," Colin said as he went past her.

By the time they got down the stairs, David had already opened a beer and was gulping down the contents.

"Why did the fuel blow up?" Colin asked, a mix of anger and confusion on his face.

"We didn't cause that explosion just by draining a few silos!" Wolf replied, both men standing motionless near the door, out of reach of David's anger.

"Which one of you cunts did it!" he screamed, slamming the bottle into the bar's surface.

There was no answer from the two men.

"Which one of you idiots fucked up?"

"Neither of us, you saw what we did," Colin said.

He noticed blood was starting to seep from his leg wound again and hobbled into the room to sit down.

"Make sure you don't bleed on the floor or the sofa!"

"Screw you! I'm in pain and bleeding here!" Colin screamed back at David, his face turning red with anger.

He sat down and pushed the coffee table away with his good leg.

"Get me something to clean and bind it, instead of accusing us of shit!" he added.

His rage overcoming him, David threw his beer bottle at Colin, but he saw it coming.

Ducking, he managed to avoid being hit full force but it caught his ear.

"You bastard!" was all he managed in reply before David ran from behind the bar and directly at him.

Wolf chose to no longer stand by and let the scene play out.

As David got level with him, he dove forward and grabbed him.

Using the momentum from his forward motion, he spun David up off the floor and over his body.

In perfect Judo style he went with the movement and the two men slammed down into the coffee table, splintering it into shards of wood and glass.

David screamed. Wolf felt the impact and thinking of David being crushed between the glass and himself, it felt good, like a release after so many years of being on the receiving end.

Wolf got up and saw cuts on his hands, but David was worse.

He was winded from the impact, struggling to breathe, making a wheezing, rasping sound.

A small piece of glass had fractured into a cruel-looking point and was stuck in his left cheek.

He whimpered with the pain and took the shard in his hand, easing it out, blood pouring from a one-inch gash.

"Well, at least now you'll shut the fuck up and listen. Now sit down and don't *bleed* everywhere!" Colin said, goading him in return for his earlier comment.

Wolf went as casually to the bar as he could, surprised at his reaction and quietly relieved that David hadn't been more injured.

He got them all a fresh beer and handed David some napkins to use on his face.

"Back in a sec, let's get you some first aid."

A few silent minutes passed before Wolf returned with Mary, who was equipped with a first-aid kit and towels.

She finished patching the two men up as best she could. Tapes held David's cheek together and a dressing now stemmed the bleeding from Colin's leg.

When she finished, she walked away from the men and sat down, then started to roll a joint as her habit and nerves demanded.

Wolf stood before the two men. "All we did was open some pipes," he said.

"Really?" David replied, nodding back to Mary, to question the wisdom of talking in front of her.

"Well, she obviously knows something's wrong, not much point in repeating it all when she bombards you with questions later." Wolf said. He continued, "We opened some pipes and let some stuff out, that's all. What else happened?"

"Someone else was there," Colin said.

David turned to him. "The guard we nailed?"

"No, not him. The guy we saw running away from where the silos were. You all saw him."

"Colin's got a point," Wolf said. "Who was that and why was he running from the Silos before we went in? Where was he running to?"

"He ran to the helicopters," David said in a quiet tone, staring at the floor. "He ran to the helicopters, and they weren't dropping off, they were picking up. And they weren't police either."

"What? How can you know this?" Wolf asked, now lost after David's deductions.

He continued to stare at the floor. He felt tired and drained.

"The police don't arrive like the army, they drive in cars with flashing blue lights and sirens, through the gates. We didn't see a single copper running at us or in the area when we got back up into the woods."

"I wasn't looking," Colin said.

"I was. When we were running to the fence, before the blast, I turned and saw there was a small helicopter hovering just near the water. They were leaving, not coming."

The group of men said nothing, lost in their own thoughts and recollections, exhaustion and beer starting to overcome their earlier excitement.

"What does that mean then?" Mary asked, breaking the spell of silence that had fallen over them.

"If there were others there who weren't the police?" she continued.

"It means there were others there when we were. Others doing shit to cause explosions," David said, now standing and beginning to pace around.

"It means we've been set up," Colin said, staring directly at David.

The two men looked at each other and silently agreed that this must be the case.

"Mary, call Frost and ask him to come here straight away," David said.

"I can't call him now, it's one in the morning!"

"Fucking call him, I said!"

Mary was already panicking from what she'd heard, but not about the same things the men were.

"David, what if the police are after you, what if they come here? We have all the stuff here!"

It was a typical junkie response, completely missing the point of what was being said and thinking only of where the next joint, line or wrap was coming from.

David felt his blood boiling.

"Shut up! Shut up!" he shouted, walking quickly over to her and shaking her by both her shoulders. "It's not about the drugs all the time!"

He reached down and grabbed the bag of hash she'd used to skin up with.

"It's not all about your drugs!" As he straightened back up, he swung his hand upwards and slapped the bag into her face.

She screamed and fell back to the sofa.

"Now call Frost!"

He turned and left a whimpering Mary to get herself together and do as she'd been told.

"I'm going to have a shower and a nap, you guys do what you want and grab something to eat if you want as well. Meet you back here at 7am."

The two men said nothing, the violence that had returned and a sense of feeling trapped by their situation subduing them both.

∞

"Hey, boss, you sound pretty awake. Been up early, have we?" Frost said to Byford.

"Funny man. What's up?"

"Our friend rang me ridiculously early today. Wants me to head over and see him in half an hour, at 7am."

"Hmm... whatever for?" Byford joked back, both men enjoying the thought of a panicked David.

"Either you-know-what or to grill me on my excuse of having a dicky stomach. I'm guessing the former though!"

"OK, head over and see what he wants from you. Be careful though, they've got a hard-hitting incident team set up already and we need to let things play out from here."

Frost agreed and hung up.

∞

David pulled himself out of bed.

He must have nodded off, but sleep was not going to come easy after the night's events.

"Paul, sorry to call you again, mate," David said, nervous of ringing his only contact in the force so soon after getting Frost checked out.

"I need to know if I'm on the radar, I got a feeling I'm being dragged into something."

"Another call? Don't make this a habit."

David could hear his annoyed tone, and he imagined his bulldog face with the crooked nose he'd acquired from playing rugby in his youth.

They'd only met face to face a couple of times, but David always felt that Paul was about to tackle him to the ground. His posture and words were always mildly threatening, his bulldog face and intent stare used to great effect in intimidating people.

"I hear you, it won't. Just a lot has been going on lately. Anything coming across your desk about me?"

"No, nothing. What's happened?"

David hesitated. Unnerving the guy who both exploited and protected him was not a good move.

"A bit of trouble."

"What kind of trouble?" Paul asked, his tone rising and speech quickening.

"Nothing to do with the business, that I know of anyway. That's why I was calling you."

David described what the team had been up to the night before, leaving key details out like it being prompted by Lauren and how things such as the improvised ladder and tools had been made available for them.

"You let them do this eco shit on a fuel plant, half killed a guard and don't expect the police to get involved?" Paul asked.

David just sighed, not answering the rhetorical question.

"The stunt you pulled last night is obviously the event of the year in the office already. I can't protect you from this one if they come knocking on your door. Every senior copper who can get involved will get involved. Solving this one is instant promotion, even the local councillor has been here this morning already."

"Is that likely, getting a knock on my door?"

"David, who knows. Keep your head down and do some spring cleaning. That's my advice."

With that, Paul hung up.

"We're wanted in the war room. Chief Inspector is paying us a visit. ASTU are in on this one apparently."

Paul looked towards his fellow detective and nodded in acknowledgement.

A few more presses on his phone's screen and the call was deleted from his call log, along with David's number. Not a foolproof way to remove the data that would still be sitting deep in his phone's memory, but at least it wouldn't just be sitting there plain as day to incriminate him.

He put his phone away and followed his colleague to the so-called War Room, where the senior staff were waiting.

Chief Inspector Aggard was standing at the head of the meeting room table, and to her side were a man and woman Paul didn't recognise.

"Thank you all, I don't need to tell you why we're here. This is Operative Melissa and Operative Nelson from ASTU. We'll be assisting them in their investigation."

∞

The doorbell rang and Mary checked her watch. Frost was exactly on time.

"Hey, morning," Frost said cheerily as she opened the door to him.

"Oh! Thank you for coming, they're downstairs."

"Are you OK?"

"I'm fine," she replied, raising a hand to her mouth as if to prevent herself from crying.

Of course he knew exactly why he was here, but seeing Mary upset darkened his mood.

From the urgent call he guessed things were moving along as planned. The sooner this was over the better.

He followed Mary down into the basement where the three men were finishing off breakfast.

"Morning, hiding away, are we?" Frost said trying to project the confidence he figured they wanted from him.

He reached over and gave David a firm handshake, but didn't do the same with Colin or Wolf.

It was a trick learned over the years, to keep an association with the leaders and a distance from the followers. A posture he wanted to exploit.

The tension in the room was palpable, and he noticed that the table between the sofas was now supporting a three-foot square board.

"So, what's up? Everything go OK last night?" Frost asked, though he knew full well how it had gone. "Again, sorry about ducking out last minute, I was in the toilet all night! And what happened to your face?" he asked, pointing at the gash that was now taped closed.

David thought for a second.

"I tripped up and broke the table."

"Tea?" Mary suddenly asked, taking everyone by surprise.

"Err, yes... Thanks," Frost replied, reaching for the mug she'd just offered across the bar.

David saw red.

"Tea? Come on, Mary! Get upstairs!"

Ignoring the altercation, Colin broke his silence.

"We did the job as asked, but there was another team there!"

"Another team? How do you know?" Frost asked.

"We saw them and their helicopters, that's how we know. We also didn't blow anything up. We went with an old carpet and a wrench, for fucks sake!" David said.

Frost got the men to recount how the evening had gone. They explained what they'd done and how they'd seen the helicopters, barely escaping before the explosions went off. It sounded like amateur night from start to finish.

"Do you know anything about this?" David asked, starting intently at Frost.

"Are you suggesting I set you up?" Frost asked.

"Well, it seems a bit odd! You were all for it, then at the last minute you duck out, leaving me to do the dirty work. You knew we were relying on you. You're the one who's got the experience in all this!" David said, raising his voice

"David, mate! I was just ill or I'd have been there too, you know that. Just calm down and tell me what happened."

David stared at him for a moment longer, and then began to tell him the story.

"OK, it does seem odd," Frost offered once they ran out of tale to tell. "I can do some digging, but I'm not sure what I'll find out," he said, absolutely confident he was going to find nothing out for them.

David didn't look reassured. He put the tea down and patted him on the shoulder.

"Don't panic, mate, I'm sure this is just some, very odd, coincidence. Let me see what I can find out," Frost said.

"OK, but find out quickly. Come on, I'll show you out."

The two men walked up the stairs to the front door.

David stepped through the door with Frost and grabbed his arm.

"Look, I'm not blaming you. I just know we've been set up, that lawyer bitch must be in on it. It was her that asked us to do the job! What should we do?"

"Do nothing. You weren't there and nothing has changed in your lives, so change nothing. Start doing odd things and it will get noticed. Make sure those two down there say nothing and do nothing too."

He patted David on the shoulder again to reassure him and walked off.

What a dick, Frost thought as he walked away.

David went downstairs and saw Colin and Wolf were ready to leave, making idle chit chat to Mary, who had come downstairs yet again.

"You guys off?"

"Yes, nothing more to be done here," Wolf said.

"How's your leg?"

Colin reached down and removed the towel that he'd been soaking the blood up with.

"Looks bad but the pain has settled down, just a lot of skin wounds, nothing a few days healing won't sort out."

"OK, you two get off. Say nothing, act normally and I'll see you in a few days."

The men left David and Mary alone.

∞

"What did Frost say?" Mary asked.

"Just relax, Mary. We carry on business as usual."

David sat down and placed his feet on the wooden board over the table. He felt his body sink into the sofa and realised how exhausted he was.

The stress of the night had not been diminished by the brief nap he'd had earlier.

He felt the need to fully unwind, mentally and physically.

"Mary, come here," he said and she walked over to the sofa.

He stood up in front of her and pushed her down, first sitting and then lying down.

She knew what this routine was.

As he pulled open her jeans buttons, she lifted her backside, allowing him to pull her trousers and knickers down and off, in one rough move. He knelt into position between her legs and put himself a little way inside her. He then dropped his body forward and over her, pushing out her thighs and grabbing her elbows as he did so. Pinned down, he entered her roughly and used her without any thought for her comfort or feelings.

When he'd finished, he climbed off and sat back on the sofa, leaving Mary to gather her clothing and deal with the mess he'd made.

"Go and run me a bath, Mary."

She left and as usual did as she'd been told.

Sitting back in the sofa, he imagined himself already in the bath, the warm water surrounding his aching limbs and the heat soaking into his muscles.

He could smell the scent of the water and the relaxation of being naked and out of the grimy clothes he'd put back on when waking earlier.

He touched his neck.

"Where the hell did I lose you," he said under his breath, hand still on his throat where the locket should have been.

He looked around the table, moving the wood to check underneath, then got to his knees to look on the floor. Nothing.

"You bastard," he said aloud, thinking of Wolf throwing him down.

∞

Morning, again," Frost said into the phone.

"So, how did it go?" Byford asked.

"David is very concerned, as are his friends. I had a right story from them."

"What was your advice?"

"I told him to carry on as normal and keep calm. I'm figuring we need him in a holding pattern until certain people put two and two together."

"Yes, true, and I don't think it will take them long, days at most. Listen, Frost, keep your head down and stay away from David until I get word of what our friends in blue are up to."

"Sure thing," Frost replied, understanding that he needed to let things play their course.

"By the way..." Byford started hesitantly. "Did you see Mary?"

"Yes, she was a bit upset about events but nothing too bad. I think a little domestic incident had taken place. I'm sure they'll kiss and make up," he said, hiding what he'd seen.

"Not sure I want to hear that."

"Sorry, sorry. Bad choice of words. I just mean he'll calm down when nothing happens over the next few days."

The call ended and Frost headed home.

~ 25 ~

Melissa and Nelson arrived at the refinery and were met with a scene of devastation.

Around ten fire engines with crew and supporting vehicles were still on site, some continuing to damp down the last few minor fires.

Police and ambulance crews milled around their vehicles and equipment. No one seemed in a panic now, but last night must have been chaos.

In front of them was a charred mass of fallen pipework, broken walls and the remains of metal storage tanks and wooden buildings. Thick clouds of black smoke still billowed up from the remaining fires and steam filled the air as the fire crews turned their hoses onto them.

Every inch of the area that had been destroyed was blanketed in debris and soot or was steadily being trodden on or covered in water and foam.

"Jesus, that's a hell of a messed-up crime scene," Melissa said, taking in the scene before her.

"Certainly is. We should suit up, even though I don't think there's much point."

Nelson drove up to the main gate, where an armed police officer was standing guard.

"ASTU," he announced, holding his badge out for the officer to see.

The officer took note of the dual MI5 and ASTU crests.

"Inspector Weis is running the incident, he's at the mobile unit just over there, sir," he replied through the open window.

He pointed to a large black truck parked some 150 feet away in the refinery complex.

The truck was marked with 'Mobile Incident Unit' in large white letters.

"Ah, that one?" Nelson asked, mocking the officer. "Thanks, and she's with me," he added, nodding across to Melissa, who was sitting to his side.

"Ah, I did wonder," the officer replied, matching Nelson's sarcastic comment.

With that, Nelson drove forward and headed to the mobile incident truck.

"Who was that?" asked a second officer, who'd been silently watching the exchange.

"An ASTU wanker," came the terse reply.

Nelson pulled up at the truck, which was being guarded by another couple of armed officers.

He thought they looked more military every day.

Paramilitary clothing, fully automatic machine guns, Kevlar armour, side arms, mace spray. All they needed were daggers and a few grenades.

What kind of battle they imagined these officers would get into was beyond him.

They'd have to radio in just to shoot off a few rounds, let alone take out some grand attacking force, who it seemed had been and gone anyway.

ASTU meanwhile had been granted 'Freedom to Fire' authority and Nelson looked forward to using it one day.

"Come on, let's suit up," he said to Melissa.

They opened the car door and were hit with a stink that almost made Melissa wretch.

"Ugh, what the hell is that?"

Nelson sniffed the air cautiously.

"Hydrogenated vegetable oil, ammonia, crude and some other crap if I'm not mistaken."

Melissa looked back at Nelson, surprised by his ability to identify smells.

"My old man used to work at one of these factories," he said, pre-empting her question.

"Ah, OK. Well, look at the state of this," Melissa said, looking to the ground.

The ground they were about to step on was a mess of foam and water from the fire crews, with oil and dirt from the refinery.

"Wellington boots and masks, gloves and forensic the suit then," Nelson said.

They stepped away from the car and walked carefully to the boot, where the forensic suits and evidence-collecting equipment were stored.

Once equipped in their paper clothing and masks, boots and other equipment, they went over to the incident unit.

"Nelson, thanks for coming out. Bloody mess here, literally."

Weiss was an older man, perhaps 55 Melissa thought to herself, sporting a light tan and with that softening physique common of men his age, for which exercise is defined as golf and lifting a few pints.

The two men shook hands and this time, Nelson didn't even bother with introductions for Melissa.

She felt the usual sense of being pissed off.

Nelson had a great way to make her feel like an unimportant child and she was coming to the end of her patience with him.

"I see you're properly attired, but I'm not sure there's much point. Practically burnt to the ground, this place," Weiss said.

"What do you know about what's happened?" Melissa asked Weiss, knowing it was stepping over her boss, but she was happy to annoy him.

They both looked at her and she returned their glances with a flat expression and steady gaze.

"Brief us on what you know so far," she said.

Weiss got the message; either that or he decided to humour her.

"Yes. Well, as usual, eyewitness accounts aren't worth a damn and CCTV was cut, so we have little to go on except what we see on the ground. There was a guard on the gate over the other side of this area, they shut the main gate at night and have just the side one for late-shift staff to come and go. About 10pm last night the guard heard noises from near the tanks, just over the building there. He was on his patrol."

Weiss extended his arm and pointed to a set of three large storage tanks, the tops of which could be seen to be broken and charred.

One was split almost in half, each side leaning away from the other and looking like it would fall over at any moment.

"There were six, the other three blew up or collapsed, you'll need to be careful around them. The fire crews will let you through, but at your own risk."

"What caused the fires?" Nelson asked.

"Not sure what the root cause is yet, fire crews are still waiting until the last of the fires are out and the structures have been checked for safety."

"Fine, but what do you and your boys think happened?" Nelson said.

Melissa didn't miss the reference to the 'boys'—it was yet another seemingly minor point to everyone else, but it was something that made her blood boil.

Joining MI5 and then ASTU, she'd hoped to join a progressive force.

While it was in some ways, sexism and machismo were all too prevalent.

She sensed Weiss had again picked up on her thinking when he replied.

"My team believe some kind of explosives were used, the storage area is pretty much destroyed. The guard was badly beaten by what he describes as a ragtag group of about three. They looked like 'lefties' according to him, dressed scruffy and not carrying equipment. They attacked him as he and his colleague went out on their separate patrols. He figured they were here to vandalise the place. Environmental protesters, maybe. Thankfully, though they smacked him around, they put him back near the cabin. His colleague found him when he came out to see what the explosion was, otherwise he'd be dead now. Looks like they came in over the beach along that bay over to the other side there. We found that the fence was cut."

Weiss again pointed out an area of the plant about a thousand metres away, in the opposite direction of the destroyed storage tanks.

They could see a collection of buildings, some burnt down, others in reasonable condition.

Beyond them, there was a perimeter fence and wall and in the distance a large harbour, framed all around the coast by other industrial installations.

Nelson and Melissa shared a look of silent understanding between themselves.

Environmentalist groups generally expected to get caught, it was part of the publicity. Whoever did this clearly didn't, and that was worrying.

This was no environmentalist protest gone wrong—it was too much, too daring.

"OK, thanks, sir. We'll get going and take a look around before the fire crew stomp all over everything," Nelson said.

"All right then, just be careful and report back in before you leave," Weiss said.

Nelson agreed they would and they set out towards the harbour side of the installation.

"Let's have a look over there first, Broer should already have been checking things out," Nelson said.

"What? Why is Broer here, I thought he was assigned elsewhere," Melissa said.

"He was, but as soon as I got the call on this one it was obvious it was more than just a bunch of Eco idiots causing trouble. Local police had complaints about helicopters flying over houses in the local town, thinking it was the police disturbing everyone's sleep." He turned to her and continued, "Shortly afterwards they get calls saying people had heard explosions and the place was on fire."

"You haven't answered why Broer is here."

"He's here because I asked him to be here. We need his military experience in looking over this scene," Nelson replied, in a way that told Melissa he'd had enough of her stepping out of place.

They walked in silence for the next few minutes, Melissa feeling the anger burning inside her.

She tried to push it away and focus on what she was seeing. Focus on honing her skills.

All around her, most of the ground was covered in a brown-black sticky substance, like burnt cooking oil or watery syrup mixed with dirt, soot and oil.

It gave her the impression of being in a stinking, rotting swamp.

With each step, their boots squelched in the morass, leaving an indistinct trail of footsteps behind them.

After a few minutes of continued walking, they heard a metallic groan in the distance behind them and turned just in time to see one side of the split tank fall to the ground.

Crashing metal and shouts from fire or police crews could be heard.

"Well, glad we didn't start over there then," she said.

"Yeh, lucky that," Nelson replied, then turned and carried on the way they'd been going a moment before.

Melissa didn't move, instead continuing to look back towards the tanks.

What had caught her attention was the pattern of destruction she could now see.

She could see the storage tanks that had just collapsed even more had been the epicentre of the attack.

The destruction radiated out from them.

Buildings, storage areas, the network of pipes and towers, even the ground itself became progressively less damaged the further out from the silos she looked.

Turning back towards the harbour she realised the ground was no longer as rank as it was before and the buildings around them were hardly damaged at all.

"Melissa! Come on, we need to meet Broer!"

The sound of his name brought her out of her reflections.

Melissa turned fully and walked towards the waiting Nelson. In the distance, standing near the perimeter wall, was Broer.

"Aw right, brought yer girlfriend along this time, Nelson?" Broer said in greeting as the two of them approached him.

"Less of the lip, Broer," Nelson said in reply. "What have you found out?"

"All right, mate, just joking with you, eh? How you doing, bokkie?" Broer asked, directing the last comment to Melissa.

The girlfriend comment was already loaded and referring to her as an immature springbok was his not-so-subtle way of saying that she was too young and inexperienced to be playing with the big boys.

Of all the people she'd met at ASTU, Broer, the cocksure ex South African Defence Force Sergeant turned policeman, was the most annoying. It didn't help that within weeks of joining ASTU, she'd embarrassed herself by getting laid by him during a drunken celebration at the end of ASTU selection.

"Fine, what have you found out then, old man? And why aren't you in forensics?" she said in a weak attempt to even the field.

"Relax, both of you, I only just got here too and there's no point in dressing like that, there'll be nothing left after this inferno. I'll tell you what I do know. They swam in from the bay, avoiding the harbour walls around the dock to this place. There's marks on the beach and sand on top of the wall. They obviously wanted a quieter way in than bursting through the manned gate," Broer said, demonstrating that he had been doing useful investigation.

"But they didn't worry about getting *out* quietly; the guard on patrol to this side reported two helicopters coming in just before the first explosions."

Nelson said nothing, continuing to take in the scene around him.

"How long between the explosions and the helicopters arriving?" Nelson asked.

"I've no idea, long enough to get back here to the choppers obviously," Broer said.

Entry via the sea meant they had a boat and possibly swim gear, timed explosive meant military-grade equipment and two helicopters meant that the team was four to eight strong.

This wasn't eco warriors, it was a military-level operation with some well-equipped backers.

"Activists, Greenpeace or something else?" Melissa asked.

"Something else. Espionage," Nelson said.

"Well equipped enough to destroy the place and get out—well-chosen extraction point too, must have known where it was going to be safe to bring the choppers in."

"Have you found the extraction point?" Nelson asked Broer.

"You're standing on it!"

"What... shit, Broer!"

"Everyone just stand still!" Melissa shouted. "If we want to count numbers and start our evidence trail we need to preserve the scene!"

"There was nothing here, I checked all around!" Broer replied.

"You mean to tell us you've trampled on a crime scene, maybe the scene of a terrorist attack?" Melissa bellowed.

"Look, I checked this area and I can read tracks better than anyone. All there is are some scuff marks on the shore behind the wall and some sand on the top of the wall, that's it," Broer said.

"How many people came in?" Melissa asked.

"I count 3 or 4," Broer replied.

"Melissa, go and have a look, walk to the edge here," Nelson said, directing Melissa away from the centre of the area where they were standing.

She retraced her steps, careful to avoid causing any more damage, and moved around to the edge of the nearest building, heading to the wall opposite.

Nelson squatted down to look at the ground from a different angle.

He could see the dirt had been blown up onto the edges of the buildings.

There was room for a small helicopter to land, but given the lack of marks on the ground he figured it hadn't actually touched down.

Looking past where Broer was standing, he could see that the unkempt grass next to the steps into the nearby building had been trampled down to the ground.

"Nothing here you say? Look over there," he said, pointing to the steps. "Three of them were there and one was injured."

"How do you work that out?" Broer asked.

"They dragged him to the helicopter. Look at the two lines where his feet were scraping the ground. They end here, where the chopper was. One person can't drag a man across the ground and yank him into a helicopter, so that makes three for starters. You're not the only one who can read tracks," Nelson added as a strike against Broer's all-too-common arrogance.

Broer shifted on his feet, feeling uncomfortable about being proven wrong that the scene held no clues.

"Given that we have two helicopters and only one here at any one time, that makes a team of five at the very least. Two in the second, no one uses a helicopter alone," Nelson concluded.

"You guess," Broer said.

"Better than what you've come up with so far," Nelson replied.

Melissa had reached the wall and pulled herself up on top of it.

She was able to hear the two men talking but was not able to make out all that was being said.

Despite that, she could tell that Nelson was pissed at Broer and that was enough for her right now.

Looking across the top of the wall, she saw the sand Broer had mentioned.

Balancing her way along the top of the wall she walked over to it and sat down, legs astride the wall.

Opening her forensic kit, she took out an empty vial and a small brush.

She carefully filled the vial with sand and labelled it 'Sand 1 – Harbour Side Wall.'

Looking down from the wall at the chain-link fence, no more than 10 feet away, she saw where a hole had been cut to let the raiders through.

On an instinct, she turned fully around and looking the other way and spotted what she'd anticipated.

A second hole about 30 feet away from where she was.

"Two groups, two holes," she said, smiling to herself.

Once again, she carefully made her way along the wall and, on getting closer to the second hole, saw more sand and dirt on top of the wall.

After collecting a sample of this, she dropped down from the wall and headed towards the gap in the fence.

"Where'd she go to?" Nelson asked partly to himself, partly to Broer.

"Melissa!" he shouted.

"Over the wall! Jump over and take a look at what's here," she shouted back.

A moment later, the two men appeared on top of the wall opposite the first hole.

"Jump down and stay at the hole," she said.

They jumped down and positioned themselves on either side of the hole Broer had mentioned.

"Look," she said, "there's another hole where I am, and on the beach I can see partial marks from flippers."

"Fins," Nelson said, correcting her failure to use their correct term. "Yes, well spotted. Half-sized ones by the looks of it, they couldn't walk on full-length from the water," he said.

"Whatever. The marks are here on both sides. It seems they came out of the water and to where the holes are in the fence, cut the fence and went up and over the wall. When I approached the wall on the other side, I could see the ground was pressed down there, on both sides," she said.

"Well, Broer, looks like you missed crap loads," Nelson said, noting that Broer had said nothing.

"There's more," she said.

"Look towards the middle of these sets of marks. There was one more person."

"The team leader," Broer offered.

"Insightful," Melissa replied, with no attempt to hide the sarcasm in her voice.

"OK, so this already doesn't add up," Nelson said. "If they swam in, there was a boat off shore. The bay is at least a mile to the other side and we're talking about what, four or five team members with full scuba gear, equipment and explosives, likely weapons too."

"What doesn't add up?" Broer asked.

"Jesus, have you had a knock on the head?" Nelson asked, which was met with laughter from Melissa.

Broer gave a laugh too.

"All right, mate, what am I missing?"

"Where are the changing rooms?" she said.

Nelson looked back at Broer, who just raised his hands in the air and pulled his face to show he didn't understand.

Melissa continued, "The guard said there were about three scruffily dressed people who attacked him. No scuba gear, equipment, etc. They didn't change and go running about, pop back here and pick up their kit then get spirited away—there were two teams!" she said, practically shouting at the end.

Broer made a slight noise to show that he'd got the point.

"The team the guard saw was probably a distraction. Let's head over to the silos and side gate back there and see what we can find out," Nelson said.

The three of them retraced their earlier steps and headed to the storage tanks.

Before they even arrived at the centre of the attack, the scale of destruction was apparent.

The ground around 150 feet out was strewn with large metal pieces from the tanks that had been destroyed or fallen down.

Pipes and towers, for power and lighting, were either in the twisted piles of metal dotted around or were dangling out into mid-air, ruptured and broken.

Buildings nearby were variously entirely burnt to the ground or had a complete side missing.

As they got close, they saw a wall surrounding the storage tanks was no more than charred and smashed rubble in most places, leaving just one corner intact, propping up yet one more piece of burnt and twisted metal.

Everything, including the ground, had been burned, charred, melted or covered in the thick black porridge they were now wading through once more.

"Wow, this really is a mess," Melissa said.

"Certainly is," Broer added.

"Right, you two, being careful, let's have a closer look and see what we can work out," Nelson said.

"Broer, check inside around the storage tanks, see if you can work out how the place was damaged and turned into this heap of scrap metal. Melissa, scout around. There are no bodies here, so the second group got out. Find out how, check towards the side gate and fence," Nelson said, waving them on their way.

Standing alone, Nelson surveyed the damage. It was extensive, and effective. The fuel that had been contained in the silos was no more than treacle at his feet.

Whoever had done this was going to be found, and he had a few hunches as to who it might be. While he had no hard evidence so early in the investigation, this reminded him of the Barton Incident. Multiple teams, explosives, professional.

He gave a deep sigh and, pulling out his mobile, called in to his Commander. "Nelson, how's it looking?"

"Complete mess, sir, literally nothing left. We're not going to get anything from this scene we couldn't guess just looking at it," he said.

"Very well, and the vats?"

"Completely gone, as are the research offices nearby, sir," Nelson said.

"As we suspected. OK, carry on, Nelson. Full report on your return please."

He hung up and headed over to where Melissa had gone.

"Found anything?" Nelson said.

"Footprints heading from the storage tanks to the fence," she replied.

"No hole this time?"

"No, they climbed it," she replied, pointing to what looked like a black pile of melted plastic. "It's on top, too," she said.

Nelson looked up at the fence, where a ring of barbed wire ran along the top. There, he could see some of the wire had melted and buckled. In places it had what looked like black, melted plastic stuck to it.

"What was it?" Nelson asked.

"A carpet, I'm guessing. It's on old trick at border crossings. Double it up, cut foot holes and throw it over the barbed wire. It acts like a rope ladder and the barbed wire holds it in place while protecting the climbers from the wire," she said.

"Hmm, OK. Simple but effective. How many?" Nelson asked.

"Three to four I'd say."

"OK, let's go and check on Broer, see what he's found."

The two of them made their way back to Broer at the storage tanks.

As they arrived, they saw Broer standing on the broken wall surrounding the tanks, talking on the phone.

"Broer, busy?" Nelson asked as they approached.

"OK, I'll see what I can get," he said and hung up.

He turned to them both.

"Not much here, boss. I took refuge on the rocks here as this shit is soaking into my boots," he said. "Did you guys find anything?"

"Melissa did, yeh. Second group for sure, they went out the other way, back over the fence they came in from," Nelson said.

"Get down off there. Let's check this place thoroughly, it's where it all happened so there must be something here. Let's walk it," Nelson said.

They entered the storage area in a line, about 20 feet away from one another, walking slowly and inspecting everything around them.

Melissa called out a blast pattern that could be seen in some pipes and the base of one of the storage tanks still standing.

"OK, good," Nelson said, "keep going."

In just a few minutes they had reached the other side of the storage area and turned around at the wall.

"Look, another blast pattern. Same place as the first one," Broer said.

"Right, let's sweep it again back to where we started," Nelson said.

The three of them retraced their footsteps and searched again for any meagre clues.

Melissa saw Broer tilt his head to an angle and look under a section of pipes. He walked over to it and bent down and inspected the ground.

"What do you see?" she asked.

"Looks like a lay pattern, not clear with this crap covering it but it's there. Someone hit the ground hard," he said.

"You can make that out?" she asked, leaning down to look but seeing nothing.

"Aye, sweetheart. You spend time in the platteland like I have, you learn to notice things," Broer replied.

Melissa recalled Broer telling tales of tracking vagrants and gangsters through the countryside and mountains back home. She felt suddenly unsettled by the idea that he could hunt people down this way.

"That'll help explain what we saw at the buildings back there. No doubt the injured person hasn't gone to any general hospital, but let's check it," Nelson said.

Back at what was left of the gateway, the three of them stood looking at the wreckage. "Certainly did the job," Broer said.

"Yeh, but doesn't give us much to go on," Melissa added. "Just some explosive remnants."

"Look around here and check the fence out again. Broer, go left and around the wall here. Melissa, right. Decide which way the team went and note anything you see," Nelson instructed them. "I'll pull off what's left of the casings from the explosives."

They left as instructed and walked slowly around the wall, at times ducking under the broken silos and scrambling over the rubble of the wall.

A few seconds later Broer shouted, "I see tracks this side!"

"Good, keep looking," Nelson shouted back, his voice coming from within the walls.

Melissa turned the corner to the rear of the storage area just as Broer did.

For a second her eyes met his and their gazes locked.

Melissa felt her heartbeat and her breath go shallow, an anger rising inside of her.

Sensing it, Broer looked down and carried on walking towards her.

"Nothing special that side, just footprints to the fence here," he said, pointing up to the burnt carpet she'd discovered earlier. "Sweep around and have a look for yourself."

She took a few slow steps as he passed her, saying nothing in response.

As she went to turn the corner she looked back at him and saw that he was crouched down, about to reach out for something with his bare hands.

"DNA!" she shouted, but she was too late.

He picked the object up and spun it around in his hands.

"Hey, bokkie, the heat from the fire will have destroyed any DNA," he said, dangling the chain and pendant in his hand.

"What do we have here then?" Nelson asked, holding his hand out to receive the find.

Mark J Diez

~ 26 ~

Byford walked through the main doors of the Centenary Club and was greeted with clipped courtesy from the doorman.

No need for checking of names or membership here.

Based in the heart of the city, the Centenary was one of London's oldest and most exclusive clubs, owned by Hannover. Hence why the Handler felt safe meeting here.

Unlike the Hannover Club, the public face of Hannover hiding in plain sight, you were unlikely to know the Centenary existed.

You were even less likely to get through the door, unless you were the right kind of person, knowing the right kind of people.

This place was not for outsiders and not for casual meetings to get IT equipment, as was done at the Hannover Club.

Separating operations and planning was a safeguard, in case one day Hannover became a target themselves.

The doorman guided Byford through the reception area, towards a panelled door of heavy oak.

He held the door handle for a second.

"He's waiting for you in the Grange Room, sir," Byford was informed and the door was held open for him to pass through.

He took a few steps forward into the main hall as the door was shut behind him.

Free to find his own way, he looked around, recollecting his memories of the layout of the club, its décor and the times he'd been here before to give his debrief.

Only once had he dreaded that event, but this time it was all good news, as far as he knew.

The hall was smaller than he remembered.

A double staircase rose to his left and on hitting the wall, split into single staircases turning to each side to reach balconies on opposite walls above him.

Large oil paintings of historic club members hung from ceiling to floor. Marble busts of prime ministers and generals were dotted around.

Here and there, other members were gathered together, standing as if ready to move off somewhere else or sitting in the collections of sofas, drinks in hand, clearly settled in for a while.

No one paid the slightest attention to him.

He headed up the staircase and to the far balcony, turning left at the top and into the east wing.

A little way along the east-wing corridor he stopped, took a deep breath to collect himself, and then opened the door to the Grange Room.

"Ah, Byford, it seems your project went rather well."

The words, both a statement and a greeting, were from a familiar voice hidden behind a large chair at the other side of the room.

The Handler stood up and came around the chair to meet Byford.

"Thank you very much, sir. It was a reasonably straightforward objective, if somewhat convoluted in its planning and execution."

The Handler noted but ignored the barbed comment.

"A new team and lots of other pieces to put in place, Byford. But, you know how these things go."

He knew only too well.

No job with Hannover was straightforward.

Whether he'd find out what all the other pieces were was doubtful; he'd be told what he needed to be told.

"Tell me how it went. I see the objective was achieved, but any issues or problems along the way?" the Handler asked, pointing to a chair for Byford to sit in.

Byford ran through the events of the night and described it all as it had happened.

"Good, so the team proved themselves and the mission was a success. You must be pleased, Byford?"

"Of course, sir, but as I said it was a simple one this time, so not much scope for issues. Well, except for Carlson failing at gymnastics. Any word on him, by the way?" he asked.

"One of our boys told me he was in a car accident," the Handler said, practising the lie that had been concocted. "Nothing serious, but a nasty bump on the head saw him spend the night in hospital," the Handler said.

"You sent him to hospital? Didn't we have someone to look at him?"

"Obviously it wasn't a public hospital, Byford. Besides, it allows us to create a paper trail in case we ever need it."

This was Hannover all over, always turning a situation into an opportunity.

If by some remote chance Carlson was ever questioned about his whereabouts that night, he'd have an alibi. One less piece in the puzzle for the other side to build the whole picture.

As for where the rest of the team were now, including Carlson, that was not for him to know.

"I imagine we've had a notable response to last night. What's the reaction?" Byford asked.

"Big, as expected. An incident team set up that includes ASTU."

"So they're treating it as terrorism straight away?"

"Don't be surprised, Byford. The government have been warned to expect a physical or cyber-attack on infrastructure of some kind since 9/11, so they'll need to bring out the big guns just in case. Even that useless, expenses-leaching councillor Vangen or Vanden, whatever his name is, has been down there this morning."

"This is expected then?" Byford asked.

"Byford, yes. All of this has been modelled and planned for. They'll investigate, find the explosives and with a little help, they'll put two and two together and come up with five."

"Right," was Byford's response.

Just in the use of that phrase he knew Hannover were manipulating more people and events. Two plus two equals five was a way of saying Hannover would guide people to the answer they wanted.

"Well now, all that aside, the Sponsor is of course very pleased with events. A couple of other things got affected by your actions, as you no doubt expect."

"This *is* Hannover, sir."

"Indeed it is. So everyone's happy. Except you, of course," the Handler said, giving a half smile to Byford.

"Well, count me as 30 percent happy. I'm also pleased that we got the team together successfully and completed the mission. There was the matter of our friends being there, which was fun."

"But what happens next, Byford? That's the question, eh?" the Handler offered, knowing what was on Byford's mind.

"Precisely. Recovering my reputation wasn't the primary reason I accepted the job."

"I understand, Byford, but the game's not over yet and there are a few more rounds to play before you get to take the prize home."

"I just want her back," Byford said softly.

The Handler saw a look of longing and despair come across Byford's face, and he reached forward and held him by the arm.

"We will get her, Byford. The rest now is icing on the cake for us. You've done your part, we let the dust settle and it's checkmate. You win in just a few more moves."

"Sir, I'm concerned about the follow up with David and how he will react. What's more, ASTU will find him and when they do, they find Mary," Byford said, worry etched on his face.

"Once again, I understand, but if we were not old friends, I would wonder about your concern for these other people," the Handler said flatly.

Byford let the comment rest with him for a moment and gave an audible sigh.

"You know why, sir."

The Handler looked down at his hands, thinking what to say next.

"As hard as it is to hear, however David reacts and whatever he does to Mary, he's done it a hundred times already. In a few days it will be over, for all three of you."

"So, what next?"

"You go home and wait. I'll call you."

~ 27 ~

"Chief Inspector Aggard," Nelson said as a greeting to the woman who'd just walked into the operations room.

As he walked over to her he noticed her police uniform was pristine, her posture upright and strong. She emanated the power of her character and position. It unsettled him.

Set up less than 24 hours ago, the operations room was now a hive of activity.

Photos of the scene were pinned to the story board. Grainy stills from CCTV cameras, pictures of the site, guards, sticky notes and bits of papers with names and questions populated it.

It all formed a collection of facts and brainstormed guesses, put together as fast as possible.

"Nelson," the woman replied, extending her hand and completing the greeting with a firm handshake.

She turned to the story board. "What do you have?"

"Just bits at the moment. No real breach of the perimeter fence, we're assuming they climbed it. Fuel released and then a set of explosions set off. Around 11pm, midnight latest," Nelson began.

"OK," Aggard said, with a tone indicating she expected him to continue.

"The guard was attacked by two assailants and we found this."

He turned back to the boardroom table that was laden with laptops, notebooks and coffee cups.

Moving some of the items aside, he retrieved a sealed plastic bag with a small chain and pendant inside of it.

"What's this then?"

"We're assuming it came from one of the assailants."

"Lucky find. Given its importance, why is it scattered with the coffee cups and papers on the table?"

Melissa looked up from her laptop, enjoying the uncomfortable moment Nelson now found himself in. With typical ease however, he turned the situation away from himself.

"Melissa, show the Inspector what we have."

"I had the necklace scanned and 3D rendered," Melissa said, showing an image on her screen. "Due to the fire, there was no DNA or other materials to retrieve."

"Interesting, but what use is it then?" Aggard asked.

"I'm collating advertisements and CCTV camera images from jewellery stores in a 50-mile radius to see if I can find where it came from. In addition, I'm rendering images from local government and police CCTV and photos from social media sites, for people in the local area wearing a necklace like this. With these I can run an algorithm I wrote this morning that will use the database of images to compare our rendered image to."

Aggard looked at Melissa for a moment, trying to take in what she'd been told.

"I think I see what you're doing. The chances of that working?"

"If there are enough elements of the necklace showing in the image, it will be found."

"OK, impressive. Erm... how do you know those responsible are from within 50 miles of the site?"

"They usually are, so it's the most optimal criteria to use for an initial search," Melissa replied flatly.

"Right, well…" Nelson interjected, noticing Aggard needed rescuing.

He led them both out of the War Room and into the hallway.

"She's a bright one," Aggard said.

"Yes, very. But she's also a smartass."

"Makes you wonder, whatever happened to the old-fashioned approach of talking to witnesses?"

"We're doing that too," Nelson said. "We have a statement from the guard that was attacked. He's sure he saw three men in total; he's given a very general description. Usual stuff: it all happened so fast, it was dark, et cetera."

"So three men, one wearing a necklace that was lost in the struggle, from the local area. That's all we have, is it?"

"So far, yes," Nelson lied.

Aggard held his gaze for a few seconds, saying nothing.

They both knew he was lying and it was her call on what to do about it.

"I see. Well, you were brought in to use your clever approaches, so let's hope for both of our sakes they pay off," she said, choosing to give him the space to operate as he wanted—for now, at least.

Well played, Nelson thought.

He knew that if the more visible ASTU failed, if he failed, she'd win. If they succeeded, she'd win, too. He could see how she'd risen through the ranks.

"What else are you doing?" she asked, now moving off down the hallway.

"The scene is being combed, a number of groups and individuals are being investigated to see if we can get any hint of motives for doing this. We had the refinery owner, Daler, on the line this morning too. Seems he's a friend of Councillor Vangen."

"Of course he is. What did he have to say?" she asked.

"Naturally, Daler was deeply shocked and offered his full support with our investigation… blah, blah, blah."

"Usual stuff then."

"As always," Nelson said, pulling a face that reflected his lack of regard for Daler's insincere concern. "What about the Councillor, do I need to do anything there?"

"No, don't worry about Vangen, he works through us. I'll deal with him. He's asked to be kept informed, but he won't want any real work or responsibility. Just a feeling, but check Daler out along with the others."

Nelson nodded his agreement, the two of them shook hands and Aggard disappeared down the hallway towards some waiting officers.

"Not showing her all the cards then?" Melissa said as she heard Nelson come back in the room.

"How do you know it's me, without looking?"

"You always let the handle up the instant the door opens, most people wait until they're through the door a little."

"Hmm, very Sherlock of you. And yes," he said, sitting down next to her, "I'm not telling her everything and she knows it."

Melissa turned to him.

"A cut fence, entry from the sea, helicopters. She's going to know about the reports of the helicopters at the very least. They're her police officers that got called after all. Why aren't you telling her these things?"

"We need a head start, that's all. She is technically in charge..."

"Is *actually* in charge," Melissa said, interrupting.

"Yes, of the investigation, but not of us. We're ASTU, and I'm in charge of our work. We work with, not for," he added.

"Not how you put it in the meeting the other day. But anyway, you haven't really answered my question."

Nelson stared at the wall for a second.

"As we've established from the site, there were two groups. One lot was just some amateurs pratting about, and the other group did the damage. Necklace boy was with the prats. So hunt away, but him and his two mates are not the real targets," he said.

"So who is?"

"Haven't got a bloody clue, but this is exactly why ASTU was formed and I'm not handing this over to the regular forces on a plate. Good luck with the necklace, though, it's the only lead we have now until Broer's field agents come back with something."

As if summoned by mention of his name, the quiet conversation came to an explosive end as Broer appeared in the doorway, pushing the door wide open and raising his arms in the air in greeting.

"All right, you two!"

"Hey, Broer!" Nelson said loudly in return, standing and swinging a smacking handshake to the man.

"How's the hunt going, tell me you have something."

"I have something and nothing," he replied.

He tossed a see-through evidence bag down on the desk.

"Boom! Mine casings. Indian army. Well, Chinese made, but supplied to the Indian army."

"Yeh, something and yet nothing we didn't see when we all had a look around," Nelson said.

Melissa looked at Broer, confused.

"So the Indian army are attacking chemical plants?"

"Come on, bokkie, you can do better than that. Someone has contacts with either the Chinese manufacturers or the Indian army. Your guess as to which is as good as anyone's, but my money is on the manufacturer. Indians are too busy with their shops and curry houses."

Melissa raised her eyebrows at Broer.

"Amazing how you manage to stereotype two nations in one easy sentence."

Nelson ignored the comment—it was the usual way a conversation went between these two.

"Though you may be right. It's not unheard of for them to run a slightly longer batch and sneak the extras out the back door," Melissa added.

"Now you're thinking," Broer said.

Nelson lifted the bag to inspect the contents, but before he could add his own thoughts, a pinging noise from Melissa's computer got their attention.

Nelson looked at Melissa.

"Done?"

She turned to the computer and scrolled through a list that had appeared on her screen.

"527 results," she announced.

"That's a lot of people wearing T-shirts in October, are you sure it's right?" he asked.

"This is for the last six months and there will be duplicates, the same person caught on several cameras. Some false positives too, from low-grade images. I'll have to filter them out and come up with a list of uniques. Not sure how to do that other than manually going through them."

"Big job, we might leave you to it," Nelson said.

"Are you using Gait Mapper?" Broer asked, leaning past them both and looking over some of the images.

Melissa and Nelson cast a glance to each other, but the comment was lost on them both.

"What's that?" Melissa asked.

"Gait, as in the way a person's body moves when they walk. It creates a unique signature you can't hide. We used it back home to spot the ANC lot sneaking off to attend rallies, disguised in their stupid get-ups. Not hard to spot them the way they walk. You should have seen them Kaffirs, moving around like they'd just learned to stand..."

"OK, OK, we get the idea!" Nelson interrupted, just as Broer was about to ramble on and had started walking with his arms drooping down.

"You really are an arsehole aren't you?" Melissa said in disgust, prompting a laugh from Broer.

Nelson held a hand up to prevent any further comments.

Broer being Broer once again.

"What's Gait Mapper?" Nelson asked.

"We call it GM. It's experimental software the techs have been trialling on the Anonymous lot. Techies wanted my experience using the one we had in the Defence Force. Those hackers can wear all the Guy Fawkes masks they like, we'll still know who they are eventually. Don't bother filtering your list, just feed in the pictures and source videos to the GM server and it'll do your matches for you. If one of your bods there are in the system already, you'll have all sorts of info on them in a few hours."

"I'm impressed, Broer, I never knew you were such a techie," Melissa said.

"Hidden depths, sweetheart," he replied, giving her a wink.

"Yeh, that'll be it. We'll leave you to it, Melissa. Make the request to tech services and tell them it's an immediate request. Any pushback, call me straight away. Broer and I are off to the site again. Before Aggard paid a visit, I got a report that one of the helicopters landed in a farmer's field on the other side of the bay. Let's see what he can tell us."

With that, the two men left Melissa alone.

∞

"Thanks for the walkthrough. How long will it take?" she asked the technician.

He didn't respond, lost in the task he was completing.

She watched him finish putting her data lists together and clicked the 'Run Batch' button on screen.

"Varies, I'd guess about two hours with a set this size. Once you have the matches though, you'll need to manually review. Do you know who you're looking for?"

"Not really, I just have one lead," she replied.

"OK, Gait results match people to places. It only tells you that person went to those places. To find out *who* they are, you'll need to dig deeper and identify them by their use of police records, credit cards, ATMs, mobile phone records and whatever else you find. It means watching a lot of video and doing more digging, but the pieces will come together."

∞

The farmhouse was small, but comfortable. A small fire crackled in the hearth, ready to be built up when the evening chill came. Out of the rear window, Nelson could make out the refinery, in the far distance, across the bay.

The farmer returned to the dining table and took a seat.

"Sorry about that, age makes the call of nature a slow affair," he said.

"No problem. The tea is great, and thanks for the cake. You bake it?" Broer asked the farmer, in a tone of civility that took Nelson by surprise and brought his attention back to the situation at hand.

"Aha, no, my wife does all the cooking. She's in town with her sister right now."

"You keep stock?"

"Just farming. Grains and beets mostly, a few other things for the market and we have a nice hazel stand too."

"Did I see flax?" Nelson asked, in part to show he knew at least a little something about plants.

"Yes, that's just a side line we're trying this year, but given that the helicopter landed on it, we'll not get much from it I'm guessing."

"Yes, unfortunate, I believe you can be compensated," Nelson said.

"Not worth it," the farmer replied dismissively. "Anyway, you want to know what I saw?"

"Yes please," Broer said, again maintaining his unfamiliar civility.

"Aye, it was just after 10.30pm. We were in bed of course, and then we heard an almighty bang from that factory over there. Always said it was a bloody danger! Them ships coming and going with god knows what and the spill a couple of years ago caused a ruddy mess. Stank to high heaven it did. We complained to our local councillor but he's a waste of space, don't know how he stays in office!"

"I see, so the explosion was between 10.30 and 11.00pm?" Broer asked to get the farmer back on track.

"Oh, aye. Actually it was several explosions, the ones that woke us up and them two we saw go off. Shook the windows, they did!"

Nelson leant forward and pointed a pencil at the farmer to help him focus.

"And the helicopter? How long until it landed afterwards?"

"Two minutes? If that. It was already flying towards us before the explosions, I'd seen them in the air lit up by the ruddy fireballs!"

"Them? I thought you said there was one helicopter?" Nelson asked.

"That's what I was telling you. One what landed in my field and another what stayed out over the water," the farmer replied.

"Ah, Sorry. I see now," Nelson said.

"I see that one coming at us, the other out near the boat and then it gets here and four of them get out and run towards the road. Well, one looked a bit ropey, but they were all as good as running."

Nelson and Broer looked at each other for a second, absorbing what had been revealed.

Before they could follow up with more questions, Nelson's phone rang.

"Melissa, how's it going?" he asked.

"We have a match on necklace man."

"OK, on our way back to you."

The pair spent a few more minutes clarifying what they'd been told, then left the farmer and headed back to the car.

"You know a lot about farming," Nelson said.

"That's what I was before the country went to shit," Broer said, alluding to the post-apartheid era that had seen him lose his land and head over to the UK.

He'd mentioned it in passing before, but talking to the farmer was the first time Nelson had seen Broer properly smiling, with joy instead of sarcasm.

It explained a lot, he thought.

"What's Melissa found?" Broer asked.

"A match on necklace man was all she said, let's go see."

∞

"Took your time," was the curt greeting as the two men came into the office.

"Yeh, just giving you space to commune with technology. So what do you have?" Broer asked.

"Someone you may have seen already," Melissa said.

Turning to her screen she pulled up a paused video. The frame showed an image of a man in the centre of a crowd, who in turn were surrounded by police.

A white cloud was forming near his feet, keeping the crowd away and making a space around him.

"You may have seen this already, if you were watching the anti-capitalism marches a week or so ago," she said, hitting play and rolling the video.

A scene from a news team camera played out.

Through the growing cloud of gas, they saw the man reach down and throw at the police lines what was apparently a tear gas canister.

"Necklace man or, more accurately, David Rhett, known activist," Melissa explained.

They watched as an instant later another man ran from the crowd and threw an arm around David.

She paused the video.

"And who's that?" Nelson asked.

"No idea, no matches on him. I'm running his image through the systems now to see what comes up," Melissa replied.

They carried on watching the scene unfold, entranced by the riot police now coming into play.

However, Broer felt his breathing stop. He could hardly believe his eyes.

It was Frost.

An image of Byford filled his mind, and his thoughts raced back to his last mission with him and the trouble they'd had.

All down to Frost.

Byford has defended him, but he hadn't been the one depending on Frost to do his part.

If he hadn't been so well trained in his earlier career, Frost would have gotten Broer killed too.

That was his view, and he hadn't come this far for someone to change it.

He'd sworn then to pay Frost back and here he was, smiling and larking about like he had no worries in the world.

He snapped out of his reflections.

"Whoever he is, we need to track him too," he said, doing his best to keep an even tone.

"Do we have an address for this David Rhett?" Nelson asked.

"Several, it's not clear which is the correct one. I've made a request for his arrest record; as you can see from the video, he was pulled out by a riot team. It should have his most current address on, but no guarantee. However, that aside, I have something more interesting and worrying, a call that he made recently,"

"A call to whom from who?" Nelson asked.

"We identified his mobile number before his address? That's screwed up," Broer said.

"Mobile calls were being intercepted during the riot. Aggard's intel team had that data cross-referenced to David just sent here, but had no reason to do any further analysis," Melissa explained.

"Right, but what call and to whom?" Nelson asked.

"To Detective McGail. Paul McGail, who's here in the office, assigned to this investigation."

"Now that is interesting," Nelson said, walking away from the screen and around the other side of the desk, biting his bottom lip in thought.

"You two go and pull our new friend Paul in and see what he knows about David. I'll have a chat with Aggard to make sure he's ours for as long as we need him."

∞

"Right now?"

Broer leant in towards the man.

"Listen, ya kont, you've got about 20 seconds to stand up and walk out nicely like, before I lose my temper and I drag you out of that chair."

Paul got the message.

He stood up, picked up his mobile and jacket and headed to the door.

"Very sensible," Melissa said following him out.

Minutes later, the three of them entered the interview room.

"Take a seat," Broer said to the man, pointing at a chair on one side of the desk.

"Why am I here? You can't just hold me here without telling me why."

"You're collaborating with a suspected terrorist. We have the phone records and other details about your activities with him," Melissa said, elaborating the truth for effect.

"Who are you talking about?"

Broer slammed his fist down onto the table in front of the man.

"David Rhett!" he shouted.

"Now why are you helping him commit terrorist acts?" Melissa asked.

"I don't know what you're talking about!"

"So you deny knowing him?" Melissa said, continuing her quick fire questions.

"No, no, OK, I know him. I arrested him about a year ago for dealing drugs, that's all."

Slowly and calmly, Broer sat on the edge of the table next to Paul.

"That's all, eh? So what's he calling you for then? What are you two chatting about?"

The man looked down as if thinking about what to answer. Before he could, Broer's old-country habits kicked in.

He reached down, grabbed the lapels of Paul's jacket and wrenched him out of his seat and through the air.

The chair hit the floor and the journey ended with Paul slamming against the wall.

Broer screamed at him again.

"Ya fokken domkop! What's your relationship with David? Why you protecting him? How much you taking, eh?"

"Broer! Stand down!"

Broer dropped the man at the sound of hearing Nelson shouting his order.

"Jesus, man, you're supposed to question him, not attack him!" Nelson shouted.

Broer stepped away back to the table and let Paul recover himself.

"You come to ask me if you can question one of my detectives and you're already assaulting him? Is this how you go about things in ASTU?" Aggard asked in an accusative tone.

"No, not at all. What's gotten into you?" Nelson asked.

"Sorry, boss," Broer replied, his mind still regressed to earlier years.

Broer knew he'd gone too far too quickly, but he was closer now to Frost than he had been for years.

The image of him in the riot was playing on his mind. He imagined himself as one of the Riot Police, smashing his baton into Frost's skull.

He sat down without saying a word and shook the thought from his mind.

"Paul, are you OK?" Aggard asked him, as he straightened his clothes and sat back into to his interrogation chair once again.

"I'm fine."

"You better tell us what's been going on," she said.

Paul leaned back in his chair and composed his thoughts, everyone waited.

"Is David your informant?" Nelson asked, unable to wait for the man to start talking.

"Yes, kind of. Since I pulled David a year ago I've become *entangled* with him, shall we say. My brother had a gambling problem a way back and David knew the people who he owed money to. David straightened things out, and in return I gave him a heads up on the September raids we did last year, so he didn't get arrested. That's it, I swear."

"Bullshit," Melissa said, taking the room by surprise with both her outburst and the untypical form of it.

She stood up, pushing her chair backwards, placed her fists on the table and leant into the man just had Broer had done earlier.

"You had at least one call from David in the last 24 hours, and other calls in the last week. Your relationship with him is current. What were the calls about?"

"No more hiding the facts, Paul. If you help with the investigation, certain things don't need to leave this room," Aggard said.

This was the first time he realised that this was not a proper interview room. As such there were no audio recordings being done and no cameras in the room.

While he saw the benefits of later on denying what he might tell them, he felt suddenly more nervous about his situation.

"OK, he called me about a new guy in his team. Someone called Frost that he'd met at the demonstrations."

Melissa pulled out her tablet PC while he continued talking.

"We know about him, what else?" she said, again elaborating to encourage him to say more.

"He wanted him in the group and I ran a background check on him. He called me yesterday to ask if we had him on the radar for the attack that took place. That's everything."

"What details did you get on this Frost guy?" Broer asked.

"All a bit odd really. His background had been sanitised. I'm guessing he was police or military previously. There was nothing criminal, so I told David he was probably OK."

"And what do you get out of this? Drugs, money, women?" Melissa asked.

"Whoa! Hang on, don't answer that. I don't care and we don't need to know," Nelson said. "Do you have an address for David?"

"Sure, he lives at the top of Colchester Road, that dual carriage way..."

"...off the Harden roundabout," Melissa interrupted, spinning her tablet PC around.

A zoomed image showed two people on the doorstep of a house, one man grabbing the other's arm.

"Traffic camera image from just a few days ago. Looks like David and Frost have been getting quality time together."

Seeing where the conversation might go, Broer stepped in.

"Interesting, but we have nothing on the Frost guy. Let's bring David in for questioning though, he's up to his neck in it."

"Agreed. Aggard, this man is yours," Nelson said, pointing to Paul.

Coppers taking backhanders and a little dope were of no interest to ASTU.

He was screwed anyway, now that Aggard knew what he'd been up to.

"We need a warrant and some of your officers. We'll pay David a visit today," Nelson added.

"No problem, it'll take a few hours to get the paperwork and rally the people needed, of course."

"That's fine."

Nelson turned back to Paul.

"What will we find?"

"Just drugs and maybe four or five people there, but no one dangerous."

"OK, Broer, your suggestion, so you head this one up. Let Aggard's team do the work but you take charge of David and bring him into custody. No funny business with the suspect this time!"

"Sure thing," Broer said, feeling Frost was just hours away from finally being found.

"Let's go. Get some rest, it's going to be a long night," Nelson said to his team, and left the room.

~ 28 ~

"In the side office there," the officer said, pointing his thumb to a darkened room off the corridor.

Nelson sat upright on the sofa he'd moments ago been snoring on.

"Hey, sorry, I must have fallen asleep."

Melissa held out a piece of folded paper to him.

"Want to check it?"

"No, Aggard will have made sure it's fine, give it to Broer."

"Are you really trusting him to bring Rhett in unharmed, after what we saw earlier?"

"Melissa, we've been over this a dozen times. Give the warrant to Broer and get ready to interview David when he comes in."

∞

Two lines of officers stood either side of the hallway.

"11 officers," Aggard told Broer.

"More than I expected, but an odd number, isn't it?"

"You're number 12. I doubt this Rhett is a problem, but as we saw, he has friends and this is serious. I don't like my men being taken by surprise, so I've given you two groups."

Broer looked over the assembled officers. All but two were dressed in full protective equipment. Those two were female officers. They had stab-proof vests and soft caps on; standard-issue uniforms for the street, not for a raid.

"What do I have and why are they not equipped?"

"The two at the front there are your doormen," Aggard said, pointing to two officers holding steel battering rams. "The two female officers are not front line. If there are any females in the house they will assist with them. Detention and searches, etc."

Broer looked down the hallway which ended in a wide, open door. Outside, he could see two vans with their rear doors open.

"Those my vans?"

"Obviously," Aggard said.

He walked towards the door, between the two lines of officers, inspecting them like they were on show parade for him.

Thinking forward to how the raid would take place, a nagging concern came back into his mind. Leading the raid would help him get closer to Frost, help him get into their space, but what if Frost was actually there?

He reached the end of the line and turned back to Aggard.

"No firearms?" he asked.

"No," Aggard replied flatly.

Next to him were his two sergeants, Sokolof and Chester.

He quickly checked and saw it was Chester's line that was an officer short.

"Chester, take front and go up. Sokolof, you take rear and go down. Your female duty officers go in last. I'll go in right behind your last man in," he said to the sergeant.

It was the only way he could think of being involved as Aggard expected, yet giving time to have everyone arrested, including possibly Frost.

"Shouldn't you stay outside to command the op?" Chester asked Broer, who glanced at Aggard for confirmation.

"It would be normal protocol," she said, answering her officer but directing the comment to Broer.

"OK, fine. In fact I'll stay in the van until you're done if that helps?" he asked, jumping on the opportunity they'd just offered up.

"Works for me," Chester said.

"Good. Load up!"

Responding to Broer's command, the officers headed down the corridor and loaded themselves into the waiting transport.

"I'll see you when you get back," Aggard said to Broer, and slammed the van door shut.

∞

"A few minutes and we're on location," the van driver shouted back to the officers.

They continued on at the leisurely pace, which Broer was beginning to find maddening.

He could see that the officers were occasionally casting glances over to him, no doubt expecting him to give them orders to follow on the raid.

This was as expected.

In truth, though, he wasn't interested in directing the raid. They could follow their sergeant's commands and do what police do.

For him, David was the prize. He was the gateway to Frost.

He thought about whether Frost would be at the house. If Frost saw him, there was nothing he could do surrounded by 11 other coppers, then Frost would vanish for a few more years for certain.

He felt the van slowing.

"Sir, we're on location!" the driver announced.

"Sokolof, lead your team out first," Broer replied.

"No last minute instructions?" Chester asked.

"Yes, anyone arrested I want cuffed and facing the floor. Let's not have these terrorists remembering faces. Go!"

"Let's make this quick!" Sokolof shouted, swinging the doors open and jumping out.

His doorman and the rest of the officers ran behind, towards the rear door of the house.

"Sokolof, in position?" Chester called out into his radio, almost at the front door.

"Call it!" came the reply.

The backdoor entry team had just that second gotten into position, and their doorman was holding his steel battering ram two feet back from the door lock, ready to smash it through for the waiting officers.

"Up and through," Chester said to his team as they continued running, led by the doorman.

"Make entry!"

He stood out of the way as the battering ram was swung back, the officer skipped a foot forward to carry the momentum and the ram slammed into the door. It burst open with a crack of wood and ring of metal.

In the distance, Sergeant Sokolof's ram could be heard as a faint thud.

The doorman pinned himself against the wall and the squad poured past him and as ordered, ran upstairs.

As he ran in, Sokolof was shouting.

"Police! Police! Stay where you are!"

Chester heard a woman scream from the back of the building.

The house wasn't empty, then.

He sprinted up the stairs behind his team, just in time to see the doorman sending his ram through what looked like a normal interior door.

To the doorman's surprise, this one cracked under the force, leaving a ragged hole where the handle had been, but the top and bottom stayed in position.

"Bolts! Must be locked from the inside," he shouted and prepared to swing low and destroy the bottom bolt.

The other officers were clearing the rooms in pairs, shouting "Clear!" and then re-emerging to head into the next room.

The doorman swung but failed to break through.

"Get it open!" Chester shouted to him.

The other officers were now standing ready to burst through, anticipating rushing in and apprehending whoever was in there.

∞

In the darkness of the room, David crept up to the door and looked through a slight crack between the door's wooden panels and its frame.

Beyond it, he could just make out the back of a policeman standing in the kitchen doorway.

He could hear a female voice talking firmly but calmly to a crying Mary as the banging and shouting carried on upstairs.

For now she was saying nothing, but he knew he had to make a move and fast.

He realised one set of officers must have come through the front door and straight upstairs, the others through the back door and into the kitchen, checking the main room by going through adjoining French doors.

By a stroke of luck, no one had actually gone into the hallway yet.

Had they done so, they'd have seen the cellar door he was now peering through.

As it was, only a coat rack obscured it from the officer in the kitchen.

∞

"Hang on, hang on!" Chester shouted and the doorman put his ram down.

Three more smashes had damaged the door, but had hardly moved the bolts.

Chester stepped into the doorway of the adjoining room and saw what he had suspected.

Kneeling down he prised off a 1-inch plastic disc that looked like the decorative covering of a screw or bolt holding the wooden frame on.

"Deadbars from this side," he said.

Understanding, another officer checked to the top and saw the same thing.

Deadbars were an uncommon but effective trick.

Where two doorways sat together, thick steel bars were fed through holes in the wall and doorframe of the adjoining room.

The bar would pass behind the door to be protected and then sit in holes on the other side.

With the bar running behind the protected door, secured in the wall from either side, it made it nearly impossible to break down without smashing the entire door to splinters.

The bar was flush with the wall, meaning it couldn't be pulled out by hand.

There was, however, a drilled hole through the end, in which something could be inserted.

"Great," Chester said, realising they would need a tool to pull out the bars and also that no one was inside the room.

"You four, go downstairs and look for a tool box or a thin, wire-like tool," he said to the officers.

In perfect bad timing, David felt his moment to escape had come.

Quietly lowering the handle, he sprung the door open and rushed from the cellar.

The officer at the kitchen door reacted immediately, turning around and reaching out to grab David.

"Stop!" he shouted.

In running forward, though, David had pushed the coat stand towards the officer, who became entangled with coats and scarves.

Even though he'd managed to grab David, his instinct to protect his face meant he lost balance and headed to the floor.

David was dragged down, making wild noises and striking out at the officer's hands.

He freed himself and, pushing away, stood to run.

Hearing the commotion, officers from upstairs started to come down the stairs towards him. He sprinted for the open front door.

Broer stepped into the doorway and landed a fist squarely into David's cheek.

A blinding flash filled his vision and a rush of noise filled his ears.

∞

The tool looked like a Bale Hook. A smooth bar of wood to fit in the hand and a hook protruding through the fingers.

It could be easily mistaken for something innocent, which was no doubt why it was in the kitchen drawer with the wooden spoons, cork screws and garlic crusher.

Chester fed the hook through the hole in the bar and pulled hard.

The bar slid towards him and he grabbed it, feeding it all the way out.

With both out of the way, the door opposite popped open.

Sokolof went through first.

To the untrained eye it looked like a regular study or office: desk, lamp, etc. But there was an unexpected amount of drawers. Almost one wall was full with 4 sets of 3 drawer units.

There was also a familiar, sweet smell.

Chester and Sokolof went over and pulled out various drawers.

Inside was what they were looking for.

A pack of coke that was easily 1kg in weight, resealable packs of white pills, wraps of what looked like heroin and in another set of drawers a mix of resin blocks, leaf and buds.

"What do you reckon?" Chester said.

"15 to 20 years for this lot, he's no kingpin but this is bigtime supplier territory," Sokolof said.

An officer with a video camera came over to the drawers and filmed what had been found.

"OK, you all search around and see what else you find," Chester said to six other officers waiting at the doorway.

"Let's go down and see if David's awake," he added and Sokolof followed.

By the time David finally woke up, most of the officers and all of the evidence had already left the scene.

The female officer was finishing putting suture tape across David's cheek.

The bleeding had stopped again, but while Broer's fist had landed squarely on David's temple, the facial skin had pulled, rupturing the wound once more.

It had been suggested that an ambulance should be called, but Broer had refused.

He squatted down in front of David, bringing their faces level.

"Well now, you're in deep shit, aren't you? That's a lot of dagga and other gear you got up there, eh?"

David said nothing.

"We also heard you've been a naughty boy these last nights."

On hearing this, David looked up and stared Broer in the eyes.

"Yeh, deep shit, mate," he said smiling.

"We should hold the questioning until they're both back at the station," Sergeant Sokolof said.

Broer looked around at Mary, who was sitting on the sofa, and stood up.

"OK, let's seal this place up and get the teams back. Take these both into custody."

Chester and the female officer led Mary out and Sokolof grabbed David's arm and led him away.

The carpenter who'd been called to fix the doors swung the front door open. The wooden frame was repaired and the door patched so that it could be locked again.

He held his arm up and dangled several keys in the air.

"Two sets, who wants them?" he asked.

Broer took them from his hand.

"I'll take them, these guys are a bit busy right now."

∞

Nelson, Melissa, Aggard and Broer all stood watching David through the one-way glass.

"You know the drill. You have 72 hours to place him at the scene or you'll have to let him go," Aggard said.

The usual for terror suspects was at least seven days, but they understood she was being cautious.

"We could charge him with the drugs we found, couldn't we?" Melissa asked.

"Sure, Class A, intent to supply. He could get life, but it's not preferred. Not if you want to pin the attack on the refinery on him," Nelson said.

Broer stepped forward to the glass and stared at David, who was slumped forward onto the desk, his head in his hands.

"Can't we pin him for both?" he asked.

"You'll need evidence of both. Let's be clear, ASTU don't care about the drugs, but the police do," Nelson said.

"So, we question him about the attack and see what he spills?"

"Hang on," Aggard interrupted, raising her hands to indicate that they should stop talking. "It's a hell of a haul. We can hardly just let him go now, not after finding so much."

"I agree, but if we assume that he's not the ringleader for the attacks, however involved he is, we need to find out who is. We can suggest a deal, he talks and the more he gives us the more we set aside the drug charges," Melissa said, offering a way forward for both sides.

"OK, right now he's just been detained, not formally arrested. It's a fine line, but Melissa and Broer, formally arrest him now for the attack and question him. If we get nothing, set him loose on the 72 hour mark and I'll re-arrest him for the drugs."

Nelson turned to Aggard, surprised at her flexibility with the legal aspects.

"Thanks," Nelson said to her. "Get to it, you two."

~ 29 ~

"You see that mark on the wall over there?" Melissa asked David, tipping her head towards a small dent in the plaster. "That was where the last person he had in here bounced, before they hit the floor. I only mention this because I can see he's a little tired, a bit cranky. You might want to keep an eye on him."

Melissa and Broer dragged out the chairs opposite David and sat down.

Broer leant forwards towards David and extended his arm, as if reaching for David. He reached to the side and clicked 'Record' on the interview recorder.

"David Rhett," Melissa began, "I am arresting you under suspicion of terrorism. You do not have to say anything, but it may harm your defence if you do not mention when questioned something which you may later rely on in court. Anything you do say may be taken in evidence. Do you understand?"

David looked dumbstruck.

Not having been formally arrested yet, he'd been hoping beyond hope this was about the drugs, that Paul would come to his rescue and that he would be home soon.

Now he felt himself go cold and his diaphragm tensed as he resisted the urge to cry.

"Yes," was all he managed to say.

"We have you, your buddy Frost and the naughty copper Paul." David's eyes went wide. "We'll have your mates soon enough too," Broer said, carefully avoiding stating how many mates, given they didn't yet know.

"We have you at the scene too," Melissa added.

Broer retrieved a clear bag from within his document folder. He dropped it on the table in front of David.

David tensed again on seeing the necklace.

"I thought you'd recognise that. So, given we've also got half the contents of your sock drawers in the evidence room..." Broer said, placing photos of the drugs onto the table, carefully spreading them out for maximum effect.

"The best thing you can do right now, is start by telling us what happened the other night," he continued.

David sat back and raised a hand to the wound on his cheek.

This opportunity had gone wrong very quickly.

The guys acting like idiots was one thing, but it was clear to him now that he'd been set up from the start.

He thought about Lauren offering him the so-called sponsorship when he was at the police station.

Whatever sponsorship it was meant to be—free money to supplement his drug dealing, he'd hoped—that was now gone.

There was no way they, whoever they were, would support him now.

What about Frost?

He was the only other new person in David's life.

Either it was Lauren or Frost who'd set him up.

Where Lauren was he had no idea, but Frost was another matter.

It was 50/50 who was to blame, and right now he needed a scapegoat.

"Well?" Melissa asked, interrupting David, who was staring at the table with glazed eyes.

He looked up at them and said nothing for a few more seconds.

"OK, you've arrested me for terrorism, not for the drugs, right?"

"Well that's just a technicality. The drug issue is still on the table," Broer said, waving his hand across the photographs.

David gently gathered up the photographs, as if doing so carefully and slowly would mean they wouldn't notice.

The two of them watched, curious to see what he was up to.

"But can we strike a deal and then we can take these off the table perhaps?" he asked, placing the stack of photos face down near him at the edge of the table.

"Someone is getting into trouble for the adventure at the refinery and the drugs. That much is for sure," Melissa said.

Broer reached out and moved the photos next to him.

"What deal are you thinking of?"

"Do you have Mary here?"

"Maybe, but you didn't answer my question."

"You need to keep hold of her. I'm not the dealer, Mary is."

Melissa burst out laughing.

"Sorry..." she said, composing herself.

"David, she looks like your drug-addled whore. You obviously like her that way and the bruises on her face speak volumes. So don't bullshit us," she said.

"Right, ten minute break," Broer announced and stopped the tape recorder.

Standing up he walked slowly over to David's side of the table, give a sigh and sat down on the corner.

"Dear me, bru... I thought we had you with us, but you're beginning to piss me off."

"Broer! Let's not do this every time!" Melissa said.

Melissa sensed this was a game, but she was taking no chances. She hit record.

"Interview resumes," she said.

Broer stood up, moving forward so that he loomed over David, staring at him with clenched fists.

David was visibly scared, his eyes wider then before and his upper body pushing back into the chair in an attempt to escape.

Broer noisily expelled a lungful of air through his nose and walked back to his chair.

"Tell us about what happened the other night, why you and your friends were there and what part you all played," Melissa said, trying to get a grip of the situation.

Scared and intimidated, David surrendered to his situation and began to tell them everything.

At several points he came close to choking up.

Melissa's training told her this was either where he felt he'd been set up or he realised it put him deeper into trouble. Either way, it seemed he was now telling the truth.

He told them about his first encounter with Frost, the visit from Lauren and the subsequent phone call. He continued right up to the night he and his two activists climbed the fence and emptied the fuel onto the ground. He recounted seeing the running man, the explosion and sound of helicopters.

A few details, like beating up the guard were obvious omissions, but it was the mention of Lauren that was of interest to Melissa, whoever this was she was important.

"Have you ever met this Lauren?" Melissa asked.

"No, just spoke to her on the phone and I have no way of contacting her."

That bit of information set Melissa's mind thinking.

They wrapped up the interview and had David escorted back to his cell.

∞

Now alone, Melissa and Broer looked at each other in the eyes, as if trying to divine what the other was thinking.

She saw Broer's eyes move from hers to her mouth and to her eyes again; it made her unexpectedly flush with an almost instinctual arousal.

She quickly turned away.

"What do you think?" she asked.

"He's a drug-dealing liar of course, but that's all. It's clear he was set up by someone. He has no reason to be at the refinery with his boys."

"So now what? If we don't charge him with the terrorism offence..."

Broer spoke over her.

"We have 72 hours before Aggard comes checking on us, right? Which is bullshit for detention of terrorist suspects by the way."

Melissa looked him in the eyes again.

She hated not being able to second guess him, to think ahead of him.

He'd changed since they'd had their brief time together.

Now he more like when they'd first met; insular, harder. Broer the Boer, as he'd put it.

"So?" she asked.

What she couldn't realise was the direction he wanted this to go in and why.

"We let him go."

"Are you crazy! This is not the movies, we can't let him walk away. He's guilty by evidence or admission of either terrorism or drug dealing. I get he's not the ringleader for either, but there's a producer and a mastermind behind him. He can lead us to them!"

Broer grabbed her arm.

"Melissa, exactly. He's a pawn in either case. Let him go and see which way he runs. We have his clothes and his phone with the property officer, right? Get her to give you them and we'll bug them both, then we can track him day and night."

She pulled her arm away and he let her go. Standing straight and defiant, he awaited her response.

Melissa thought hard.

As Nelson had made clear, ASTU didn't care about the drugs. They weren't Vice, they were anti-terrorism, here to resolve the attack—and pinning it on David was a false victory.

If in a few months or years when whoever it was struck again, there would be hell to pay.

She closed her eyes and let out a long sigh, realising she had to act against her instincts.

"OK, Aggard's shift lasts for another two hours. Go to the property officer for David's stuff just before shift change. Keep her busy so she can't do handover. Then as soon as she goes, we release him. The new shift officer should be clueless. If she asks questions, tell her Aggard agreed. We'll answer for it in the morning, though!"

"Now you're talking."

She turned to Broer.

"Let's be clear. What I just said was a hypothetical example of what could be done. It's your stupid idea and I don't support it. If things go south I'll point to the confusion you caused and blame you."

Broer was in no doubt there was only sincerity in her voice.

"Understood. I'll see you in two hours."

"Fine, I'll get him moved to a quieter cell, out of the way. Oh, and what about Mary?"

"She's nobody, just look at the state of her," Broer said

"Let her go now, then?"

"No, hang on to her for a few more hours. Better they're kept together."

With Mary and David safely tucked away, Broer made his way back to their house.

As hoped, the place was locked up, with no police presence.

He parked and made his way around to the rear door.

Retrieving the key from his jacket, he unlocked the door and carefully opened it.

There was no real need for such caution, no one but the police had keys and he'd taken one of each off the full set.

He'd near subconsciously checked the windows, too—all were closed.

Still, better safe than sorry.

Inside the house was quiet, it smelt of wood dust from the recent smashing and repairing of doors.

He walked through the large double doors to the sitting room and took in the set-up.

It was as cluttered as he remembered it from earlier.

A lot of dealer houses were, it was often the first way to spot them.

Too many seats and cushions, ornaments and pictures, rugs on the floor and boxes. Like they were trying too hard to project a normal family life, but overdoing it.

Always the fokken boxes, he thought to himself.

Looking over the pictures, he saw one with Mary, and standing next to her was Byford.

"Ah, there you are, mate. I'm surprised David allows this picture, naughty girl."

He turned his attention to the reason he'd come to the house.

Kneeling down in front of the TV, he pulled out the multi-plug adapter from the wall.

From his backpack, he removed one that was a close match and replaced the plugs and unit back into the wall.

No one would know the difference.

The difference with his, though, was its ability to listen in to conversations.

Containing a GSM device, he could silently call it like any mobile and hear whatever was being said in the room.

This wasn't where the interesting stuff would be said, though; to capture that, he headed down into the cellar.

It was wider than the upstairs, being almost the size of the house.

To make sure he could learn what was going on, Broer selected two wall sockets. One on the wall near the bar, the other behind the sofas.

He carefully unscrewed them, removed the wires and then fitted the wall-socket covers.

It wasn't a perfect fit, but they were secure.

He sat on the sofa and called all three units, confirming that they were working.

Satisfied with his work, he checked his watch.

"Move it, Broer!" he said out loud, zipping his backpack up and heading upstairs.

It was less than half an hour until shift change at the station.

~ 30 ~

"There they go. You got the tags on him, right?" Melissa asked.

"Don't worry, bokkie, all snugly hidden away on his stuff and the system's logging his movements since before he left," Broer said.

"Well you cut it a bit fine, where the hell were you?"

"I had some errands to run."

Melissa's attention was drawn to the vibration of her phone.

"Just now, yes," she said into the handset.

"You told him?" Broer whispered.

Melissa covered the microphone.

"Of course I told him!" she whispered back.

Melissa turned away from Broer and continued with the call. "Go ahead. Sorry, sir, you broke up a little there."

After a few minutes she hung up and walked back to Broer.

"Right, it seems GCHQ have passed us a report from DECC. They're concerned about a certain Dr. Kirby, who's been looking to sell trade secrets to Standard Oil."

"Clear as mud, who's DECC? Who's Dr. Kirby?" Broer asked.

"DECC are the UK Department for Energy and Climate Change, Dr. Kirby is a chemist and Standard Oil is where he works. They are a competitor of Terminal Fuels."

"You have a department that helps with climate change? I thought we were trying to prevent it."

"Yeh, hilarious. Nelson wants us to go and pick up this Dr. Kirby, find out what he's been up to and get whatever he's been trying to sell."

"Backup?" Broer asked, pointing his thumb to the police officer at the front desk.

"No. We'll make a home visit ourselves now."

"Now? Shit, I had plans to keep an eye on David. You were so concerned about losing him five minutes ago!" Broer said, visualising the devices he'd planted in the house.

"Broer, we need to go now. David can wait, he's only going to go home and get stoned."

"Jesus, fine. Let's get this guy quick then!"

Broer stormed out of the police station, rapidly followed by Melissa. *Here we go again*, she thought to herself.

∞

"Dr. Kirby?" Melissa asked, holding out her ID wallet. "ASTU."

Kirby looked dumbstruck.

"What, who are you?" he asked, lowering his glasses and peering at them both.

"ASTU, the S is for Standard and the T is the Terminal. Mind if we come in?" Broer said, stepping forward.

The look on Kirby's face changed instantly.

"Ah, yes fine. Come through to the study, my wife is in the lounge watching TV."

They entered the house and followed Dr. Kirby as he shuffled his way along with the aid of a walking stick.

"Who is it, dear?" a woman called out from behind a closed door.

"Work, dear, won't be long," he replied and guided his guests into a room on the opposite side of the hall.

"Yes, err… take a seat," he said to them, lowering himself into an armchair.

"So, you've come about the business with Terminal Fuels and my chat with Federman, I presume?"

It never ceased to amaze Melissa how often people just gave information away, believing the police already knew.

"The very same, yes. It's been reported that you tried to sell some research belonging to Standard Oil. You do know there was an attack on Standard's facility?" Melissa asked.

"I saw the news, but I don't see what the connection is."

Broer stepped in, not wanting to waste any time.

"The connection is there was an attack, and you were reported as trying to sell company secrets to a competitor in a monitored industry."

Melissa had no idea what a monitored industry was, but it sounded impressive.

She saw Kirby's hands were shaking and seeing her look at them he placed them together to steady them.

"This is a terrible mistake," Kirby began. "I went to see an old friend for dinner and we got to discussing our work. I used to work for him, you know? I explained about the bio-fuel research and joked he should get his hands on it, adding he couldn't afford it. It was just witty banter between friends. I assume now he thought I actually wanted to sell it!"

A thought came to Broer.

"What's really striking," he said, "is how you collect this research, and then a few days later the plant goes up in smoke. Coincidence?"

"I didn't collect anything, it was just a conversation!"

Melissa could see Kirby was beginning to shake more, holding his hands together on his knees.

"Are you OK, doctor?"

"Not really, I'm awfully sorry. I was just about to take my medications when you arrived. I tripped down the stairs a few days ago and hurt my leg and ribs. The pain is quite terrible. Would you mind? They're in the kitchen just here. Won't be a second, I'll bring them in."

"Please go ahead, but return quickly," Melissa said, smiling to him.

The old man struggled to lift himself from the seat, pulled his cardigan closed and shuffled once again across the floor and out of the room.

"Good god, he looks like he's about to keel over again. One foot in the grave and half a brain there too. This is going to take all night and we don't have all night!" Broer said.

Melissa raised her eyebrows and smiled at the state of the man.

"Wow, what is he, sixty going on a hundred? Must be all the chemicals."

Broer looked at the ceiling, and then turned to Melissa.

"What did Nelson say DECC told him?"

"Kirby had tried to sell research."

"Virtually or physically?"

Melissa cast her eyes down and visualised Kirby turning up at his friends.

"Damn it!" she said aloud, realising her gut feeling was Kirby had turned up with physical items, not being of the computer generation.

The sound of her expletive had barely died before Broer leapt from his chair and through the door.

He turned and ran towards the back room where the alleged kitchen was.

Melissa followed as fast as she could.

He entered, not into a kitchen but a reception room, where Kirby was kneeling in front of an open fire, feeding printed pages into the flames.

"Stop! Now!" Broer shouted.

Kirby dropped the papers reflexively in response to the sudden outburst.

Fearing another attack on his person, he curled up into a ball.

"No, please! No more, I didn't do anything more!" he shouted.

Broer heaved the man off the floor and, kicking a chair out from a table, dropped him down into it.

"Where are the rest of the papers, what else do you have? Start cooperating or you and your wife will be down in the station and this place will be turned upside down!" Melissa said, raising her voice to a shout near the end.

"OK, OK, I'm sorry! I thought you were Hannover again! I have these and some items in my study upstairs."

Broer's ears pricked up at the mention of his old employers. So they were behind this.

"Get up, let's go," Broer told the man, pushing him to ensure he got that a sense of urgency and immediate compliance was expected. They marched him back to the room they had been in moments earlier.

Melissa wasn't sure if Broer caught the reference to Hannover, but if he had, it didn't show.

Her mind raced with the thought of it.

Hannover had been mentioned during ASTU training, but they were dealt with like Anonymous or a spontaneous people's movement.

They were accepted as real only in that people made it so by using the label—it was an us-and-them idea to rally around occasionally. There were no headquarters, known leaders, formality.

Yet here was someone implying it was real.

Kirby's wife appeared at door.

"What's going on?"

Melissa pulled her badge out.

"Mrs Kirby, your husband has committed a serious offence, sit down," she said, pointing to one of the chairs.

The woman gave a mousey squeak and sat down as instructed.

"Is there anyone else in the house?" Melissa asked them both.

They confirmed it was just them.

"Do you have anything else, doctor?" Melissa asked.

"Yes, in the study."

"Broer, help the doctor fetch whatever else he has."

Broer pressed his hand on Kirby's back. He stood and they headed from the room.

"What's my husband done?"

"Stolen secrets and tried to sell them it seems. What can you tell me about that?"

"He doesn't talk about his work. Well, except recently about his new job at Standard Oil. Went on and on about it. Complaining he was being pushed out, how he had no choice to go, but how he'd show them."

"Who are 'they?'" Melissa asked.

"I've no idea, Cosgrove Research I suppose."

Broer came back in with Dr. Kirby and a laptop bag slung over his shoulder.

Under instruction from Broer, Kirby now sat down again, obediently sorting through the documents that had been saved.

There were three large manila wallets of papers: a mix of notes, letters, and diagrams of chemical compounds and other items.

To Melissa it looked like everything someone would need to copy whatever product this all related to.

"Melissa," Broer said, tipping his head to the door.

They both went outside the kitchen and closed the door. Broer grabbed her arm and pulled her to the front door.

"What are you doing!"

He let go of her and proceeded to shove her further down the hall.

"Get your hands off me!"

She tried to dig her heels in but couldn't stop him moving her forward. She could feel a panic rising in her.

He eventually stopped shoving her along and she turned to see him tight mouthed and panting.

"Who do you think you are, shoving me about!"

Broer raised both hands towards her, as his arms went up Melissa winced, expecting to be hit but instead he grabbed her shoulders and squeezed.

"Forget this guy! We have the research, he didn't sell it, no harm done. I need to get back and monitor David right now!" he said, letting go of her.

"Calm down! What's got into you?"

"He's on the loose and we're dicking about with this guy! That's what's got into me!"

He raced to the door, stepped out and slammed it closed behind him.

"God almighty," she said aloud, running her fingers over her brow and temples, trying to relax her face.

They of course would have heard everything and now she was alone to deal with it.

Walking back into the kitchen, she saw the Kirbys looking at her with open mouths.

"It's a tense investigation," Melissa said flatly. "Have you finished sorting the papers?"

"Yes, but some of the formulas and compound models aren't here," Kirby said.

"Well it's just evidence, we don't need the actual information," she replied, gathering up the wallets of documents.

"Actually…" Kirby began.

Melissa's intuition leapt ahead of what Kirby was about to say.

"This is just a paper copy right?"

"Yes and no. The data at Cosgrove was all deleted."

"Deleted?"

"Yes, that was part of the agreement. I'd take a full copy and then they'd delete the rest. There was this paper copy and the files on the laptop."

Melissa was now the one wide eyed as she heard 'they' once again and realised what Broer had just walked out with.

She put the papers down on the table, pulled out a chair and sat down.

"I suggest you talk me through this, from start to finish, and explain who 'they' are and what you've been doing for them."

~ 31 ~

Broer slammed the front door behind him and made straight for his study.

He moved his own laptop aside and replaced it with Kirby's.

Firing it up, he found that the man had set no password and Broer went straight into the recent documents.

"Thank you, you idiot," he said.

Having confirmed Kirby's data was there to be taken, he calmed down a little and remembered the other pressing matter.

Turning back to his own laptop he went to the monitoring software and waited for it to show where David was.

A map rendered on the screen and a central dot travelled across the page, tracking movement data from the first point when David had been released until now. Broer held his breath, anxious about where the current point would be.

"Come on, you kont."

The map stopped moving and started to zoom in.

Colchester Road. He silently cursed Melissa.

She'd been right, David had gone straight home and hadn't moved since.

The tension eased from Broer's body. He half stood up to fetch a celebratory beer from the fridge, and then remembered his outstanding task.

From the detritus scattered on his desk he found a data stick and inserted it into Kirby's laptop.

Scanning through the files and folders he found a well-organised set of files, selected them and began to copy them down to the data stick.

Now he gave into the need for the beer.

Via his laptop, he dialed into the devices hidden in David's house and put on his headphones.

There was nothing but white noise.

Satisfied, he turned the laptop screen towards an old rocking chair in the corner of the study.

He whipped the headphone cables over the table and sat down with his beer.

Sliding down into the comfy chair, he squinted his eyes and settled in to watch and listen.

Basically like fishing, he thought to himself.

∞

David woke up, face down on the sofa, staring bleary eyed at a boarded-up table, an ashtray full of joint butts and an array of beer bottles.

The rapid consumption of large amounts of liquefied and gasified drugs, combined with tiredness and stress, had brought about the precise effect he'd hoped for.

The world had faded away as quickly as his senses and he'd now woken where he'd dropped.

His mind was blank for the first few minutes, and then the thoughts came flooding back. He sat up and looked around. Nothing had been touched down here in the basement.

He hadn't thought anything of it when he pulled the working box from under the table and rolled the joints.

Despite the raid, using the new keys and having been shown pictures of his drugs, he'd come home as if everything here was just as it had been.

Jesus... I'm an idiot, he thought, realising the stress of the last few days had overwhelmed him even more than he had realised.

The police had raided the house but had not cleared it fully.

His mind went to his upstairs strong-room and again to the photos he'd been shown.

Racing out of the cellar, he ran through the hallway and up the stairs to the room.

David cast a glance around the door frame. Of course they'd found the bars to get in, why was he even checking!

The door was smashed up, but the room inside was intact, allowing for him to see the completely empty drawers.

He'd seen the photos, but seeing the room empty made his heart sink.

That was about quarter of a million in street value that should have been there.

Suddenly it seemed Mary's concern at keeping so much in one place was right, though he'd never imagined getting raided given he had Paul's protection.

He thought of Paul and wondered what part he'd had to play in all this. If none, he was going to be another problem to face.

Walking into the room, he went over to the half-opened wardrobe and swung the doors wide.

∞

The helicopter's blades made a low *thud-thud-thud* sound as it swept overhead. Broer looked up from the lake and to the sky, balancing the fishing rod in one hand. Everything seemed to be moving in slow motion.

Broer jerked forward in the chair, realising he'd nodded off and was dreaming.

Experience told him he'd been woken by a real noise coming through his headphones, that noise prompting the dream.

He blinked and tensed his eyes hard to clear his vision and checked his laptop screen—the red dot that was David was still at home. A creak of wood through the headphones told him that David was up and on the move.

He switched from the rocker and back to the desk chair, closing his eyes to focus on the sound and try to picture what he was hearing.

∞

David pushed again on the corner of the cupboard base.

The wood creaked and the board, supported slightly off centre underneath, tilted just enough for him to get his fingers under the corner nearest to him.

He lifted the board and let a sigh of relief out as he saw that the money was still there.

Taking out a few bundles of cash, he dropped the board down again and closed the doors.

Broer heard David returning downstairs with a *thud-thud-thud* noise.

∞

Over the next half an hour Broer listened in, the devices working perfectly.

A few eavesdropped phone calls later, Broer had learned who the other two people at the attack on the refinery were.

His interest, though, was piqued at the sound of hearing the name of Frost being mentioned.

David was to have the three others over tonight, seemingly to get more product via Colin, but also to get advice from whoever Wolf was and from the man of interest, Frost.

Broer checked his watch. He needed to be back to monitoring for when they started at 7pm.

He thought about Melissa and whether Nelson or Aggard were on the warpath. Right now, he'd have to leave David to himself again and deal with his ASTU world.

He also wanted to see what Melissa had found out.

Grabbing the laptop bag, he headed out of his house and back to the war room.

∞

A browbeaten Melissa continued to stand where she'd been for what already felt like a lifetime.

If at any point in the previous 20 years she'd ever felt like the naughty child, it was now. Having Aggard standing there too just increased the feeling.

Nelson was red with rage.

The moment Melissa had returned to the station, he'd spotted her and for a second time that afternoon, she had been physically manhandled by an ASTU colleague.

He'd appeared out of nowhere and literally dragged her aside into his temporary office.

The first 5 minutes had been spent being told how stupid her actions were and getting interrogated as to what the hell Broer and her were up to.

"Who authorised his release?" Aggard asked.

"Your duty officer?" Melissa said, regretting it straight away.

"Don't get smart! You're on your last chance on this investigation as it is. Messing up like this as a rookie might be your last chance with ASTU too! You let a prime suspect in a terrorist attack go free. You do remember what we're here for, don't you?"

The forcefulness of Nelson's words left her in no doubt that he would happily take this further.

"I'm sorry. We saw no further benefit from holding them here any longer. Broer wanted to have them on the streets so that he could contact whoever he's working with. Either on the drugs side or related to the attack."

"So you're blaming Broer for your act of professional negligence, for aiding a suspected terrorist?" Nelson asked.

"No, we're both to blame. It was Broer who suggested it and said if we got into trouble like this I could blame him. Which I'm not doing."

∞

Broer's mobile rang for the third time. He rejected the call again and realised he was out of time.

"Fok!" he shouted aloud several times, while slamming his hands into the steering wheel.

He'd not thought through what he'd say when he arrived back to the ASTU team.

By now, Nelson would know David was gone and given his outburst at the Kirby's, Melissa would have put the blame squarely on him.

What's more, he couldn't just hand over the laptop.

His new paymasters were pleased at learning they'd got a bonus out of their ASTU mole.

It was an unexpected way out for him and they'd cut his balls off if they knew the research was anywhere but in their hands.

He gave a long sigh. Things were moving faster than expected and he needed to keep focused.

A few hours ago he'd been in control, events had played out to his benefit, but he now realised he'd got overconfident and was in a hole.

It was pointless trying to maintain his story at ASTU now, it had always been a means to an end anyway. If he went back they could prevent him watching over David and finding Frost.

They'd want the research, too.

His whole exit plan could easily fall apart, but right now he had the upper hand.

"Fok it!" he said again, and then slowed and turned the car around.

∞

"Do we know where he is now?" Aggard asked.

Melissa thought back to him storming out with the laptop.

"As I mentioned, he was at the Kirbys', we argued because he wanted to go and monitor David. He left with Dr. Kirby's laptop. I assumed he was coming here."

Nelson was about to jump in again but Aggard raised a hand, the look on her face telling him he'd missed something.

"How? How is he monitoring David? We have a plainclothes unit watching the front of the house and they haven't reported seeing anyone."

"He said he'd bugged his clothing."

"What! Without authorisation and setting up a monitoring station here?" Nelson shouted.

"I'm sorry, sir. He's the senior officer. He said he'd bugged the clothing and I assumed that meant the monitoring would be done here," Melissa said, adding in a little truth with her lie.

The desk phone rang and Nelson picked up.

"OK, send a Collection Unit to his house and pick him up, if he's even there!" he said and hung up.

"His phone is ringing out, more likely rejecting the calls. Tracking says he was headed this way 20 minutes ago but is now heading back towards home."

Melissa realised the severity of the situation.

ASTU were already treating Broer as a rogue operative. The so called Collection Unit was a snatch squad, the ghosts hidden amongst the ghosts.

At best, Broer would be detained, brought in and questioned.

At worst, he'd resist or run and they'd invoke ASTU's unique Freedom to Fire permissions, the ultimate authority to prevent subversion and terrorism. Then he'd vanish from memory and record.

The call was an insight for Melissa.

"Other than your rank, I'm guessing you're not just an ordinary member of the force, ma'am?" Melissa said to Aggard, offering her a new level of respect.

There was no way Nelson would have let her overhear what she'd heard in this room and on the phone now, unless he felt safe doing so.

"No, I'm not," Aggard confirmed. "There are many layers to this organisation, Melissa. Some stretch in and others out. You don't need to know the nuances, but rest assured that we're on the same team."

Nelson let out a burst of air.

"Are we! We might be, but is she?" he said pointing to Melissa.

"I think we can relax about her. Beyond your basic account of Kirby trying to sell research, is there anything else you want to tell us?" Aggard asked.

"No, ma'am, that's all he told me. It was an opportunistic theft, made more valuable by the coincidence of the attack."

She hoped she sounded convincing.

Kirby's talk of Hannover wasn't a nugget of information she wanted to hand over just yet.

Nelson turned to Melissa, clearly wanting to end this conversation.

"Fine, we have nothing else on Kirby anyway, he came up clean on background checks. Aggard's team will take over dealing with him for theft of intellectual property. You need to get back on this case, alone for now until we find a replacement. Report back to me in a couple of hours with your game plan. Now get out."

When Melissa had left, Aggard turned to Nelson.

"And what's your game plan?"

"I was hoping you had one! All we have is David, as he's already back in the wild, so we have the choice of leaving him there for now, but not for long."

Aggard understood. "Processing paperwork technicalities before we re-arrest him."

"Exactly. Watch his house, see where he goes, who comes to him. Unless you have any new leads or ideas to chase?"

"Nothing clever from my team, we're too busy being the public face of the operation as usual. Are you sure you don't want me to arrest him for the drugs?" she asked.

"We're not interested in that, are we? The Home Office will want a report in a few days, it better be with them before Councillor what's his face raises the topic in Parliament and makes the Home Secretary look an idiot."

Aggard laughed. "The Home Secretary always looks like an idiot!"

"True, but unlike me she's not chasing promotion. Whoever they are, we have a terrorist group using Chinese-made explosives and destroying research. Not finding them could be very career limiting for me."

"Do you think you're overreacting to Broer? Maybe he'll come in," Aggard said.

"No, his actions are insubordination at the least, putting the whole investigation at risk. I've turned a blind eye to his ways before, but not this time. By definition, he's up to something and he's not allowed to be."

Nelson checked his watch.

"Can't be long now. Shut the door and let me fire up my laptop. We can log in to the comms dashboard and see if our friends are having any luck finding Broer."

Several mouse clicks and password checks later, they had the right communications dashboard in front of them.

They announced themselves when challenged and the dashboard rendered all of its screens.

Nelson plugged in a pair of headphones and passed one earplug to Aggard.

A map showed Broer stationary at home and the Collection Team heading towards him.

They watched and listened.

∞

Running as fast as he could upstairs, Broer burst into his study and threw a large sports bag down on the floor.

He moved quickly, gathering up the monitoring equipment, laptop, data pen and other electronic necessities and started filling the bag. Pulling out the desk drawer, he grabbed a wad of cash he kept there for emergencies.

The sweat was running down his back and he visualised Nelson driving towards his house. He didn't want to be here when he arrived but if he was, he'd have to knock the guy down and probably tie him up.

On thinking this he realised he was still play pretending being ASTU, still pretending he had options, which he was definitely out of.

He shot out of the room across the hallway and into his bedroom. There, from the top shelf of a cupboard, he pulled down a large shoe box. It always felt like a cliché keeping his mementos in this way, but it was also the easiest.

Pulling the top off he saw the folded flag of South Africa, not the current one, but the old one, the 'real' one.

He lifted his beret out and smelt it. He was instantly transported back, his mind filled with visions of South Africa.

"Broer the Boer," he said to himself. The feeling of the land being tied to his blood had always been there, and always would.

He removed it and saw what he was looking for. An 8-inch-long field knife. Better than any gun he'd ever used in service. He pulled it out of the sheath and lingered on the feel of it in his hand.

Bright, sharp steel with a wound leather handle. Perfect. He slid the knife back into its sheath, put the box back and headed to the study for his bag.

∞

The convention was no chatter on the line—this wasn't a NASA mission with a need for constant updates and checks. Once a command or update was given, it was radio silence until absolutely needed.

After around ten minutes of hearing nothing and watching a dot on the screen do nothing, the silence was broken.

"CT in position, awaiting green light," came the voice.

Aggard and Nelson looked at each other.

"Here we go then," he said.

A moment later the reply came.

"CT, you are confirmed go, channels are open," was the response.

Now with the Collection Team's microphones open there was background noise, muffled voices, metallic noises, footsteps, the scraping of cloth against microphones.

Someone would have a video view, but that required higher clearance. For Aggard and Nelson, they had to be content with audio only and the unmoving dot on the screen.

A noise that sounded like keys and a door opening.

"They're inside," Nelson whispered.

More muffled voices, footsteps, other noises they couldn't determine.

"Phone," they heard someone whisper.

"Check the car."

More sounds of footsteps and what sounded like a door being unlocked, then confident steps on a path.

Aggard pulled her face to show she didn't understand.

"He's not with his phone, so where is he?" Nelson replied, narrating the question the team were likely asking themselves.

"Not with the car, heading back in."

Nelson leant forward in his chair.

"I hope he's in the bloody house!" he said.

Broer threw the bag on the front passenger seat and closed the driver door as quietly as he could.

This was officially worse than expected, but at least he was completely clear on where the situation now stood. He just hoped his Chinese friends did too, but that was a worry for later.

He eased off the handbrake just enough to get the van rolling and slowly the vehicle crept forward.

Being parked between the back of the houses, he'd have a good 30 metres of pitch-black back alley to coast down before he needed to start the engine.

Even if the team caught up with him there was a good chance they didn't have guns.

He thought about what he'd heard they carry. It was more usual to carry mace spray, Tasers and old-fashioned batons.

They'd want to detain him, whereas he'd kill them without a second thought.

He felt a little excitement at the idea: it'd been a while.

The van reached the end of the alleyway, and he released the handbrake fully and took a hard right as he coasted onto the main road. Dropping the clutch, he did a perfect jump start and accelerated away.

Laughing as he felt the tension release, he headed to his favourite quiet spot to enjoy an evening's eavesdropping.

"Search complete. Location Empty. We're pulling out. Repeat, pulling out. Close channels."

Instantly, the audio died and the on-screen dashboard closed, leaving them staring at a bunch of icons on the PC's desktop.

Both listeners sat stunned for a few seconds.

"What the hell just happened!" Nelson said.

He ripped out the earpiece and staggered backwards, pushing his chair out of the way.

"They've lost him," Aggard said, stating the obvious.

She turned to see Nelson had both hands on his head, eyes closed, head tilted backwards.

"What the hell is he up to!" he said.

"I don't know what he's up to, but he's officially rogue. You know what that means."

"Yes, I know what that means and he can kiss his ass goodbye for all I care. But again, what the hell is he up to and can we stop him before he does it?"

Aggard stood and walked around to Nelson.

She fixed her eyes on his in a determined look.

"You need to take charge of this directly, you with Melissa to reinforce the continuity of the team," she said. "Blame the release of David and Mary entirely on Broer, he's gone rogue and stolen the research. He's to be stopped on sight. I'll pull David and Mary back in as soon as the paperwork goes through. It'll take a day or so given the explanations I'll have to make."

Nelson again saw how she played a better political game than he did.

Right now he needed to cover himself, and her advice was the best he had.

"I'm not protecting Melissa, she's a liability too, but let's focus on Broer and get those two other idiots back in our hands," Nelson said, making the decision that Melissa would be offered up if needed.

~ 32 ~

Colin greeted Mary at the door.

"Downstairs?" he said, walking around to the cellar steps.

"Ah, no, he's upstairs, doing some tidying up."

From the whine of an electric power tool, the tidying up sounded more like DIY.

Colin ran up the stairs to see David putting the finishing touches to the door that had been smashed in recently.

David turned the machine off.

"Wow, they really did a job on you, eh?" Colin said.

He realised that not only was the door in need of some attention, but if it had been part of the raid, the room beyond would also be in need.

"Fiberglass?" he asked, as David pulled his mask off and used his hand to dust off where he'd just been sanding.

"Yeh, bars inside the door this time with a new lock, American safe-room design."

David showed him how a decorative central door knob was in fact a lever to lock the door.

"Look, rotating a quarter turn one way and back, positions or removes the bars."

"Wow, quite cool. Will it stop them getting in next time?" Colin asked, the stupidity of what David was doing clear in his mind. He couldn't believe David would think hiding the stuff in the same room was a sensible idea.

David looked at him for a second, pulling an odd expression.

"Jesus, don't say that, mate, they've already cleared us out."

He put down the sander and, lifting a wet cloth from the floor, rubbed the repair down.

"Good as new, I'll paint it later. Come inside, we need to sort out our stock situation."

The two men went into the room and David took a carrier bag off a far shelf.

"Ten thousand pounds here. It's not much but it'll get us started again. If we stay low at 20 percent mark-up, we can move a lot of product and make sure our suppliers regain confidence in us again."

Colin noted the frequent use of 'we' and 'us' from David. He'd never done this before.

It had always been clear that David was in charge and Colin was to do the donkey work.

He decided to push the situation to his advantage; the balance had been too long tipped one way. He picked up a bundle of cash and nonchalantly tossed it down.

"20 percent is too low, and just ten thousand? You telling me they cleared you out of cash too? We need to double those figures. The risk-to-return ratio is too low, mate. They got you, I could be next on the list."

David was taken by surprise. His mind went to the extra cash hidden nearby, but there was no way Colin could know about it.

He hadn't expected Colin to do anything other than agree with him; this was new territory.

"OK, so what are you looking for?"

Colin thought for a second. David was in a weak position and given their wrestling match the other day he doubted he could try anything physical again.

"You need to stay out of it. I'll store the drugs and we'll split profits 50-50 on a mark-up at 40 percent, you lose nothing then."

David went to protest but Colin aggressively pressed home his advantage.

"David! You must be mad to jump straight back into dealing! Look at you, fixing the door and talking about restocking with product. Did you get a bump on the head? You think that is going to fool anyone?" Colin said, pointing at the door and tools. "You don't even have the sense to move your gear. They're going to come crashing back through that door and next time, send you straight to prison!"

David stood, speechless, his anger and frustration building.

He knew Colin was right, but accepting it was another thing.

"Arrgh! What else am I supposed to do? If I stop dealing I get hammered. If I carry on, I get mugged by the coppers again!"

In the back of the darkened van, Broer leant back in the chair and kicked his feet up on the desk. He loved listening into conversations and this conversation was as entertaining as they came, like listening to a late-night radio drama.

He took his field knife out and sliced a piece of biltong to chew on. His regression to the pre-ASTU Broer was now complete.

The argument carried on growing.

"Listen to me, you idiot!" Colin said, leaning into David. "You cannot deal anymore, your business is over. I'm taking charge of the drugs and you'll keep the deals going with your contacts. That's the only way we're going to *keep making money!*"

Colin screamed the last few words at David, causing him to reel backwards to escape the sound. He stepped back, but was not about to give up.

"Who the hell do you think you are! You can't do this, they won't let you deal direct!"

David stepping back triggered a primitive attack reaction in Colin, and he grabbed David by the collar, twisted the cloth around his hands and pulled David towards him.

To his surprise, David did the same and the two men's sweating faces came into contact.

Colin pressed his forehead into David's, a look of intense anger on his face.

He wanted to hurt David, to dominate him, but David was still fighting him.

"What now, eh?" Colin asked.

"Get the fuck off me!" David squealed in protest, wanting to get away but still hanging on with the instinct to protect himself.

Colin hooked his foot behind David's lower leg and sent him to the floor. They came down hard and David released his grip, using his hands to try and protect himself, and he landed square on his back. Colin heard the crack of his head on the floor.

David let out a cry of pain.

Uncaring, Colin held on, pressing David to the ground.

"Are we clear now?" he shouted.

"Yes, yes, OK!"

Colin released his grip and stood up over a prostrate David.

David rolled onto his front, got up and stepped over to the near wall, downcast and seething with anger.

Closing his eyes, he took a few long, deep breaths, but it did no good. His heart was pounding and he could feel the blood throbbing in his skull.

He recalled again that a week ago, everything had seemed under control. Now another piece of his life was spinning away from him.

He checked his watch: 30 minutes until 7pm.

Going along with the situation, he rang Wolf and they agreed the group would meet in a few weeks.

Frost, however, still needed to come, despite what Colin might want.

This was a different matter.

Of anyone, Frost might be able to offer advice on what to do, about the police and the attack on the refinery at least.

Other things were still confidential.

Broer was listening intently, excited to realise Frost would now be going alone.

That meant three people to deal with at most, and hopefully he'd have Frost man to man.

A noise suddenly exploded in his ears.

"Jesus!" he shouted.

Broer pulled off the earphones as quickly as he could, his hearing again assaulted by the high-pitched whining of the sander.

∞

"Hey, mate! Good to see you again," David said to a relaxed-looking Frost.

They shook hands.

"Likewise, how are tricks?"

David raised his arms in the air, smiling and making a 'huff' noise.

"Ha, yeh, it happens, mate! You guys are OK though, yeh? You got out pretty quick, didn't you?"

"Yeh, we did, tell you all about it downstairs."

The men headed to the cellar and cracked open the customary beers. Giving each other a toast, they took their seats.

"No one else here tonight?" Frost asked.

"No, with what happened I thought we should keep it quiet for a while. I called the other guys and told them not to come."

"Well, probably best now. My advice to keep things normal didn't really account for much."

They talked about the raid on the house, getting arrested and the questioning.

Frost asked about the rumour of drugs being found, but David explained it away as a few joints and wraps.

While Frost was politely listening to what he knew was a preamble to the real reason he was here, something caught his eye.

"Whoa, sorry! Let me stop you there," Frost said, taking David by surprise. "Sorry, buddy, I really gotta use the toilet. Curry belly if you know what I mean!"

"Aha, OK, be my guest," David replied and dropped back into the sofa.

Broer winced and wondered if the device upstairs was going to pick up any disgusting noises.

Frost took three paces from David, turned fully around and with a finger over his mouth mimed a 'Shush!' several times.

The look of Frost's face made David obey immediately.

Frost tiptoed back in the direction of the table and, supporting himself on the sofa, leaned over to place his mouth directly over David's ear.

"Say nothing," he whispered so low that David could barely hear him.

Frost realised that he'd made a wrong move. Whoever had put the device on the wall would have put others elsewhere.

He took comically large paces from the room back towards the cellar steps, climbed them as quietly as possible then started walking normally. Whoever it was that was listening could fill in the gaps.

Upstairs, he passed a closed door that David must have been working on and spotted the toolbox. Grabbing a selection of screwdrivers, he proceeded to the toilet and, a few acted-out noises later, he headed back downstairs.

"Hey!" Frost said as he came back into where David was, more to announce his whereabouts to the listeners.

He slammed the fridge shut and clanked the beer bottles as further ear candy.

"Blimey, what happened to the light here? You can't leave the wires hanging out like that, mate!"

David looked at Frost, confused.

Frost rotated his hand in a circle to indicate for David to 'roll with it, say something.' David got the cue.

"Oh that, it's been like that all week. I was going to fix it, but events overtook me."

"I can fix that in two minutes."

Broer heard some more footsteps, and then the noises they were making became more distant. The device in the room stopped working.

"Shit!" he said aloud.

Fortunately, the ones upstairs were still operating and given their sensitivity he could at least hear that they were still in the house.

As if to assist his listening, David and Frost came upstairs and Broer picked up the conversation again. What he hadn't heard was Frost instructing David to look for any other devices that seemed 'odd.'

"So that's what I said to him," Frost said as they entered the kitchen, making complete nonsense conversation. "Running like that was always going to give him shin splints, it was crazy."

They both wandered out of the kitchen to the front room.

"Yeh, but why didn't he listen?" David said in reply, now warming to the charade.

Frost started saying something just as the multi-plug near the TV caught David's eye.

The plugs were in the wrong order. Nearest device to the right, furthest to the left.

He always did it this way so that he knew which was which.

David pointed it out to Frost.

Broer pulled off his headphones. When the second device went silent, his ability to surveil from a distance was at an end.

He yanked out the field knife from the desk, where he had pinned it earlier after slicing his snacks, and placed it in the sheath on his belt.

There was no operating in secret anymore, so it was time to act. He dove into the front seat of the van and headed to David's house.

∞

Back in the comfort of his own home, Frost dipped his toast into the warm tea and enjoyed an early supper.

The phone started ringing and Byford answered, connecting the call. After a few pleasantries they got down to business.

"Yes, it was a quick release, but as expected he's still on the hook. Sorry, mate, but I guess that means Mary too. They'll have him on two counts now, but for her it'll just be related to the drug haul," Frost said. "I still don't get why they were released so quickly."

"Someone wants to see which way he runs. ASTU or the regular force will be watching the house. Are you sure you weren't followed?" Byford asked.

"I switched cars at the supermarket underground car park. Standard protocol!" Frost said, attempting to reassure Byford.

It wasn't foolproof, but no one had followed him in, so he was happy enough that no one had followed him on his way out.

Byford left that point there.

"Right, I'll do some digging and see what's happening with David. Be extra vigilant from now on."

"Always. Listen, boss, there's another thing, quite a big thing actually. I pulled out two audio surveillance devices from David's place."

"You tell me this now! Can you place them?"

"Not really, they're pretty standard but they are professional units. Mains powered with GSM cards. It means the listener could be anywhere. The installation was good. This looks professional, someone else is watching and listening."

"Did you sweep the place?"

"No, I just spotted two and removed them, not sure if that was a good move or bad. Leaving them in there doesn't help us though."

Byford thought about this new situation.

It confirmed David had been released in order to monitor him, though it was unusual given the seriousness of the crime he was being accused of.

"Something's afoot here and it doesn't seem like ASTU or the force. Neither of them would have gotten the approval or through the bureaucracy to get surveillance set up so quickly. Watch yourself until we learn more. They've heard your voice and assume you've been seen, even if you think you gave them the slip."

"No worries, I'll go back to my daily routine and wait to hear from you. You sure your Mary's OK if someone else is paying David attention?"

"Not sure. If she's not, I'll need to call in some big favours, that much is for certain."

"Hannover owe you, call it in, boss."

The call ended and Frost added it to his collection.

~ 33 ~

From the look of the van ahead, Broer knew he wasn't the only one interested in David's house.

There was no way he could park on the street and not get seen. As he drove slowly past, he noted that the suspension of the van was sitting low.

It could have been full of tools and materials, but for safety he'd assume it was full of equipment and police officers.

Broer saw a lay-by on the opposite side of the roundabout ahead and drove up to it. A closed fast-food van offered the perfect obstacle to park behind.

He switched off the van lights, swung it around and parked behind it, sticking himself out just enough to see past the van, over the roundabout and to David's front doors.

Wish I had night vision, he thought to himself, now forced to stare into the yellow-orange light cast by the street lamps.

If the other surveillance van hadn't been there, he'd have at least turned on the tracking software on his laptop, allowing him to make sure David and Mary were still in the house.

Doing so meant there was a chance he'd be detected.

The next hour or so, then, was going to be good old-fashioned observation.

As it was, David and Mary were both definitely staying in.

David walked into the bedroom where Mary had been for the last couple of hours. Judging by her groggy state, she hadn't been awake for long after the injection he'd given her.

"Are you comfortable?" he asked her, stroking her hair and moving it from her face.

With the gag in her mouth, all she could manage was a muffled whimper and a cry.

"Don't cry, Mary, we've both had a tough day, but at least you got to enjoy a few hours' magic journey. I bet that was a good one, wasn't it? I hope you enjoyed it."

His odd, playful tone unnerved her even more.

Mary whimpered again, anticipating another theatrical ritual of abuse that was about to play out.

"I, on the other hand, have had a shit time," he said, raising his voice.

He pulled on the rope binding her ankles, which drew them up to the back of her thighs, locking her into a foetal position. With her arms already tied behind her back, it was a perfect combination.

Everyone else might have gotten the better of him today, but one person was not going to.

Broer checked his watch; it had been two hours.

At some point, someone had to leave the house or he had to go in.

What's more, he was now seriously bored and his concentration was starting to lapse. As it turned out, he wasn't the only one.

The street-side door of the van he'd passed earlier slid open. Someone stepped out and then slid the door closed again, but not before Broer saw the dim light coming from inside.

"I knew it," he said.

That was a complication, though. If he was to go in, he'd have to make extra sure he wasn't seen by these police or whoever they were.

This was no spy movie; he was trained for taking on one or two people, that was fine, but a loaded van was another matter.

Another half hour or so passed and his patience ran out.

Broer started the van and pulled out onto the roundabout. Flicking his lights on, he accelerated away and after a few more yards turned down the road that would lead him behind David's house.

He drove the full length of the back street but saw no suspicious vans, no one hiding in cars or standing on street corners. He supposed they could be in an opposite building, but the likelihood was low.

Satisfied, he spun the van around and came back, pulling up directly outside David's back gate.

The back door to the house opened easily, and thankfully they hadn't thought to lock it fully.

On coming through the gate he'd seen no lights on downstairs, just a gentle glow upstairs. That was perfect—it meant he could get into the house fully before being seen.

Now inside the kitchen, Broer closed the back door quietly and stayed crouched down in the dark.

He could hear faint splashing noises from upstairs. It sounded like someone having a bath.

That was one person accounted for, then, but where were the other two?

He walked slowly through the kitchen to the double doors leading to the living room. It was pitch black except for the dull orange glow of street lights soaking through the curtains.

Broer half expected to find someone asleep on the couch, but no one was there either. Looking over to the corner of the room he saw the plugs scattered on the floor where his listening device used to be.

He silently cursed them for finding it.

Still crouching, walking on the sides of his feet to minimise any noise, he retraced his steps and this time went to the cellar door and listened.

Nothing, no noise and no light.

Broer realised that Frost was gone.

He stood to his full height and drew his knife.

The only ones to face here were David and Mary.

Standing at the bottom of the stairs, there was no doubt one of them was in the bath, the other probably in bed.

Broer went to place his foot on the first step and stopped. Lost in a day dream, he replayed the noises he'd heard listening to David, through the surveillance devices.

He heard the *thud, thud, thud* sound again, which he'd dreamed of as being the helicopter blades.

In a revelatory moment he could now imagine David leaving the living room and climbing the stairs.

Thud, thud, thud as he ran up.

Broer made his way up and stopped when his head was level with the landing.

To one side was the bathroom, where someone was moving about occasionally in the water. To the other side was a darkened room with the door ajar, but directly in front was a door so pristine it stood out like a beacon.

Nodding to himself, he admired how quickly David had repaired it. Clearly, there was something new or something they'd missed still in the room.

As for whoever was in the bath, they could be easily overpowered. Instead, Broer crept forward towards the bedroom. Slowly he peered around the door into the blackness and, as expected, saw someone with their back towards the door asleep on the bed.

He rushed in and slapped one hand over their mouth and raised the knife to the side of their head.

The sleeper woke as he'd seen others do. Snapping awake with a start and a muffled scream, jumping at the shock of finding themselves restrained and then stopping stiff on realising they had a knife waving above their face.

Broer felt the gag under his hand just an instant before he realised the person was Mary. A moment later, he saw the ropes and let go of her.

"What the fuck?" he said in a whispered tone, pulling an evil-looking smile.

Her eyes went wide and he smiled again.

Raising his hand, Broer put a finger to his mouth.

"Shusshh... I'm not after you," he said and winked at her.

He turned and casually walked from the bedroom.

Though her mind was filled with fear, she lay quietly and closed her eyes, too exhausted to fight anymore.

Broer was smiling as he opened the bathroom door, walked in and sat down on the toilet.

David sat up as fast as he could, sending water onto the floor, a look of panic on his face.

"Don't get up, mate," Broer said, enjoying David's vulnerability.

"I just want a word, that's all." He pointed at David with the knife. "Where's Frost? And if you pretend not to know, I'll bleed you out into that bath of yours."

"He left about an hour ago."

Broer sat forward and spun the knife in his hand.

"I can see he left, but I didn't ask you that. I said, where is he now?"

David started to speak but barely got the first sound out when Broer leapt towards him and aimed the length of the blade at his throat.

Unfortunately David reacted, raising his hands to protect himself and sinking down into the bath.

Broer turned the knife so that it was handle-side down and pummelled David's arms, grunting with anger.

David screamed out as the metal heel of the handle struck the bones of his forearms and hands again and again.

After many hard blows, Broer stepped back to hear David crying and saw that David's arms were shaking from the pain, blood dripping into the bath.

"Stop your crying! You're lucky I didn't stab you to death!" Broer said, now easily placing the blade's edge against David's undefended throat.

"Now answer the fucking question. Where's Frost?"

David gasped for air in an attempt to overcome the pain and speak.

"Home... He went home."

A few encouraging words later, Broer had the address.

"I'm impressed, I didn't think you'd know that," he said. "I think I'll let you live, but if I get there and he's out, maybe tipped off, I'll come back here and gut you like a hog."

Broer sheathed the knife and stood to leave.

He saw David relax his arms closer to the water, anticipating being left alone.

Faster than David could anticipate, Broer slammed his fist into David's cheekbone, causing David to cry out.

"Don't let your guard down, mate!" he said, laughing loudly as he left the bathroom.

Broer went back into the room where Mary was, walked over to her and grabbed the ropes around her arms.

With a practiced movement he pulled out the knife and sawed through the ropes. He did the same with the rest of the ropes and, as she straightened herself out for the first time in several hours, the pain made her wince.

"You want to get yourself a new boyfriend, sweetheart."

He turned and walked to the landing. Placing a foot on the step it triggered the memory of the surveillance sounds again.

"Oh yeh, I nearly forgot in all this excitement."

He turned back to the pristine door, inspected it for a few seconds, then turned the large, central door knob.

With a click the door opened.

"Helps if you lock it!" he shouted at David, who he saw was reaching cautiously out of the bath for a towel.

The room looked bare. Broer inspected a few of the drawers but no new product had appeared.

He wandered over to the wardrobe in the corner and opened the doors.

The sound seemed right.

Running his hands over the back of the cupboard, it all felt solid. He did the same on the floor and again it felt right.

He was about to give up when he noticed that, in the far corner at the back of the cupboard, there was a small patch of shiny wood.

Reaching in, he pushed down on the far corner and, taking him by surprise, the side near him titled upwards.

Pretty cool, he thought.

Lifting the board, there was what he was looking for.

David's stash of ready cash neatly laid out in two rows of five, except there was a gap where two others stacks would have gone.

"Don't mind if I do," he said, snatching them up and shoving them down the front of his jacket.

This was turning into a good night.

∞

Broer watched Frost wandering about his living room. He hadn't even closed the curtains.

Now parked outside Frost's house, he could see everything through the grand Victorian picture windows.

Frost really had settled into a civilian lifestyle and judging by the way he was going about his evening routine, David has said nothing to him either.

For an operative of Hannover, this was unbelievable.

Broer enjoyed the spectacle for a while longer, thinking about how he'd get in the house.

Frost would be no pushover, but he'd clearly gone soft.

It had been a long time coming, but whatever Broer did now didn't really matter.

All being well, a few hours from now he'd be one old adversary down and heading out of the country.

He looked back out of the windscreen and, down the street, saw his inspiration in the shape of a fast-food shop.

Broer walked out with the pizza and placed it on the front passenger seat of the van.

"Hey, mate," he called over to one of the delivery boys waiting near their mopeds at the side of the shop. "A bit of a strange request, but can I borrow your jacket and helmet for a few minutes? I want to pull a prank on an old friend up the road there."

The two young men looked at each other, unsure what to make of the unusual request.

"Listen," Broer said, pulling his wallet out, "I'll give you 50 pounds and when I'm done I'll bring your stuff back, promise. I get it's weird, but it'll kill him when he sees it's me!"

He held out the money and the man still hesitated, looking back at his friend for guidance on what to do.

"Go on..." his friend said at last, and with that he took the money and handed over his helmet and jacket.

"Be quick though, yeh? I'm still working tonight."

"Great, mate, back before you know it!"

Broer put on the tight-fitting jacket and climbed back in the van.

At the door, Broer pulled the helmet down over his face and turned his back to the window, showing the pizza shop's logo and text to Frost, should he look out of the window.

The door opened.

"24?" Broer said, looking down and fumbling with his back pocket as if searching for an order slip.

"Ah, no, this is 26, you need the next door."

As he spoke Frost stepped forward, pointing to which side number 24 was on and Broer seized his chance.

Lifting the pizza box to Frost's face, he pulled the knife from its sheath and lunged forward at Frost's unguarded stomach.

Broer felt the wet, meaty resistance of muscle as the tip of the blade found its target, but Frost staggered back, stepping into the house, avoiding further injury.

He tried to close the door, but Broer quickly followed, throwing the pizza box aside as he advanced.

Frost had his hand on his stomach—the wound was slight, but the shock of the attack was still to be overcome.

Now inside, Broer kicked the door shut, pulled off the helmet and dropped it to the floor.

"Long time, mate, long time!" he said through gritted teeth.

He tore off the jacket and stood tall before the bleeding Frost, revealing the cruel knife fully for the first time.

"Are you insane! What are you doing here?"

"I've been looking for you for a long time. Must be two or three years now, but who's counting."

"Listen to me, Broer," Frost said, struggling with pain and shock. "What happened wasn't my fault!" he said, now leaning with his free hand against the wall to relieve the pain in his opposite side. "They were nearly out! It was you who sent them down the wrong tunnel!"

Frost stepped back, away from the slowly advancing Broer. His heart was racing and he could feel the bloody bile leaking from his wound.

"Byford gave me that map, it was him who marked it up," he said.

Broer had heard this before.

When the team had got the hostages out of the city and to the border, the tunnels into Egypt were the quickest way out of Gaza. As far as Byford was concerned, Frost had done no wrong.

It wasn't Byford who had gotten the blame, though.

The incident and injury had ended Broer's time with Hannover and while Byford had quit later for other reasons, Frost was still riding high.

Not for much longer—he was about to pay.

Broer shouted, "They got killed because you couldn't read a fokken map! I got taken out because you put us in the wrong place! Six months I was in rehab, do you know what that feels like? I couldn't piss standing up for the first two months. You're all the same, you land niggers and sand niggers. Blaming everyone else when things get messed up, never taking responsibility!"

Much closer now, Broer suddenly bent at the knee and stabbed forward at Frost.

The blade sank into Frost's upper thigh, and with a defensive reflex he swung his fist in a great arc towards Broer.

At the same instant, Broer had straightened up and positioned himself perfectly for the full force of the blow.

His head snapped sideways and he reeled around and away with the force.

Shaking off the pain and shock of the strike, he turned again and spat the blood out at Frost's feet, wiping his mouth with the back of his hand.

"Nice one, mate. It's good to go out fighting."

Frost saw a look of finality in Broer's eyes and turned to run.

From behind, Broer gave a guttural cry of aggression and ran forward.

Much quicker than the injured Frost, he was upon his quarry before he'd gone even a few feet.

Jumping in the air, he raised the knife and brought it slicing down into Frost's back. The blade sank deep between his shoulder blades, thudding into flesh and cracking through bone.

Frost buckled and fell to his knees. Broer grabbed his head and yanked it back.

"Say hello to my team," he said, then slid the knife across Frost's throat.

Blood poured out of the wound, forming a pool on the floor.

Frost gave a final sigh and fell to the ground.

~ 34 ~

"Oh, you're finally in!" Nelson said as he rushed past Melissa.

Arriving at 9.30am wasn't late, normally, but in the middle of an investigation it was practically the middle of the day.

"Sorry," was all she managed before he was out of earshot.

Melissa would have been in earlier, but last night's wine was both welcome and stupid at the same time.

He turned around to face her.

"Get into the war room!" he shouted and continued on his way.

Melissa hesitated for a second, trying to decide if a strong coffee or doing as told was the priority. The coffee won out.

When she arrived to the morning meeting, virtually the whole team was there. Nelson greeted her with a look of mild disgust.

"OK, settle down," he said from the front of the room. "We've had a development. It seems last night someone, a known associate of David Rhett or Rhett himself, paid this guy a visit..."

Nelson turned and tapped a photo of Frost that was hanging on the wall with other clues, pictures and notes.

The photo was just of his face, his eyes closed and his black skin looking dull and flat.

He pinned more photos on the wall, prompting murmurings and noises of disgust from the team.

"I know, it's grim and bloody but this is what we're dealing with now. As you can see it didn't go well. I believe this is related to the group David runs. As of today he's the prime suspect."

An officer raised his hand.

"How do we know it's David? Frost was one of his own, wasn't he?"

"Yes and no. There was a pizza delivery at the time our observation teams were doing handover. They didn't see the delivery boy leave but it doesn't seem significant. What is significant is that a van which was seen leaving David's house was possibly seen on the road where Frost lives, and then arriving and leaving David's house again in the early hours. Whoever is in the van is connected somehow. This guy was killed last night or in the early hours this morning and whoever did it came from David's house."

Another officer spoke up.

"Sir, are we pulling David and Mary back in?"

Nelson put his hands on his hips and let out a sigh.

"No, not yet. The other piece of news is the Home Secretary has ordered a hush on all reporting and questioning while she looks over the case notes."

This news caused even more of a stir than seeing the bloody mess that was Frost.

"I know, I know. But this just got more serious, it's suspected terrorism and murder now. She doesn't want us to rush in, if this is part of something bigger. If this is a UK terrorist cell, she's involved whether we like it or not. I need you all to go back over case notes and info we have, then see what else we can find out. We also have another lead, may be something or nothing. The interesting part of this is that the spooks at SIS got a report from Sanmobile of encrypted voice traffic on their network. Tracing it back to the originator is still ongoing, but I'm betting it's someone we already have our eye on."

"SIS?" someone on the audience asked.

"Secret Intelligence Service, MI6 as they still get called," he replied. "They rebranded. Anyway, what we need to care about is where the calls ended up, they bounced off a mast in the Shetlands. As well as looking into Frost further, I need you communications guys to look into this. SIS are on it, but if they find something funky they might not share, so I want you digging. OK, get lost!"

Nelson waved his arms in the air to dismiss the assembled team.

"Melissa, not you," Nelson called to her before she left the room. "Let Aggard's team do the donkey work, we have another lead. It's a long shot, but there was a repair of a compressor for diving tanks about three weeks ago for a diving instructor up on the Shetlands. He had some guests with him too. Kept to themselves so we've been told, but they were seen doing some odd training for people on a diving holiday. There was a report to local police by some old farmer that he thought some army were up there training, but they dismissed it."

"You think the calls were to the diving instructor?" she asked.

"Come on, don't act dumb! We know one or two of the *other* team went into the sea. They came from the shore's side, too, so they may well have swam in. Like I said, a long shot, but we're going to check it out."

∞

The weather was rainy, cold and windy. Judging by the relaxed demeanour of the ferry crew, this was just another day of regular weather.

"God almighty," Melissa said, her hands deep inside her jacket's pockets.

She tried to pull the coat around her more and dipped her face into the neck of the fur-lined collar.

"It's nay warm, es it?" Nelson said, doing a bad impression of a Scottish accent.

"Why exactly did we need to come here?" Melissa asked.

"What exactly did you do at MI5? Sit behind a desk all day? I thought those guys were always out and about."

"You're getting confused with MI6. I just sat behind a desk all day, breaking into electronics, a little hacking, doing analysis and writing reports."

"Well, in answer to your question, we're here to do old-fashioned police work. We can't leave questioning to the local police. Anyone who encountered the team will remember them and I want us to know about it first. All we have now is some encrypted phone traffic."

"Have we got anything from the office yet?"

Nelson checked his phone. Scanning through his emails, he saw nothing new.

"I guess not, but then signal comes and goes here."

"What will Aggard do when she finds out you've crept off up here?" Melissa asked.

Nelson continued to look at his phone. He'd been avoiding thinking about Aggard.

Now that the Home Secretary was involved they were all meant to stay put; the investigation was essentially suspended. Aggard had made it clear that she would follow orders.

That included chasing down anyone who didn't.

So long as he could stay ahead of her and solving the case, it would be fine.

Nelson sighed deeply and put his phone away.

He pulled out a small notepad from his inside coat pocket, bent the cover back to the next blank page and retrieved a small pencil from the book's spiral bindings.

Melissa watched with a sideways glance and a look of disbelief on her face.

"Really?" she said, screwing up her face in disapproval.

"Yes, really, what have you got?"

"A tablet PC."

"Good luck using that in the street, when it's raining," Nelson said.

He turned his attention back to the notepad and started to write something Melissa had no interest in.

She wanted to be back in the office, behind a computer.

"We're here," Nelson said, knocking Melissa on the arm and snapping her out of her sulking.

When the other travellers had left the ferry, Nelson went to the cabin and presented his badge to the captain.

"We need to ask you a few questions," he said.

"You have jurisdiction here?" the old man asked.

"What? You've been watching too many movies, and last I checked you never went independent. So, yeh, I have jurisdiction. You want to help us here or down at the station?"

"Fine, ask your questions."

Melissa stepped forward, judging that the man needed a gentler touch.

"Think back around two weeks. We believe you would have ferried some visitors."

The man did everything he could to show this was all a lot of bother. He tipped his cap backwards and leant forward against the wheel, letting out a grating sound that Melissa assumed was meant to show he was thinking. "I ferry a lot of people, darling."

Melissa smiled as if finding some hidden wit in the acerbic comment.

"Of course. They would have come as a group, heading for the scuba-diving school."

The man gave another thoughtful growl.

"Now you mention it, I did see some swimmers in the back bay. Didn't get close enough to recognise them, but there were four of them in the water."

"Where would they have been headed?" Nelson asked.

"They seemed to be messing about a lot given it was getting dark. The only property up that end is the old lighthouse cottage. There, I guess."

"And how do we get there?" Melissa asked.

"Take a cab?" the man suggested, pointing back to the dock area where a cab was parked waiting for a fare.

They thanked the man and headed onto the docks.

"Look," Nelson said, pointing to a diving equipment shop.

He flicked through his notepad again, consulting various pages of scribbles.

"Yep, that's our repair man."

They walked into the shop and found the shop owner idly leaning against the counter. After some preliminary questioning, the conversation turned interesting when the he confirmed he'd fixed the tank.

"Can you describe who it was?" Nelson asked.

"I can do better than that, I'll have him on camera." The shop owner pointed to an LED light in the wall. "That's one of them high-definition cameras. My son fitted it, right the wiz with all of this he is. Come back in a few hours and I'll dig out the footage for you."

Melissa and Nelson thanked the man and left the shop, hardly able to believe their luck.

"Now, that is why we needed to have come here!" Nelson said.

Melissa started towards the cab.

"Let's push our luck and get to the house," she said.

Nelson stood back and inspected the exterior of the house.

"Completely locked up and no one here, then."

Nelson's conclusion seemed to be correct. They'd rang the bell, tried the doors and looked through the windows as best they could, but the place seemed empty.

Nelson wandered off down the gravel path, and then a little later came back with a large, jagged rock.

"Are you going to do what I think you're going to do?" Melissa asked.

"Yep, not like the police are going to be coming any time soon, is it!"

Nelson stood in front of the main window and threw the rock as hard as he could.

Instead of crashing through the glass and landing inside the house, breaking furniture and scattering furnishings, it bounced off the window and hit the ground.

"What the hell!" he said.

"Try again," Melissa said softly, already suspecting what may be wrong.

Nelson did as told and the effect was exactly the same.

"It's armoured glass, might be bulletproof," she said.

"Great, so how do we get in?"

∞

The Hannover technician saw the flashing alert on her screen and confirmed the location.

"OP7 advising—we have a possible intrusion attempt," she said into her microphone, informing the supervisor of the event on her screen.

"Location?"

"North 1," she replied, using the ID for the Shetland Island safe house.

The supervisor checked a list on her own screen and saw it was present.

"It's not in use, but call it in, please."

The operative did a mental shift, adopting her fake persona, and dialed the contact number now presented to her by the supervisor.

"Operations, which service do you require?" came the response from the emergency services operator.

"Police, please."

A few clicks later and another voice.

"Police operations, ID and nature of your call?"

"Hey, Proguard Security room here, partner ID is 'Foxtrot Romeo dash two seven four.' We have an alarm going off on one of our properties. Looks like a break-in attempt is taking place. We believe the house is occupied by a lone, elderly gentleman."

"OK, dispatching a unit now."

The call ended and the operative assumed her more real persona once again.

"Response sent, monitoring now," she said to her supervisor.

∞

"Try the door," Melissa said, "surely with enough force you can break the lock off?"

"Why do I think not," Nelson said, lifting the rock to try again anyway.

"Shout if you get in," Melissa said, now walking off around the building to inspect it further.

From the side of the house she could hear the solid banging sound of Nelson trying to batter the door down.

Inspecting the side of the house, she saw what she was looking for.

Built out onto the side of the house was what may have been a toilet or store room in times past. It meant there was a way to climb towards an upstairs window.

She picked up a stone the size of her palm and threw it as hard as she could at the window.

This time the glass shattered.

Nelson came running around to where she was.

"You broke it?"

"I've seen this before. Lower windows made safe and the rest normal. Look here," she said, pointing to an old metallic drainpipe running up the well where the building walls met. "Climb up and go inside and open the door."

∞

The operative spoke again into her microphone. "OP7 escalating—we have a breach."

∞

Nelson climbed onto the low roof of the attached building and, jumping for the window frame, kicked and pulled himself onto the window ledge.

A few grunts and brute-force movements later he had the window opened, and he dropped inside. Melissa ran to the front of the house and a minute later heard the door locks clicking off. They were both inside.

"Look around, we should be as quick as we can," Nelson said.

They split up, Nelson downstairs and Melissa upstairs.

The kitchen area was clean and tidy, looking unused for weeks. He ran a finger across the kitchen table and lifted a very fine layer of dust.

He inspected the rest of the downstairs. Except for some fancy equipment lockers, there was nothing out of the ordinary.

"Nothing!" he shouted upstairs.

Meanwhile, in what looked like the master bedroom, Melissa's attention had been drawn to a small pad of stolen hotel note paper on the bedside cabinet.

She held it up to the light coming through the window and saw the impression of a set of numbers.

"Nothing here either, still looking!" she shouted back over her shoulder.

Nelson went back to the front door and out to the front path.

"Stay where you are!" a voice to his side shouted.

Another came from his other side: "Don't move!"

Two police officers ran towards him, arms outstretched, ready to detain him.

Melissa heard the shouts and bounded down the stairs. Looking through the front door she saw one of the officers cry out, convulse and drop to the floor.

The other pulled out his baton and swung it at Nelson, who ducked and stabbed forward with something.

This time he missed and the officer easily knocked to the floor whatever it was Nelson was trying to attack him with.

In another easy move, he grabbed Nelson's arm and pulled it behind his back.

Nelson tried to free himself but his disadvantage was too great. The officer dragged him backwards and, twisting, sent Nelson down onto the gravel drive.

"Go, go now!" Nelson shouted.

Melissa ran out of the door and past the two men.

As she went by, the officer reached out for her, but keeping a hold on Nelson was his priority.

On the ground she saw what Nelson had used: a Taser stick.

She thought about picking it up but the struggling Nelson again shouted for her to run. A few yards away she hesitated, unclear where exactly she was meant to be running.

"Towards the slope!" Nelson shouted after her.

Looking ahead she saw two fresh sets of footprints in the grass—or, more accurately, in the wetness of the misty rain the grass was now layered with.

She ran on, and as she approached the top of a slope where the lawn disappeared, she saw a police powerboat further down, tied to a rickety-looking mooring at the beach's edge.

She finished her run and scrambled in, breathless and panicked.

Melissa took the wheel and started the engine, thanking her luck that the officers had left the keys in place.

Slowly she moved the boat forward, making sure she didn't sink herself in her ignorance of how to drive this thing. Her thoughts racing, she decided that the priority was to get to the shop for the video evidence and then get off the island.

As she picked up speed and headed for the docks on the other side of the bay, she hoped Nelson was OK. Were they real police, or maybe terrorists too?

Police would still be an issue, but Aggard would be able to sort that out once she'd gotten over being lied to. Terrorists would be another matter.

In the powerboat, the trip across the bay took only a few minutes.

Melissa slowly pulled it up to a spare mooring, bumping it into a row of old tires and attracting a few looks from the locals.

Aware she was still visibly shaken, she composed herself and headed to the diving shop.

∞

Lauren waited for Byford to say something, hearing only background noise over the phone.

She knew the news would hit him hard and as the one in-between camps, it was her job to tell him.

"When did this happen?" he asked in a quiet voice.

"Looks like it was last night or this morning, it just got posted today. The pathologist is doing an autopsy, of course, but the cause is obvious."

"Any idea on who it was?"

"The thinking is it was David Rhett, but it doesn't stack up."

Byford jumped in.

"Idiots! There's no way he did it, he's frightened of his own shadow. He abuses women and druggies, not trained operatives."

There was a pause in the conversation and Lauren allowed him time to fill the silence.

"If he's the prime suspect, he could act irrationally. That's a liability for us. Has there been any response on that?" he said at last.

Lauren smiled to herself. The planning and probabilities she'd reviewed several weeks ago had already factored in the idea of David going loco.

The ace card for Hannover was Byford and his special interest.

"It's been considered, and we're working on a response. I suggest you hang on for an update from the Handler."

"Right," was all he said in reply.

"Byford, it's known you and Frost were in contact and that he was in David's group for a reason. Returning a few favours, shall we say. Trust the process and we'll be in touch."

Byford agreed and ended the call.

He closed his eyes and thought of his old friend.

When his job was done and Mary was back with him, he was going to kill whoever had done this.

~ 35 ~

Not entirely surprised, Lagis saw Buckby across the street.

He'd forgotten how attractive he found her dishevelled look. Tall and slim with shoulder-length dark hair in loose tangles, it was a look he preferred in his women.

She was fidgeting and walking up and down slowly, probably as uncertain about agreeing to meet as he was.

Byford was to be here in a few minutes, assuming he wasn't already observing them before making himself known.

Lagis thought back to the quiet conversation he and Byford had during training. Totally against protocol, but it was welcome.

For Lagis, a team leader taking a personal interest and asking for a way to stay in touch was job security.

It meant Byford would request him on one of his teams in the future and as greenhorn, it meant he was now secure in Hannover. Clearly, it was the same for Buckby too.

Lagis saw her pull out her phone and check the screen for something. A moment later, his vibrated and he saw a text message had come through.

'Westlocks in 15' was all it said.

He looked up and saw Buckby heading off and cut through a pathway between two houses.

If she was on foot she'd have to run to reach the restaurant in 15 minutes. He would have liked to have got her attention and give her a lift, but he thought better of it.

Best to find out what Byford was up to before pushing things further.

He arrived at the Westlocks car park and parked slightly out of the way.

Walking towards the restaurant, he saw Byford at the back of the building, gesturing for him to come over.

Lagis extended his hand and Byford gave him a firm handshake.

"Great to see you again, Lagis. Buckby is already here," Byford said and guided the new arrival inside.

Lagis walked into a small room with four tables and a roaring fire.

At the far table was Buckby, smiling and securing her hair behind her ears.

"What took you?" she asked.

"I'm impressed!"

He walked over to her and kissed her on the cheek.

It was a gesture that seemed appropriate, if overly friendly towards a fellow operative.

"We OK here?" Lagis asked when they were all had sat down.

"The owner may or may not understand who we are and what we do," Byford replied.

"Ah, I see, but you couldn't possibly say," Buckby added, giving a smile.

"Indeed. Now, thanks both of you for coming. As this is business, we have coffee or coffee for you to enjoy," Byford said, reaching out to a flask he brought, then pouring himself a coffee into a disposable plastic cup.

"OK, better than nothing," Buckby said, taking the flask Byford offered and pouring herself a drink.

"You two were the best of the recruits on the mission, despite a few snags along the way," Byford began. "When I took your phone numbers I said I'd be in touch. The reason I've asked you here is I have a problem and I need your help."

"I take it this is off the books?" Lagis asked.

"Completely, yet as with all things Hannover, it's connected with what's on the books."

They settled in, enjoying the warmth of the coffee and fire.

Conversation ranged across the death of Frost, the link to David and the raid and the reason why Byford had been tempted back to active service.

"Wow, the threads we weave," Lagis said when the conversation came to a natural end.

"Despite David's current state of paranoia, he has to maintain a public face by carrying on as normal. There's his usual Wednesday night open house tomorrow. A thing he does with other groups, so you won't be the only strangers there. As in, you both need to get in there and see what's happening."

They discussed what Byford wanted from them being there: mainly intel on Mary and the state of David and his group.

They parted ways and agreed to be back in contact in the next few days.

∞

Melissa opened the door to her apartment and welcomed the silence. The journey out from the Shetlands had thankfully been uneventful.

Since seeing Nelson face down on the gravel, she hadn't heard anything from him.

That was just under 12 hours ago.

She guessed he'd either kept quiet to give her space or was already on his way back, having pulled his ace card of being ASTU.

Either way, neither Nelson nor anyone at the office had been in touch and she was grateful for it.

She ran upstairs, kicking off her boots and throwing her coat over the banister, focused only on deciphering the one piece of information she had gathered from the house.

On her desk she had a homemade piece of equipment that had come in handy several times.

Placing the scrap of paper from the Shetlands on its metal plate, she scattered a mix of graphite, iron filings and other brighter coloured but electrically sensitive material.

She switched the machine on and watched.

Slowly the powder mix started to separate out, heavier material to the bottom and lighter material to the top.

It was like an electrically driven form of gold panning. But in this case, the gold was whatever impression was on the paper.

After a few minutes, she saw the rough lines that formed a phone number.

Starting up her ASTU laptop, she opened the dashboard showing what software she had available.

Selecting the phone number search, she entered the mobile number and initiated a search.

"Who are you?" she whispered to herself as the search started.

∞

Andrew was angry and embarrassed in equal measure. At least Nelson was back, but where the hell was Melissa?

As the head of ASTU, Andrew wouldn't hesitate to have her detained once he found her.

Aggard stood to the left side of Andrew, arms crossed and looking seriously pissed off.

"So once again, where is she?" Andrew asked down the phone.

"I guess she's at home, if she's not in the office. Have you checked?" Nelson said.

"Spare me the wit, we don't go chasing our operatives around. That's what Collection Teams are for. Just be warned, you're in no position to push it right now. They think that officer you attacked had a bloody heart attack. Add to that the fact you weren't authorised to leave here or go breaking into private property!"

Nelson masked a sigh. At 24 hours with no contact, Melissa would officially be AWOL.

If Nelson had a second operative go missing or rogue in the space of a few days, he'd be finished.

Andrew spoke again.

"You need to get a grip, Nelson. She's your responsibility and I don't think she's shaping up. Find her and both of you report in to the operations room."

∞

Melissa stared at the screen, trying to understand what she was seeing. The results had come back and it looked like there was a pattern already.

The mobile number was showing as receiving calls in both the Shetlands and, more recently, southeast England.

This was an interesting enough coincidence, but even more interesting was the fact that calls to the mobile were encrypted.

Had Frost made the calls and, if so, was he playing both sides? Not only part of David's Eco group, which they already knew, but also in touch with the terrorist group?

She needed evidence of what Frost had been up to. She reflected on the conversation with Dr. Kirby. He'd mentioned Hannover in relation to them directing him to steal the bio-fuel research.

What game were they playing?

Somewhere between David's group, the terrorist cell, and Hannover, there was a connection, and she was determined to find it.

Melissa was startled by the door bell ringing.

Her heart started beating harder, the tension in her body rising. ASTU hadn't wasted any time coming for her after the mess up with Broer.

She headed downstairs to her inevitable detention and questioning.

"Coming!" she shouted and made her way to the front door.

She swung it open but instead of an ASTU Collection Team, it was Broer standing there.

Before she could slam the door shut, he advanced on her and forced the door open.

"Hello, bokkie!" he said, following her into the house as she tried to back away from him.

Broer closed the door behind him and went to say something, but Melissa reacted.

"Are you insane? Get out, stay away from me!" she shouted, feeling her fear rising.

"Hey, Melissa, I'm not going to hurt you am I, not you, eh?"

"How do I know what you're going to do!" Her mind was racing with what to do next, but for now Broer remained standing at the front door, coming no further into the house. "Did you kill Frost?" she added.

"Listen to me, Melissa. Yeh, I killed Frost, but for good reason. I'm not here to explain why and I'll be gone soon, so you don't need to worry about me coming back here again."

"What…what…what did you come here for then?" she asked, shocked by his admission to a question she'd asked only to unsettle him. Now she was on the back foot, doing her best to steady her trembling voice and process what she'd just been told.

"To give you a message for Nelson. I'm going and I won't be back. You tell him not to try and follow me or find me. If he does, I'll come back and look for him; right after I do full disclosure and drop the whole organisation in the dirt."

"You know if you disclose, they'll kill you?" she said softly, regaining her composure a little as she heard a touch of desperation in Broer's voice.

"Listen, ASTU aren't the ones to worry about. But don't panic, lovely, I'm one step ahead of them too," he said.

"Hannover?" she said, wanting to test his response once more and from what she saw, that was a correct guess.

He straightened and looked her directly in the eyes.

"Good try, but go and talk to the doctor if you want to know about them."

She thought back to her solo conversation with Kirby and was sure she'd never related anything to Broer afterwards.

So he knew about Hannover too. The pieces were really starting to come together, but not in the way she'd imagined.

He turned and opened the door.

"Tell Nelson what I said."

He held her gaze, attempting to project strength and a silent warning, but she saw something different in his eyes.

He turned to leave.

"Why did you really come here?" she asked.

It seemed he was about to speak, but instead he looked down. "I came to say I'm sorry," he said, his voice hoarse and low. Eyes still on the floor, he opened the door and left.

Melissa stood rooted to the spot, his words swirling around her mind.

She shook off her stupor and checked her watch.

There was still time to make one more visit, before she really had to report in and be back under Nelson's watchful eye.

~ 36 ~

Melissa walked up the short pathway to Frost's front door and to the officers posted there.

"ASTU, I'm with the investigation," she said, showing them her badge. "You have the house locked up already?"

"Yes, forensics were too busy to come yet," the officer replied.

"Since when!" Melissa said, knowing as the officers did that a scene needed to be processed as quickly as possible.

"Since the Home Office got involved is the rumour. We're to wait for their team."

Melissa needed to act quickly, to get in before they asked too many questions.

She went back to her car and, opening the boot, retrieved one of the forensics kits she kept there.

Returning fully dressed, except for shoe covers and gloves, she approached the officers again.

"Well, open up then. I'll do preliminaries before the main team get here."

The two officers hesitated and Melissa jumped in before they could start blocking her.

"There were two shields on that badge. Who do you think ASTU belongs to?" she asked, pulling on her gloves and trying to emanate an air of unchallengeable authority.

A glance between the officers showed the ruse had worked, and the door was opened.

Melissa placed on the shoe covers and stepped inside, straight into the living room.

She half turned and impatiently waved her hand at the nearest officer.

"Close the door please! We need to preserve the environment."

He bought the made-up concept and did as instructed.

From outside, Frost's house looked large, but now Melissa could see it was an extreme version of a townhouse design.

Three stories up and one down, but shallow to the point of looking like there was a room missing at the back of the house.

From where she stood in the living room, she could see the pool of blood that had carried Frost's life away with it, still where it had formed near the doorway to the kitchen, but now hardened and black.

There was so little space there was no hallway, and the stairs to the next floor were at the back of the living room.

She walked slowly from the front door into the middle of the room, taking her time to get a feel for Frost and how he might have lived.

The room was furnished in a contemporary way, but sparsely. Probably on account of the space, she thought to herself.

On the far wall, under the stairs, there was a small phone table with a simple handset. She lifted it and heard the dialing tone, but the phone was so basic it would hold no secrets; there wasn't even a redial button.

Melissa shook her head to pull her thinking together.

"Come on," she said to herself, walking quickly to the stairs and jogging up them.

They led to a small landing where she saw the two rooms here were the bathroom and bedroom, not what she was looking for.

She ran up the next flight and emerged in an attic area that had been converted into an office, and here she saw the prize.

∞

"You were lucky he didn't throw the book at you," Aggard said to Nelson as he washed his hands.

The conversation may well have been private, but her following him into the men's toilets hadn't been very subtle and had been more than a little off putting.

"Have you heard from her yet?"

"You know I haven't," he replied, now drowning her voice out with the sound of the hand dryer.

She switched it off at the wall.

"In three hours she's AWOL and it doesn't look good even now. She's looking like an amateur, or she's hiding something."

Nelson said nothing in response.

All he knew now was they hadn't found her at home or been able to reach her on her phone.

No matter what amount of time had gone by, she was already making him look bad.

First they let David go, then Broer went off the rails, followed by the Home Office interest, and now Melissa.

This investigation was not going the way he had hoped.

"I get it, but Melissa is probably just mentally recovering or something. She's very highly strung. I expect we'll see her soon and we can deal with it then."

"You're still making excuses for her? You're screwed if she messes up, you do understand that? Andrew's already taken over at the Home Secretary's request, so I'm in no position to help you anymore."

"Yes, I understand and I thank you for getting some breathing space off Andrew. Let's go and see him. Maybe we can pull David in, process Frost's place, chase up the call tracking or just pull one of this investigation's loose threads together!"

∞

"Shit," Melissa said aloud as she stood from the desk.

She'd looked over Frost's laptop for anything useful, but found nothing.

That was a very complete and suspicious nothing too, the computer was as clean as if it had just been installed, which meant she was missing something.

It had definitely been used though, that much she was certain of from the scratches on the keyboard and Frost's fingerprints on the screen.

She checked the computer's file system and there on screen was confirmation of her suspicions.

The hard disk was more than half full. Even with this being a small notebook, a clean install of the operating system didn't take this much space.

That could only mean one thing, there were a lot of hidden files, but how to access them was eluding her.

She wracked her memory for what she was missing, thinking back to the computer forensics course she'd done when with MI5.

With a determined look on her face, she held the computer with both hands aside the screen.

Hidden on this laptop were files she needed access to, but the tools to do that were not here, they were at her home.

"All done," she said cheerfully to the two officers as the front door was opened.

She tied the arms of the suit around her waist and pulled off her cap.

"Find anything of interest?" one of the officers asked.

"Nothing. Except for a blood stain, the place is as clean as a whistle. I'll report that in and make sure they bring the full forensics kit. Keep it closed up until we get back."

She thanked them and walked back to her car.

Sitting on the rim of the car boot, Melissa untied the arms of her suit and let the laptop drop gently behind her.

She whipped off the rest of the suit and placed it on top of the stolen device, then slammed the boot closed.

As she walked around to the driver's seat, she saw the officers weren't even looking at her. She jumped in and headed to the station in search of more clues.

∞

Andrew looked up from his desk and eyed Nelson and Aggard with caution.

"Sir, have we got a green light on David yet? I was hoping we could…"

"Could what," Andrew asked, "mess up even more? Have you got you girl back yet?"

Nelson lied almost as a reflex.

"Yes, sir. She's investigating a lead from the Shetlands. I had a call from her about an hour ago. Apologies, I thought that had been fed back to you."

"Well, about time! But no, no one told me! Get her back here and a report written up as soon as possible. Now, we have more important things to address than some greenhorn."

Andrew picked up then tossed down a manila folder of papers onto the table.

"In answer to your earlier question, the Home Secretary has responded with her team's analysis. She's authorised the paperwork for David, naming him as the lynchpin for the terrorist attack and naming his group a known terrorist organisation."

"Do we really think that?" Nelson asked.

"That's not for you to question, is it, Nelson? Get in there and arrest him if you can. He ceases to operate by any means necessary."

Andrew flipped open the folder and on top of the papers was the signed order to detain David and authorising the use of deadly force if necessary.

"So we've lost control of the investigation?" Nelson said.

The question was ignored as being a point evident to everyone.

"Right then," Aggard said, moving quickly in the new direction they'd just been pointed, "I'll make the preparations with the firearms team."

"No, you'll provide the regular force," Andrew said to her surprise. "The armed officers are being specially provided for this one."

They both looked at Andrew for a second, expecting to be told more.

"Use your imagination," he said softly, as if talking to a pair of slow-witted children, closing the manila file.

They both made positive noises as if having a clear understanding and turned to leave.

∞

"ASTU, I'm with the investigation," Melissa said for the second time this afternoon.

Receiving a nod from the receptionist, she replaced her badge into her coat and stood waiting to be guided to the storage room.

"We've laid him out for you," an assistant said as she appeared from around the corner, indicating to Melissa she should follow her.

They arrived in the autopsy room, and in the middle on a shiny steel bed was Frost.

"His effects are here in the tray," the women said. "I'll be outside when you've finished."

Melissa walked over to Frost, who was fully covered with a crisp white sheet.

She pulled the cloth down and saw the slash across his throat that had been the source of the blood in the house and cause of his death.

"Jesus," she muttered on seeing the injury, and pulled the cloth back over his face.

Turning to the items in the tray she tried his mobile first, but the battery was drained.

"Great," she said aloud, tossing it back in the tray.

She took out his wallet and emptied the contents, carefully laying them on the table the tray had been placed on. It was all the usual stuff: bank cards, a coffee card and a few notes.

She was about to close the wallet, when the light caught a small rectangular raised area of leather, at the bottom of a pocket.

Running her fingers inside, she retrieved a miniature memory card.

"Now why are you keeping that there?"

∞

"Why the hell did you just lie to him?" Aggard asked.

"I don't know, it just came out and anyway what am I supposed to do? Tell him I've lost control of my other senior team member? Broer and Melissa aren't the only ones working on this you know!"

Nelson tipped his head to the investigation team working in the war room behind them.

"I need to arrange a team to go in and get David, supporting whoever the armed team are," Aggard said.

"When will you do it?" Nelson asked, wondering how long he had to straighten things out.

"Too late for today, probably tomorrow afternoon or early evening. Assuming Andrew agrees."

Aggard leant into Nelson and lowered her voice to avoid the team overhearing.

"You need to find Melissa, get her back in here and pull your part of the investigation together. Rescue what you can. Once we have David, the spotlight will be on you to wrap this case up."

They parted ways and Nelson walked off into the War Room.

He checked over the incident board. A few items had been added, more lines had been drawn to make connections between information and evidence, but it was nothing conclusive.

He sat at his desk, lounging back in his chair and pushing his feet into the desk's edge. He felt the need to comfort eat to ease the stress. That or drink.

Melissa was hopefully just being Melissa and would come back with something soon.

"Nothing on Broer?" he shouted across the office.

Various replies confirmed Broer was still out in the wild somewhere.

Dropping his feet off the desk, he leaned forward and placed his head in his hands, closing his eyes and taking the strain off his neck. He could feel the start of a migraine forming.

What are you doing, Broer? he thought to himself.

Nelson thought through what he knew about Broer.

He'd seemed like a good friend once, but in the last 12 months or so a distance had grown between them.

As if far away, he heard a voice calling his name and returned his mind to the office.

"Yes?"

"Sir, the shift log at Frost's house states an ASTU Operative visited them earlier."

He jumped up from his chair.

"Right, good work," he said and bolted from the office.

∞

Now outside the mortuary and back in the relative privacy of her car, Melissa threw the laptop onto her knees, pushed the memory card into the side slot and turned the computer on.

A spinning globe appeared on screen.

"Yes, come on," she said to herself, seeing her belief of the laptop having a dual-boot system was proving correct.

The globe disappeared and was replaced by an empty oval shape, traced as a simple black outline.

She waited, wondering what was to happen next.

The webcam switched on and she appeared on screen within the oval. Red dots danced across her face, searching for key facial features. Two came to rest on her left eye and turned green, but the rest remained red.

The oval itself now turned red, the computer beeped twice and shut down.

"Shit!" she cursed aloud.

Her thoughts went to Frost, his dead face staring up from his temporary death bed.

She could take the laptop in and place it in front of him, but then she'd be inside with this valuable asset.

A better idea struck her.

She leapt out of the car and around to the boot. There, in a small box, was the impression kit.

She grabbed it and headed back in to see Frost once more.

∞

"What did she say she was there for?" Nelson asked.

"She showed us her badge and said she was there to start the forensics work on the house, just like my end of day report says."

The officer stood there with a blank look on his face, determined that whatever trouble the woman was in, it was none of his fault.

"Did you see her take anything?"

"Nothing, she left as she went in."

"OK, thanks. You can head home."

The officer nodded to his inspector and left.

"Seems your girl is doing her own thing then?" the inspector asked.

"Yes, looks like it. Well, thanks for your time."

Nelson gave him a handshake and left.

Exactly what threads Melissa was chasing he didn't know, but chasing up leads alone was not on. ASTU couldn't risk loners in the team.

If she was following leads on Frost, there was one more place to try.

∞

The combined structure of Alginate and bandages was not quite dry, but Melissa was beginning to get panicked at how long she'd been in one place.

She had to assume someone would find her and if they did, the laptop needed to stay in her care. Further evidence for the man in the photo at the diving repair shop, links to who Frost was connected with and possibly something more on Hannover were likely all hidden on it.

This was her moment to break a case singlehandedly and she wasn't about to blow it.

She could almost feel the congratulations and praise, imagining a promotion at long last and an end to being seen as the odd one in the team.

Just the thought of it gave her a warm glow, causing her to smile.

She tested the mask again and decided it was hard enough. Pulling at the corners and prising it off gently, she started to free it from Frost's face.

His skin remained stuck to it in places and pulled, risking breaking the mask.

She poked and held his flesh with her fingers and the feel of it repulsed her.

A few tugs and pulls further, the mask came free.

Melissa inspected it and while not perfect, it was a good enough reverse image of Frost for what she needed.

Packing up her equipment once more she placed the mask in a plastic bag, pushing it up inside to help stop the mask deforming.

With one last glance at Frost, she pulled the sheet back over his face and left for her car.

With everything secured back in the boot, Melissa smiled again. Despite the risks, it was a good day spent feeling free. Finally she was doing what she'd wanted to do.

A solo operative, investigating, chasing clues, using her know how and technology to solve the mystery.

It was why she'd studied such varied fields in university, why she joined MI5.

She checked her watch and saw her solo time was nearly up. It was the perfect time to report in.

Lifting her phone from her pocket, she pulled up Nelson's number and dialed.

It rang and she heard a strange echo of the ring tone in her other ear.

"Melissa!" a voice shouted from a short distance away.

There, across the car park to the hospital, was Nelson.

Melissa was dumbstruck for a moment and then a mild panic set in as she thought about what was in the boot of the car.

"Where the hell have you been? Your phone has been off and you haven't been home!"

"What, I have been home!" she lied. "I got back from the Shetlands and went home. I thought it was better than rolling into the office without you and having to explain, especially after your actions up there!"

Nelson was fazed for a second by the way she'd reflected her absence into it being his fault.

He recovered his senses.

"What are you doing here?"

"Old-fashioned policing, as you advocated, remember?"

"Why didn't you call in or something? You're presumed AWOL. Tell me you found something?" he said, the frustration with her evident in his voice.

"Nothing, there was nothing at the house and just his dead mobile here. I have no way to charge it, so I left," she said, gesturing to the hospital.

"Right, that's just great. We'll get his mobile collected. What about the video imagery from the shop?" he asked, chasing one last thread of hope.

Her stomach and chest tensed, in the way it sometimes does when your physiology knows you're going to lie before your conscious has registered it.

"It was too blurry. The camera set-up was next to useless."

Nelson threw his arms up in frustration.

"Damn it!" he shouted, as if trying to expel the bad news from inside himself. "We have nothing then and they're going in for David tomorrow!"

"For questioning?" she asked.

"No, Melissa, to end the case and give the Home Office a win. From tomorrow, this investigation is over."

~ 37 ~

"Yes, of course. As always, these investigations never quite go as planned."

"Yes, well, that's why we make alternate plans, we can't always know what people will do or how things will unfold. Are you sure you can pull her out at this time? A little bird tells me things are coming to a head," Steven said.

Andrew thought on the question for a few seconds. Pulling team members off an investigation and changing the course of it midway would usually raise questions.

In this case, however, the Home Office had made a call and he could say he was just re-aligning to that. With Melissa's recent behaviour it would probably be expected.

Anyway, the investigation be damned.

David was always there as a potential fall guy, even if he wasn't the actual culprit. Hannover wanted to take advantage of the Home Office meddling as much as he did.

They'd get the outcome they wanted and eyes off their people, and Andrew's debts would be squared away. Everyone wins.

"I have the perfect window. And your man is ready, is he?" Andrew asked.

"He will be on a moment's notice. He's been biting at the chomp, as they say, for weeks. Let's get him in there and wrap this up, shall we?"

"Let's do that, wish me luck with my performance!" Andrew said.

Steven laughed. He always appreciated that there was a level of acting needed in all they did, and it was good to see others sharing that understanding.

"Break a leg!" Steven replied.

Andrew thanked him and hung up.

∞

Nelson walked around his desk, threw his car keys down and dropped into his chair.

Thankfully, Melissa had made it back before him. Though given she'd made zero progress the last couple of days, this wasn't something to celebrate.

"Sir, the boss wants to see you," the officer said, slightly out of breath and clearly having been told to find Nelson quickly.

"What the hell is this about? We were just in with him," he said, referring to the recent conversation with Andrew that was still playing on his mind.

"No idea, he just said to get you urgently."

Nelson thanked the officer and made his way to Andrew's office.

"You wanted to see me, sir?"

"Yes, come in, sit down."

Nelson did as he was told, but prepared himself for a lecture.

Andrew had come around to the front of the desk and leant back on it, screwing his face up and looking to the floor as if in deep thought.

"This investigation has not progressed as I expected. It's making me and the ASTU look bad. What's worse is that it looks to me like you have no control over it," Andrew said.

Nelson was about to speak but he was stopped.

"Hang on!" Andrew cautioned. "I don't want you to reactively defend yourself! Let's look at this rationally. You have no leads, just a smattering of evidence that may or may not be connected. Your right-hand man, Broer, has gone missing and is a possible suspect in the murder of Frost. Your main suspect to the attack on the refinery, linked only by a necklace, that will never stand up in court, was released without charge and we're left to pull him on drugs."

Nelson held his hand up to interrupt, but Andrew did the same to silence him.

"A major terrorist attack on UK soil and what have you got? Nothing! A dead man and a necklace!"

Andrew stood and walked to the back of the desk, remaining standing when he got there.

Nelson saw his gap.

"Sir, we have other leads. We know there was another team at the refinery and this isn't what David and his friends do."

"Nelson, you're not hearing me, I'm pulling the investigation. Wrap up anything your team have and box up the war room. Once we pull David in—with help, I'm embarrassed to say—the whole thing transfers to the regular forces."

Nelson sat back on his chair, finally accepting defeat.

The last few weeks he'd been doing all he could to keep the investigation on track, but he'd felt it falling apart almost from the start.

He felt he was supposed to argue against the decision, but he already knew they had run out of time. Sitting there, he felt beaten up by the events of the past weeks, and he was almost relieved it looked to be coming to an end.

Since the Barton Incident, which had been the catalyst for the formation of ASTU, this was only the first of now three major terrorist attacks they had made no progress on.

It was just what the older forces had been waiting for after ASTU's earlier successes. Unfortunately, the failure had happened on his watch.

"Fine…" he said, letting out a blast of air as if finally letting go. "I'll wrap up and start the clear down."

"Good. One more thing before you go. Melissa. I'm not happy about her. Melissa is off the rails, she's unstable. She can't be part of ASTU anymore."

"Sir? She joined us only recently. This is only her second investigation. Her work on her first was exemplary."

"Agreed, but it looks like beginner's luck. She was kicked from MI5, did you know that? Now I'm kicking her from ASTU. Bring your girl in, and debrief her," he said.

"Sir?" was all Nelson could manage as he took in the magnitude of what was happening.

"It's you or her, Nelson," Andrew said, sounding more like he was advising than threatening.

"Debriefed, sir, are you certain?" Nelson asked to confirm that this was it for her.

"Certain."

∞

Melissa looked up from her desk and saw Nelson, walking to her with an expression of frustration and embarrassment on his face. The two others with him were unknown to her; they were in plainclothes, wearing black polo shirts, and she figured they were technicians and her heart leapt.

Had they found the laptop?

Nelson stepped forward and stood to her side but slightly behind her, facing her desk.

"Melissa, I've been instructed to advise you..." Nelson cleared his throat. "You're to leave your system as it is, clear your desk and hand over to IT here."

"Clear my desk? So I'm off the investigation?" Melissa asked with surprise in her voice, though mentally she'd already prepared for this.

"Yes, what's more you're to submit yourself for debrief."

Melissa stared wide eyed at Nelson, the full meaning of the words taking time to sink in.

"I'm sorry," he said, holding his hand out.

Her body froze and mind went blank. For a full three seconds she stared at Nelson, appearing not to notice his outstretched hand, before taking in a ragged breath. She reached into her jacket and took out her badge holder and handed it to him. He turned and walked away, leaving her alone with the technicians.

Melissa grabbed what few personal items she had on her desk and nodded to one of the technicians.

There was nothing else to give up except her door pass. He guided her out from the desk and she walked ahead of him towards the exit.

Outside she felt the cool air hit her face, and tears forming in her eyes.

An overwhelming feeling of loneliness swept over her as she walked to her car. A feeling she had lived with most of her young life.

Here it was again, an empty coldness.

No words came to her mind, just feelings and images.

She sat in her car and leant forward on the steering wheel, hitting it several times with her fists and letting the tears fall.

For the first occasion in a long time, she thought about her parents and the sadness mixed with anger. She'd had a mother who had barely cared to raise her and a father who had vanished from her life before she had a chance to know him.

She thought of her joy at joining MI5 and the sense of validation and purpose it had given her, then how it had turned out to be nothing like she imagined.

Now ASTU was abandoning her, to what future she couldn't even imagine.

Eventually the tears ran out and the images stopped.

She sat back in her seat, feeling calmer, wiping the wetness from her face.

There was one possible way forward, just an idea, but it was all she had right now. Maybe a crazed idea born of desperation, but there was nothing to lose in trying.

Starting the engine, Melissa headed for home, aware that the clock was ticking on her future.

Melissa pulled the car into the garage and made sure the garage door was closed before getting out of the car.

From here on, she couldn't take any risks or make any mistakes.

She opened the boot of the car and retrieved the laptop and plastic bag containing the fragile mask.

Heading upstairs to her bedroom she set the items down on her bed.

After a few minutes rummaging in the cupboard she found what she was looking for—an old wig stand that had held a sharply cut, jet-black wig in her teens.

She turned back to the bed and took the fragile mask in her hands.

Looking inside she saw for the first time the ghostly image of Frost's face formed by the white Alginate and the impression being a reverse image.

Snapping herself out of the spell the mask had put her under, she shot downstairs to the kitchen Unlike most people, who might have cleaning products under their sink, she instead kept the rest of her investigative supplies there.

She found the latex liquid that would be needed for the next step.

A few minutes later she'd rigged up a place on the kitchen table to hold the mask horizontal and secure.

Melissa spent the best part of the next hour smearing in thin layers of latex and drying it with a hairdryer. This would be a weak mask, but it would serve the purpose she needed it to.

Carefully teasing at the upper edges of the latex, she freed the freshly made mask from its marginally sturdier mould.

She took a knife and carefully cut eye holes and slit the mouth.

To complete the final step, she raced back to the bedroom with her new creation.

Heading to the dresser again, she placed the mask over the wig stand and dragged her make-up sets closer.

∞

"Anything from her system?" Nelson asked.

"Nothing, it's pretty clean. She kept a very structured file system and version controlled everything. There's nothing on here I don't think you're not expecting," the technician told him.

Nelson struggled with the words for a second but decided he understood what was meant.

"OK, great, compare it with the intranet documents and anything that matches, delete off here. Anything new, back it up please."

Nelson saw Andrew waving at him from his office. He walked over to him, leaving the man to do as asked.

"Andrew," Nelson said as a greeting when in the office.

"The occupational psychologist is available for Melissa tomorrow morning," Andrew said.

"For?"

"What do you mean, for? For debrief of course."

"We have a psychologist doing that now? I thought it was just someone in HR," Nelson said, sounding genuinely confused.

"Maybe when you first started, but now it's all moved on. That's your problem, Nelson, you've fell behind the times."

Nelson thought he might be right, he didn't even know what an occupational psychologist was.

"Right, got it. Do you contact her or do I?" he asked.

"No, Nelson, they do! For god's sake."

∞

Melissa stepped back and looked at the mask.

For having a mix of spray paint, acrylic paint from an old hobby kit and make up on it, the mask looked unmistakably like Frost, at least to her eyes.

It was a strange thing to see his disembodied head floating a few inches about her dressing table.

She pushed it aside, turned and grabbed the laptop from the bed.

Switching it on, she saw it starting in the hidden operating system it was now using, as the memory card was still in place.

Quickly but carefully she lifted the mask from the stand and placed it over her face. The fit was loose, but it stayed on.

Unlike before, her face didn't appear on the screen, but instead her creation of Frost's did.

Red dots danced around the image in front of her, one by one they turned green and then the oval surrounding the image turned green.

Melissa's heart skipped a beat.

She was in.

She took the mask off and set to work.

The number of files on the system was more than she had imagined, and they painted a long and complete picture of what Frost had been up to.

In memos and emails there were full details of what seemed to be his current mission, getting in touch with Byford out in Spain, where Byford could be found, mention of reuniting Byford with Mary as his motivation to come back to service.

There was a brief mention of Mary's connection with David and a memo to tell Byford she was now under David's malign control.

Looking at the dates of emails and those stated in the documents, Melissa started to see how what she was reading and what they'd gotten from the investigation could start to be fitted together.

It was clear that she was closer to the real people who'd orchestrated the attack; these were far more organised than David's group ever could be.

She turned her attention to the audio recordings and for the next two hours listened with excitement as more details became clear.

Several times, the name of Hannover was mentioned. Now there was no doubt they existed and she now knew two of their operatives and a doctor that was involved.

Her excitement built at her growing insight and, listening on, she started to piece together the true relationship between Byford and Mary.

Frost must have literally recorded every call.

She cursed herself for not having gotten Frost's phone.

Melissa's eyes went wide and she stood up with the shock of realising that this was her way in—she could help finish Frost's mission.

She paced her room for a few minutes, her mind racing with what she could do next.

There were dangers, but she was adrift with nothing to lose and maybe, just maybe, they would forgive her intrusion and be favourable to her for intervening.

Melissa saw the self-image she often held, a lost child unsure of being in danger, being insecure and taking risks. That hadn't got her anywhere so far except abandoned at every turn.

"Fuck it," she said and, sitting back down, opened the email client and typed 'Byford' in. His email address was automatically filled and she began to write.

∞

The senior security agent peered over his junior colleague's shoulder, taking in what was on screen.

That agent had just been alerted to the fact a dead operative was sending emails.

"OK, I want a freeze on any communications that aren't between Byford and Frost's account."

"Confirming you don't want a complete block?"

"No, the damage is done now; let's see what else we get."

"Understood. Rerouting all other network traffic away from the subjects."

The senior security agent stepped back and looked over the screens in the operations room.

From here he could see live threats to the network, data movements and a host of other information. Allowing for a dead man sending emails, nothing looked out of place.

"Any location or identification yet? Tell me it's not those blood hackers SorceSek!" he said.

"Sorry, nothing yet. It's coming over our encrypted network, so we're just getting data as it arrives and leaves right now. It's definitely not a SorceSek hack though."

"Good, a hacking attempt again right now would be all we need! OK, so strictly the network is secure, we just have a compromised unit which we can kill on command. Alert the operative, Byford, and hand this back to him."

The junior member of staff pulled up an application on screen and sent Byford a text message.

∞

The phone next to Melissa lit up and vibrated against the desk. She stopped the latest audio recording she was listening to and read the message that had just come through.

It was simple, 'Debrief at 0900 tomorrow', along with details of what office to go to.

She had no idea how long or what format an ASTU debrief would take or even who it was with, but everyone knew what it meant.

So that was it. She felt her heart sink.

Turning back to the laptop, she checked the emails again but there was nothing new.

Going back to the audio file, she continued to listen.

∞

Byford raced to his system and opened up his email. There, as stated in the text he'd just received, was a new one from Frost's account.

It was entitled 'A friendly outsider.'

He opened it and read the message.

> Byford,
> My name is Melissa and for the next few hours I am an ASTU operative. As you will have guessed, I have access to Frost's laptop.
> Reading through the files on this system, I am now aware, to some degree, that Hannover are a key part of what ASTU are investigating.
> It is not my intention to reveal any information about yourself or Hannover. I am, however, interested in how I may be of assistance to Hannover.
> As proof of this I will tell you that I have kept the following hidden from anyone at ASTU:
> - You were seen on the camera at the diving repair shop in the Shetlands
> - I have Frost's phone number from an impression on the hotel pad you used

In addition to assisting you by hiding the above, I would also tell you there is to be an armed raid on David's house tomorrow. Given your relationship to Mary, I believe you would want to know this.

I hope the above helps you trust me enough to get in contact in some way.

Melissa – (05555 827 194)

Byford read over the email again, trying to ensure he'd understood not only the content, but also how someone other than Frost had been able to send it, whatever their motivation really was.

No one had ever approached Hannover like this as far as he knew. It was always Hannover that did the contacting.

The girl had even left her mobile number. She was either dumb or desperate.

His mind went to the line about the raid on David's house and his tension rose.

Mary would be there and a firearms raid was not what he wanted her in the middle of. An image of her being shot flashed into his mind.

He wanted to call Melissa, to believe he could do something.

This was not an option though—the person on the other end of that email could be anyone.

He replied to the text message, 'Kill the system.'

The expected 'failed to send' message text came back, but he knew they had received it.

His thoughts went back to Mary.

The raid was well timed, many people that probably needed arresting would be there.

The extra problem was, two of them were there because he'd sent them and they absolutely couldn't be arrested.

∞

Melissa tore the headphones off her head as fast as she could, but not before the high pitched squeal had made her leap from the chair.

The headphones pulled and swung against the dresser.

"Jesus!" she shouted as she stood up, holding her ears.

She looked back at the laptop and the screen was completely blank.

Checking the power the laptop was off. A few minutes of testing confirmed the system had been fried.

∞

"System killed," the security engineer said aloud to his supervisor.

"Good, did you get the shot beforehand?"

"Yes, two actually. Miss Daisy was falling asleep by the looks of it."

The engineer showed the two web camera screenshots he had taken. One of Melissa's face full on, eyes closed and headphones on. The other was her leaping from the chair, arms flailing and headphones mid-air.

"That's a classic," the supervisor said. "Better get the first one over to operations ASAP."

"Whose group?"

"Byford is with Anthear right now."

The engineer nodded his understanding and sent the image on.

~ 38 ~

"I'm here for debrief," Melissa said as she entered the office.

"Come in, take a seat."

Melissa walked over to the chair being pointed out for her and sat down. She looked up at the woman, who was dressed in a smart, dark business suit and white blouse, with her hair tied back and glasses on.

She thought she looked more like a lawyer, not an HR person or psychologist or whatever these people really were in ASTU.

"Melissa, isn't it?"

"Yes, that's right. I've been sent for debrief, whatever that is, doctor... is it doctor?" Melissa asked.

"Ah, no, sadly I am not a doctor. I never got that far with my studies," the woman said, removing her glasses and smiling. "Just call me Lauren."

Melissa visibly blanched at the mention of the name, but shook away the idea of it being David's Lauren.

"Melissa, I'm guessing you know what Debrief means?" Lauren asked.

"It means I'm being kicked off the team."

Lauren smiled at Melissa's directness, taking it as a measure of how she could speak directly to her in return.

"Yes and no. Strictly speaking you've already been kicked off, this is preparing you for what's next. I want to see where you are now and where you want to go next. See how ASTU can use you next," Lauren said.

"If at all, I assume you mean?" Melissa asked.

"That is always a possibility, and in truth the most likely outcome. Life with ASTU is stressful and some people come and go quickly. I've been told you've already had some stressful events happen," Lauren said.

Now someone else had confirmed that she really was getting kicked out, the truth of it sank in fully. An image of no longer being with ASTU momentarily flashed before her mind.

She wondered if Byford had received her message.

The feeling of cold and loneliness overcame her again.

Lauren waited for Melissa to bring her attention back to the room, it was interesting and insightful seeing how she was reacting already.

"When you think of what's happened recently, how you've arrived at this point, what comes to mind?" Lauren asked in a soft and mild tone.

Melissa thought about the question, running through the emotions as they arose in her.

"Anger, disappointment, frustration, loneliness," she said in a slow and determined way.

Lauren sat back in her chair and left some silence at the end of Melissa's answer.

"Can you recall, when was the first time you felt these emotions?"

Melissa looked at the woman and wondered where these questions were going. This was psychoanalysis, not an exit interview.

"When my father left," she replied directly, surrendering to whatever process was being played out.

"I'm surprised you remember," Lauren said.

Melissa looked at her directly and tilted her head to the side, studying Lauren's face.

"I see you know more about me than you're letting on," she said.

"It's our job to do so."

Melissa knew that was the case, but it was still alarming in a way how much they did know.

She sat back in her chair.

"I don't, to answer your question. I don't remember him leaving, I remember realising he'd left and what that meant."

The two women talked for the next hour, going over Melissa's history and coming up to the current time with the incidents in ASTU.

Lauren skillfully played on Melissa's insecurity, her obvious sense of loss and lack of place in the world.

It was mostly textbook, but Melissa, being as bright as she was, proved to be a tricky quarry to direct to where Lauren could deliver the final strike.

Lauren started the build-up, using an artful blend of word skills, metaphors and psychological principles. Melissa seemed to be focused and listening intently.

She decided to push it.

"Sometimes we have to draw a line and say that was me then and this is going to be me now and in the future. There's always a way forward and that means leaving what you know behind, stepping forward into the unknown a little. We do this every day, but usually by accident. Instead of the meandering way that happens so often in our lives, do it on purpose this time."

"I thought I had found a way forward, then and now," Melissa said, alluding to her jumping over to ASTU and now risking contacting Hannover.

The more she thought about that the more she convinced herself what a stupid move it had been. She'd be lucky if they just forgot about her and somehow got the laptop back, never mind recruited her.

Melissa made an audible tutting sound.

"Something you want to share, Melissa?"

"No, no, I was just thinking about where I go from here. It's all well and good you saying move forward, but where to? That's the question."

"It's not for me to say, Melissa. Do you know where you want to be going ahead?"

"I want to be doing what I do best: investigation, solving mysteries, and I want to be part of a team that wants to be a team."

"Have you any ideas where you could do that? No options you've uncovered or tried to approach lately?" Lauren said, continuing to play her.

Melissa felt her face flush at the suggestion. She remembered again what Kirby had said about the subtle approach first made to him and how David had mentioned a Lauren.

It felt like subtle probing and clues were being laid out.

"No. Don't you?" she asked. "Do you have any suggestions, any feedback?" she added, just in case there really was a game being played.

"Well, as you ask, I know people in the industry of course, but if you decide to move forward you have to do it yourself, as I've already said. I could at best only show you a path, but you need to choose to walk it."

Melissa was lost in thought for a time. Lauren left her like that, waiting for her mind to fix on a yes or no.

"I'd need to know where the path led to," Melissa said after some time.

"Naturally, you wouldn't hand over your future to just any organisation," Lauren replied.

"OK, how do we do this?" Melissa asked at last.

"I'll introduce you to someone, you have a chat and make your decision. We could go this evening if you would like?"

Melissa paused again and after a second replied.

"Yes, please introduce me."

Lauren smiled and reaching forward, touched Lauren on the hand.

"Great. This will be the right direction for you, Melissa," Lauren said.

Melissa took a moment to translate the words to what she believed she'd heard, not what was said, then smiled.

Lauren stood and extended her arm towards the door, indicating the conversation was over.

As Melissa stood and turned, Lauren linked her arm and placed her free hand gently onto Melissa's upper arm. A connected, warm, anchoring action that was all part of Lauren's box of tricks and no part real friendliness.

"Oh..." she said breathlessly as they walked slowly across the office.

At the door she turned to Melissa.

"And bring Frost's laptop. They'll want it back."

Melissa made a slight noise showing agreement and nodded, too surprised at the implications of the simple statement to say anything meaningful.

∞

"How did the interview go?" Steven asked.

"I wasn't aware it was an interview," Lauren replied.

"Yes, well, OK, it was and it wasn't. I'm guessing you worked your magic on her?"

"That you have to even ask, Steven, really? You won't catch someone so useful in both the perfect mental state, ready to accept a new direction, along with perfect circumstances that make it the right time to approach her."

"Right, well that sounds perfect. Did you say what was next?"

"Of course, I told her you'd be in touch. Why not do it right away?" Lauren suggested.

"You don't think that looks a bit eager?"

"You are eager! Anyway, it'll work for her. As she's already contacted us—well, Byford at least—it'll look like we're super keen on her. You'll make the poor girl happy."

"Well then," Steven said," I always like to make the girls happy!"

Lauren gave a quiet laugh.

"Very true, sir. I'll collect her this evening and bring her over to you."

∞

Melissa finished putting on her makeup, placed the lipstick back in its place on the dresser and checked her watch.

Lauren would be here in a few minutes.

She stood and looked at herself in the dress mirror. She'd chosen to wear a dark blue business suit for the meeting.

The knee-length skirt was modest but feminine, and the white blouse framed her neck and reflected a little light onto her face. With her hair gathered up into a bun, she always thought it completed a look straight out of a 1940s war film.

Though unclear if it was an interview, a dinner or something else, dressing like this made her feel oddly safe and grounded.

She stood and stared into her own eyes.

Images of the recent events played out in the air between her real and reflected self.

The feeling she had was of sorting them, discarding some and keeping others. Letting go of who she thought she was or had been, building a new image and sense of herself.

For the first time she had a feeling of being her own person, a grown up, freed from the memories and emotions of the child she had been.

The ethereal images cleared from her eyes and she looked at herself fully for the first time since she couldn't remember.

Her figure, her hair, the colour of her skin.

She looked back into her own eyes and saw a maturity there she had not seen before.

Smiling to herself, she brushed her hands down the skirt and walked downstairs to await Lauren.

∞

"Melissa, this is the Handler. Consider him to be our manager in the organisation. I will leave you together, with your permission, sir," Lauren added, playing her role perfectly.

"Granted, thank you, Lauren. No need to wait, I'll have Melissa seen safely home."

"Very well, sir," Lauren replied.

"Melissa," she added, giving an almost imperceptible curtsey to them both and heading out of the room. It wasn't the convention, but it was a quirk of behaviour Steven had noted her doing before.

Steven guided Melissa to a comfortable lounge chair and indicated for her to sit down.

"Tea or coffee?" he asked her, picking up a small teapot and pouring for himself.

"Oh, I'll have tea please, Han... sir," she said, a little uncertain as to how she should refer to him.

"Sir is fine, I'm not knighted but it's the convention. Convention is something we enjoy here, by the way. It can seem a little stuffy at times," he continued as he poured the tea. "However, it's all part of who we are."

He stirred Melissa's tea briefly and placed it in front of her.

As she reached for it, he leant forward and gently cupped her hand in both of his.

Though unexpected, Melissa felt comforted by the action.

"Melissa, what I'm going to explain to you I will never repeat and nor are you to do so. I won't threaten you 'on pain of death' or anything dramatic. I just want you to give me your word," Steven said softly to Melissa sitting back and releasing her hand as he did so.

"You have my word, sir," she said.

"Gracias, Melissa."

"Oh, hablas Español?" she asked him.

"Si, un poco. Pero, ya no practico ahora. *Sin embargo,* I know you do. Like you, I had a mixed upbringing, though unlike you, I don't have a mixed heritage. My nanny was from Madrid."

"I thought you were a bit continental in your demeanour, she had a big influence on you I think. You must miss her and her cooking?"

"Ah, yes! The cooking especially," he agreed, giving a smile.

"But, that's not why we're here. Let me tell you of who we are and why we are," Steven said, becoming more serious.

"Melissa, the world, as you may have noticed, is a rather messed up place. Hannover dream of a day when racism, sexism, wars, poverty, inequality… you name it, are all gone. Over the generations we have fought to eradicate these destructive aspects of human society. Of course, to some this looks like Big Brother meddling, but we never interfere with the free choices of individuals. Never limit them, subjugate them or punish them as governments do. Governments are the biggest destroyers and killers the world has ever seen, and their ways are not the Hannover way."

Steven paused for a moment to ensure Melissa was listening and seemingly on-board with what he was saying.

"Melissa, the Hannover world would be one in which divisive ways of living no longer existed, but where diversity of the human experience would flourish. If you wanted to be a mixed-race, gay, pagan couple, with two adopted kids from Asia, that would be just fine. Because, why shouldn't it be? That may seem radical to some quarters right now, perhaps extreme, but once realised, it would seem rational and normal. In terms of scale and longevity, I won't bore you with a history lesson, but we've existed for hundreds of generations."

Steven took a long sip of his tea, lost in thought. Melissa chose not to interrupt.

"Recently, we were responsible in part for the European Union, the creation of European law and the European currency, for the creation of Esperanto too. Though I'm afraid that wasn't so successful, but in any case Zamenhof's driving principles continue to be applied today."

Melissa sat back in her seat, cradling the tea and reflecting on this world view.

"A great big harmonious family of humankind," she added.

"Precisely! Imagine the possibilities! Imagine if the Dark Ages and the two world wars had never happened. What if in human history we had never reduced women to chattel, criminalised homosexuality, discriminated due to race. Where would humanity be now?" Steven said.

Melissa believed he was genuinely getting both angry and upset with humanity's short-sightedness.

"Of course to achieve this, you'll essentially need a single world government, a global army, police, economic system. You'll need quite a forge to form that, maybe one fuelled by biofuel research perhaps. That's not very utopian, is it?" she said, interested to see the Handler's response.

"Good points and a good example, if not very subtle," he replied. "However, all coming from a naïve perspective as could only be the case right now. Thinking of how we achieve our aims and how current governments do, was anyone killed? Was a city or nation decimated for generations? Did society break down and get replaced by terrorists? No, none of that."

"Frost, David," she said, answering the question of who got killed and who was about to be arrested.

"Frost was murdered by someone who was well out of Hannover and we genuinely mourn him. David is a drug-dealing, abusive vile man who society is better off without and whose absence will bring about some other positive changes we're still working on," Steven said.

A realisation flashed across Melissa's mind about David and the raid—that should be taking place as they sat and spoke.

It had always been Hannover's intention to pin the attack on him. It was another glaring insight into how deep their influence ran.

"What has happened, Melissa, is that the world has become—will become—a better place, because we took direct action to make it so."

"When the good sit idle, tyrants prevail?"

"Precisely!" Steven agreed.

Melissa sipped her tea and reflected again on what the Handler had said.

The world was messed up, that was for sure. She wasn't convinced it was all down to governments, but the current system was clearly broken.

On balance though, what Hannover seemed to be up to was nothing compared to world governments and outright terrorists.

It sounded like a naively utopian goal, but at least it sounded like a benevolent dictatorship. Something she'd secretly thought was just fine, and maybe a little of what the world needed.

"You mention taking direct action, that's the heart of achieving your agenda. What action would I be involved in?" she asked.

Steven smiled to himself, he had her.

"As I hope you've picked up on by now, nothing that you didn't want to be, let me be clear on that. You have unique skills and abilities, a psychological profile all your own, beliefs and ideas about the world. We would look to utilise the whole you, though only in a way that was acceptable to you."

Melissa ran the words through her mind.

"You haven't answered my question."

"Very astute," Steven replied. "You will work to bring various groups around the world over to our cause, by fair means or foul. You will help enhance those that stand for us and remove those that stand against us and our goals."

Melissa smiled. An indistinct thought was forming in her mind, constructed of what she knew were incomplete and likely false memories from her past. Ideas of an imagined future self, standing tall and powerful, a leader in her own right. An image of her father came to mind, or at least what she imagined he would look like. She felt she knew where her path was leading and Hannover would be the ideal stepping stone.

"I will expect to be challenged and very well rewarded," she replied, signifying her acceptance of what was being offered.

"Oh you will, you have my word."

~ 39 ~

The Wednesday meeting at David's house was going well, despite most people having learned that he'd been raided just a few days earlier. It hadn't put them off.

Brother Wolf was playing host and Mary was doing the usual thing she did, hiding in a corner with a few trusted friends, drinking and smoking joints.

The wisest thing David had done was to fit an extractor fan with some ducting he'd taken from one of the bathrooms. It was now keeping the smoke and general smell of people under reasonable control.

David, however, was nowhere to be seen and Colin was beginning to wonder if he would come down at all. Despite everything, David needed to maintain some semblance of normality.

As Colin was taking more of a hand in the business now, David's behaviour mattered to him.

He looked over at Wolf and saw two faces he didn't recognise.

They'd been speaking to Mary earlier and the guy had brought some gear with him, so had fit right in when he skinned up and offered it around.

The woman seemed uncomfortable, though, like she was on edge.

From behind the bar that he was leaning on, Colin watched everyone for a while, having never really done that before.

Everyone was pretty much wrapped up in their own thing.

Busy being part of their little cliques. Half of these were already customers, but the others needed hooking and reeling in.

An image of him being a vampire came to mind, as if he was looking over his cattle down in his crypt.

It made him smile, and he decided to start increasing his herd.

"Hey! Brother Wolf," Colin said, greeting the man and giving him a strong handshake.

"I'm Colin," he said to the new arrivals.

They both shook hands in return and the man introduced them.

"I'm Lagis, this is my girlfriend, Buckby," he said, putting an arm around the woman's waist and pulling their hips together.

She laughed but Colin again noticed she seemed stiff and distracted.

"Don't you have first names?" Colin said, smiling at the odd introduction.

"Ah, sorry!" Lagis said, giving a soft laugh. "I'm Daniel, this is my girlfriend Louise. We were in the Air Force together, force of habit."

"Whatever you like. Wolf, show Lagis to the bar and grab some drinks, mate," Colin said, then turned to Lagis. "It's an open house, so make yourself at home. I'll introduce a few of the girls to your misses."

With that, Wolf walked Lagis off and Colin came closer to Buckby.

"You know Mary?" he asked, nodding over to her.

"No, just met her tonight. She's the host, right?"

"Yeh, kind of. The host is her boyfriend David really, but fuck knows where he is," Colin said as he wandered over to where Mary was sitting.

She was cross legged on the sofa, sitting behind a large fake-leather foot rest or poof or whatever these things were called. He was never sure, but what he was sure of was this made a great table to get a captive audience.

"What do you like?" he asked Buckby as they walked over.

"A bit of charlie, some smoke. Nothing too exciting."

"You don't want some pills or something? You seem a bit edgy," he said to see if he could probe what she was really after.

"Nah, just a bit of charlie would do the trick. Since moving here we've lost our normal contacts if you know what I mean."

"OK, let's see what the others want and I'll go get some."

They both approached the women on the sofa and after some pleasantries, Colin had their orders.

"OK, you ladies carry on and I'll go get the shopping in. I'll see where David is, too!" he said and walked away upstairs.

∞

The controller continued to fuss about, tugging this and tightening that.

"Is everything fitting OK, you all happy with your kit?"

"Yes, it's all good. Don't you think it's a bit odd though? Having the three of us armed and the rest of the team as her regular bobbies?"

"No, it'll be fine, in fact they'll be nervous about asking too many questions," Steven said, "Though I do appreciate that you're stepping in amongst the lions a little bit."

"A little bit completely," Byford added.

"Look," Andrew said, "I've told Aggard this has been taken over by MI5. They don't allow questions and you don't ask them. Aggard's bobbies will crack open the door and stay out of the way until you're done. Call them in when finished, then get the hell out of there as fast as you can," he added, sounding like he was both advising them of the plan and convincing himself of it at the same time.

The two other Hannover operatives assigned to Byford had said nothing since they'd arrived for briefing and gotten their equipment.

"And what about Morecambe and Wise here?" he asked.

"They're not there for you, they'll run interference if any comes up," Steven said.

Steven was pleased that at least now he saw why they'd brought Andrew into the fold. He could be relied on to do his part when needed, if not to stay out of debt, which now would all have to be squared away.

"Let's get you to the van. You know the drill…"

Byford interrupted Andrew before he could start talking again.

"Aye, we have it. In and out."

∞

Colin stood over David, looking at him sitting on the floor and leaning back against the bed.

"I thought you didn't use your own products?" he said.

"I haven't, I just had some beers and shots," David managed to slur.

Colin went to the bedside cabinet and laid out some of his best powder that had been intended for the girl downstairs.

"Get up, get that inside you and sober up," he said to David, who was still lolling about on the floor.

"Get up!" he said again, and David started to move.

A few minutes later, with assistance and insistence from Colin, David had ingested a couple of lines and was back on his feet.

He walked across the other side of the room and immediately grabbed the can he'd been drinking from earlier.

"I don't want to play host!" David protested.

Colin flew across the room at him, grabbing him by the scruff of his clothes as he had done just recently, determined to stop this in its tracks.

"I told you once, I'll tell you again! The game has changed!"

David tried to pull away but found he was stuck fast by a determined grip. He swung the can at Colin, trying to bash him in the head with it, but his arm was blocked by Colin's elbow. Colin forced him against the wall.

"You don't fucking learn, do you? Don't try the same shit again!" he hissed.

David spat into his face and Colin instinctively let go, ducking and lifting his hands to protect himself from more spit.

Seeing his gap, David began swinging his arms in wide circles, striking his fists down repeatedly on Colin's head and arms, grunting and pummelling with all his strength. This windmill movement may have been effective when David was stronger in his twenties, but right now it was barely delivering any force.

Colin twisted and rose, swinging his fist up under David's arms and landed a forceful blow into his solar plexus.

David cried out and crumpled to the floor.

Stepping back, Colin slid out his thick leather belt from his jeans, wrapped the free end around his hand a few times and let the buckle end hang down.

"I'm going to beat you like the bitch you are, so you learn once and for all!"

∞

Lagis looked over to see Buckby was now well in with the girls and talking to Mary.

She was animated about whatever the conversation was, touching Buckby's hand and leaning forward and backwards with each new snippet of gossip, as if adding extra emphasis to her words.

Wolf droned on for another couple of minutes about activism, protecting the planet and other stuff that was equally boring to Lagis.

He felt a vibration in his pocket and pulled out his phone.

A short message had come through.

"Excuse me a second," he said to Wolf and walked over to where Buckby was.

"Hey, darling," he said, standing next to her as she perched on the corner of the footrest that was still hosting a collection of grass and resin, plus other illicit items.

"Message from the babysitter," he said, showing her the phone.

'Be clear in 15 minutes' was all the text said.

"Oh, great! Was hoping we'd have longer."

Mary was just about to ask what the matter was, when the whole house heard the screams and shouts from upstairs.

"Now!" they heard Colin scream.

A heavy crash told them someone had fell or been thrown down the stairs.

Lagis readied himself.

"Shit," he said, half to himself and half to Buckby, cursing the timing of this event.

David burst into the room.

"What?" he said loudly to everyone and went straight to Mary.

Lagis stood in front of him and blocked his advance.

"What the fuck do you want?" David shouted.

"He's a mate!" Wolf said, already halfway around the bar and heading to the two men.

"He's no one, what's he doing here!"

"It's cool, it's open house, remember!" Wolf said.

David wasn't listening and instead went to grab Lagis. He pulled Lagis away and tried to push him further, but being bigger Lagis had the advantage.

He pulled David's arms off himself and after some squirming and struggling, managed to get behind him and wrap his arms around David.

David kicked backwards and tried to reverse head butt him, but these were all things Lagis had seen before.

"Get the fuck off me and get out of here!" David shouted in different ways several times.

Buckby had to act and fast.

With the two men shouting and struggling, she turned and leaned into Mary, putting her hand around the back of Mary's head and pulling her close as if to kiss her on the cheek.

"Whatever happens next, stay in the corner, stay out of the way," she whispered.

She pulled her face away and looked into Mary's confused eyes.

"Stay in this corner," she said again, then let go and stood up.

"Stop it! Stop it!" Buckby shouted, giving her best impression of a distraught and frightened girlfriend.

Lagis let go and Wolf immediately came around to prevent David from doing anything foolish.

"OK, OK! Let's go!" Lagis said, grabbing Buckby's arm heading quickly for the door.

∞

The van continued to speed along and Byford, the two other assigned team members and a regular police officer sat in silence.

He could feel the heat around his face from the black balaclava he had on. The tactical helmet and ballistic vest added to the feeling of being encased.

He closed his eyes and thought of Mary when she had been younger. He could hear her laughter and see her running along in the park they would visit each Sunday.

An aching began to build in his heart and he forced the images from his mind.

In a few minutes all the waiting would be over, this project would be completed and he could get back to doing nothing.

Byford released the magazine from the Glock 17 he'd been issued and checked the number of rounds. There were 15 instead of the 30 he was hoping for, which meant he'd been issued the standard semi-automatic.

His other two colleagues didn't seem concerned, still doing and saying nothing.

Whoever they'd chosen, they were disciplined at least.

"IC1 male and IC1 female leaving the premises, detain?" they heard over their police radios.

"Is it the subject?" Byford responded.

"Negative."

"Then let them go, we can't pull everyone in."

He hoped he knew who it was that was leaving.

The van came to a halt and the officer slid the side door open.

Byford readied his weapon and spoke into the separate radio system he and his two armed assistants had.

"Morecambe, you stay inside the front door. Wise, you stay at the top of the stairs," Byford said. The two men spoke for the first time, verbally confirming their understanding. He saw the officer who was playing doorman run up to the front door and position himself to swing his ram through David's door lock once again.

Other officers were getting into position and running around the back of the house. Byford wondered what the neighbours would be thinking this time.

"We hear mixed screams and shouting," a female officer's voice said over the radio.

Byford pressed the talk button on his radio.

"Knock knock!" he said and leaping from the van, sprinted towards the door.

He heard the bash of the ram and the door burst open in one hit. The timing was perfect. As it rebounded, he was in the doorway, pushing it aside as it swung towards him.

A second earlier and he'd have crashed into a locked door.

Morecambe followed behind and hooked around the open door, slamming it shut as Wise came through.

Wise followed Byford as he headed straight for the cellar where Lagis had reported the party was taking place.

Before reaching the door, they could already hear David shouting and other people screaming and shouting back.

In a stroke of luck, Colin had been weighing out grams of charlie upstairs when he heard the door being bashed through.

He threw everything aside, went to the landing and on seeing no one, dashed into the toilet and locked the door.

Byford opened the cellar door and raced down the stairs.

The room was in chaos—he saw people looking on in horror at a larger group around the sofas against a far wall.

Byford came to the foot of the stairs and aiming his gun forward, shouted as loud as he could several times.

"Armed Police! Get on the ground! Get on the ground, now! Move now, get down!"

A man ran towards him in obvious panic. Byford kicked forward, booting him in the stomach.

Byford let off a round into the soft ceiling and screams erupted.

The few who were still standing hit the floor.

He heard the shot being reported on the police radio, and his two officers remained silent.

With the crowd moved away, Byford now saw what the commotion was about.

In the corner, scrabbling about on the sofa was a desperate, wide eyed and sweat soaked David.

In a choke hold was a weak-looking woman, with the back of her head pressed to David's chest.

David was half sitting, pressed up against the wall.

In one hand was a collection of what looked like pills and powder. By her glazed expression, rolling eyes and bleeding mouth, it was apparent that David had been violently forcing the woman to consume the mix of drugs.

Byford levelled the gun at David, who pulled the woman closer and further over him for protection.

"Let her go, now! Let her go! Let her go!" Byford commanded, taking a few more steps forward, further pushing the bystanders to move backwards with a mix of screams and whimpers.

"Leave me alone!" David screamed. "Leave me alone or I'll kill her!"

Byford shot forward, staring David in the eyes as he did so and saw him for the coward he was.

He quickly twisted the gun around in his hand and slammed the butt of it down onto David's head. A white-hot pain shot through David's skull, causing him to scream and release Mary.

As he fell sideways, she fell forward.

Byford raised the gun again and squeezed the trigger three times in rapid succession., blasting the life out of the bastard who had long abused Mary.

"Good fucking riddance," Byford said as the blood leaked from David's corpse and soaked into the sofa.

Byford put the weapon away, turned and picked Mary up in a fireman's lift.

"We have a casualty and a female needing urgent medical help. Get me an ambulance right now!" he said into the police radio.

Running as fast as he could up the stairs, he left the shocked crowd with David's corpse.

At the front door, police officers had already arrived with a stretcher.

He handed Mary over to them and with his two armed officers climbed back into their van and left the scene.

~ 40 ~

"How is she doing?" Steven asked the nurse on the other end of the line.

"Good, sir. She's starting to get her strength back now the immediate withdrawal phase is over with. She was out of bed for the first time yesterday and is eating more now."

"I'm grateful, thank you for your good work. I'll call again in a few days."

The nurse ended the call and turned to her colleague.

"Our mystery bill payer checking on his favourite patient again."

"Has she had any visitors yet?" the other nurse asked.

"Not yet, but she'll be out in a week or so and someone will need to sign her out."

∞

"Byford, come in," Steven said as he greeted him at his office door.

Byford walked into the office, the same office he'd been in just a few weeks before to accept the project. The two men took their seats and Steven waited.

"I just want to thank you, sir, for helping to get Mary out of there and for looking after her these last weeks," Byford said, the words laden with more than just thanks for paying some hospital bills.

"It's my pleasure, Byford. You've been a good and loyal member of our family here over the years. You've never asked for anything and it's only right that when we see a way to help like this, then we do so."

Byford thought over the words for a few seconds.

He wondered if this was more about Hannover's desire to control people and outcomes or it really was an opportune coincidence to do a project that also led to emancipating Mary. In any case, why they'd waited so long was a question for another time.

"As I'm sure I've said before, don't overthink it, Byford. Everyone wins in situations like this," Steven said, as if divining Byford's thoughts.

"What's important is, what's next?" Steven said, changing the tone of the conversation and wanting to use the opportunity to check Byford's intentions.

"I'll go to the hospital and see her next week."

"You're hoping for a reconciliation then?"

"Yes," Byford said flatly.

Steven looked thoughtfully at Byford for a few silent seconds.

"You know, better than most I imagine," Steven began, "I spend half my day dealing in lies, saying one thing to one person and another thing to another. Crafting stories and perspectives, looking over scenario probability data and psychology reports. Dealing with this person who is one of ours and that person who isn't but who we can manipulate as if they were. I get to the end of some days and I don't know what's real and what's make believe."

Steven paused, reflecting on his situation, a half smile on his face as he looked down at the floor.

He raised his head and looked directly at Byford.

"It may surprise you, however, that there is one person to whom I never lie, someone who knows the truth when I don't. The only person I really trust. That's my wife."

"You tell your wife everything? But, I didn't think she was part of Hannover?" Byford asked, the surprise evident in his voice.

"No she's not, but without her I would forget what was real in this world. We all need that, Byford, and you can't tell me you've not felt adrift these last years. We've done what we can, now it's up to you. I suggest you are open and frank with Mary. Open your heart to her so she is never again in any doubt about how much you love her. You said yourself she never got over losing her mother and now with these last two years and the events these last weeks, she needs you, the true you more than ever. Trust me. You're all she has."

∞

"They want to let her out in a couple of days. Apparently she's healing well, the pills had little time to do much damage. She'll need time to recover from the other forms of abuse though," Lagis said.

"Well, of course, but at least that's good news in itself! I guess it's time to go and talk to her then," Byford said.

"Visiting time is an hour from now, I'll pick you up."

Lagis hung up the phone and headed out to collect Byford.

∞

Lagis pulled the car into the hospital car park and switched off the engine.

Byford had been quiet the whole journey, making just a few comments about how far the hospital was, if he should have brought a gift and how the late autumn rain was already tiresome.

Lagis tactfully acknowledged his conversation, but essentially ignored it. He'd been around enough to know when people weren't really making conversation, but instead distracting themselves from what was really on their mind.

"Sure about this?" he asked Byford.

"Yeh, no time like the present, eh?"

"True, and no, I'm not coming in with you. Just before you ask."

Byford looked to Lagis but said nothing.

∞

Byford closed the door softly behind him and walked quietly over to the bed.

Mary opened her eyes, waking from the half sleep she had been in.

"Hey, how you doing?" he asked, standing apprehensively about two feet from the bed.

Mary went to push herself up into a sitting position and Byford stepped forward to help.

"It's OK," she said with a strained smile. "I'm healthier than I've been in years. They're still insisting I take sleeping medication to help me recover, hence the afternoon nap."

"Ah, well that's good then," Byford said, too tense to say anything meaningful.

"Mary," Byford said, his voice hesitant. "You were always my world, Mary. When my mother passed I had no one left, and I didn't know what to do. Then your mother passed and I didn't know what to do for you. All I did was cause you pain when I should have been there for you."

Byford's voice trailed off as he broke Mary's gaze and lowered his eyes.

Despite all that had happened, standing here he felt impotent and pathetic.

Mary stared at him and felt something deep inside change, like her heart had cracked at his simple admission and his humility towards her.

The pain of the years the man had suffered was suddenly apparent to her.

The emotion threatened to overwhelm her and with a tear in her eye she reached out and took Byford's hand in hers.

"It's over now," she said, a slight smile forming on her mouth. "I'll see you at home."

The words made him catch his breath and for a moment he thought his knees would fail him.

"OK," he said, smiling and forcing himself not to cry.

He lifted her hand, held it to his cheek for a second and kissed her palm.

"I'll see you at home."

That's it then, Byford thought to himself, feeling a new future opening up ahead of him.

His mind was clear, things felt done.

He walked down the hospital corridor and out to the entrance.

Lagis was leaning against the car. He stood up, looked at Byford and saw things had gone well.

"Sure about this too?" he asked.

"Yes, drive me to the Centenary, would you? I have a final debrief to give a slightly less important person," Byford said climbing into the car.

"Rather you than me," Lagis mumbled to himself, feeling an apprehension Byford seemed to be ignorant of or hiding well.

~ 41 ~

Byford stepped out of the room and wandered slowly away, feeling the weight of the last few weeks, the last few years, lifted from his shoulders.

For the first time in months he felt he was now back to the person he remembered himself to be.

"Hello there, Steven," he heard called from the hall in front of him.

Byford looked up to see an elderly man, walking cane waving in the air in greeting.

He was flanked by a middle-aged man, well dressed and with the healthy glow of someone who had too much money.

Confused at who was being called out to, Byford turned to look up the opposite direction of the hall and realised that the Handler had silently stepped out of the room at some point.

So his name is Steven, is it? I'll have to remember that, Byford thought to himself.

Trapped in between the advancing old man with his companion, coming up the hallway and the Handler behind him, Byford stepped backward to the wall, allowing them to come face to face.

"I hear you handled the last project extremely well," the old man said to the Handler, as if unconcerned Byford was trapped between them.

"Very tidy conclusion," he added, as if summarising the most important point.

"Kind of you to say so, sir," the Handler replied.

"Well, carefully handling projects is his job," Byford offered to the old man, feeling he could use the moment of pleasant conversation as a way of introduction to the stranger.

The Handler shot Byford a look of surprise. Byford had never overstepped the mark before, but then he certainly didn't know who he was talking to at this time.

The old man turned casually to Byford and with an entirely blank expression, looked him straight in the eyes.

Byford felt his heart suddenly flutter and though he tried his best to hide it, the feeling made him catch his breath.

The more contacts a person had the better off a person was in this field of work, but sometimes it was better not to know who some people were. Byford hoped he hadn't made a parting mistake.

"Yes, true," the old man responded to Byford with a slight smile, "but of course we've you to thank for the success of execution, from start to finish, haven't we, Byford."

Holding out a thin and blotchy hand towards Byford, the old man's demeanour softened.

"Lord Durran," he stated as an introduction. "And this is Sir Anthear," he said, gesturing to his companion.

Byford took the man's hand and shook it with some care due to him seeming so fragile. He noted how soft and slightly cold the skin was.

"Thank you, sir, I aimed to give good quality of service," Byford said, trying to maintain a light-hearted tone in the face of meeting such senior Hannover figures.

"Oh, I know," Lord Durran said quietly, with what seemed to Byford to be a slightly threatening tone. "I've been your well-wisher for many years, Byford, but of course protocol doesn't allow me to work with you directly. I'm sure you understand," he added.

Before Byford could answer, the Handler took the opportunity to break the impromptu conversation and get Byford on his way out of the Centenary.

"Well," he said as an interjection. Pausing for a brief moment, he turned to Byford and gave a subtle nod of his head. "Very good, Byford, do carry on."

Byford took the hint.

"Yes, thank you again, for everything, sir," Byford said to the Handler.

"Lord Durran… Sir Anthear… good day, sirs."

He was about to turn and leave, when he added, "and goodbye."

Mirroring the gesture the Handler had made, he nodded to the two men and turned and headed away down the corridor.

Lord Durran watched for a few moments, and when Byford was at a suitable distance he turned back to Steven.

Steven raised an eyebrow and smiled to Lord Durran.

"I thought he'd say that," he said.

"So he quit on you again, did he?" Lord Durran asked rhetorically. "They do that," he added with an amused tone.

Brushing the words aside as if insignificant, he turned back to Steven.

"Do you think he's *ready*, Steven?" Lord Durran asked, standing rigidly with both hands resting on his cane and looking questioningly at him.

Steven knew this casual encounter had all been planned by Lord Durran, to briefly meet Byford and then get to this point.

A passing introduction like this was always the first step, it had been the exact same for him almost 15 years ago. Now he guessed his relationship with Byford was about to change. Steven smiled inside at how easily things had moved along.

"Yes, sir. I believe he's ready. He's proven himself on many projects now and with the events of the last project"—he paused momentarily to choose the right words—"I think we can be assured he's very positively minded towards us."

Durran nodded in seeming approval and, stepping forwards, linked arms with the Handler.

It was something he'd done only once before, an odd gesture that seemed overly familiar given their relationship and unequal position in Hannover. The same as when he called him Steven, it made him feel personally closer to a man he didn't want to be personally close to.

Lord Durran began to walk them both in the direction Byford had gone. Sir Anthear silently fell in behind and followed them.

He hadn't said a word in the entire encounter and the Steven wondered if ignoring him was something to worry about.

"Very well then, I have a new and important project for you, Steven," Durran said. "Anthear will come and see you first thing tomorrow."

With that, Lord Durran patted the Handler on the arm a few times and then separated from him.

Reaching for Anthear, Durran turned, waved his cane in the air and called back.

"Have a good day, Steven."

He watched as the couple headed away from him.

Standing alone, he thought about Byford's last words.

"Goodbye, eh, Byford? Not a chance, my friend, I've not finished with *you* yet."

~ 42 ~

Byford stepped out of the Centenary club and felt the cool air on his face.

It had recently stopped raining and for a change the stale London air was crisp and damp, just like his native Scotland, he reflected.

"That's it, I'm done," he said to himself as he stood there.

He half believed it and half doubted it. He'd thought he was done before, but he would have never guessed they'd find Mary.

This time the sense of finality was as invigorating as the fresh air filling his lungs.

He hailed a cab and headed home.

With a cheery 'thank you', Byford waved the cab driver goodbye and climbed the steps to the front door of his house.

Swinging the door open he was greeted by a view of Mary in the kitchen, at the far end of the hallway.

"Hello, lovely," he called out to her with a bright and happy tone. The sense of relief at how things had worked out was beginning to sink in even more.

Here she was, like a mirage, standing in his home, in the kitchen, as if no time had passed.

"Welcome home, dinner's nearly ready!" she called out to him.

The words were unfamiliar, strangely civilised, but he felt the happiness rise in him, in a way he'd forgotten after so many years working as he did and living without her.

Nothing could bring the lost years back, but at least he'd found her again.

Dinner was a relaxed affair; Mary recounted many of the things she'd been up to over the years with David and the Eco group.

Some good, a lot bad.

"David always seemed so sure and so passionate about what we were doing and why we were doing it," she said at one point.

Byford noticed the look of sadness come across her face and he reached out to her hand, resting around her wine glass, holding her gently he gave her a reassuring smile.

He let go after a few seconds, not wishing to push the newly re-established relationship too much.

Important to give her time, he'd thought to himself several times that evening.

"People like David are very convincing. Remember, he'd practiced for years to be good at the role he played. At first he would have been using you like the rest of those eco warriors; no doubt in time you grew on him."

He looked her in the eyes and felt an ingrained surge of love for her.

"My gut feel though, from what you say, is there was something real there, some genuine feeling for you at some point."

He hoped the words would help comfort her, but her face changed almost immediately.

"He was a lying manipulative bastard, who used everyone around him. What strange kind of love causes you to try and kill someone with an overdose," Mary said, as both a statement and a question.

"Hmm..." Byford replied and silently thought for a moment, taking a sip of his wine as if trying to imbue some extra wisdom, while Mary continued to look at him awaiting a response.

"But that was the last moment of a cornered and frightened man," he said at last, meeting her gaze. "People do extreme things when what defines who they are and what their life is about is taken away from them."

Mary reflected on what Byford had said.

She realised he wasn't just talking about David.

If David hadn't tried to overstep who he was, hadn't been fooled by whoever Lauren was, hadn't been trying to kill her when Byford arrived, maybe he'd still be alive.

"I felt you'd abandoned me and left me with him. Early on I knew he was manipulating, brainwashing people, but later, it all seemed so right. I felt David really loved me. I can't believe I thought that way now," she said, a soft despair creeping into her voice. "Whether you knew what he was like, if I loved him or not, would you have killed him anyway?" she asked, to Byford's surprise.

He got up from his dining chair and grabbed the bottle of wine, motioning with his arm to the sofa.

"That chair's killing my arse, I know that much," he said, deflecting the question.

His mind was spinning and a sense of guilt was building. He thought about how he'd stopped searching for her all those years ago, how he'd now found her again and killed the person she felt she had been in love with.

The idea he'd torn her life apart twice made his heart feel like lead.

He dropped into the sofa and filled his glass; Mary sat beside him and offered her glass up to him to do the same.

"Would I have killed him anyway?" he said, coming back to her question.

He took another sip of wine and let a few moments of silence pass between them.

"Given what he'd done to you, to get you free and back in my life, yes, I'd have killed him anyway," he said.

She leaned into him and he hesitated for a moment before putting his arm around her and kissed her on the forehead.

"Thank you, dad," she said to him in a tired tone.

Minutes passed, her breathing became heavy and he realised she had fallen asleep in his arms.

Byford's emotions overwhelmed him and he felt a tear course down his cheek.

Closing his eyes, he pulled her tight.

"You're welcome, my beautiful daughter."

A few moments later, he joined her in a comforting sleep.

End of Direct Action

Epilogue

Black Dragon Protocol

~ 43 ~

Lord Durran sat politely on the dark wooden chair placed directly opposite the Home Secretary, who was staring at him over her glasses from the other side of the desk.

"Well, Home Secretary, I can't fault you on your timing this time. The gap you created to get Byford in on the raid was a great help," Lord Durran said, hoping to convey his genuine appreciation.

"Spare me the charm, Durran. As one of Her Majesty's favoured, you're afforded some accommodation, but let me remind you not to step beyond what I'd be able to support."

Durran nodded, confirming his understanding. She sat back into her chair and continued in a less stern tone.

"Anyway, I'll overlook your little sub-agenda, as usual; it got us all where we need to be."

Getting Mary back into Byford's arms had been essential and he'd explained that early on, cautiously demanded it even. It was never wise to force the Home Secretary into doing something she didn't support. Thankfully, he'd always been respectful of who she was and tactful in his dealings with her, and as such she'd had always been on his side.

"Where is everything now?" she asked.

"We have the bio-fuel and enzyme samples, along with the few papers that were rescued from Dr. Kirby. Once he joins Standard in a few weeks…"

"Once he recovers in a few weeks, you mean," she stated accusatively.

"Yes, ma'am, when he recovers, then Standard can start to test and produce the fuel."

"Good, we'll see what we can get out of DECC for the favour."

"Ma'am, may I ask, something that has puzzled me is why DECC wanted to stop working with Cosgrove."

"Money. It was no more mysterious than Daler told you. The board of directors at Cosgrove decided they wanted to sell the fuel and make money by being first to market. You know the dangers of doing that. Our Saudi and American friends would not be amused. The board at Standard are a little wiser."

"Now, moving on," she said in a brighter tone, "are your pieces set up for the next project?"

"We're almost there; Steven has the team coming in today."

"Well good, inform me when you're ready to go."

"Yes, of course," he replied.

His tone warned her there was something else and she again peered at him over the rim of her glasses, silently interrogating him.

"And?"

"Err… yes. There is just one small thing, Home Secretary. I still need your help in locating Broer."

"Fine. I'll speak to my friends in SIS and see what they have."

∞

Byford stepped from the car and looked at the doors of the Centenary Club. When he last left, he'd imagined there would be a long time elapsed until he was here again, if ever. It had been just about a month since he'd had the inconclusive conversation with the Handler.

Now he'd been called in for a chat, which, as always with Hannover, was not going to be a purely social event.

Even Mary had been surprised when he'd spoken about ending his time with Hannover. She was probably right in her view. At 52, it was perhaps better to stick with what he knew, instead of trying to go into private consultancy as he'd been thinking.

There were offers, but it all seemed like a lot of uncertain ground when considered seriously.

He sighed and walked towards the door, which was smartly opened for him by the doorman. A concierge met him on the other side of the doorway, guided him through to the main hall and directed him to the room where the Handler was waiting.

A routine as timeless and familiar as many things in Hannover.

He entered the room, but to his surprise Sir Anthear was also there.

"Gentlemen," Byford said, acknowledging them both.

"Byford, I believe you met Sir Anthear in passing a few days ago."

"Aye, how are you, sir?" Byford replied, shaking Sir Anthear by the hand and giving a polite nod.

"I am well, Byford. Perfect timing by the way, we're just about to have some tea."

Byford looked over to his left and saw a pot and three cups sat on a small table, in front of the chairs the men must have been sitting in before he arrived. His arrival when tea had been served was hardly coincidental timing—he'd been told to arrive here at this time. Just one more Hannover ritual, he told himself.

"Tea would be nice, thank you."

Sir Anthear took the far chair and Byford the middle, placing himself between the men. The Handler poured the tea.

"The reason we've asked you here today, Byford, is to talk about your future with Hannover," the Handler said.

"Just to check, do you know who I am?" Anthear asked.

"I know your name of course, but if you mean what you do here, then no, I don't know who you are, sir," Byford replied.

"In simple terms, I am the one that gives instructions to your Handler. He in turn instructs a Lead, yourself in this case, who runs a project team."

"I see, so you're the Sponsor?"

"Correct, Byford. I am the Sponsor."

The Handler handed the men their tea and sat back in his chair.

"Sir Anthear and I were concerned when last I met you that you appeared to desire to leave us. Would this be true, do you feel your time in the field should come to an end?"

Byford was not surprised by the question in front of Sir Anthear. Though Byford had made it clear that's what he meant, the Handler had asked him to think over the decision. At the time Byford had thought it strange how unconcerned the Handler was.

Perhaps it was a common thing for people to quit after missions, or perhaps he was about to find out why there was a lack of concern. In any case, he was now asking for an admission to a broader audience.

Things had changed again however, even with the short amount of time since last meeting.

"I've had time to think about that. When I completed the last mission successfully, on top of getting Mary back..."

"You thought you'd quit while you were ahead?" Anthear interrupted.

"Exactly, but now it's kind of sunk in that things are real, secure."

"It's perfectly understandable, Byford," the Handler said. "After having made up for that unfortunate fiasco in Israel and then getting your daughter back, it's no wonder you'd want to call it a day and just enjoy the moment."

Byford took a few sips of tea and stayed with the thought for a moment.

"Yes, you're exactly right. I just wanted to live it for a while. But, that uncertainty has passed. What I remain uncertain about is what I do next. I'm 52 after all and running about blowing things up is a young man's game."

"I agree," the Handler said in a bright tone. "In fact, Sir Anthear has a proposal for you."

"Indeed I do," Anthear said.

Byford placed his tea cup down and leaned forward to listen more intently.

"Do tell, gentlemen."

"Fortunately, as you were so successful this time around, I am moving onwards through Hannover. Lord Durran has accepted he won't be around forever and has taken me as his protégé, in readiness for when his final day comes."

You can join, but you can never leave, Byford thought.

Anthear continued, "And Steven here is moving up too. That means we need a new Handler and the Inner Council has chosen you for this role. You will be mentored through your next project by Steven and, when ready, you will leave active service in the field. This is a good compromise, is it not?"

Byford said nothing, running through what had been said.

At one point he had been planning to leave, the next content to continue running teams, so long as they would let him, and now he was being promoted.

"What to say…" he said, smiling. Then the words Anthear had used hit him. "What project?"

~ 44 ~

The text came through from his contact in SorceSek. 'Cat Club, 11pm.' That was it, but it was enough for Broer to know what to do next.

The Cat Club was the required haunt of the hackers he needed the help of. A place where they could wallow under the protection of Black Dragon.

He'd been to the club just once before and it was a typical Chinese gangster nightclub, hidden away at the back of a legitimate-looking casino. A memory of the place came to mind. Loud music, flashing lights, Asian hookers and slouching, fat, sour-faced Chinese gangsters.

"Just my kind of shit hole," he said to himself.

Broer put Dr. Kirby's laptop into a small backpack, checked the laptop bag pockets once again and being sure there was nothing further of interest, threw it behind him onto the hotel bed.

He stood up from the desk and headed to the shower to clean up and get ready for his visit.

∞

Broer walked into the casino and immediately saw the minders watching the crowds. Though reasonably out of the way, they were there if you knew what to look for.

He'd been trained to know what to look for.

Security wise the set-up was good. It was impossible to get into the casino floor without being seen by the minders. The building's entrance led to a hallway which ended in a flight of stairs down to the casino floor.

They'd already know he was here, a little early, but that was always good manners.

Given the backpack he was carrying had just been inspected at the door, they'd know he had his trade with him too.

He saw one of the minders looking over to him and gave a slight nod to show he'd also seen the man. It was something and nothing, but he didn't like the idea of them thinking he wasn't also in control of things a little.

Walking down the stairs, Broer headed over to the bar area, took a stool and got himself a whisky and soda. He checked his watch: 11.40pm.

10 minutes more to let the word spread, he thought, knowing the news of his arrival would have been relayed to the boss already.

Sitting there, Broer looked around at the casino floor.

It reminded him of an arena, with people eating and drinking around a sunken central area, which they could then descend into and revel in a battle against the odds. The odds he knew were stacked well towards the house wherever they could be.

Gambling machines were arrayed on the far wall, poker tables in front of them and nearest him were the roulette wheels. That was his preferred game, being harder to fix, and given he was too lousy at card counting to play poker.

On one roulette table was a cliché straight out of a novel.

A skinny, young Chinese girl with a low-cut red dress and long hair, hanging off a rich-looking white boy. The table would clean him out first and then she'd finish him off later.

Broer laughed at the thought and soaked up the whole scene before him. Unlike the dangerous part he'd be in the middle of shortly, this was just fine.

From the far corner, he saw a minder work his way past some diners and down onto the floor.

The man was typical.

Just under six feet tall, but built like a bull. His neck was so thick it blurred the lines of his anatomy. At this distance it was hard to tell where his bulging shoulders ended and his fat head began.

His face was so puffed up with muscle, it squeezed his Chinese eyes even more closed than Broer guessed they naturally would be.

The man came up the stairs to Broer's right and walked up to him.

"Mister Broer," the man announced, giving a slight bow.

Broer had realised early on in his dealings with the various Chinese groups how to tell the natives and the highly educated apart by the way they said his name. This one pronounced it correctly, showing he was born outside mainland China—it was unlikely to be the refinement of education.

Anything sounding like 'blower', it was the other way around.

Broer finished off his drink, stood and acknowledged who he was.

"Come this way, please," the man said, though Broer knew exactly where to go from his previous visit a few weeks ago.

The two of them walked past the gamblers, up the steps from the floor and towards a door at the back of the dining area, where another minder was waiting.

As they arrived he swung the door open, allowing them both to pass into another small, dimly lit corridor, oddly lined with red curtains along its full length.

Broer could hear the distant thud of music emanating from the end of the corridor, where yet another door and two minders awaited them.

They walked forward the twenty or so feet to the minders and Broer raised the backpack for them to take and inspect.

Unspeaking, one of the men took the bag and did as expected.

Broer unbuttoned his jacket and opened it to reveal his trusty field knife, strapped to his side under his armpit.

The second man made a disapproving sound, likely both for the fact Broer had brought it and that he'd gotten this far with it. Broer pulled off the Velcro straps holding the knife in place and passed it to the man.

After being patted down to make sure he wasn't carrying anything else, they handed him the backpack and opened the door. A wave of noise washed over Broer and he and the man with the fat neck walked into the hidden Cat Club.

Broer stepped into the side room he'd been guided to and remained at the door awaiting an invitation to enter and be part of the assembled guests.

Though it felt artificial, he was determined to show whatever respect and cultural know-how he could. After all, he was out of options and already in the dragon's mouth.

The trade and deal couldn't go sour.

The Boss, Guang Yue, was seated at the back of the room, behind the round, rotating dining table.

He was facing the door as he always did.

It always appeared to Broer that he looked like a Shaolin monk who had gone to seed. His thick arms and chest made him look like he was about to wrestle you whenever he approached.

As was also always the case, he had to his side his second in command, a middle-aged man who Broer knew only as the General.

Someone more opposite to Guang would be hard to find. The General was a tall, thin man who was always immaculately groomed and unerringly polite.

He'd been in China's People's Liberation Army all his life. As a PLA lifer, he was a hard-line traditionalist. Always careful to never offend a guest, but inflexible in his view of how things should be run.

When Broer had first met them, he had thought him to be the softer edge to the boss's hard-faced approach. He'd later learned they were two sides of the same coin.

Broer assumed the other female guests to be prostitutes or mistresses and the twenty-something-year-old men to be SorceSek.

The Cat Club was no place for wives and regular acquaintances.

The General's face lit up and he stood as an acknowledgement of Broer's presence, but remained silent in deference to Guang.

"Blower!" Guang bellowed across the table, not bothering to stand.

"Nǐ hǎo, sir," Broer said in his best Chinese accent, giving a smile and bowing to the man ever so slightly.

Guang waved his arms towards an empty seat opposite him and Broer moved into the room.

"Good to see you again, Broer," the General said at last.

"And you too, General. It's been too long."

Broer turned slightly to the General and tapped the side of the backpack that was hanging off his shoulder.

"Ah, very good," the General said and signalled to a minder who stepped from the corner of the room. Walking to Broer, he relieved him of the gift he'd brought.

"Sit, sit!" Guang insisted.

Broer sat and instantly a plate and set of chop sticks, along with a bowl of steaming, sticky white rice appeared in front of him.

"Join us for something to eat!" the General said.

"Ah, thank you, I will," Broer said, starting to fill his plate with some of the food on offer.

"Our technicians here will have a look at the item and let us know later."

"Very good, General. I'm sure it'll be very interesting to you."

By rights, Broer should be speaking to Guang directly, but he needed help from the hackers to secure the data and present it in trade.

At this time then, he was a guest of SorceSek, who would mediate his request to the Boss.

Thankfully, it was just protocol so that no one lost face—the Boss wasn't going to sit back and let the kids run things. What's more, as he knew the Boss and the General from before he had left South Africa, these SorceSek youngsters wouldn't dare try anything stupid.

These two groups working together was, as far as he could tell, a love-hate relationship on both sides.

SorceSek were a bunch of antisocial youths who got their fingers into too many sticky pies back in China or for various Chinese sponsors, then got found out.

In what was becoming a common turn of events the world over, the Chinese government gave them a way to avoid jail by allowing them to join the PLA Cyber Warfare team.

Just like the US government, with its own hackers; the ones that didn't end up in jail for going public at least.

Of course, the Chinese government's honourable intentions were a great way for ex-PLA members turned gangsters to exploit this expertise for themselves.

Just as was happening now.

"You lot go! Get that package sorted out. Kuài, Kuài!" Guang said to the rest of his guests, in his typical direct manner.

The General smiled and nodded at them as they stood to leave, thanking them for something, perhaps leaving civilly. As if they would do anything else.

Once the room was cleared, Guang turned his attention back to Broer.

For the first time he sat straight and looked directly at the new arrival.

"How long we know each other, Blower?" Guang asked.

"About five years I think, since the first engineering job we ran protection for your boys in Jo'burg."

"Ah yes, a fine job, Broer, as were the others after that," the General added.

"Yes," Guang said in agreement, his eyes squinted as if deep in thought. "We have you in ASTU for us was useful, but now I hear you cause trouble and you bring gift for me. I'm confused, I'm thinking what for? You want me in the middle?"

Guang stared with an expressionless face at Broer, waiting for him to answer, while as usual the general sat politely with a hint of a smile.

"I just evened up an old score, that was all. He wasn't even an ASTU…"

"Am I idiot? I know this!" Guang said, dropping his meaty fist onto the table. "He was Hannover and now they look for you and you in my club, with this thing you stole! I'm thinking, what the fuck you doing here! Ah? What the fuck you doing, Gwailo?"

A few tense moments passed as Broer tried to think of a good response.

Guang pushed his chair out and stood, a belligerent air about him.

He walked slowly around the table to Broer and stood in front of him with his trademark, intimidating, flat expression.

Then burst into laughter.

"Ahah! Look at the Gwailo, he's white like ghost!"

The tension released, and the other two men joined in the laughter.

"Eh, you pee your pants like schoolboy?" Guang taunted him, slapping him on the shoulder several times.

"Fok'in 'ell, bass. I shit myself then!" Broer said, reverting to his native accent with the stress of the moment.

Still laughing, Guang poured Broer a glass of beer from the carafe on the table.

"Eh, you always loyal, Blower, and now you bring this for us…" Guang said, giving a smile and gesturing to the door where the laptop had vanished earlier.

"This is very good for us, now we be good to you," he added.

Guang waved a hand at the General, prompting him to take over the conversation, then leaned on the table.

"We already heard that it would be difficult for you to return to ASTU," the General said, using the word difficult in the polite Chinese form meaning 'completely impossible.'

"That's true, and of course Hannover is not an option."

"So, you have come back to your friend for employment?" the General asked, tilting his head over to Guang.

"Yes, General."

"Good, Broer, because we have a special offer of employment for you. Something only a man of your skills and experience can help with."

"Someone with your skin colour!" Guang added, to the General's amusement.

Broer smiled weakly at the joke, more concerned as to what the special offer would entail.

"All right then, gentlemen, so how can I help you?" he asked.

"There is an American company called Cytech Systems, operating in Shanghai. They are experimenting with neural augmentation technology. They claim it is for education and video gaming, but we suspect it is military."

"Virtual Reality?" Broer asked.

"No, in fact we think it is more like mind control, but not in the way it's usually thought of."

"This is not American MK Ultra programme!" Guang threw in, not that Broer had any clue what that was.

The General continued.

"It seems to be more about targeted neural stimulation, via implantable and wearable technologies to, shall we say, focus and enhance the performance of willing subjects."

"Sounds cutting edge," Broer offered.

"Yes, it is very advanced and would be excellent military technology. Stealing this would give us something valuable as a bargaining chip with certain people, along with helping our own."

"You know how that works, Blower!" Guang said.

"All we need you to do is infiltrate Cytech in Shanghai and secure a copy of the research, maybe some examples. No more than you did with Cosgrove!"

Broer wondered if they were aware, but were ignoring the fact that he'd merely grabbed the research after it was stolen. He was happy for it to remain an unspoken truth.

"How do I get in?"

"A little social engineering and we have a contact on the inside who is hiring. With your military and police knowledge you will be a believable recruit. You'll go in as an advisor and technology consultant. That will give you access to the information we need," the General said.

Broer dropped his eyes to the table, thinking of what was on offer. On paper it should be simple enough and low risk, but it was still mainland China and what the hell was a US company doing there?

A foreign company developing anything remotely like a military technology in China would definitely have government eyes on it.

He thought about ASTU and Hannover. He could feel them drawing closer and his time running out. It was only a matter of time until one of them caught up with him.

Broer felt his heart sink a little. He thought of Melissa, of her face when he'd said goodbye.

There were times he wished he were a more regular person who could have just settled, just stayed where he was, but it wasn't his nature.

He always a needed to be challenged, to fight, to keep moving into the unknown and prove he could defeat whatever was thrown at him. The thought of settling down felt like being defeated, like waiting for death.

Broer the Boer. It was in his DNA.

"OK," he said at last, "I'm your man."

"Good, good! But, you can't do this outside the family," Guang said, walking over to the General.

Guang raised his glass; the General and Broer stood and did likewise.

"To our new brother in Black Dragon."

"Gān bēi!" the three of them toasted.

On cue, the doors the other guests had left through earlier swung open.

Two of the women who had been at the table held open the doors, keeping their heads bowed.

Guang walked ahead towards the door and with a sweep of his hand, the General indicated Broer should follow.

At the doorway, Broer could see two blue lanterns on the floor and to the back of the room beyond, a small altar with a red staff lying across it. Behind the staff, the stern-faced statue of Guan Yu, the Saint of War, looked down, holding a halberd in his left hand and extending his right arm, as if beckoning Broer towards him.

The similarity to the saint's name and the Boss's wasn't lost on Broer.

Guang reached the doorway, stopped and turned. Broer stood before him and looked the man in the eyes, anticipating his words, but it was the General who spoke.

"This is the Black Dragon," he said, gesturing to Guang, "servant of Guan Yu, whom we all serve. Before you walk through this door, you must know, there are oaths to be observed. Should you fail to do so, your life will become forfeit. You have wandered from your chosen path before, so think carefully. Do you accept this burden and promise to bear your oaths of brotherhood and righteousness?"

"You have my word," Broer replied without hesitation.

With that said, Guang turned and walked towards the altar.

Standing at the gateway to the dragon's den, Broer needed no prompting to follow.

He stepped beyond the lanterns, leaving his past behind.

The end

The Hannover Game

Afterwords

Thank you for reading The Hannover Game. I hope you enjoyed reading this first full length novel in the Hannover series, as much as I enjoyed writing it. However, the good news is that your adventure into the world of Hannover doesn't end here!

As you own a copy of the book - more adventure and intrigue awaits at my author site.

www.MarkJDiez.com

Become a Hannover Member, ASTU Operative or a SorceSek Hacker!

The website is not only a source of information about the Hannover world, but also a portal to the World itself! On the website you can join Hannover, ASTU or SorceSek and play through a growing set of games, puzzles and challenges. As you do, you'll win points and shift the balance of power to your team! Join up today and get involved!

Reader Community Mail Group

Come and join the reader mail group to keep in touch with what's happening in the Hannover world. The mail group allows me to send you updates on new novels and short stories, details of special offers, box sets, author visits and more.

Hannover Wiki

There is a rich Wiki being built with details of people, places, events and information about the Hannover world. Be sure to visit the website and click on the Wiki link. Don't worry there are no story spoilers!

Find it all at

www.MarkJDiez.com

Coming Next...

Black Dragon Protocol

Book 2 in the Hannover Series

The hidden forces within Hannover look East, seeing the time has come to shift the balance of power and advance their generations' long goals.

With their pieces in position and events moving more swiftly than they could have hoped, the time has come to strike at the heart of the dragon.

Meanwhile, in the East, Black Dragon pursue their own agenda and with the arrival of the traitorous Broer, seek to acquire a precious prize that will elevate their power.

Will the Black Dragon Protocol be harshly tested in a clash of civilizations, a fight for supremacy? The space between East and West will become a place where feuds, family, history and the future will all be to fight for – the only outcome; survival or destruction.

www.ingramcontent.com/pod-product-compliance
Lightning Source LLC
Chambersburg PA
CBHW051431260626
47162CB00001B/37